AN
HONORABLE
PLACE

AN HONORABLE PLACE

HENRY TAYLOR MILLARD

gatekeeper press™
Columbus, Ohio

AN HONORABLE PLACE

Published by Gatekeeper Press
2167 Stringtown Rd, Suite 109
Columbus, OH 43123-2989
www.GatekeeperPress.com

The editorial work for this book is entirely the product of the author. Gatekeeper Press did not participate in and is not responsible for any aspect of this element.

Library of Congress Control Number: 2021934981

ISBN (hardcover): 9781662910555
ISBN (paperback): 9781662910562
eISBN: 9781662910579

For Sandy and my grandchildren

CONTENTS

PART III

PROLOGUE

Commandancy of the Alamo
February 24, 1836

To the People of Texas & all Americans in the world-

Fellow citizens & compatriots-

I am besieged, by a thousand or more of the Mexicans under Santa Anna—I have sustained a continual bombardment & cannonade for 24 hours & have not lost a man—The enemy has demanded a surrender at discretion, otherwise, the garrison are to be put to the sword, if the fort is taken—I have answered the demand with a cannon shot, & our flag still waves proudly from the walls—I shall never surrender or retreat. Then, I call on you in the name of Liberty, of patriotism & everything dear to the American character, to come to our aid, with all dispatch —The enemy is receiving reinforcements daily & will no doubt increase to three or four thousand in four or five days. If this call is neglected, I am determined to sustain myself as long as possible & die like a soldier who never forgets what is due to his own honor & that of his country –

Victory or Death.

William Barret Travis
Lt. Col. comdt.

Travis' letter, as it is known to the People of Texas and *should* be to all Americans in the world, is emblematic of the power of the written word. It represents all we hold honorable from a time when twenty-six-year-old William Barret Travis inspired the creation of a new nation with his mighty pen and sword in hand. Travis City, Texas, recognizes a citizen in their small town each February 24th, the date of the document, to read The Letter at high noon on the town square. It has been read by teachers, bankers, cowboys, welders, secretaries, students, nurses, and even a few politicians have been selected for the honor. Each one has stood where it began by proclamation of the city council in 1886, the fiftieth anniversary of The Letter. The Letter is engraved in granite in the town square and printed copies are posted in the schools, courthouse, and churches. It is omnipresent in the town.

It is said history is written by the victors, but it is also told by the ones who sacrifice their all. The martyrs with Travis inspired others beyond their graves dug by their killers. Each one was a volunteer and could have left at any time, or never come at all, but they stood beside Travis until the last man fell. Their immeasurable sacrifice created the Republic of Texas less than two months later. In Travis City, The Letter is taught in fourth grade Texas history and again to seniors in high school. It is emblazoned on the hearts of the citizens of Travis City, and if you ask any of them, they will proudly say The Letter never leaves them.

I am besieged . . .

"For I know the plans I have for you," declares the Lord, "plans to prosper you and not to harm you, plans to give you hope and a future."

Jeremiah 29:11

PART I

CHAPTER 1

March 1989 Travis City, Texas

A NAMELESS COMPACT SEDAN with a missing hubcap pushed north against the darkness of the Central Texas landscape on a warm spring night. The kind of car no one notices in the kind of place no one notices. A long stretch of black highway interrupted occasionally by the twin white eyes of oncoming cars and trucks interrupting the void. Who are these people out at three thirty in the morning, and why are they here? Some are working to take care of a family, some are lovers that abandon their senses to see each other, and some are evil, using the darkness to hide their sins.

* * *

Debbie greeted Karla with her usual tired smile at Don's Quick Stop. Debbie had been on her shift since eleven last night and was happy to see some help. Karla was the cook for the store's deli. She arrived at four thirty to get the breakfast prep going. Debbie and Karla were first cousins and grew up seven miles east of the of the interstate in Travis City, Texas, a town of 6,419 at last census of 1980, about the same population as the last four times the count was done. Debbie was twenty-three and single and described herself as chubby. Karla was twenty-seven and married with a young son and described Debbie as butter butt in a cute loving way reserved for close friends.

"I gotta go take out the garbage. I had no chance all night since that idiot Marvin didn't show up or call. Guess Don will fire his lazy butt, and I hope he does," Debbie grabbed a handful of black plastic garbage bags from under the counter as she stomped out the front doors toward the gas pumps. There were four trash cans under the fluorescent lit canopy stationed between the pumps that she needed to pull out the full bags and replace with fresh ones. Insects buzzed above her against the unnaturally bright lights. Don demanded all the trash cans be emptied and in the dumpster before the trash truck came each morning. She gathered the four bags with various amounts of empty beer cans, soda bottles, snack bags, Whataburger sacks smelling of strong onion, and baby diapers. Debbie thought to herself as the odor assaulted her nose, "I will never have kids."

There was a lone security light casting an eerie green glow in the rear of the store where the steel dumpster sat as Debbie pulled her load across the gravel drive that circled behind the store. She noticed the lid was open and she said to herself, "I thought I saw this closed when I came to work." The sound of the trash truck could now be heard downshifting as the diesel engine blasted loudly in the quiet early morning—right on time. She quickly tossed the bags in as the truck pulled into the front drive and she scooted to the side. As she turned to walk away, she heard a small weak voice say, "Mama?"

Debbie rushed around the other side of the dumpster to locate the sound. Was it a doll? Was she hearing things? And then again, "Mama?" She peered into the dumpster on her toes to look inside, and she saw the outline of a small leg pushing out from under the black plastic bags.

The big truck was lined up with long imposing prongs to pierce the side collars of the steel bin to raise it and shake out the contents into the compactor. Debbie ran frantically waving her arms toward the driver's door.

"Mr. Ray! Stop! Stop!" The driver stared down through his window far above her in the tall cab and immediately stopped the truck with the air brakes hissing, and the huge truck lurched to a stop.

"Come here and help me!" Debbie pleaded, turning, and running to the sound of the child.

The diesel engine slowly coughed and faded to silence as the driver door swung open and the short man exited and followed her to the dumpster.

"Help me up, Mr. Ray! There's a baby in here, and it's alive!" she impatiently pulled herself over the lip of the open trash bin. The man pushed up her ample backside as Debbie pulled her waist balancing against the coarse metal. She leaned in and reached for the little leg and gently pulled it toward her—a body and now hair and face of what looked like a three-year-old girl. Blood was dried and matted against her black hair as Debbie carefully cradled her head.

"It's okay, baby. It's okay; I got ya now," Debbie spoke sweetly and softly as she pulled the girl toward her bosom. She lifted her up as high as she could to clear the debris-stained interior wall of the dumpster and rotated as Mr. Ray delicately lowered Debbie and the child to the ground.

"Someone threw a baby away? Oh, my Lord," the driver's voice broke as he thought of his own precious children.

Debbie walked briskly to the front of the store as her mind raced on what to do next. She held the limp body against her and laid the tiny face on her shoulder. The driver walked behind her mumbling a prayer. "Please God, save this child. Please God. I could have killed that child. Oh Lord!"

Debbie pushed through the glass door and called out to Karla, "Call 911. We just found a baby in the dumpster!"

"What?" Karla darted from behind the deli counter with a ten-inch knife in her hand. "My God! That's a kid!"

"Just call 911! We don't know anything 'cept we just found her. Looks like she has a bad cut on the side of her head. Hurry!" Debbie ordered her cousin as the bell above the entrance door jingled announcing someone entering. Karla looked at Mr. Ray, and he was visibly shaken.

Debbie could hear her cousin saying the store's address as she entered the tiny ladies' room. She sat on the toilet next to the vanity and positioned the child on her right thigh. With her left hand she turned on the water and then pushed the soap dispenser allowing the soft foam to gather in her left hand. She then ran the warming water over her soapy hand and begin to wash the child starting at her bare feet and legs. Debbie just now noticed in the bright light what she was wearing. Faded blue shorts and a pink T-shirt with a simple white flower on the front. Her thin arms and legs showed a few scattered abrasions against her olive skin.

She gathered more soap and water and cleaned her carefully where the skin was exposed. She reached across the vanity and began aggressively pulling paper towels to dry the washed areas. Karla opened the door and looked at the little, dirty bundle sitting on Debbie's lap. The tiny head lifted up and pitifully said, "Mama."

Karla had a plastic bottle of apple juice she opened and placed against the bottom lip of the child. The tiny mouth instinctively opened like a baby bird as she slowly tilted the juice into her mouth.

*   *   *

William Barrett Downs III crossed over the cattle guard hearing the familiar rumble from his tires rolling over the spaced pipes below him. He left his house early each weekday morning dressed in a Brooks Brothers suit and silk tie with his Open Road Stetson sitting atop his balding head. Polished handmade black alligator boots looked odd against the cheap plastic floor mat of his ten-year-old Ford F-150. He was six-foot and carried more weight than he should, but the suit fit his rounded waist in a good way. At least he thought he looked good. He was teased about his truck by his friends, but he didn't care. It got him to work and back. Billy, as his childhood friends called him, was fifty-two years old with a circle of thick graying hair against his tanned head and was always clean shaven.

He was a man of routine. Up by four thirty, out the door by five fifteen, and driving to his bank Monday through Friday. Saturday morning was dedicated to the ranch. He would meet with his long-time foreman and plan the week ahead. Sunday morning was church, lunch with the family, and an afternoon nap.

The bank had been in his family for three generations. Mr. Downs, as almost everyone addressed him, was a fifth generation Texan. The first of his family came to Texas as part of a Mexican Land Grant in 1830 and later fought the good fight for independence, helping to establish the Republic of Texas. Banking, real estate, ranching, mineral rights, and old money drove his pickup down the driveway to the two-lane highway to turn right when he saw the flashing emergency lights coming from town.

He waited at his driveway for the swirling red lights to pass, an ambulance. He thought, "Probably a wreck," and then he hoped it was not caused by one of his wandering calves.

Mr. Downs headed east to town on his daily five-mile drive. He probably could make this trip in his sleep, and some days he seemed to do just that as he would park his truck and not remember the drive in to work. This morning was the same as the thousands before with only the ambulance causing a disturbance in the routine. He made the left turn on Maple Street and another left into the rear parking lot behind the bank. He sat for a moment in the still predawn atmosphere which was suddenly disturbed by the bright headlights of a car turning quickly behind him. He swiftly reached in the glove box and pulled a .45 Colt 1911 pistol and aimed at the driver side window where the car was screeching to a stop next to him.

"Hey, sum bitch!" the man in the car grinned as he shouted to Mr. Downs through his window.

"Damn it, Randy! You scared the crap out of me, and you nearly got shot. And, hey sum bitch, to you too." Mr. Downs chuckled to himself in relief, returning the gun to its safe place. The two always greeted each other that way, when no one who would be offended was around, and had done it so long the reason had been lost over the fifty years of friendship.

Randy Weyers and Billy Downs grew up together, played little league baseball, high school basketball and football, went fishing and hunting, chased girls, went off to the University of Texas and were roommates for four years, and never had an argument that they could recall. Except the one over Janet, Billy's wife. They competed and pushed each other to be better. Iron sharpens iron was how Billy's dad described their relationship. Randy moved to Fort Worth after college and made a pile of money selling oil and gas services and built a real estate empire with his wife. But he always stayed close to Travis City where his mom and dad lived. His siblings had also moved away so caring for the aging parents usually fell to Randy. Randy was about six-two—if anyone asked—and fit. He had a thick mustache which was now getting gray as his abundant head of black hair was turning salt and pepper. He was a handsome man in a rugged way with round glasses and round brown eyes. Quick to smile and just as quick to fight when the times called for action.

"Why didn't you call me and let me know you were in town?" Billy asked his friend.

"Sorry about that, but I got a call from Daddy yesterday afternoon, and he said Mom wasn't breathing, and he had called an ambulance. So, I tell Vickie, 'I got to go, *now!*' You know, thinking the worst. I take her fastest car and haul ass down here making funeral arrangements in my head as I drove. Well, I get to the hospital and turns out she *was* breathing. He just can't *hear!*"

Billy started laughing as they both sat in their vehicles. "Come on in. Dawn gets the coffee ready the night before, so all I got to do is turn it on."

The two friends made their way to the back door, and Billy began the process of turning off the alarm system to enter the old building. He walked the brick walled corridor flipping on lights as he went as Randy followed behind. The break room was on the left side, and they entered to find the coffee pot ready to go. Billy pushed the red button and heard the familiar sound of water heating.

"Well, is your Mom okay?" Billy asked as he leaned against the counter waiting for the brewing process to finish.

"Yes and no. She was breathing, of course, but she did have very low blood pressure—60 over 30. Turns out she needed to go to the hospital, so kind of a blessing. Should be just fine with some meds adjusted."

The aroma of coffee filled the little room quickly as both men stared at the stainless pot awaiting the hot stream of brown morning nectar. The pot filled quickly, and each poured themselves a white mug of black coffee.

"Let's go to my office and solve the world's problems," Billy said as he headed out of the room.

William Barrett Downs the Third's office was his father's before him and his grandfather's before that. The room was large and traditional, and the entry sat in the rear of the room with the desk at the other end. The kind of space that evoked stability and wealth. A table accompanied by four Chippendale chairs with padded cloth seats of green, blue, and red stripes looking like a fraternity member's tie, encircled a polished five-foot round wood table at the entrance of the room. The paintings on the walls were of Texas bluebonnets and Hereford bulls posing against a backdrop of lush green pastures. Black and white photos of men in Fedoras posing for pictures in front of the bank building established the affluent history. One of the photos had handwritten names above each head, with 1,2,3, the first three William Barrett Downs's when Billy was about two years old. A color photo from 1978, when the bank was remodeled, looked a bit too modern in the mix with men in colorful wide ties and plaid suits. A younger Billy, with long sideburns, stood next to his father with a proud smile of accomplishment. The rich wood paneled walls rose ten feet to ornate dentil crown molding. The deep blue wool carpeting softened and silenced the steps of heavy boots of cattleman needing a short loan and high heels of attractive ladies selling check stock and computers. Twin chandeliers balanced over the rectangle shaped room creating odd slivers of light and shadows on the wood walls.

A heavy brown leather sofa covered with cracks caused by the weight of countless farmers, ranchers, businessmen, or anyone needing money had left a bit of their dreams in that cowhide. Two upholstered navy wingback chairs on each side sat angled toward a rough-hewn coffee table made of an antique barn door with a few neatly fanned magazines about cows and finance and Texas. An imposing eight-foot by six-foot mahogany desk created a barricade between the banker and his guests. An aged brown leather swivel chair sat between the center of the desk and the matching credenza and hutch that reached to the ten-foot ceiling and was the eight-foot width of the desk. To the right of the desk, in the corner, stood a stained wood hat rack where Billy hung his Stetson each morning.

The tabletop of the credenza was the same height as the desk and two feet deep. Above were open compartments of various sizes. Family photos, diplomas, snapshots of dove hunts with friends, Billy holding a large redfish and grinning in a floppy hat. A photo of a whitetail buck lay on the ground with a rifle laid across the trophy's body and a smiling Billy holding up antlers. In the lower right corner was a University of Texas football helmet sitting on a wooden base with 1963 National Champions embossed on a brass plaque. The large desk was a bit cluttered with legal sized note pads of handwritten scrawl that even he had a hard time deciphering. Several neat piles of manilla folders with colored tabs and typed names with crooked sticky notes in yellow and green lined the desk.

A silver frame with an eight-by-ten photo of his wife, Janet taken on her fortieth birthday, sat on the front right corner facing his chair. It was his favorite picture of her. It was a candid moment of her sitting on their back porch in her gardening clothes, hair messed up by wind and sweat. On a day when most people want attention for a milestone day, she had preferred to plant flowers and stay home. He saw everything good about her in that natural, unposed photo, and she hated it was the one he chose for his desk. She would say, "I look awful. Please throw that thing away." It was three days after the photo when she fell.

This was Mr. Downs' sanctuary, protected from the outside world of disappointing family members and sickness. He could control the world that lived in this room. He was the boss of this space. People looked up to him and respected him and maybe feared him. He loved the person he was in this room. What a rare gift, he had thought so many times before.

Randy sat on the navy wingback chair to the right and placed his cup on the coffee table. Billy sat in his chair and held the cup with both hands in front of his chin to smell the aroma of the brew.

"I wonder what the ambulance was about?" Billy pondered aloud, still wondering if it was part of his herd causing the morning disruption.

CHAPTER 2

THE MORROW COUNTY ambulance lights flashed red against the white metal, south facing walls of Don's Quick Stop amplifying the emergency when they came to a stop. The driver had not turned on the siren as there was no need to alert the very few others on the road or awaken townspeople. Martha was in the back and Gregg drove. The pair normally spent an early Monday morning sleeping in their clothes and not being disturbed. Both were startled by the ringing bell that awoke them at the small building designated for the two man shift ambulance teams. If another ambulance was needed at the same time—which was rare—the fire department would send theirs.

Martha Stall grew up in the county and wanted to be a doctor, but finances as well as a surprise pregnancy at nineteen had limited her. But she was only twenty-three, and she still dreamed of a path to her medical career. Gregg Dunning was forty and preferred the usual shift of no emergencies. He was a good gunsmith and spent most of his shifts cleaning and repairing hunting guns or whatever the public brought by the station.

Martha was tall and athletic which Gregg appreciated for lifting purposes. He had been against a woman being hired but had grown to respect her for her smarts and attitude. All of it, she had earned. Martha ran ahead with a response bag as Gregg parked the truck, and he quickly followed her in the store.

"Where is the child?" Martha asked Mr. Ray who was seated in the deli area sipping some coffee with his head down, still upset, and praying.

"Ladies' room," he answered, pointed, and again bowed his head.

Martha reached for the door as it opened, and she came face to face with Karla and the little girl on Debbie's lap.

The room was too small for three people, much less to properly assess the situation.

"Please move," Martha said to Karla. "Let me check her for any broken bones." She ran her hands over the child.

"I don't think there are any breaks or bruises. Just this cut on her head," Debbie said trying to be helpful.

"Let me have her, please." Martha reached for the child who was alert, but probably in shock as fear consumed her eyes.

Gregg had a blanket which he lay on the floor outside the ladies' room in a private hallway stacked with soft drinks. Martha took some medical shears and delicately cut off the clothes examining as she went. She lightly felt her legs and ribs and neck, looking at the little face for signs of sudden pain. Debbie and Karla stood above the two EMTs and waited for orders desperately wanting to help the child. Martha checked for any sexual abuse and was quietly relieved she saw nothing obvious.

"What's your name, baby girl?" Martha asked with as much kindness as possible. The response was only a blank stare.

"OK, Gregg, I don't feel anything broken. The bleeding has stopped on the head wound. She was in the dumpster, but appears clean of debris, except her head." Martha looked at the cousins.

"I cleaned her up, best I could. She weren't real bad, but her feet were the worst. And the blood on her head," Debbie stammered out quickly.

"Okay, thanks for taking care of her. Let's get her to County." Martha looked at Gregg and the unspoken role of good partners went to work. Gregg lifted the little girl wrapped in the blanket and walked to the ambulance as the Sheriff's car arrived and parked on the side of the building next to the ambulance.

The driver got out of the brown and white Chevy Malibu with several antennas bouncing back and forth from the abrupt stop. He was a tall lean man in starched wrangler blue jeans and a white long-sleeved shirt with a Texas flag patch on his left shoulder and a USA flag on the right shoulder. His belt rivaled Batman's as there appeared to be some type of leather case or holster in every spot available surrounding his thirty-four-inch waist. A wide brimmed silver belly Resistol hat sat straight on his head with brownish gray hair circling below the brim. His ruddy complexion looked like someone with a continuous sunburn, and he wore prescription yellow lensed Ray-ban glasses. His face was clean shaven only because he could not grow a mustache. He had tried and been ridiculed.

"Morning, Gregg. Heard we got a bad mess here," Sheriff Elvis Stanley said trying to evoke as much authority as possible.

"Yep, Elvis. Martha and I need to get her to the hospital. You should interview the girls inside. The good news, she apparently was not in the dumpster very long, is my guess. I have her clothes bagged up here for you." Gregg handed him a clear plastic bag with the blue shorts and the shirt with the flower.

*   *   *

Randy sipped his coffee and looked around at the office for anything new to comment on. The black and white picture of WB Downs the First standing in a cattle pen created a topic.

"Hey, you ought to get a picture like this of you. That would be cool," Randy said nodding to the black and white photo. Billy's grandfather wore khaki pants and a light-colored long-sleeved work shirt and a Stetson slightly tilted on his head. He stood between two yearling Hereford bulls in a wooden corral, and it appeared to be in the nineteen thirties. A wooden feed trough held hay in the forefront as the old man stood behind the bulls leaning on his ever-present walking cane used for bad hips and bad cattle.

"I should. I probably won't, but I should," Billy said. His mind still on the ambulance and a possible escaped calf.

"How's Janet?" Randy asked scared of the answer in some ways. Her health was the only topic they discussed it seemed lately.

"Some good days and maybe some new treatments possible. I hate when she gets so depressed with the pain but getting our hopes up can be worse. She will read where someone in Italy took a bath in bird crap or some crazy thing and ask me if she should try. She's just frustrated, but she never complains," Billy answered and tried to laugh it off. "How's Vickie?"

"I see her about twice a month, and that's on some billboard. Selling more houses than any realtor in Texas, but we both knew she would. My Lord, that woman doesn't know how to stop working. The only vacation she takes is to lead the number one producers in the agency on some week-long, high-class trip to Europe."

"You are the only man I know who isn't afraid of her. My favorite thing she did was to some poor guy trying to hit on her. When that idiot gave her his business card in the bar, she responded with her cynical smile, 'Thanks, they are out of toilet paper in the ladies' room.'" Both men laughed.

"Poor bastard never knew what was coming. You want to switch? I would rather have Janet than that crazy woman."

"Oh no, that was your choice, my friend. When we walked over to those two thirty years ago, *you* said, 'I want the blonde.'" They laughed as if they had not said it a thousand times.

*   *   *

The ambulance wailed to a stop at the lone hospital in a forty-mile radius. Martha opened the back door and softly stepped out carrying her patient. Gregg joined her as they walked through the emergency room door. The pediatrician on duty, Dr. Alan Bergman, had received the call at home and made his way urgently to the hospital. He was a tenderhearted man which was sometimes difficult when dealing with sick and hurt children, but he had quickly earned a great reputation for his skills. Medical school teaches you to not become attached emotionally. He had ignored that class.

"What do we have, Martha?" the doctor greeted the EMT as she cradled the child against her, and they walked to the open exam room.

"Appears to be blunt force trauma above the right ear. I don't see anything else, and her vitals are good." Martha was glad Bergman was there. She admired him and had a bit of a crush on the handsome man. She lay the little girl on the examination table.

"Is she verbal?" the doctor flashed his light back and forth in her eyes thinking of his own daughter about this age.

"Not really. She said mama a couple of times, but no real crying or words to speak of. Probably in shock." Martha stared down at the child who remained quiet looking back at Martha with a blank expression.

"OK, let's try and get her cleaned up better." A nurse appeared now by his side, and Martha knew she should leave, and normally would by now, but she saw the child latching on to her eyes.

"Has anyone called CPS?" a voice from the hall asked.

* * *

Monica Downs felt her toddler's forehead and thought to herself, "He has a fever." She was married to William Barrett Downs IV called Four by almost everyone since he was born. He had one childless older sister, Daisy, in California who was married to a new age healer. Whatever that was. Four was still asleep in the master bedroom as Monica dealt with their two children. Monica had married Four when they were both in their early twenties living in Austin. She had been a beautiful waitress, and he an heir apparent. They both got what they wanted out of the marriage. Monica had intellectual curiosity and a great work ethic. Four did not. She was an avid reader and could converse on any topic. He was reclusive and lacked ambition.

Monica sat her soon to be three-year-old son on her lap. William Barrett Downs the Fifth, they called him Barrett. His sister, Janet Ann, was two years older and sat cross legged on the floor of the den in front of the television watching Sesame Street. She was named after Four's mother, Janet and Monica's deceased grandmother, Ann—an allowance of naming rights for the first-born daughter. Monica sat in her pink silky pajamas with her hair pulled back staring ahead at her life. She loved her children, but she spent most days worrying about her husband.

She looked down at the blonde curls of her son and stroked his head, still staring ahead. She and Four moved into the two-story Victorian house on Main Street in Travis City the year before, after his grandmother passed away. She had been given permission to update it, but her in-laws kept a close eye on her plans, so very little was her choice. She did get a beautiful kitchen and den, and her master bedroom and bath with real closets. She knew she was spoiled, but she sometimes wondered at what price.

Her son began squirming to get down. When she released him, he wandered in his Ralph Lauren pajamas to sit with his sister. She knew she needed to take him to Dr. Bergman just in case there was something wrong. The housekeeper would be there soon, and she could watch Janet Ann while she went with Barrett to the doctor.

*   *   *

Dr. Bergman gingerly brushed back the wet hair of the child after the nurse finished washing her hair in a bowl of warm water. He knew he needed to cut the hair around the wound.

"Have you ever cut hair?" he asked his attending nurse.

"Sure, I have two daughters; I can do it. What do you want?" the nurse responded confident of her beauty skills.

"I need to clear this area only, but I don't want it to look awful," Dr. Bergman said.

The nurse nodded she understood and sat the child up in a sitting position on the side of the exam table. She combed as much of the hair straight down and took the surgical scissors and circled around her head removing the long black hair into a pixie cut or at least that was the goal. She cut bangs as best as she could, and the child remained very still while the nurse hummed a lullaby as she snipped.

The doctor watched and seemed impressed at her barbering skills. He had retrieved a wound kit and prepared to sew a few stitches.

The state social worker stood outside the door and peered in to see the little girl. Margie Gillam was in her late fifties and presided over the local county child welfare office. She had dealt with abused children, but nothing like this case. She knew nothing about the parents, or any family for that matter, and worried about the child being thrown into a system which did its best but certainly had its faults.

The doctor finished the stitches after applying the topical numbing medicine. He kept a low comforting tone with his tiny patient. He applied an antibiotic and a bandage. The child never grimaced or cried.

"Do we know her name?" Margie asked the doctor.

"No, she has not said anything or even cried." He looked at the child, "She is just perfect and so beautiful."

"Hi, my name is Margie. What is your name?" the older lady in the rust-colored pantsuit asked the child with her new haircut.

"Can you say hi?" she tried another question.

"Hi," a weak voice replied.

"Hi, to you! Do you have a name?" Margie raised her tone with a bit of excitement at the response.

"Lo tus," she replied in a meek dry voice.

"Low dus?" Margie said with some confusion, "Oh, I bet it's Lourdes."

The little face just looked at her with exhaustion.

"How old are you, Lourdes?"

The little girl lifted her right hand with her two fingers, then she changed to three fingers extended with her thumb and pinky locked under them.

"Oh my, you are a big girl. Do you know where you live?"

The child just stared at her with confusion. She was too young to answer any questions that could provide much information. Names like Mama were not proper clues for anyone.

"Based on her teeth and other factors, my guess is right at three years old. Bring her by my office as soon as you can this morning, and I'll make sure to get her some clothes and that she receives any immunization shots needed. Her head injury will cause her some foggy moments for a while. She should be fine, just needs a lot of love right now," Dr. Bergman said and left the hospital to begin seeing patients at his office.

The nurse returned to the room with a t-shirt which was too big but would be something for her to wear.

Margie began her plan for the child, and it all depended on a parent or family member being discovered. She did not have any direct experience with child abandonment with the intent to dispose of the child in such a gruesome manner. If a parent did show up, were they involved? She knew the proper protocol and it bothered her soul to throw her from a dumpster into the system. The doctor was right, she needed love and affection and urgently.

*   *   *

The sheriff photographed the dumpster area and any tire or footprints visible in the rear of the store. He had spoken with Debbie and Karla; they had not seen anyone. A careful assessment of fingerprints was attempted on the dumpster and the push stick used to lift the heavy lid with no real results. Don was on his way to pull the video and all were hopeful the security camera positioned over the front door would catch a glimpse of the crime. Mr. Ray was still upset, so another driver was on his way to relieve his shift on the trash truck.

Don Warner pulled in the store parking lot that now had become busy with normal morning traffic. Two cowboys appeared pulling a twenty-foot gooseneck trailer with two saddled horses in the front compartment of the trailer and a hyper Australian Shepherd bouncing back and forth in the bed of the truck. A mother stopped needing gas on her way to ferry three kids to school. A delivery van for potato chips sat on the side, away from the traffic, with back doors open as the driver carried a large box toward the store. Seeing the lawman present and yellow crime scene tape stretched around a large portion of the rear of the store and dumpster, left all of these people to wonder if the store had been robbed earlier.

"Morning, Elvis. Well, this is a crazy thing, ain't it?" Don said as he got out of his pickup and extended his hand to the sheriff.

"I'd say so, Don. How you been?"

"Alright, I guess. Just can't keep help. Everybody says they need a job, but half of 'em don't show up. Come on in, and we'll try and see if we can see something on the tape." He motioned Elvis to follow him into the store. The patrons watched with curiosity as the two walked with purpose past the restrooms toward the closed off rear storage area and the small, locked office. Don pulled out what seemed like fifty keys on a key ring and sorted through until he settled on the one to unlock the solid wood office door. A small, cluttered desk with two old diner type red vinyl and rusty chrome chairs sat against the back wall. Above the desk was a crude plywood shelf with a video recorder and small black and white monitor. Don began to rewind and hit play looking at the time stamp on the top left corner of the screen. They began watching at eleven p.m. when Debbie said she remembered seeing the lid closed at that time when she started her shift. Don hit fast forward to speed the process.

An occasional customer of the twenty-four-hour store created brief excitement for the two men, but no one went to the rear of the store. Fifteen customers between eleven p.m. and four fifty-one a.m. when the child was discovered. No one went to the rear. They changed their strategy to only look at the left edge of the picture. Normally people pulled in from the south, so they went through it again.

"There! Stop it right there, Don!" Elvis said with excitement. There was a brief flash of something at three forty a.m. "Go back again and play it in slow motion, if you can."

The two men stared intently at the black and white screen. The picture was from the only camera over the front door and clearly showed the gas pumps and a bit of the frontage road. The peripheral views were not as big as the store footprint of paved concrete and faded out at the edge of the pumps. The cameras were set that way to catch anyone stealing gas. There were no customers, but headlights appeared to show on the left side of the screen and only the bottom third of a car was briefly seen at three, forty-two, and twenty-nine seconds.

"Freeze it there! What's that look like to you, Don?"

"Looks like a small car, and it's missing a front driver side hubcap, but that's all we can see."

"Let's keep watching, maybe we can see on the right side when they leave." Elvis was hopeful.

At three, forty-four and seven seconds only lights were seen exiting. Nothing else. Easily enough time to stop, raise the lid, and dispose of the child.

"I'm going to need the tape for evidence. I will send it to Austin and get the Texas Ranger's involved. They got people who can tell us all about that car . . . I hope," Elvis said with cautious optimism and thought to himself, "I bet they thought the kid was dead."

CHAPTER 3

MARGIE GILLIAM SAT the child in the front seat of her state issued plain Ford sedan. She buckled her in careful to miss the head wound. She needed to think about this case and what she could do that was best for Lourdes. She stopped at the red light at Main Street and looked at her precious passenger. Margie's eyes were drawn to the child's fingers that appeared to be counting or typing or playing an imaginary keyboard. She smiled at the girl with the short black hair and dark eyes as she finalized her plan.

Margie drove home first and not to the office. The child needed food, and she had some milk and cereal. She would feed her a little breakfast and make a couple of calls. She carried Lourdes inside and sat her at the kitchen table. She then retrieved a throw pillow from the sofa for her to sit on so she could reach her breakfast. Margie hummed a nameless tune to assure Lourdes she was close by as she pulled down the box of Frosted Flakes reserved for her own grandkids when visiting. She poured the cereal in a bowl and reached for the milk, opening it she sniffed it to make sure it was fresh. She sat the bowl and spoon in front of her guest, and Lourdes nodded in appreciation and began to eat.

"Hello, Father Michael, this is Margie Gilliam. We've met a few times over the years . . . Yes, I do live next to Pam and Otis . . . Oh my, great people . . . Listen, the reason I called is I have a child in need of a loving home . . ." Margie walked with the phone extension cord pulled to its limit to make sure Lourdes could see her as she ate her cereal sitting on the Panda bear place mat.

"Can I come to the church and speak with you today? . . . Great, I will see you later this morning . . . You have a couple in mind? . . . They sound perfect, and that puts my heart at rest. You have no idea . . . Yes, it is one of those God things!" She hung up the phone and allowed herself a hopeful smile.

* * *

Dr. Bergman walked in the rear entrance of his office with its diagonal window on the painted brown wooden door. He had purchased the practice and the 1960s building from the prior pediatrician, Dr. Wilma Dunlevy. Doc Wilma, as she was normally addressed by the townspeople, had done it all for kids in the area for forty years and people were slow to change from the beloved lady to this young upstart.

"Good morning, you have a busy day. Monica Downs called and asked if we can work her in. The little prince has a fever." Kathy, his office manager, assistant shot giver, and chief transition officer, since she also worked for Doc Wilma, greeted him. Kathy Carr was around forty and knew everyone in town—at least the ones with kids. She had begun working for Doc Wilma out of high school, no nursing school or medical training, but after over twenty years of on-the-job training, no one asked for credentials.

"Call Monica back for me, please, Kathy. I need to ask her a favor." He just remembered Monica had a daughter around five.

"Line two," Kathy called down the hall from her place in front to the doctor's office.

"Hello Monica? This is Alan Bergman; can I ask you a favor, please? I know Janet Ann is about five. Do you happen to have any of her old clothes from when she was three or four? . . . Wonderful! I have a child, a three-year-old girl, who was abandoned . . . I know, just horrible. If you could bring whatever clothing you have when you come, socks, underwear, shoes. She really has nothing . . . that is so nice of you and thanks again. I knew you would be the perfect person to ask."

Monica hung up the phone and started up the staircase to the unfinished spare bedroom used as storage for now. She had boxed up the kids' clothes when they moved a year ago and had intended to donate them but had not gotten around to it yet. She sorted through the stacked cardboard boxes and found three marked JA for her daughter. This would be a great start for a little girl, and Monica felt good about helping. She carried the boxes downstairs and set them by the back door.

She checked on her children who were occupied by the television and went to her bedroom. Four was still asleep, or passed out, and she quietly closed her bathroom door behind her to take a shower and get ready for the doctor visit.

*   *   *

Margie sat the little girl in the too big t-shirt back in her sedan. They both had eaten and used the restroom before leaving the house. Margie could take her to the doctor and then to the church, but where would Lourdes stay tonight?

Margie drove to Dr. Bergman's office and pulled in the parking lot the same time as a white suburban with a beautiful driver. Monica had made a stop at Walmart and bought some socks and underwear and three different sizes of tennis shoes, with Velcro straps. She took the gray plastic sacks off the front seat and got out as Margie retrieved the girl with the bandage on her head above her ear in the parking space beside her. Monica set the bags on the ground as she unbuckled Barrett from his car seat and pulled him free on her hip. She reached down and grabbed the bags and used her free hip to close the door.

"Are you Mrs. Downs?" Margie asked as the two with toddlers walked together toward the entrance.

"Yes, I'm sorry, have we met?" Monica responded politely.

"No, but it's a small town, and you have Downs 4 on your license plate." Margie smiled.

"Oh, that makes sense! Is this the baby who was abandoned?"

"Yes, how did you know?"

"Your car has CPS on the side of it, and Doctor Bergman called and asked me to donate some clothes for an abandoned three-year-old girl. I have more clothes in the car."

They both chuckled and Margie opened the door as Monica walked into the waiting room.

"Welcome, Doctor Bergman is expecting you both. Miss Margie, please come on back to room one. Monica, you and Barrett can go to room two." Kathy lavished all her Texas charm on the ladies.

Margie took the child to the examination room with colorful balloons painted on the wall and a cartoon elephant balancing on a beach ball on his trunk. The doctor entered and leaned down to be level with the child.

"Hi, Doctor Bergman. Me and Lourdes came for our checkup like you asked," Margie said seated next to Lourdes with her arm around the child.

"Hi there, Miss Lourdes. We are going to get you all better and healthy." Alan Bergman meant every word.

After the two children had been seen, Monica brought the boxes and sacks of clothing to Margie, and together they dressed Lourdes in her new wardrobe. The broken child seemed somewhat happier at the clothes and sweet attention. A baby blue dress adorned with white ribbons was selected and white lace trimmed socks and white sandals which fit her perfectly. Monica dug through another box and found one more accessory. She placed a large white bow above the bandage, which covered the wounded area completely from the correct angle. The ladies smiled at each other as the good feeling of new clothes was universally true whether you are sixty or thirty or three. Three grown people stared at the dressed-up child, all of them thrilled to see the first smile from the little girl.

*　*　*

Maria Sanchez walked as fast as her short legs could carry her through her neighborhood of small wood frame houses to Main Street to head east to the welding shop where her husband Danny worked. She praised God for her answered prayer as she walked. Father Michael had called minutes earlier and she immediately ran out the door to tell her husband in person. There was a child in need of parents! She had been praying for eighteen years after so many failed attempts at getting pregnant, and now today, maybe she would get her miracle. Father Michael had specifically prayed with her only yesterday after Mass.

Danny was in the back of the shop with a welding helmet over his head when he heard, "Danny! Maria is here and seems to be very upset." He released the welding rod and lifted his helmet to see his wife standing by the open garage door of the shop with her feet nervously shuffling and holding both her open hands over her mouth. He rushed to her and began to think the worst, "Who died?"

She lifted her hands above her head, "A baby! A child! Father Michael . . ." She could no longer speak and threw her arms around her husband and sobbed uncontrollably into his shoulder as he hugged her tight. He began to cry as well.

He heard his boss behind him say, "Go with Maria. You go on home, Danny. We got this for as long as you need." And three grown, tough men from the shop all joined in the happy tears but doing their best to make sure no one saw their happiness leaking down their hard faces.

It was no secret that Danny and Maria wanted children and had been disappointed for years. Danny grew up in Travis City as a Baptist. Maria was from Mexico and Catholic. She was not close to her family and Danny's parents were in poor health. He had a younger brother who worked for a trucking company, but not married. She was desperate to be a mother and the years had passed with no luck. She refused to go to a doctor, afraid what they would say. Could the doctors tell what happened to her so long ago?

The happy couple got in the family car, a fifteen-year-old pickup, first going home to change clothes and then to meet Father Michael at Saint John Catholic Church. Maria cleaned houses and occasionally sold tamales. Danny worked as a welder, fence builder, and mechanic. Today they received a new title, parents.

* * *

The two men finished their final duty, tamping the loose ground with the shovels they had brought from home. Ashes and burned bits could be seen if you looked carefully, but no one would be looking down the abandoned gravel road. The gas can was put back in the trunk of the old sedan. The older man nodded toward the car with the missing hubcap for the young man to drive. The night had finally ended, and it was over. The two vehicles drove back to let them know it was done.

CHAPTER 4

1996

MARIA SANCHEZ WEAVED her way around the chatting parents to the front of the Travis City Elementary School cafetorium with her new camera in hand. It was the last day of school and the award ceremony for the fifth graders who were moving on to middle school next year. Maria was excited and nervous for her daughter because she was hopeful of receiving an award. Three of Lourdes' teachers had told her to invite her parents which should mean maybe an award was possible. She did have the highest grades in three of her classes—that she knew of—and her math teacher praised her constantly.

Maria found a seat in the front closest to the stage as other parents began streaming in to display their genetics against those of other townspeople. Most of the crowd were white mothers who did not work, and Maria felt a bit out of place.

Rows of small seats were set facing the stage leaving a large space open for the students to sit on the floor. The school had maintained the same size of approximately one hundred and twenty students for each grade kindergarten through five for many years. The small size was beneficial. The teachers knew almost every student by name by the time they were fifth graders. Donna Benítez had been the principal for twenty-four years and loved every day—especially this day.

The children now came marching in from the hallway door closest to the stage. They spoke in a low buzz as they entered. Each searched for a parent as they walked to take their place. They sat on the floor in rows squirming and turning to wave at proud, smiling parents. Mrs. Benitez waited for her fifth graders to be fully seated, while she surveyed the one hundred twenty-seven children like a rancher looking at prize cattle. She then walked the wooden stairs four feet up to the raised stage and strode to the center podium.

"Welcome parents, to our year end award program." She began applauding and the crowd joined her.

"We will begin by awarding the best students in each area of studies: Math, Science, Reading, and Social Studies. We also have some other special awards, so let's get started!"

Maria had located Lourdes sitting on the second row close to the middle, but Lourdes had not searched for her mother. She sat smiling and talking with another girl in her class who Maria did not know. Lourdes hair had been so pretty when she left that morning with a yellow bow to match her daffodil yellow polo shirt, yet now her mother looked at a crooked bow atop black hair going all directions. She wore khaki shorts and white tennis shoes and looked like the other girls which supposedly was the goal when dressing ten-year-old girls. Lourdes had bright brown eyes flecked with black, and a sweet face that looked like it was about to smile all the time.

"We begin with our award for our Math Genius student . . . Lourdes Sanchez," Mrs. Benitez announced and waved the little girl, now standing to come to the stage as the crowd applauded. Lourdes walked up the stairs and received the ten-inch-tall gold plastic trophy, and quickly turned to go back down to her seat.

"Not so fast, young lady." Lourdes turned and worried she had done something wrong and froze on the top step. "Lourdes has also won the Excellence in Science category!" She extended her hand to give the smiling and relieved girl another trophy.

The seated kids clapped loudly again with the parents. Lourdes now looked at Mrs. Benitez for permission to leave as the crowd chuckled.

"Just stay where you are, Lourdes. You also have won the Reading award," Principal Benitez said handing her another award. Lourdes was now very embarrassed and feeling thankful but weird about all the attention. She balanced the three trophies in her hands and looked again at Mrs. Benitez for guidance.

The principal smiled at her and used her left hand to guide her back to her seat. Lourdes returned to her friends who were all smiling and shaking their heads up and down quickly in enthusiastic applause.

"Now this next award is really for three subjects including History, Geography and Culture, so please give a nice round of applause for our Spectacular Social Studies award to . . . Claudia Bergman."

Claudia accepted her award wearing a white dress trimmed with a navy-blue collar, cuffs, and hem. The applause was quieter from the children's section but seemed louder from the parent's section. Her shoes were navy blue sandals and all appeared the latest fashion. Her hair had been brushed and freshened prior to the ceremony by her mother as Dorothy Bergman was in the hallway when the students were marching from their rooms. The perfectionist mother had to ensure her daughter's appearance was up to her expectations before she entered the cafeteria. Claudia accepted the award and smiled at her headmaster and waved the trophy at her mother with pride.

Four more awards for various categories were given to individual students as the children came and went with various reactions from shy to showing off. Barrett Downs won most athletic boy and Shara Boyd, who was at least a head taller than anyone in the class, won most athletic girl. When Shara walked to the stage, she pushed her head down between her shoulders to try not to be taller than Mrs. Benitez. Barrett stood beside Shara for a picture, standing on his toes as the kids laughed along with Shara.

"I know that as parents and teachers, we want to award all of our students, but if we give an award to every child, it cheapens the efforts of the most deserving. It is dangerous, in my opinion, to flatter the mediocre. I will say this—and this is extremely important—I have seen average students in the fifth grade become high achievers in middle school or high school or even college. Where we are in life at age ten or eleven, will not, and *should not*, define who we are later in life. But elementary school is when they are mine. These first six years are mine and my teaching staff's responsibility. I see them come here as kindergarteners full of all things wonderful about children. Our last award is for Student of the Year and is selected by the teachers. In my twenty-four years, I believe this is our first unanimous vote in all categories. This young lady is an excellent student—a once in a career student. This is also very important: she is kind and sweet, and I am honored to have been a small part of her life so far. Please welcome our Student of the Year, Lourdes Sanchez!" Mrs. Benitez exclaimed and pointed to Lourdes.

Lourdes stood to walk to the stage and all her classmates stood and clapped as she made her way up the stairs. Maria stood applauding her little girl with happy tears streaming down her cheeks.

"I also want to bring up Mr. Timmons our math teacher." Mrs. Benitez waved the young man of around thirty-five in black frame glasses and wearing a blue plaid shirt and brown polyester pants. He waved his hand high in the air as he walked up the stairs and the kids applauded the fun teacher.

"Mr. Timmons and I have a demonstration for you today. Do you have a calculator?" Mrs. Benitez asked her colleague as Lourdes stood between the two on the stage. He pulled a small calculator from his shirt pocket and waved to the crowd.

"Now, I need some assistance from the audience. Can someone give me a three-digit number?" Someone shouted 123.

"Now can someone give me a four-digit number?" And another voice shouted 7,472.

"Ok, Lourdes. Can you multiply one hundred twenty-three times seven thousand four hundred and seventy-two?" Mrs. Benitez looked down smiling at the crooked yellow bow.

Lourdes looked up at her and flatly said with absolute conviction, "Nine hundred and nineteen thousand and fifty-six."

Mr. Timmons entered the numbers as the principal spoke and raised his calculator in the air and exclaimed, "She is correct!"

The kids all erupted with applause and each one grinning because they already knew she could do it. But the parents were stunned and looked at each other in amazement and joined in the applause.

"Now, you can see why this girl is amazing. It has been my privilege to know her these past six years, and I know she'll do amazing things in her life. This concludes our ceremony and thank you all for being here today." Mrs. Benitez leaned down and hugged Lourdes.

Lourdes walked down the stairs and was greeted like a rock star by her classmates and teachers. Maria waited patiently for her daughter to address her admirers. Maria felt a hand on her shoulder, and she turned to see a beautiful lady smiling at her.

"Hi, Mrs. Sanchez, we have never formally met. My name is Monica Downs. I just wanted to say that your daughter is just a treasure. I'm sure you are so very proud of her. But, oh my, I think the whole town is proud of her! I know you need to go see your child. I just wanted to say hello." Monica shook the short lady's hand smiling sweetly at the proud mother.

Twice a year Monica had been sending Maria a box of her daughter's used clothes, along with several new items, through the priest at the Catholic Church. She had followed Lourdes through the years and heard she was special from the teachers. It was a nice thing she did, but Monica was a nice person, and it seemed wrong if people knew she helped the little girl. True charity is anonymous.

*   *   *

Martha Stall walked through the Morrow County courthouse, comfortable in her white medical coat as the new Physician's Assistant for the Morrow County Health Clinic. The building was completed the year she graduated and became the first director. A federal grant along with a sizeable charitable donation helped to make the facility very nice. Local physicians volunteered time to help and a nearby nursing school had an endless supply of students learning on the job.

Through a scholarship and Martha's own determination, she had reached her medical status as a PA, but for most of the county's poorest, she was their doctor. She walked into the Sheriff's office with a question for Elvis Stanley who was entrenched in his fourth consecutive term.

"Hey, Sheriff, got a minute?" Martha asked curtly.

"Sure, always happy to assist the fine folks at the clinic," he answered cheerfully even though knowing by the tone, it was not going to be friendly.

"There's a young woman in my clinic. She's beat up bad. Her whole body looks like one damn bruise. Are y'all going to at least try and catch the son of a bitch who beat her up?" she asked with her nostrils flaring and fists clinched.

"I know this makes you mad, Martha. Hell, it makes us all mad and you are fixin' to get a whole lot more pissed. We caught him, locked him up by ten this morning and went by to see your beat-up patient. We spoke with her—guess you missed us. She won't file charges."

"Are you kidding me? I talked to her myself! I had her ready to go. She told you she isn't going to put that bastard away?" Martha yelled and paced back and forth like a caged tiger.

"Now settle down, Martha. I get it, but this is considered assault. Her cooperation helps, but he isn't getting out anytime soon," Elvis said doing his best to calm her.

"It's just that it becomes a revolving door of busted faces, broken bones, and fearful hearts. So sad. I know you do your best. It just makes me sick." Martha slumped in the industrial metal chair across from Elvis's desk succumbing to the brutal facts.

"I know, honey. The little ones are the hardest for me. Children abused by the one who is supposed to protect them. That's what gets me. I don't know how many more of those I can see." Elvis looked down at the floor reviewing the history of broken children passing through his mind. They never fully left his memory.

Martha looked at him lost in his trance somehow understanding where his mind had gone. She was trained after years of watching the expressions of tormented women and children and hearing sickening lies from the oppressors. *She fell, or he was on his bicycle when I heard him cry, or I was protecting the family.*

Martha did not stay in that loathsome place for too long. It would kill her if she did. No one saw her crying alone in her car on those days when it was overwhelming, trying to purge the evil before she came home to her own child. A thought from the past crossed her, and she looked at Elvis to break both of their trances.

"Hey, I've been meaning to ask you. Was there anything ever found out about the little girl in the dumpster at Don's a few years ago?"

"Nothing in years. I sent the video to the state lab in Austin. Came up a 1980 Toyota Corolla. Analysis showed two cars pulling behind the store, but only could see the one. Faint headlights on the second car is all but showed there were at least two people involved. No family ever claimed her was the strangest part. The little girl's picture was sent around TV stations around the state. Nothing ever happened. Chased down a few leads on the car, but all checked out. Very strange. My thoughts are some drug deal gone bad. Kid was in a mule's car somehow and became disposable. Who knows? But she's fine now . . . I hear." Elvis did not want to let on he knew where she was.

"I hear that too, and I'm very pleased. At least one young life found a path of hope." Martha smiled.

CHAPTER 5

MONICA DOWNS' LIFE had settled into a routine over the years of school functions, coffee with friends, church, and spending time with her mother-in-law. Four was trying to be a better husband. He would go months without drinking and then binge for a couple of weeks, but he was never violent. Each sober period was nice and normal, and he was a good father and husband until he wasn't. Each binge brought her closer to the contempt she worried would take her over her ivy-covered fences away from what she loved. Her only relief was that he spent more time at their beach house in Port Aransas where his drunkenness was hidden from the prying eyes of the chattering townspeople and his own family.

Monica had grown up in a small town in East Texas. An old oil field location that boomed it up and busted it back down when oil prices dropped. She lived there in the down times. Her mother had raised her with her grandparents in that dead little town, and she thrived there.

She was smart and popular and adored by her grandparents. They were poor, but so was everyone else it seemed. Life was good until her grandparents both tragically died in a car wreck when she was sixteen. She had been devastated by the sudden disappearance of the two people who loved her the most, and her mother was grieving with alcohol to soften the loss. She had a half-sister a couple of years older who had been raised by that sister's other grandparents and moved off years ago when Monica was a baby. Monica did not have that option. She was told her father was a Russian mobster in prison for life. She had never met him and that was as good a story as any to tell a child asking who her daddy was.

Her mother hired a slimy billboard attorney to represent her in the grandparent's fatal wreck. He was the kind of lawyer who dressed in wrestling tights on late night commercials saying he body slammed the big insurance companies. The spring Monica graduated high school, her mother collected fifty-eight thousand dollars after attorney fees. She was a great student and was encouraged to go to college by counselors. No one in her family had ever graduated from high school, much less a university, so the path seemed impossible. Monica received three thousand dollars and a dark blue used Ford sedan with a yellow driver door and no working air conditioner from her mother and was told to go out in the world and make it. Mama needed some time away from the obligations of motherhood. Monica had been to Austin once on a field trip, so she chose to go there with thirty crisp one-hundred-dollar bills in her purse. With no fiscal skills or life skills, she just knew she was the wealthiest she had ever been.

She found a one-bedroom apartment in a semi-safe part of east Austin where rundown cars were parked on narrow streets. She opened her first checking account at a community bank where the banker seemed very interested in assisting her. With utility deposits, a phone, some lightly used furniture, and a couple of cute outfits, the once great pile of money disappeared fast.

*   *   *

Monica was very proud of herself as she sat on the used brown corduroy couch surveying her own kingdom complete with a queen size mattress with a new colorful striped comforter on the floor of the bedroom, a framed print of a New York City skyline she found by a dumpster, and a single setting of antique silverware she bought for eighteen dollars in a fancy store with nice things.

Her own attraction was in stark contrast to her surroundings. Monica was a stunning beauty. Her light brown hair hung just below her shoulders and parted on the left with the right side of her face seductively covered. Her eyebrows framed her haunting blue eyes with an unexpected openness. Her nose matched her perfectly symmetrical features and pointed to her naturally pouting lips. Her face was a soft square with high cheek bones and a balanced chin. She was beautiful.

In the small town she did not realize her potency. But in a college town, full of young men, she was empowered. She exuded sex appeal whenever she wanted to unleash her full arsenal. She could also downplay her looks with baggy clothes and no makeup, and she preferred that over the painted, look at me approach. But she needed to work, so look at me was her strategy for interviewing.

Monica dressed in a lightweight gray V-neck sweater, her best fitted jeans and black heels. She wore a black belt pulled tight across her hips, and enough makeup to get the point across—but not too whorish like her grandmother used to say. Just enough cleavage showed off her generous bust and just tight enough jeans showed off her curvy backside with the heels lifting everything in their sexiest place. She looked in the bathroom mirror and thought, "I would hire me."

Monica worked for two different bars and one restaurant by the end of her first week in Austin. Her days began at six a.m. through the lunch rush at a diner close to her apartment on the east side. She worked with mostly older women who gave her a week tops at the early morning shift Monday through Friday. They were wrong. She loved the job and started making enough in tips to pay her bills. She worked part-time at two bars on Sixth Street and that is where she met her first real boyfriend. His name was Brandon, and he treated her like a queen . . . in the beginning.

He was the bartender at a pub with forty different beers on draft which only created delays in ordering as young people tried to impress their friends and dates with their beer knowledge. She was a naïve beauty who a predator could impress. She was eighteen when they met and he was thirty. She thought he was sophisticated and mature, and he saw a path to use her for his own desires.

No one is brainwashed overnight; it is a long process. In six months, he was living rent free at her apartment. In a year he had been fired again, and she was fully supporting them both. In two years, he was abusing her and suggesting she use her beauty for more than selling food and drink. He made sure she had no real friends and no place to flee. She was desperate and living with a psychopath when she met William Barrett Downs the Fourth.

Four, as she learned to call him, became a regular at the diner and, not like most students, a big tipper. He came in around ten a.m. and was usually alone. Most college students were in class at this time of day, but he always seemed to be free. He remembered her name each time and would casually flirt. She thought he was nice and cute in a nonthreatening way. The two developed a friendly relationship through the weeks of pancakes and over medium eggs with Tabasco sauce. She began to look for him and found herself sad if he did not come. He lived across town and his first time at the diner was with a friend who recommended the food. But he continued to come back for her a few days every week. They were the same age of twenty when he asked her about the bruise on her arm visible under a flared left sleeve of her uniform.

"What happened to your arm?" Four asked as he sat at his now usual booth.

"Oh, I don't know. I think I bumped into a door." She looked embarrassed in her quick response and was horrified at the fact the wound was visible.

"Oh. Well, if you need softer doors, you can stay with me. I had all my doors padded for safety," he said trying to be kind and funny. He had seen the outline of a handprint on the purple bruise.

He was dressed in Levi jeans and worn Topsiders and an untucked pink Polo shirt. His hair was parted on the right and trimmed recently. He had perfect teeth and soft brown eyes. She immediately saw him in a different way because of that one sentence.

"Now don't say something you don't mean," she answered in an awkward flirty tone.

"When do you get off work?" he summoned his courage to give her an opening.

"Maybe twenty years the way things are going in my life," she nervously chuckled. "Really . . . um, let me check if they need me for lunch, and I will let you know." Her mind swirled at the thought he may give her a way out.

She gathered hope for the first time in a very long time. There had been plenty of men flirting with her, but he seemed different and was sincere, maybe even sweet. She thought he was sophisticated but not arrogant. Her fantasy of escape needed to get back to the reality of her terrifying life. She asked the manager if she could take off the lunch shift and he agreed.

"I can leave now if you like. Do you have a car?"

"Great. I'm done eating, so let's get out of here." Four grabbed the check off the table and walked to the register not believing how fast things were going. He was thinking, "How lucky am I to be with the most beautiful girl in Austin or Texas for that matter."

After he paid the tab and she clocked out whispering to one of the other waitresses, they left the restaurant. As they got in his new Mustang, she was silent and sat looking around for her old car to pull in the parking lot. "I must say this is surprising, Monica. That is your real name, I hope," Four said thinking how bizarre this seemed.

Monica quickly looked at him and nervously smiled. "I have to tell you something, Four. The bruise on my arm was not from a door. He beats me." Suddenly Monica was sobbing into her hands.

"I know. I'm so sorry. He will never touch you again." Four was surprised at his response but he meant it. He didn't know why the beautiful stranger had affected him, but he needed to do the right thing. He gently patted her back as they drove to his apartment across the Colorado River on Riverside Drive.

Monica moved from Brandon to Four that day and soon it felt like destiny. The two snuck over late one night, and with the extra keys she had in her purse she took her car back and hid it in the enclosed garage at Four's apartment. They watched her old apartment until they knew he was gone and retrieved what she could. She called all the utilities and had them cancelled as she smiled at the thought of that bastard suddenly sitting in the dark. She told the apartment manager she had joined the military and would be shipping out the next day. She whispered to her friend at the diner to pass on the message of an uncle from Houston coming to take her away. Maybe confusion would keep her safe. When you are told, *I will kill you if you leave me enough times*, it is difficult to feel safe immediately.

She stayed with Four in his apartment for six months, and he paid for everything. They kept a low profile and stayed out of bars and cafes she thought Brandon may visit. Four had a stocked liquor cabinet with drinks ready for all his friends who came over. A party was always at their apartment which was fun when you are young.

The neighbors were invited to the parties including an exotic looking student named Anika Laghari. The foreign student was amazed at the Texas and American culture and she and Monica quickly became friends. Anika's family had moved from India to Corpus Christi, Texas, where her father was an engineer for Dupont. She was expected to become an engineer like her overbearing dad. Anika was twelve years younger than her only sister and had adapted to America much faster.

Monica opened up to Anika about Brandon's abuse, and it was nice to make a friend and be able to confide her fears. Anika spoke of how strict her culture was and the girls laughed at how bad things had been and how fun their life was now.

The whole complex seemed to rotate in and out of Four's apartment. International students with strange accents, wealthy white boys in starched oxford button downs, hippie chicks in hip hugger bell-bottoms, sorority girls in colorful sundresses, and one older stoner guy called Creepy Bob who had been in school for ten years. It was an amazing time for Monica. She was enchanted by all of these different people. Four was rich and looking for an excuse to party and enjoy his youth. He was pleasant and not a mean drunk. But once he reached a certain buzz, he would disappear to his room leaving Monica to be hostess.

As Anika and Monica became closer friends, both learned from each other's culture. Monica never really knew she had a culture, but Anika asked her about everything: education systems, money, foods, and mostly sex and boys. It turned out men were the same on both sides of the world, but Anika had a much more severe code of ethics. Monica confided how wonderful Four had been as her true knight in shining armor. The two girls hung out when Anika was not in class or studying. Her roommates were a bit too boring for Anika who was now a senior in college and for the first time she was feeling rebellious.

One warm afternoon, Anika came to Four's apartment to escape her studies. Monica opened the door wearing a bright pink two-piece bathing suit as she was heading to the apartment complex's pool. Anika had never worn a bathing suit, and she was embarrassed at the sight of another woman with so much exposed skin.

Monica talked her into putting on one of her suits, because they were close enough in size, and they went to the pool. Anika felt naked as she unfurled the large towel she was given and laid it on the warm concrete beside the sparkling pool. Her brown skin did not require any more darkening which she knew sun tanning was clearly a white girl's game. The traffic around the pool usually increased when any girls were out, and Monica always drew a crowd of admirers. But now the black-haired beauty sitting next to her brought a new dimension. Monica was aware of her power over the opposite sex, but this was new to the girl from India, and she felt different, strong, scared, and excited.

They lingered by the pool and snuck peeks at immature young men splashing about in some ritual display for the females of the species. Anika had just become comfortable in her new role as assistant goddess, when she saw a familiar man walking from the parking lot and turn left toward her apartment.

"I have to go now," she urgently whispered to Monica and draped her towel over her body as much as possible.

"Wait. I'll go too. What's wrong?" Monica asked matching Anika's low voice as she quickly followed her friend. They entered Four's apartment and found him asleep on the couch.

"I have to change clothes and leave now. My dad is here. He would kill me if he knew I was dressed like this in front of people. You cannot say anything if you meet him," Anika pleaded.

"Sure. Wow, I know you said he was strict before, but you look so cute," Monica answered.

"But you don't understand . . . it's just different."

"I see. Sure, go change and if he asks, I'll tell him you were here helping me study."

"Great, thanks." Anika quickly changed and ran toward her apartment where she found her father sitting against her door with a scowl on his face.

* * *

Anika came to the apartment the next day when Monica was alone while Four had gone on an errand.

"Did you get in trouble with your Dad?" Monica asked as soon as she answered the door.

"I am always in trouble with my Father. But it would have been much worse if he had seen me in a bathing suit. He was mad enough because I was wearing *white people devil clothes!*" Anika imitated. her Dad's Indian accent and laughed.

"You were wearing a t-shirt and jeans! That's white devil clothes?"

"According to him!" Anika was laughing but she was serious. A knock on the door interrupted the two.

Monica got up and answered the door. It was Creepy Bob.

"Oh hi, Four isn't here," Monica said feeling uncomfortable inviting him in without Four present.

"It's cool. What you chicks up to?" Creepy Bob asked standing at the door.

"Studying." Anika walked up behind Monica for support.

"So . . . like, your name is Monica and your name is Anika, and like are you two sisters or something?"

"Yes, Creepy Bob, we are sisters. We have different mothers, but different fathers. We have to study," Anika said and closed the door and quickly locked it.

The two girls stared at each other and both covered their mouths to prevent Creepy Bob hearing the outburst of laughter. Monica looked through the peep hole and saw him sauntering away apparently unfazed.

"I cannot believe you! You called him Creepy Bob to his face. That was hilarious!" Both girls began laughing hysterically.

"I know! I've never done anything like that. I'm gonna pee my pants!" Anika bent over holding her crotch and matching her friend's reaction.

"Sisters!" they said together and sat on the sofa spending the rest of the afternoon laughing as they waited on Four to come home so they could tell him the story.

* * *

Monica bought books and clothes and had her hair cut and colored by a real stylist with the generous allowance Four gave her. She read his abandoned textbooks and absorbed the knowledge gratefully. She came home one day from a beauty salon and he announced they were going to meet his parents. Monica did not feel ready for this step. Four understood meeting the parents could be hard, but his father appreciated hard working, smart people and his mother would see how kind she was. They were going to tell them the truth about their relationship. The part about him dropping out of school would not be part of this truthful approach.

His parents did adore her, and they were hopeful she would be a good influence on their son who was prone to drink too much and shirk responsibilities. Monica was safe in the hands of her flawed prince who loved her. He had found someone his parents liked and she elevated him in their eyes. Monica would look good driving a new Chevy Suburban around town with their future beautiful children.

They were married at the First Baptist Church in Travis City five months later. Monica had no family in attendance. Anika from Austin and Four's sister, Daisy, were the only bridesmaids. The bride was a photographer's dream throwing her head back with a lacey veil cascading away from her shoulders as she pushed a square of bright white iced cake into her new husband's smiling face while all the town cheered and laughed. Her new mother-in-law thought, "I won't have to share holidays or grandkids with another family. She really is perfect."

CHAPTER 6

THE FIRST DAY of summer 1996 began early for Lourdes. The voice of Maria yelling from the hallway was not a pleasant way to greet the morning.

"Lourdes, get up! We have to be at the bank in twenty minutes." Maria returned to her kitchen where bacon was frying, and eggs were being scrambled to be ladled on to a warm flour tortilla. Danny was a morning person. He was singing and dancing around Maria playfully patting her butt.

"Stop that! I have to get this breakfast done and your lazy daughter dressed and be at the bank at five thirty," Maria said to her flirty husband.

"So, when she's *lazy*, she's my daughter? Do I get the *super smart* daughter too?" he retorted with a big smile.

"No, that part belongs to me!" She turned and quickly kissed her husband.

Lourdes came walking down the hall sliding her feet slowly as she approached her parents.

"Ew! Don't be kissing like that in front of your child this early in the morning," Lourdes lectured her parents.

"I'll take you two to the bank, so don't worry about being late. Maybe in a few weeks I can find a car for your mama, so I don't have to take her everywhere. The new job at the bank will be great steady money for us. I do wish it was not so early, but this is what your mother wanted, and *the man* is there early," Danny answered.

"Who is *the man*?" Lourdes questioned.

"That would be Mr. Downs. He owns the bank and he is very rich. He has a big ranch too with a thousand cows. My friend works for him at the ranch," Danny spoke with authority. "He gets there early every day and sits in his office and counts all his money. I've heard he doesn't speak to his children and doesn't have any friends."

"Stop talking like that, Danny. You are going to scare the child," Maria scolded her husband.

"Is he really mean like that?" Lourdes questioned her father.

"Nah, I was just teasing, baby girl. Just be nice to him, and I bet he'll be nice to you. I go to church with him and Mrs. Downs, but I doubt he knows me. He is wealthy for sure. He's not like us. Rich people are different," Danny stated his opinion.

Lourdes and her parents climbed into Danny's old pickup truck to make the trip on their first day of the bank job. The doors creaked and rattled as they opened and closed them with a hard slam. Lourdes sat in the middle staring ahead at the darkness of her familiar street as the three passed through the old neighborhood. Occasionally there would be a front porch light illuminating a sand yard with scattered bicycles and rusted barbeque pits. Most of the small wood frame houses were built after World War II for workers at a local manufacturing plant.

Danny's pickup went the few blocks to the west entry of the little neighborhood and turned south on Elm the six blocks to Main Street. Main ran east west, and the old downtown was about five blocks long lined with brick buildings constructed over the past one hundred and fifty years. Parking places angled into the building storefronts and were mostly empty early in the morning except for City Bakery where workers and a few early customers were gathered. It was a place frozen in time but charming in its simplicity.

The north south streets were named after trees. The bank was two blocks west of Elm at the corner of Maple Street. The old downtown buildings were in remarkably good shape. All were occupied with various businesses and services reflecting a vibrant community. The bank had undergone an extensive renovation twenty years before gaining a shiny modern glass façade while still incorporating the old brick. It was a symbol of old and new that stood valiantly as a beacon of success.

Mr. Downs' pickup was parked under a double carport in the rear of the bank when they arrived just before five thirty. The two new employees exited the truck, and Danny backed away but paused and waited for them to safely gain access to the bank. He saw the glass door open and recognized Mr. Downs in the doorway as his wife and daughter entered. Danny waved to him and headed to Caesar's Welding Shop to start his day.

"Good morning, Mr. Downs. This is my daughter, Lourdes. She will be helping me," Maria politely introduced her daughter.

"Nice to meet you, young lady." Mr. Downs extended his hand to Lourdes and then Maria. "I'm here each day at five thirty and I'll let you in. If you arrive here before me, just wait on the bench outside where the smokers go. I would request that you do my office last, because I may not want to have it done that day and you can go on. I expect you to complete your duties by 7:45 each morning. Our employees begin arriving at that time. Maria, the supply closet is there." He pointed to an unmarked door in the hallway.

"We will work hard for you. I promise," Maria assured her new boss.

Maria and Lourdes began their approach to the spacious lobby. From the double glass front door there was a row of four secretary desks stationed in front of enclosed offices with heavy wooden doors and glass fronts. The walls consisted of dark wood panels that reached up twelve feet high with a cream- colored plastered ceiling adorned with five three-foot-wide chandeliers. The left side was a teller line of dark mahogany and white marble with four stations where cheery ladies in dresses from JC Penney greeted customers with well-trained smiles. A hallway from the lobby to the rear door had the supply closet on the right followed by the break room. On the left was the vault, a door to the accounting department, composed of one large open room with cubicles, and the next door led to Dawn Monroe's office sitting as a barrier to Mr. Downs' inner sanctum.

Lourdes helped by emptying the trash cans and scooping up any loose crumpled paper found on the floor. She dusted desks and chairs while her mother vacuumed the offices and hallway runner. The two were so busy scrubbing and cleaning, they never noticed Mr. Downs crossing to obtain his second cup of coffee. He paused as he returned and admired the two cleaning. It was not a glamorous job, but it was a necessary job. Mr. Downs appreciated anyone who worked hard. He thought how admirable it was to see such a young person on her stomach reaching under a desk for a loose piece of trash. Most children were asleep this time of day. But not her. She was here helping her industrious mother who was such a great example for a child. He thought of his own children, and how their lives were so different and not always for the best.

When Mr. Downs' children were born, his parents had placed two million dollars in a trust for each child—William Barrett Downs the Fourth and Daisy Marie Downs. This was done in part for tax purposes by Four and Daisy's grandparents. The inheritance tax code had a way of creating diversions. The money could not be touched until they reached twenty-five years of age, and neither were made aware of the fund until that day. The trust could then be converted to an investment that paid the recipient with the goal of retaining the principle amount such as tax-free municipal bonds. The trust manager at the Executive Bank & Trust in Fort Worth was a very talented, and even luckier, man. The initial two million dollars now exceeded twenty million dollars in each one of the Downs' heirs' accounts. The twenty million each had been converted to tax free municipal bonds to provide an income. At 2.25 percent, Four and Daisy were each receiving over $450,000 tax free annually. Mr. Downs often thought how his parents, while trying to do good, had instead ruined his children's lives.

* * *

The local Catholic priest, Father Michael, would bring Maria a box twice a year filled with fashionable, gently used clothes and some new underwear and shoes. It was always a special day. Maria and Lourdes would pull out the clothes and spread the bounty on her bed commenting on style and colors. Lourdes never thought how nice this was. She assumed most people received clothing from the church. Maria understood how generous this gift was and was always surprised when a tag would show the high prices. She knew her daughter had a much nicer wardrobe than she and Danny, but clothing was not important to either of them. When Maria asked who was doing such a nice thing, Father Michael would only say the donor requested anonymity.

Lourdes wore a cute blue and white striped dress from the box that Sunday as Danny dropped them off at the Catholic Church for early Mass, while he headed to Sunday school at his Baptist Church a couple of blocks away. Most Sundays Lourdes would leave after Mass and walk to meet her father for his eleven a.m. services. It was Danny's favorite part of his week when he would see his daughter walking down the sidewalk to the front steps of his church. He would smile broadly at her from the top of the entry steps and take her hand to proudly walk into the sanctuary and sit in the left rear section.

Mr. Downs and his wife, Janet, sat in their normal place on the right side three rows from the front. Monica, Barrett, and Janet Ann joined them all dressed like an ad for a high fashion magazine. Four would occasionally come, and a couple of times a year, Daisy would travel, usually alone, from California for a visit. Daisy had no children and rarely brought a husband or boyfriend knowing her father's politics would not match anyone she would be with.

Danny never owned a suit or tie but tried to look nice in frayed black slacks and an ironed white shirt. He loved to sing the traditional hymns even though he was off key. But it was a joyful noise to the Lord, he always said. After an opening prayer, three hymns, announcements on who died, and a solo by a talented lady and the choir, they passed the plate. Danny would hand a quarter to Lourdes to give, and he would fold a bill from his pocket as they were given the opportunity to tithe. The preacher stood in the pulpit for the day's message.

He had been the preacher for three years and had been a controversial pick by the pulpit committee. He was not from Texas. He was from North Carolina, but at least he wasn't a Yankee per the pulpit committee chairman. He was a tall slender man of about forty. He was slick bald on top and thankfully kept the remaining hair closely trimmed. He had a moustache, raising some concerns among the older ladies of the church, but his wife didn't seem to mind. He had a wonderful bass voice that soothed the soul as he poured God's words out like warm syrup on a hot buttered biscuit.

The preacher began his sermon. "Today we will study a passage from the Sermon on the Mount. Open your Bibles, please, to Matthew 6: 14 and 15. *For if ye forgive men their trespasses, your heavenly Father will also forgive you; but if ye forgive not men their trespasses, neither will your Father forgive your trespasses.* This may sound easy," the preacher continued, "but have you forgiven all the people in your lives who have caused you harm? I know I have not, because it is very difficult. What if it is a family member who hurt you, or a business partner who stole from you, or what if someone hurt your child? This may indeed be one of the most difficult tenants to follow in Christianity. Why did Jesus say this in the Sermon on the Mount? I believe that forgiveness is part of healing. If you hold on to that anger, who are you hurting? You are only hurting yourself. Forgive as fast as you can and release the anger."

Each person in attendance heard the message differently because each was in a different place in their lives. The eyes looking back at the preacher were absorbing the message and thinking of those they needed to forgive. They thought of bad things they had done that needed to be forgiven. It was an uncomfortable message, and many found their minds wandering to the bad things done to them by others. The pastor walked back and forth with his Bible open for reference and authority.

The preacher spoke further, "We cannot be perfect. We *all* fall short, but we can forgive if we are strong enough. When you pray, ask God for forgiveness and ask God for the strength to forgive others. If you think about it, forgiving others when they don't deserve it is as close to God's holy grace as we can attain." The service concluded with a hymn of invitation and a prayer. No one joined that Sunday morning.

Janet stood and steadied herself holding the back of a pew and spoke to the church members as they passed by to the exit. Janet's eye caught the sight of a black-haired girl with a familiar dress she thought she remembered buying one just like that for Janet Ann a couple years ago. It seemed an expensive dress for a laborer to buy for his daughter. Monica gathered her children and stood next to her mother-in-law.

"I have a roast in the crock pot at home. We'll see you at my house in a few minutes," Monica told her mother-in-law. Most Sundays were the same. Either Monica or Janet prepared Sunday lunch and they would speak during the week to make their plan for who would provide the family meal.

"Oh yes, honey! We'll be there." Janet smiled grimacing in pain at the same time.

Monica herded her offspring through the departing crowd to get home as quickly as possible to make sure her house looked good for her in-laws. She had lost touch with her own mother after she moved to Austin. Her mother had sold her grandparent's house and moved away with no forwarding address. Occasionally Monica would ask a friend from her hometown if anyone had heard from her mother and no one ever had.

Monica's third white Suburban since she had given birth to their first child was parked in the back parking lot to allow older people closer parking. She missed driving Four's cool Mustang, but now she was a committed mother of two and she embraced the role. She made the short, few blocks drive and parked in her spot in the garage at the Downs family Victorian home. Her children ran ahead to the back door bursting through the unlocked door arguing over shoelaces because that is what siblings do.

"Go sit down and be quiet! Nanny and Pop are coming for lunch, and I need you to pretend to be normal children for ten minutes!" the strained mother pleaded knowing there was little chance they would actually respond. Monica had the dining table set the way she had been taught by Janet. The family silver was properly placed adjacent to the heirloom china. She had fresh white roses from her garden in a Waterford vase measured perfectly in the center of the inlaid mahogany table. She was standing admiring her table when the back door opened.

"Hello, where are my grandkids?" the melodic voice of Janet Downs called out as she entered the back door into the kitchen.

"Hi, Nanny! Hi, Pop!" Barrett and Janet Ann ran to the door and both hugged their grandmother. Mr. Downs came in behind her making sure she made it up the stairs safely.

"Come sit, Janet," Monica said pulling out her usual chair. Janet released her two grandchildren and reached behind her for her husband's steady hand to guide her to the dining table. Today was a tough day with her back pain. Monica had a firm bone shaped, back pillow waiting in the chair for her mother-in-law to ease her pain. She sat down and the grandchildren sat on each side of their grandmother. Mr. Downs sat across from her and Monica beside him.

The conversation consisted of what the kids had been doing and their plans for the summer in a manner of excitement, considering their recent release from their school duties. Mr. Downs commented on the sermon and how he was liking the preacher more every Sunday. Janet teased the kids, and they all laughed at silly banter completely ignoring the fact that Four was not present.

CHAPTER 7

M R. DOWNS HUNCHED forward at his desk reading a proposal for a loan. He had a certain internal score card he would mentally check as he read through a loan packet. Collateral, business history, cash flows, contingency plans, projected profitability, but most of all, his gut feeling. Would this person pay him back? It really was that simple. "If I gave this borrower a thousand dollars or ten million dollars, will they figure out a way to pay me back." Deciding who was the most honorable and had the most grit was the central role of the banker.

"Randy on line two, and tell him I'm still married . . . but barely," Dawn called out loudly from her office while laughing at herself.

"Hey, sum bitch," Mr. Downs answered leaning back in his chair.

"Hey, sum bitch. You free for lunch? I'm in town checking on Mama and craving some El Rancho deluxe fat ass platter. I can come by at 11:30," Randy said.

"Sure thing, compadre. Come on by."

"Is he coming here?" Dawn asked standing in the doorway.

"Yep, we are going for some El Rancho. You want to come?"

"Sure! If Randy sees me eating, that's all it'll take for us to be together. I am one sexy consumer of chips and salsa."

"How in the hell can someone be sexy at eating chips and salsa?"

"Oh, you poor man! Been with your bride so long, you don't have a clue how the game is played."

"Dang, Dawn. You're married . . . again . . . so you might need to tone it down, and remember he's married too."

"I know, but it's good to bait a few fields just in case. A girl has to be prepared," Dawn giggled.

At the predetermined time of 11:30, the tall trim man with a stylish new silver belly cowboy hat atop his graying head, walked into Dawn's office.

"Hello, my darlin." Randy greeted her with the smile of a confident man while taking off his hat.

"Well, 'hello my darlin' back to you, handsome. Come give me some sugar." Dawn stood and embraced her boss' best friend.

"You two break it up. We got Mexican food to eat and I'm starving." Mr. Downs walked in to greet Randy.

"I got a new truck. Plenty of room in it, so y'all come ride with me, because Dawn and I don't want to be seen in your antique truck," Randy teased as they walked out of the bank to the rear parking lot.

"My truck is just fine with me. Besides, new ones are too expensive," Mr. Downs defended his truck.

"You are so tight; you would crawl under a gate to save the hinges," Randy quipped.

Dawn laughed loudly as they got in the new four-door, fully loaded Chevy truck. The drive was only a few blocks away, but driving was easier, quicker, and most of all air conditioned on the warm summer day. The parking lot was full, so Randy squeezed his truck in a spot toward the back with just enough room to crawl out of the leather seated cabin.

Mr. Downs led the way through the double doors into the restaurant, already buzzing with chattering patrons and scurrying waiters and waitresses. The hostess in her colorful dress weaved between the green and red tablecloths on heavy wooden tables as she clutched three menus which seemed to act as an invisible rudder allowing them to reach the destination in the rear.

Dawn spoke to two nurses from her gynecologist's office; Randy said hi to four men from a surveying crew that had done work for him in the past; and Mr. Downs paused at a table to say hello to a lady from church who was with her niece in from Houston. Several others waved or nodded their heads to the man in the suit, the man in the cowboy hat, and the woman with the big hair. It was common for the people of Travis City to speak and smile to one another because all were intertwined and connected in some way through work, or school, or church, or family. It kept them civil in many ways. You had to be careful criticizing anyone. You never knew who was related. Rude behavior is punished swiftly where everyone knows your name.

The menus were passed out and a woman appeared out of nowhere with a basket of hot, fried tortilla chips and three bowls of salsa placed in front of each person.

"Who read The Letter this year?" Randy asked as he took a chip from the basket.

"Sookie Burns," Mr. Downs answered.

"Big Sookie or Little Sookie?" Randy asked.

"Big. It's a real sweet story. Turns out Big Sookie could not read a word," Dawn injected.

"My Lord! Big Sookie is old as a big tree," Randy said while looking over the menu with his reading glasses perched on his nose.

"Yeah, he's gotta be ninety. So Big Sookie's granddaughter, Miriam the schoolteacher, she's married to Jack Fields who works at the power company. Anyway, she finds out her own grandfather can't read. This was like a year ago, so she teaches him how. Word gets out about Big Sookie learning to read and The Letter Committee names him. He gets up to read The Letter and a good crowd is there. You know, because he worked for the county over forty years driving dozers and maintainers, and there were a hundred of the Burns family there . . . that family is as fertile as bottomland. I think Big Sookie and his wife DeeLight had seven kids—six girls and little Sookie." Dawn spoke without taking a breath while the two men ate chips and occasionally looked at Dawn and grinned at each other.

"Big Sookie gets up behind the microphone . . . You remember, Billy, we were standing by the monument . . . and he does it perfect. It was beautiful. I cried and half the crowd was bawling. It was my favorite Letter reading. Very sweet," Dawn finished with her eyes beginning to tear.

"I think it was my favorite, too. My father thought the world of Mr. Sookie Burns and this town owes that man. Daddy would say Mr. Burns was the greatest crop ever come out of The Bottoms. I was glad to see him honored." Mr. Downs looked at his longtime work wife with supportive kindness.

"Dang, I regret missing that one. Way better than when Margaret Collins did it forty years ago. That time was funny though. You were too young, Dawn, but Billy and I were there. We may have been fourteen or so. Well, she was a senior in high school and maybe the nerdiest human on the planet. She was painfully unattractive with frizzy red hair and a pimply face with these terrible glasses, but she was chosen because of some essay contest. So, she stands up at the microphone in some homemade fanciful dress and she starts reading The Letter. There is a storm brewing on the southeast sky with lightning and black clouds, and the crowd is starting to get nervous about the storm." Mr. Downs began giggling like a little boy as his friend relayed the story.

"Well, Margaret is almost finished reading—just about to say Liberty or Death—when a strong wind pushed through the crowd and seemed to go right under her legs and lifted her entire dress over her head. She was standing with her back up against the courthouse, and the wind could only go up. Then, she breaks and runs stage right, but she can't see because, you know the dress is over her, and she runs over and knocks down Mayor Adams. You know he's about as big around as he is tall, and she's laying on top of him trying her best to get her dress back down, but all the crowd can see is bright white legs and white cotton panties frantically squirming on top of a fat man built like a beach ball. It was the greatest Letter reading ever."

Randy concluded with Dawn and Mr. Downs laughing uncontrollably, and Randy joined in the laughter as the crowded restaurant stared at the three of them.

"That poor girl. What ever happened to her?" Dawn caught her breath and asked.

"To her credit, she showed up at school the next day like nothing happened. She was tougher than we thought. She kind of wore the event like a badge of honor in some strange way. I always admired her for that. Most people would have crumbled. I heard she lives in Oklahoma City now days and works as an accountant," Randy answered.

"We were cruel to that poor girl. I would like to think I am a better person now, but that was the funniest thing I've ever seen." Mr. Downs tried to excuse his own behavior.

The waitress came and they ordered and ate and laughed some more. Randy loved telling stories about his lifelong friend that Dawn had never heard. Mr. Downs caught himself watching Dawn eat chips and salsa. She genuinely was a little sexy when she ate. He chuckled to himself and thought, "What else do I not know in this world?"

*   *   *

William Barrett Downs IV sat on the deck of the three-story beach house in Port Aransas watching the blue and white surf crash into the white sand. The constant sound was soothing to him like listening to a mother's heartbeat in the womb. It was all so primitive. His noon meal was a few crackers with some sharp cheddar cheese and three screwdrivers in a tumbler. He stared at the half empty glass and knew a trip to the liquor store was required. He went every day buying a fifth of vodka at a time. If he bought more he had learned he would just drink it all. In some strange way it kept him more sober. And just in case he quit, there would be no temptation in the house.

The best thing that ever happened to him was Monica, so why had he done such a thing against her? But, of course, she never knew all these things he had done. He had moments of being good. Good to his parents and wife and children, but they were only moments. He had learned to hide away and punish himself for his sins his own way. The friends he had grown up with and those from college had faded away after valiant efforts to rescue the lost young man. The little church in the beach community was nice and he liked to attend, but he would come in late and leave during the benediction, so he didn't have to speak with anyone or have someone smell his breath.

He and Monica spoke every day around nine am before the alcohol took over. She had never given up, but he could tell her fight was weakening. No matter where they were, she prayed for him each call. It was always the same, "Please God, restore my husband. Heal him, Lord." He cried after he hung up the phone, because he knew he would break another promise to her and God.

CHAPTER 8

MR. DOWNS BEGAN to look forward to seeing Maria and Lourdes each morning which surprised him. He had always enjoyed his early morning time alone at the bank reading, studying, or writing letters. He wrote letters for many reasons: thank you, congratulations, sympathy, encouragement, graduation, or simply, you were on my mind. He wrote to men and women, old and young, family and acquaintances. He felt that letter writing had been discarded by society and it was so important to the fabric of life. Travis' Letter was how their town identified. Some towns it was a crop or insect or a famous event, but his town was the written word.

Dawn would be given a first draft for review. If the letter was designed to evoke sentiment, she usually would cry. It became a litmus test of sort. He would print it, lay it on her desk, give her a few minutes and return to find her teary. She would say, "It's very good." He would smile and ask if it needed any changes and she would say no or yes with the edits. Little did he know, she kept copies of all those letters in a box by her desk.

Maria could be heard vacuuming and Lourdes had walked into his office with a can of dusting spray.

"Can I clean in here? I will be very quiet," she meekly addressed the imposing man.

"Of course, but you don't have to be quiet today. I am done with my morning letter project."

"Can I ask you something?" the little girl bravely asked.

"Sure. Anything you like, young lady."

"Are you rich?"

"That is a good question. I suppose that depends on the definition of rich. What is your definition of rich?"

"I guess a million dollars. Do you have that much?"

"Let's say I want to define rich as something different than that. My definition of rich is being loved and healthy and having a safe home and something to do that contributes to the world."

"That sounds like an answer from someone who *has* a million dollars." She looked right at him.

"Ha, that was brilliant, young lady! How did you get to be so smart?" He realized he was speaking to someone he had misjudged and he leaned back in his chair and laughed again.

"I am smart. Like the smartest girl in school."

"I bet you are. And also, hard working. You and your mother are doing the best job ever of anyone cleaning the bank." He saw her mother Maria standing in the doorway shocked to overhear her daughter speaking with Mr. Downs.

"Can we have a raise then?" Lourdes asked now standing straight across the imposing desk.

"Lourdes! Don't speak to Mr. Downs like that! I'm so sorry, Mr. Downs. Lourdes, say you are sorry," Maria blurted out in a panic.

"No, she doesn't owe me an apology, but I respect you, Maria." Mr. Downs drew back a little, aware he may have overstepped his authority.

"Can we get a raise if I win a contest? Like a math contest?" Lourdes cocked her head and smiled at her boss.

"Lourdes! We are not doing that. Mr. Downs, she is very good at math and it may not be fair," Maria pleaded.

"Now, I'm very good at math myself, so I don't mind a contest. She may need to learn a lesson." He playfully smiled at his young opponent.

"Mr. Downs, she really is very good at math. She's the best her teacher has ever seen." Maria tried once more.

"I know you are proud of your daughter, but I'm fine. What are the stakes?"

"Twenty more dollars a week because you already said we were the best," Lourdes said crossing her arms in defiance.

"And if I win, you, young lady, will have to clean my truck once a week. Deal?" he extended his hand across the desk and they shook.

"What are the rules?" he asked.

"Multiplication. No calculators. No pen. No paper," Lourdes announced.

Mr. Downs figured she had memorized multiplication tables as he had done himself. He was a bit rusty but was sure he could do it in his head.

"I will ask each of you a question and you answer as quick as you can. Ok, five times five?" Maria began with an easy one. They both answered twenty-five immediately.

"Mom, do something harder. Like at assembly."

"Mr. Downs, please say a three-digit number. Whatever you like." Maria now knew the game.

"Four hundred thirty-one."

"Now a four-digit number."

"Seven thousand six hundred twenty-seven."

"Lourdes, multiply those numbers." Maria turned to her daughter.

"Three million, two hundred eighty-seven thousand, two hundred thirty-seven," Lourdes responded with heavy emphasis on the last number.

"What the . . . Let me check that." Mr. Downs turned and placed his calculator in front of him as he mumbled the numbers to himself.

"That is correct. My Lord! I have been conned by the cleaning crew!" He raised his hands above his head and laughed and applauded her.

"Now, are you going to answer my question about the million dollars?" Lourdes wanted her answer.

"Yes, is the answer, but now I'm twenty dollars a week lighter. You are a real Lulu, young lady. I believe that is the nickname for Lourdes." He smiled with amazement at this exceptional child.

"I am very impressed with you, Miss Sanchez, and I'm calling you Lulu from now on to remind me of this day. I tell you what I'll do. Anytime you have a question for me, come in and we will talk about whatever subject you like. Is that a deal?"

"Yes, sir! Thanks, Mr. Downs, for being a good sport, too. Mom tried to warn you!"

"She sure did. You have a good mother."

"Okay, sir." Maria bowed her head toward her boss knowing how kind he was being to her daughter.

Maria and Lourdes finished and began their walk to their next job cleaning Mrs. Jernigan's house just two blocks west and one south.

"Mr. Downs is very smart I think," said Lourdes to her mother as they walked under the sprawling oak trees covering the sidewalks past the nicer old homes of the town. A time of past wealth which was preserved by new families.

"Yes, he is very smart, but not quite as smart as you in math!" Maria praised.

"Ha-ha, that's for sure! But he is smarter in other things. He may be the smartest person I know. He has so many books and he went to college. He's like teacher smart. Who was your favorite teacher, Mama?"

"I don't remember. That was a long time ago."

*   *   *

The next week an additional twenty-dollar bill was in Maria's envelope with her weekly check, and she showed Danny.

"Can you believe this? Our daughter has pulled in another twenty dollars a week. We are rich!" Maria exclaimed in excitement.

"Define rich, Mother?" Lourdes mimicked Mr. Downs to her Mom who was seated in their modest living room.

"We are, my child, because we have you!" Danny answered tickling her as she laughed.

"Are we rich, Daddy?"

"Well, not like Mr. Downs rich, but I suppose it's all relative. There will always be someone richer and there will always be someone poorer than you, but what I try to do is be grateful for what we have. Being grateful is the secret, I think. That's what the Bible says," Danny answered thoughtfully.

"He said being loved and healthy and doing something important, or helping someone, that makes you rich." Lourdes looked at her father for confirmation.

"That's a good way to look at things. He's an only child of wealthy parents, though he once had an older sister who died when Mr. Downs was around eight years old. He talked about it at church one Sunday in front of everyone. Talked about how it was hard on his parents, and how when he became a father he understood. He told the story because one of the church families had lost a child and it was an unbearable pain. I don't know what I would do if anything happened to you."

Danny hugged his daughter tightly and Maria joined them on the worn sofa in a group hug. Lourdes had never felt more loved, and she briefly felt she knew what Mr. Downs meant about being rich. Right now, she was a millionaire.

* * *

Maria and Lourdes sat on the painted wooden bench by the rear entrance waiting for their boss to arrive to unlock the bank. A storm could be heard rumbling in the black sky with occasional flashes of lightning from the other side of the building.

During severe thunderstorms, Maria's mind returned to the night she walked out of her crude shack thirty-three years prior at age thirteen. That night a storm was brewing from the southeast of her village in Mexico forty miles from the Texas border town of Roma. There was no real organized law, so the mothers of the barrio banded together to create their own police force with straight razors folded carefully in their cleavage.

Lightning flashed with the sound of delayed thunder. She counted the seconds after the flash to calculate how far off the storm was. Her mother had taught her each five seconds was a mile. One, two, three, four, five—one mile away. It is amazing how much time displays across your mind from a pivotal memory, and the entire episode flashed like the bolts of lightning in the predawn sky.

Maria was the youngest of four children and the only girl. Her older brothers were out of the family home or had died from poor choices by the time she was eleven. Her mother passed away due to poorly treated breast cancer the year before, and at the age of twelve she fulfilled her mother's role, sadly in every way. The three-room house had a primitive kitchen and a single box fan to fight off the summer heat. Chickens and a nanny goat roamed in the yard with a makeshift fence of found wire and scrapped wooden pallets surrounding the stucco hovel which was the same brown color as the dirt yard.

There were great fields of grain surrounding the village, and in September, the Americanos would come and hunt the thousands of white wing doves feeding in the grain fields. Her brothers had worked as bird boys starting at age seven. Running and retrieving the killed birds like well trained dogs for the excited hunters. The boys would hide their tips, because the ten dollars paid for a half day was more than their father made all day. One of the hunters would bring dozens of boxes of donated items when he came. It was a happy day to receive the donations, and each year the nice man delivered much needed clothing and shoes.

The hunting guide, who hired the boys, would make sure the donations were distributed to all, and not be controlled by a single person, to prevent corruption. The guide grew up in Texas, but his parents were from this agricultural area, so he understood the proper rules of negotiation. Maria would get shoes and a few shorts and shirts. The boys would be given baseball caps with random business names, tennis shoes that were usually too big, and some high school sweatshirts and pants. The night she left, she packed some of the donated clothes in a cheap plaid bag and put her hair under a cap to hide her gender. She would be traveling light.

She had journeyed several times with her father to the border town of Roma, Texas, to retrieve machinery parts for tractors or other equipment or an occasional shopping trip. Her father worked in the fields operating large tractors and combines and at the end of each day looked like someone had shoveled loose dirt over him while being careful to cover each square inch. On the last trip to the border town, she did her best to memorize the route and identify markers on the way. A church with a twenty-foot silver cross, an abandoned school bus laying on its side, a wrecking yard full of discarded combines. A trusted friend had a cousin in Roma that could help. It was time to leave.

The sexual abuse was now daily, and the night before she miscarried a fetus of maybe four months. She wasn't exactly sure how far along she was. Her father was drunk when he came to the bedroom sometime after dark to find her gone. She was already a mile away so she could not hear him screaming her name. But the neighbors heard him yelling in Spanish, "Get back in here, my little whore!"

Maria maintained a steady pace to her destination as she hid from the lights of cars. She would be startled as growling dogs raced out of their yards giving her a burst of energy as she ran ahead and away from the danger. Her legs felt heavy at the first sign of dawn. The lights of a small shop appeared in front of her and she went in and bought a pineapple soda. She sat outside the store on a crude bench and stared to the east as the first streaks of light pierced the sky above low clouds that looked like a mountain range across the horizon.

She had to keep going. It would be more dangerous in the light of day. She finished her drink and ate a snack of cheese and tortilla she had packed away. The traffic was getting busier as she tried to dodge in and out of the tree line along the road trying to stay hidden. The silver cross was now in sight on the horizon just ten more miles away. She kept pushing herself driven by fear and hope. The sun was bearing down like a burning heavy weight when she saw the cluster of buildings ahead. She had made it.

As the sunrise shone through the remnants of the storm in brilliant pinks and creamy orange, Maria was only a few miles from her rendezvous. Back home, her father and tormentor was found with his throat cut. Justice came swiftly for men like her father in a small community of women with sharp knives.

Maria connected with her liaison at a small café in Ciudad Miguel Alemán on the Mexican side. She was exhausted from walking straight through for forty miles but was thrilled when the young man in the orange shirt asked her if she was Maria. She had worn a pink bandana around her neck as a signal to him. The two walked across the narrow iron bridge as casually as possible, and the young man simply stated Maria was his sister. She was now in Texas.

He had a car and drove her to a mission facility in San Antonio that took in girls like her. She was given a full health exam and provided three school uniforms. The next five years she lived with the sisters and learned English and basic life skills. She cleaned the facilities and learned how to do it properly. The nun's standards were high, but she was not afraid of work.

In her belongings that she brought across the border was a sweatshirt that was too big with Travis City High School written in black letters across the front of the faded white material. She asked if anyone knew where this was and one of the sisters knew and showed her on a map. Maria told them of a kind man that would bring clothes each year and how she would like to find him and thank him. One Saturday, that same sister was taking some supplies to Travis City and invited her to ride the few hours to the Catholic church. Maybe the priest would know.

Maria was eighteen and appeared to have reached her maximum height of five-foot nothing. Her face was sweet with dark brown eyes and shoulder length thick black hair with bangs cut above her eyebrows. She was dressed in her school uniform of an ironed white blouse, plaid skirt, tall white socks, and black and white saddle oxfords. It was midmorning when they arrived in the little town and the driver spotted a sign for a bakery and pulled in a parking spot close to the front.

"How about a treat for us both?" the sister asked her companion.

"Oh, yes. Thank you!" Maria could not believe her good fortune.

The two walked into City Bakery to the sound of a bell chiming as they entered the door to a find a winding queue of folks waiting their turn. Maria looked around at the strangers all looking back at her and Sister Ann. She felt as if she had entered somewhere she did not belong. The bell on the door sounded again, and she turned to see a young man about her age walk in and stand in the line behind her. It was the closest a boy had been to her in years, and suddenly she was flush with embarrassment and excitement.

"Hi," the boy said when she turned again to try and steal a look at him.

"Hi," she said quickly as she turned to him and right back facing forward.

"What do you get when you come here?" he asked.

"I don't know. I have never been here."

"Well, you should get a blueberry kolache. That's my favorite or apple. I like both."

"Thank you," she nervously blurted back to him as the line inched forward.

"I want a donut and coffee and she would like . . ." Sister Ann turned to Maria with a questioning look.

"Apple kolache, please."

"A drink?" the nun asked.

"Chocolate milk," the boy answered for her.

"Yes, I want that. What he said," Maria answered.

Sister Ann smiled at Maria and then the boy. She had chosen her own path of marriage to God, but she still appreciated the electricity in the air between a young man and young lady. Sister Ann paid for their treats and the two sat at a small table by the front window. The boy chose a seat close to them facing Maria.

"What is your name, young man?" Sister Ann asked as Maria's eyes widened with shock.

"Danny, Sister. And what are your names?" he tried to be cool and calm, but his heart was racing.

"I am Sister Ann, and this is Maria. She lives with me at the convent in San Antonio at Our Lady of Guadalupe. But she is not a nun, in case you were wondering," Sister Ann said enjoying her role as matchmaker and torturer of the shy girl.

"Nice to meet you both," Danny said with his mouth full of blueberry.

"I have some things I need to do at the church down the street. Would you mind sitting with Maria while I go? She can join me later." Sister Ann had decided to force them into action.

Sister Ann left with her coffee and drove the two blocks to the church. Danny happily sat in the abandoned seat with a nervous Maria staring at the car as it drove away.

In three months, they were married. The young couple started their new life in Danny's sad little rent house. They both grew up poor, but they wanted more for their future family. They budgeted their lives to the penny and saved every dollar possible. They passed on the nicer things for years and saved enough for a little house in the same neighborhood where they lived. They both worked two and three jobs and went to bed tired most nights. But they were always happy and dreamed of children.

* * *

"Are you scared of storms, Mother?" Lourdes asked.

"No baby, but I was when I was younger," Maria replied knowing her daughter did not like the occasional violent weather of central Texas.

"I don't like it, especially sitting outside. I wonder where Mr. Downs is. He's late."

"We are early, Lourdes. Caesar sent your dad to a job in Albertville, so he dropped us off a little earlier because it's a one-hour drive for your dad."

"I'm scared, Mom. Can we go somewhere else?" Lourdes said with fear in her voice.

"He will be here; he always is here on time. Just five more minutes," Maria comforted her daughter.

A swipe of bright light appeared above them immediately followed by loud thunder. Lourdes hugged tightly against her mother as the storm was now on top of them. Hard rain suddenly beat the metal roof above them and muffled Lourdes's loud scream of terror. The familiar headlights finally appeared through the sheets of rain and pulled under the cover adjacent to the bench.

The two stood and pressed themselves tight against the door with Maria shielding her daughter from the weather but allowing Mr. Downs access to the door lock. He fumbled quickly with the keys, found the correct one, turned the lock and pushed the door open. Maria and Lourdes scurried ahead of him as he waited for them to enter, went to the alarm keypad and entered the code.

"Oh, my goodness, what a storm! Are you two alright?" he asked seeing the worry on the little girl's face.

"We are fine, but it is scary out there," Maria answered.

"I was scared to death," Lourdes said making sure he knew.

"I'm so sorry that you were out there when this storm hit," Mr. Downs genuinely apologized.

"Let's go to the break room and get some coffee and hot chocolate." He ushered them to the kitchen area.

He flipped on the lights and turned on the coffee maker readied from the prior day. He opened the refrigerator and pulled out some milk. A box of assorted bakery cookies left over from the day before sat in a white box on the table. The three sat listening to the storm punish the outside world.

"You want some milk, Lourdes?" he asked.

"Yes, sir."

"What would you like, Maria?"

"Some coffee, but we need to be working, sir. We are not paid to sit."

"It's okay, Maria. Sit with me. We'll have some milk and coffee and left-over cookies. You can start working in a bit."

The storm roared stronger as the lightning seemed constant, and the thunder shook the building. Lourdes would jump and murmur fearfully under her breath while trying to be brave in front of her mother and Mr. Downs. The fluorescent light began to flicker overhead which pushed Lourdes to be more vocal in her fears.

"It's just a storm, Lourdes; we will be fine. We're in a strong building that has been here through many other storms. We are safe," Mr. Downs assured them. "If the power goes out, we have some emergency lights that will come on so we will not be in the dark." He reassured his frightened employees and just then the overhead light was gone replaced by a floodlight in the hallway.

"Ah! What's happening?" Lourdes screamed.

"It's the emergency lights, like I told you. We can go in my office. There is more light, and it's safer in there, too." Mr. Downs escorted them across the hall through Dawn's office. They sat at the table in his office which was well-lit by a flood light over the doorway clearly illuminating the area shining toward his desk and credenza.

The building rattled with every explosion from the sky, and each time Lourdes jumped seeking comfort from her mother who was doing her best to remain calm for her nervous child. Lourdes looked toward the tall custom bookcase behind the large desk and began to gaze at all the items carefully arranged in different sections. There were framed photos and books, plaques and a football helmet. Mr. Downs noticed her looking at the items as the worst of the weather seemed to be moving northeast.

"Those are some of my things, some were my dad's, and some were my grandfather's. Do you have a question about any of them?" Mr. Downs asked using the opportunity to distract from the violence outside.

"What does that brown sign in the middle say?" Lourdes pointed to a rectangle piece of polished beveled wood with black Bookman Old Style font centered on the front with two lines of text.

"That is a quote from a famous book, The Wealth of Nations, written in 1776 by a man named Adam Smith. It says, *It is not from the benevolence of the butcher, the brewer, or the baker that we expect our dinner, but from their regard to their own interest.* Do you know what that means?" he asked her.

"I am not sure; do you know, Mama?"

"Not me; I don't know any old things like that," Maria answered her, feeling uncomfortable in the conversation.

"Sure, you know, Maria, and you too, Lulu. We just have to put it in a different time frame, because truth doesn't change over time," he encouraged them and continued.

"So, what is Adam Smith saying? It is simple, yet so powerful. He says that we as people don't work for benevolence, or you could say, kind generosity. We work for our own interest or personal gain. The butcher, the brewer, and the baker work for *themselves*, not to feed you out of the kindness of their heart. This is the core of a capitalistic system. The three of us are all part of free enterprise. We get to choose how we work. We are all free to pursue our dreams." Mr. Downs passionately imparted his view.

"That seems greedy," Maria interjected.

"I understand why you may think that, but why are you here this morning and why is Danny at Caesar's? Because you both want more for your life, and I know you want as much as possible for Lulu," Mr. Downs kindly responded.

"That makes sense. Their own interest is not just for themselves, but for others too," Maria replied.

"But why are you so rich and we are so poor?" Lourdes said genuinely wanting an answer.

"Lourdes, stop asking personal questions like that!" Maria scolded her daughter.

"Maria, please, that is a question many older people want to ask but are scared to hear the answer or sometimes want a different answer. The question is simple, but the answer is very complex. The primary factor is sacrifice and time. Time to build assets. Sacrifice to gain assets."

"What does that mean?" Lourdes asked, ignoring her mother's glare as the rumble of the storm was fading.

"Let's start with sacrifice. Someone has to be willing to take a risk. The time is the easy part; it just takes many years. The more years from the sacrifice the greater the assets, normally. In 1830, my great grandparents came from Maryland to Texas for what they hoped would be a better life. There were no trains or highways or cars. They put what they had in a horse drawn wagon and begin walking fifteen hundred miles to Texas. A three-hour flight today, took months back then."

"Why did they do it?" Lourdes asked enthralled with the story.

"For land and the chance for a better life. Where we sit was Mexico at that time, and the Mexican government wanted settlers in this part of their territory, so they offered free land. There were no people in this area but a few Indian tribes who fought each other over territory."

"What were your great grandparents' names?" Maria asked becoming interested with the Mexico reference.

"Robert and Molly Downs. They risked their lives for land. This was not an easy journey. There was disease and hostile Indians and brutal conditions. They had to cross rivers, creeks, and swamps crawling with snakes and unimaginable swarming insects. Bandits could be around any corner. There were no hotels or restaurants. They had to survive on what they brought or found along the way. It was a miracle they made it here alive. Then they had to build a cabin and barn by hand. There were not many that made it here, but if you did, you had the respect of the other frontiersmen."

"I never thought about how hard it was for people back then," Lourdes said.

"Then after they got here, Robert rode off and left his wife and children to help fight Santa Ana to create the Republic of Texas. Have you studied Texas History yet, Lulu?"

"Yes, sir, in the fourth grade. The Alamo and The Letter and other stuff," Lourdes answered.

"What do you remember of The Letter?" he asked the bright girl.

"Travis' Letter was written by William Barret Travis from the Alamo to try and get help against the Mexican army. We got extra credit if we memorized at least part of The Letter."

"Can you remember any of The Letter?" Mr. Downs prodded her.

"I think so. It starts out, *I am besieged,* which we learned meant he was in a terrible spot. I don't remember what was next, but I think I remember the last line. That's the one I memorized for extra credit. It goes: *If this call is neglected, I am determined to sustain myself as long as possible and die like a soldier who never forgets what is due to his own honor and that of his country – Victory or Death. William Barret Travis."* Lourdes beamed with pride at remembering the line and emphasized the last few words and his name.

"Excellent! And did you know that I am named William Barrett Downs the Third? I was named after Travis, and my grandson is named William Barrett Downs the Fifth, but we all call him Barrett. It does my heart good to hear you know The Letter." He applauded her and Maria clapped along.

"I know Barrett. He's in my class," Lourdes responded.

"Good. Now you will remember that all the Texans who stayed and fought at the Alamo were killed. Robert Downs arrived too late to fight at the Alamo but joined Sam Houston and helped defeat Santa Ana in San Jacinto. He returned after the battle and began buying and selling land across Texas. He partnered with a friend back in New York and started a land investment business. Wealthy people back east started buying land in the Republic of Texas. After 1845 the Republic became the state of Texas. Robert Downs started a surveying company to meet the demand of interested buyers. Over thirty years, he bought and sold hundreds of thousands of acres."

"How much land do you have now?" Lourdes asked gaining interest in the story.

"Not much compared to what Robert had when he died in 1875. It has almost all been sold off over the past one hundred years. The main thing he did, however, was when he sold the land, he kept half the mineral rights. Those mineral rights are what created money for his descendants. It helped grow this bank which in turn has helped thousands of people for generations," Mr. Downs said proudly.

"Most people forget rough times because it is too hard to remember.

You do what you can for a better life," Maria spoke as if she were a child again. "I walked alone over forty miles with what I could carry from my birthplace in Mexico to the border. My cousin's friend took me across and on to San Antonio. I was only thirteen."

Mr. Downs and Lourdes looked at her surprised at her admission.

"We do what we have to do. Sometimes if you stay where you are, it is worse than death." Maria looked down to hide her emotion.

"I never knew this, Mama." Lourdes looked at her mother with hurt knowing how hard her life had been.

"Was it worth it? The sacrifice?" Mr. Downs asked earnestly.

"If I had to do it again tomorrow, I would. Especially if I knew it would lead me to where I am now with my Lourdes."

"Your mother is no different than Robert and Molly. Only she was braver. Time is now on her side. Sacrifice and time. You have a more wonderful mother than anyone I know. Never forget what you learned about your mother today, Lulu. I know I'll never forget," Mr. Downs said reverently.

The lights began to flicker on as the storm appeared to have moved on to strike the next town.

CHAPTER 9

L OURDES LOOKED FORWARD to her seven a.m. chats with Mr. Downs. She enjoyed his appreciation of her curiosity and felt grown up around him.

"Why do you always wear a suit? I've seen other employees here at the bank not wearing suits," Lourdes asked one morning.

"I suppose I view it as a tradition. It is my way to pay honor to our customers. I don't expect them to dress like this, but many feel better that I am dressed this way. I know that times are changing but it doesn't seem right to me. I think a man, and for that matter, a woman should look their best in business. If a person walks in my office wanting to sell me something and they look like they are on the way to play golf, I treat them different than the person in a suit. I just can't help it."

"I guess I understand that thinking," she observed. "When I see a teacher at the grocery store in shorts and a T-shirt it looks weird to me."

"Yep, I feel more formal and helpful."

"How does a bank help people?" Lourdes asked.

"A bank does several things to help people. It provides a safe place to keep your money and it loans money for personal reasons and businesses. Their goal is to make money. Just like your goal is to make money in your work. If a bank is not profitable, it cannot be there to help people. It must be wise in its loan practice. But insurance may be the biggest reason banks have prospered," Mr. Downs answered his now favorite curious child.

"Why insurance? That's expensive," Maria asked as she joined the discussion.

"Without insurance, banks could not loan money for a house or a car. Insurance protects in case of loss. Before insurance, there was no real middle class. There was a group of people called Lloyds of London that created our modern insurance system. They began by insuring shipments from England of goods around the world. Let's say you had a business that made things like textiles. If you wanted to sell your textiles far away and the ship sank, you lost it all. Only very wealthy people could afford to lose a ship and its contents. Until Lloyds of London helped protect people, you could be wiped out by a single accident," Mr. Downs explained. "It works when the people at the insurance company make a lot of bets. They know if they spread their bets—or risk—that the Law of Large Numbers will eventually win. This law states that over time and with enough spread, the insurance company will be profitable. It is also how gambling works in Las Vegas. Over time, with enough bets, the house wins."

"So, insurance is gambling?" Maria asked.

"Ha! Well, in a sense it is. But like all gambling, we can calculate the odds. There are people called actuaries who decide how much premium is charged to make sure they make money. They say, 'For a house worth fifty thousand dollars, we need to charge five hundred dollars a year to be profitable.'"

"So, they can charge whatever they want?" Maria asked.

"Anyone can charge whatever they want for anything." Mr. Downs looked at both of his interested employees. "But who decides the price? The buyer or the seller?"

"The person selling," Lourdes said as her mother nodded.

"No. The buyer sets the price."

"When I go to a store, I don't set any prices. That doesn't make sense," Maria made her point.

"Sure, you do. Have you ever *not* bought something because it was too expensive? If the seller sets the price, why don't you charge ten thousand dollars a day to clean?"

"Because no one would pay that much," Lourdes answered.

"So, the buyer decides the price. This is also based on competition and scarcity of the resource or service. That is the reason gold costs more than gravel. Gold is rare and gravel is common," Mr. Downs responded.

"But you said too much money at ten thousand dollars, of course that would not be reasonable," Maria responded.

"I understand, but in a free enterprise system, all pricing of goods and services are constantly changing. I believe this works best with less government regulation. The decision to buy is made based on needs and resources. You need food, but you can buy hamburger or steak. Choices are there for everyone. We are free to choose what we buy and what work we do."

"I can't be a doctor. I don't have that choice," Maria argued.

"But you could have been a doctor, if you were young enough, smart enough, and worked very hard in school for many years. It was *possible* at one time in your life to be a doctor. There are many jobs that we cannot ever have. Lourdes will never be a football player, but she is the best of anyone we know at math. She has a unique God given talent that most of the world does not have and she can use this to excel in life. What do you want to be when you grow up?" he asked.

"I don't know. I guess a math teacher because I'm good at math," Lourdes answered.

"Being good at something does not make you a good teacher. The best coaches were usually not the best players. Teaching is a skill like any other trade. Don't limit yourself to teaching, although it's very honorable. It may not be the best use of your gift," Mr. Downs suggested.

"How do people get rich?" Lourdes asked.

"The greatest wealth since the implementation of capitalism and the industrial revolution has been created by people who make other's lives better for a cheaper price. If there is no great benefit, there is no great value. To become a millionaire, it is much easier to sell a million items for a dollar profit each than a single product for a million-dollar profit. Good ideas that benefit the masses can then become publicly traded companies."

"How much money does your mother pay you?" he asked the inquisitive youth.

"Not much. Seventy-five cents an hour. It will take me forever to get rich," Lourdes answered sullenly.

"What do you spend your own money on?"

"Well, I like Coca-Cola and I like McDonalds."

"Where do you shop?"

"Walmart. Sometimes other stores, but mostly Walmart."

"Great. Did you know you can own a small portion of those companies? They are publicly traded companies which means you can invest and be a shareholder. They are all very good companies, and your investment should grow. There are risks in investing, but normally the greater the risk, the greater the reward." Mr. Downs loved teaching his captive audience. "I tell you what I will do. I will open a brokerage account for you, and we will be partners. You give me good ideas for investing, and we will see what happens."

"Deal!" Lourdes reached across the table and they shook hands.

"So, you and I are going to buy stocks. Now we look and see what the stock price is in the paper. Come sit beside me and I will show you." He spread the stock page of the Wall Street Journal on the table in front of them.

The numbers and symbols were like seeing a beautiful portrait to Lourdes. It was glorious to her mathematical mind.

"What is this?" she asked with excitement.

"This page represents the New York Stock Exchange for this day. This column on the left is the symbols for the company. Like for Coca-Cola, it is KO. If you take your finger and follow it down, you will see right here, KO."

"What are all the numbers to the right?"

"Those are the prices for different times. Opening price, closing price, 52 week high and 52 week low. So today Coca-Cola stock costs you $4.93. That will be our very first stock to buy. Now you want to buy some Walmart and McDonalds?"

"Yes, but I don't have any money with me to give you."

"I tell you what. I will need twenty-five dollars by the end of next week. Deal?"

"Deal! I have saved thirty dollars." The young girl was excited and ready for the opportunity.

"Good! You keep five dollars for cash on hand. I will buy all three stocks on your recommendation, but Coca-Cola will be our very first buy," Mr. Downs said giving her the credit for her pick.

*   *   *

A lone man stood leaning against the Toyota Corolla with a missing hubcap. The moon was hidden by thick clouds cruising like great ships above in the dark sky. His head dug against his cupped hands in an uncomfortable spasm. The pistol lay on the hood of the car loaded and ready to dispatch the sins of his past. It had been many years since that night, but the smell of the burning flesh and hair still stung his senses. He had few trips in this car in which he did not hear the young woman's screams from the back seat twisting her body to see out the backseat window.

Why was he so weak to believe he was right that night? He was just doing what he was told. Would he fail to end the torture again tonight?

There were people who knew the truth, but they would have to admit their guilt. They were as weak as he or far worse. They were proud of what was done that night.

The echoing sound of the single pistol shot was muffled by the crashing surf of the Gulf of Mexico. As the sun rose on the beach, the person who found him reported a single gunshot wound to the head, possible Hispanic male about thirty-five.

CHAPTER 10

2000

MR. DOWNS EASED back in his leather office chair with an investment summary report raised in his right hand. He adjusted the paper from his eyes to the best resolution with his reading glasses. He smiled to himself at the number on the bottom of the page. It had been good year. He had never been a believer of high-tech stocks because he did not get the big vision of the dot com era. The last year had proven him correct and the bubble had burst for most of the new age idea slingers. He was a brick-and-mortar investor and participated in things he could understand. He also studied what companies paid taxes. If they paid taxes it simply meant they made money, and they were doing everything they could *not* to pay taxes. Large companies like Exxon paid millions to avoid payment of more taxes. Smart companies hire brilliant accountants or lobbied politicians for better protection under the tax code. If companies paid taxes, they were making money and lots of it. Exxon usually paid more in taxes than half of the United States population. Progressive taxation is what the politicians called it. Of his top ten investments, five were the top taxpayers in the United States.

Lourdes had her account which he was proud of as well. He never showed her the amount of money in the account but only the gains or losses by percentage. He had funded this account with her occasional contributions to add to the original twenty-five dollars. He added three zeros to each of her payments. She never knew. The report now reflected over one hundred and sixty-five thousand dollars in various stocks. The report was simply titled LULU PARTNERSHIP, and they were equal partners. He was the sole signatory on the account until Lulu turned eighteen. Dawn was the only other person who knew of the account.

"Dawn, did you proof that letter for me?" Mr. Downs called out to the adjacent office.

"Yes hon, it was perfect, and she'll be thrilled. I'm glad you're doing that for her, and if I didn't know any better, I'd say you're getting nicer in your old age."

January 12, 2000

Dear Miss Sanchez,

It is my pleasure to report a positive year for our investment partnership. Our stock portfolio has weathered a substantial storm in the markets this past year yet ended in profitable territory. Since it is our mutual goal for this enterprise's continued success, future consideration of additional investments will be required for the new millennium. I ask you to please be diligent in your continued pursuit of those companies that meet and exceed our high standards. I look forward to our annual board meeting on Wednesday January 19, at 7 a.m. in the office of William Barrett Downs III.

Per our usual meeting requirement, Coca-Cola bought at Walmart and McDonalds' biscuits and sausage will be served. I look forward to our meeting.

Yours truly,

WBD III

William Barrett Downs III

On a frigid morning in January, Maria and Lourdes arrived with Lourdes dressed in her new formal business attire and a warm overcoat covering her neck to below her knees. Mr. Downs greeted them in his usual manner at the back door with a bow to the young teenage girl. Maria had taken her on a shopping trip over the weekend to find the closest thing to a business suit for thirteen-year-old girls. It was a black suit for teenage boys that could not be buttoned across the chest, but other than that, it fit adequately. No one knew how to tie a necktie in the Sanchez household, so a snap-on tie in a green and red stripe had to work. Lourdes wore black patent leather shoes and sheer white socks.

"Our meeting starts promptly at seven, so please come at that time," Mr. Downs stated as he turned to get his morning coffee.

"Of course, and please have copies ready for me. It's awkward to have to share like last year," Lourdes stated in an overly formal manner.

"Anything else?" he answered in the same tone.

"No, that will be all." She kept her coat on and moved to the lobby to help her mother.

Maria stepped in the supply closet door and started snickering. "You two are killing me. I cannot believe how nice he has been to us both these past four years. We got that great car for almost nothing from a friend of his and each Christmas a nice bonus. And not to mention all the work we have now because he has recommended us to his friends and employees. I will need to hire another person if this keeps up. I remember the first day. I was so scared of him. Your father had teased us and said how mean he was. I was so terrified, I thought I was getting fired any day."

"And don't forget. I got us a raise—the first one," Lourdes said smiling and hung the big coat on a hook in the supply closet.

Maria had grown her cleaning business to the point she had hired a new employee. Danny was now the shop foreman and replaced Caesar in the day-to-day operation of the business. Caesar's health was failing, and he had been having conversations with Danny about buying the shop. The Sanchez family was moving up. Sundays after church would be spent driving around looking at houses for sale. Their old home was kept nice inside, but the exterior was going down, and Maria was on Danny to sell the eyesore truck in their yard.

The two went through their routine. Wednesday was a light day: trash, dusting, vacuuming, glass cleaning. It was the day Lourdes would normally spend with Mr. Downs after seven. She would go into his office and dust and take out the trash, and they would discuss all kinds of stuff. He would ask her about school, her teachers, and people in the neighborhood which seemed odd to Lourdes. But she would always answer honestly, "I don't know that person, or he's a nice man, or she and her husband have been fighting." Gossip was abundant in the old neighborhood and kids talked and adults thought she never paid attention.

Lourdes entered Mr. Downs office promptly at six fifty-nine dressed in her suit and tie. Her mother had put her hair up in a bun to complete the ensemble.

"Well good morning, Miss Sanchez. You look especially professional this morning." Mr. Downs was doing all he could not to burst into laughter at the miniature businesswoman. He would refrain from any smirk or smile to allow her this sincere moment.

"Thank you, Mr. Downs, and you look very nice yourself. Do you have the year-end report ready?"

"Yes. Please sit. As you will note, we have made 7% in profit last year and 21% since our business began. We have added a total of nine stocks in our portfolio and all but one is doing very well."

"Yes, this is good, but we need to be thinking more about technology," Lourdes said as she scanned the single page document.

"Why technology? That sector did not do well last year. What are you thinking?"

"Video game companies. Do you know how many boys play video games? A bunch. And they spend big money on them."

"Interesting. You would know more about teenage boys than me. Anything else?"

"Cell phones are big. Did you know rich kids my age now have their own phones?"

"Amazing! But if it is only rich kids, how big is that market?"

"I don't know, but I bet we can calculate it. If we knew how many teenagers there are and what percentage are rich . . ." Lulu loved a math problem.

"It would be a big number if you calculate the whole US population. I bet in the millions." Mr. Downs was impressed with the young girl.

"I say we buy Electronic Arts. They make lots of video games boys like. I asked several players, and they all said this company was on the packaging labels. I had to ask them like three times who made the games. Boys are so stupid." Lulu was happy with her recommendation.

"Okay, I agree on the stock, and I guess the boys too. I see it's trading at $17-$18 range, so how much are we buying?" he asked his partner.

"I have forty dollars to invest," she responded.

"I will arrange the stock buy. Do we have any further business?"

"No, so I say we eat our scheduled meal. I'm hungry!" Lourdes smiled at her partner.

As they began eating breakfast, Lourdes wondered, "That was too easy. You usually make me go through more questioning. Why the quick approval?"

"I spoke with a broker who brought up Electronic Arts a couple of months ago. He was pushing it, but I had no idea what he was talking about. To be honest when you mentioned it this morning, it gave meaning to me. I trust you; I don't usually trust brokers," he answered while complimenting her.

"That's very nice of you, Mr. Downs, but you know none of us know the future. We just try and do what we can," Lourdes said mimicking his voice. They both laughed as he raised his Coca-Cola can in a toast to her.

*   *   *

Middle school ended for the fourteen-year-old Lourdes in May. She continued her exemplary work in the classroom and teachers loved her. She was becoming more popular with the other students because she was smart but not a stuck up know it all. There were no private schools in the area which meant every child the same age had been together in the Travis City School District since kindergarten. There were four groups of approximately thirty children grouped together based on test scores and teacher evaluation. It was obvious the smartest were the best students in the Gold Group. The children understood the differences and the competitive selection process. It would change each grade. For instance, the Gold Group was almost all girls in sixth grade but would be half boys by the end of the eighth-grade year. Some parents were aware of this tracking system and would lobby teachers for their children to move up. This ploy was almost always punished instead of rewarded. The teachers took pride in the proper assessment of the top students and used it as motivation. But parents would try and circumvent the reward system because *they* knew their children better.

Lourdes was dealing with a changing body and hormonal attacks that assaulted her with doubts against her usual confident self. Was she pretty enough; was her hair style like the magazines; was she too fat; was she too thin; was she too tall or too short; or were her breasts the right shape? It was so overwhelming. Her mother seemed to be more worried about her since this transformation from child to young woman. Maria needed to know what was happening anytime she was not at school or not with her. It drove Lourdes crazy; she wanted more independence and Maria wanted a full lockdown. Danny did his best to stay out of things, but he did look at his developing daughter and knew the future would bring great changes.

The summer was spent working more hours than ever before for the entire family. Maria's number of clients was growing, and she was forced to turn down business. Danny was making more money at the welding shop and was developing his plan to buy the business which was halting any chances of purchasing a new dream home. Danny and Maria sat down to go through their finances and evaluate the future. For much of their marriage they lived well below their means. It was tempting to buy a new car or fancy things, but they saved and did without while enjoying their growing savings instead.

"Caesar hasn't given me a price. He keeps saying he will, but he hasn't yet. I've gone through the inventory of machinery and supplies, and I have a good idea of the value. The building will be expensive, but if we cannot work out a deal with Caesar, I can build my own. I believe most of the customers will use me, and I know two of the guys who would work for me. I just want Caesar to sell. It would be easier." Danny sat with his wife at their tiny kitchen table with a tablet and calculator.

"I have three more houses and two more businesses that I had to turn down. The new girl, Lupe, is doing great, and I've heard back from my customers of how well she is doing. I also talked to three women from church who say they want to work, but I'm sure two of them will fail." Maria updated her business.

"How much money do we have saved?" Maria asked.

"Eighty-seven thousand and no debt," Danny said proudly.

Lourdes was laying on the couch listening to her parents.

"Why don't you talk to Mr. Downs?" Lourdes inserted from her reclined position.

"Maybe I could, but I have no idea how all that works," Danny said.

"Just ask him. He's nice and would treat us right," Maria encouraged her husband.

"That's a good idea. He likes you two, and we go to the same church. Tell him tomorrow morning when you see him, I'd like to talk to him," Danny said as the leader of the family who was gently guided by his wife and daughter.

The next day Danny sat in Mr. Downs office discussing his plan to buy the shop. He passionately spoke of new services he could add and answered many questions from Mr. Downs regarding cash flow, labor rates, optional facilities, and even Maria's business.

By the end of the month, he had made the deal with Caesar and bought additional land adjacent to the old shop. Maria had an office in the new building and two new employees by the end of summer. After all expenses including the new debt service and taxes, the Sanchez family made more money in the month of August than they had made the whole year they were first married.

A strange thing happened to them while this money was growing in their accounts; almost nothing changed. Their monetary habits were so entrenched that their lifestyle remained the same. Optionality had increased, but old habits die hard. Lourdes was never told about the good fortune, but she obviously knew their daily work had changed. Slowly a few luxuries were allowed. Danny bought a used work truck that was only two years old. Maria was seen buying clothes out of town at nicer places than Walmart.

Lourdes was starting high school in a week and had spent her summer like she had most of her life—working. There were no trips to Disneyland or even vacations to places like Sea World in San Antonio. Danny was a huge Houston Astros fan, so they did go to Houston for a baseball game where Danny bought jerseys and caps for all of them. It was the biggest place Lourdes had ever seen with the most people in one building. "My entire hometown could fit in the outfield seats," she thought doing the math in her head.

A few days before school commenced, she jogged to the high school with a proposal in mind. Mr. Downs was always encouraging her to think of creative solutions to problems, and her problem was lunch. She would need to pay two dollars each day for lunch. It was an expense she did not care to pay out of her earnings since she was urged by her parents to work for it.

Lourdes had an appointment with Ms. Charlotte Greer, the head of food services at Travis City High. Ms. Charlotte, as everyone called her, was a large black woman of about fifty years of age. She wore a white dress uniform that strained to hold her substantial body within the heavy polyester. She was adorned with a black curly wig that seemed to move about unnaturally like an ill-fitting hat as she walked toward her tiny office.

"Ms. Greer, I'm Lourdes Sanchez. We spoke two days ago about me working for you." Lourdes walked toward the woman with her hand extended and a smile.

"Why hello, young lady! You actually showed up. My goodness, a kid doing what they said they'd do." She reached out and shook Lourdes' hand with her plump fingers.

"Come on into my office." She sat in the only chair beside a desk full of delivery receipts.

"Now, you said in your email, you want a little job, but I don't have to pay ya nothing. Just give you some lunch for trade. That right?" Now seated at about eye level, she stared right at Lourdes.

"Yes, I think that's a fair trade." Lourdes stared back at her to show strength.

"I never had a kid try and work for they lunch. Most everybody wants free. You kinda brown; you can probably get free." Ms. Greer looked the girl over as she finished.

"Why would I want it for free? That doesn't seem right," Lourdes responded wondering where this was going.

"It ain't right at all! I got to feed a bunch of kids for free that say this is the only place they eat. That ain't true. If it was true, then they'd all starve to death every summer. Can't afford to because they mama and sorry daddy lazy. And worse, they teaching their kids to be lazy. But you ain't, and I know your mama and daddy sho' ain't. I think you got a great idea and it will be fair. We gonna do this deal. Welcome to the team, Lopez."

"It's Lourdes, but you can call me Lulu. My good friends call me Lulu." She smiled broadly at her new boss.

"Lulu, you come through the side door and find me when you have lunch. I need you to clean tables and help out in here sometimes. If you're lazy, I'll fire you. Understand?"

"Yes ma'am! And thank you!" Lourdes was happy with her deal and was looking forward to working with Ms. Charlotte and could not wait to tell her parents and Mr. Downs.

*　*　*

In the predawn hour, Mr. Downs lay in his bed next to Janet staring at the ceiling with Four and Daisy both on his mind. Daisy had flown in for a visit for a few days. It had been nice. She was alone, and for their own sanity, Janet and he had quit asking about her relationships many years ago. Daisy was never a problem to him. She was just spoiled. Janet and Daisy fought during most visits over trivial things like Daisy choosing to live her life away from them. It was harder each year for Janet to survive without pain. It made her unable to travel to see her daughter in California, and she was at the mercy of her child's decision to come see her.

Daisy had been married three times and the third one appeared to be ending. Her wealth gave Daisy no reliance on a man supporting her, and she had grown weary of the expected financial service to weak men. Over the years she idolized her father in arguments with her suitors but called Mr. Downs a bigoted dinosaur to his face. Daisy could be sweet and would viciously defend all her family if anyone criticized them. She could personally lambast them but no one else was allowed to say one bad word in her presence about her family. She was hard to live with. In her younger years, Daisy had chosen not to have children, and when her feelings changed, it was determined she couldn't bear a child. It left her sad and disappointed in an unexpected way, and she began to gain weight and not really care about her life. Her parents' solution was for her to go to church. Her solution was donuts.

Four had been doing better lately, but Mr. Downs heard he was gone again to the beach house. He desperately wanted his son to be sober and productive and not a source of ridicule and embarrassment. He had thought his son would be like him and life would be predictable as planned. But Four was like a stone in his boot that would roll to a tender spot and shoot a pain up his leg at the worst times.

His annual September dove hunt with Randy and the Lonely Shotgun Boys Club would be meeting this year in far South Texas known as The Valley. The event had been comically described over the years as a drinking where a dove hunt broke out. The LSBC started when Randy and he were in college. It had subsequently grown but capped out at sixty members paying a fee of one thousand dollars a year. The membership reflected their businesses of primarily financial and oil and gas people. The big dove hunt lasted four days featuring spreads of food and an open bar which caused the participants to limp away with hangovers on Sunday morning. There were no women invited as guests, but there were ladies that served meals and drinks for the raucous bunch who did very well in tips for those few days.

The year he and Monica were married, Four was showing progress, with his wife becoming a positive influence on him. He was working at the ranch but showed little interest in the bank. At least he was working. Mr. Downs invited his son to the dove hunt to introduce him to the men he had been hunting with over the many years. Randy drove down to Travis City the day before, and the three of them traveled early the next morning to the motel outside of Harlingen to set up headquarters for the event.

The Sundown Motel was built in the early sixties and was two stories with stainless trim around the windows and doorways. The original neon sign over the office still flashed in blue curved light, "Cold Air Inside." The doors were painted in alternating colors of green, yellow, blue, and red. It stretched east and west with rooms on both sides of the building. The older men were downstairs where they had backed up their trucks to their assigned rooms. The younger men were upstairs. A bar was prepared in a conference room which was actually a motel room without the bed, where members and guests registered and received their room assignments. The group had rented the entire motel for the event. That afternoon they drove out to some grain fields and had a nice shoot. The sound of men hollering out, "Over your head," and "To your right," sounded across the dusty ground as the hunters swung their shotguns at the speedy dodging birds. The group got their limit of birds, cleaned them in the field and relived their hits and misses while laughing at crude banter reserved for men reveling in the testosterone filled environment. It was important everyone had a license and obeyed all the written and unwritten rules.

That night Four became intoxicated, which in itself was not criticized, but how he behaved was not acceptable. Mr. Downs retired early to his assigned room for some sleep, while Randy remained at the party held in an unoccupied suite. Four was rude to the attendees, and even threatened to fight an elderly man who Four tripped over stumbling back to the bar. Randy intervened quickly and sent Four to his room like a misbehaving child.

Mr. Downs and Randy sat in the parking lot the next morning an hour before daylight waiting on Four to join them for the thirty-mile drive to the grain field to meet the guide for the early hunt. Randy had not mentioned to his friend what happened the night before but felt he may have to before someone else approached Mr. Downs. It would be a hard thing to tell his best friend, and he was about to say something when the back door opened and Four came out with a tumbler and gun case in hand.

Four was quiet as they drove and Randy did his best to push aside the issue and let the incident blow over. They met the hunting guide before daylight at the entrance of a grain field off a dirt road with a parade of headlights pushing their way through the boiling dust. They began to park their trucks down a fence line spacing them a hundred yards apart to set up for the hunt after sunrise. Mr. Downs and Randy got out of the truck and suddenly heard a gun blast from the backseat. Four had not unloaded his gun the day before and accidentally shot the back door of Randy's truck.

"What the hell was that?" Randy cried out.

"Did you just shoot his truck? What kind of an idiot are you?" Mr. Downs had moved to the back where Four was standing with the gun in one hand and the large drink in the other. A hole about the size of a coffee can was blown open on the opposite side door. The damage was only to the interior and had not pierced the exterior metal.

Mr. Downs took the drink from his son's hand and threw it over the wire fence into the scrub brush. He then grabbed the gun and began checking for any other shells before thrusting the weapon back into the case and glaring at Four.

"Get back in the truck. You're going home now! I will not let you embarrass me anymore. You have broken the rules, and you will pay the price. Now!" he screamed at his adult son. Randy remained silent not wanting to pour fuel on a fire.

Randy and Mr. Downs quickly left the grain field for the five-hour trek back to Travis City with a sullen Four in the back seat. Almost no words were spoken on the trip. Randy was mad, Mr. Downs was seething, and Four just wished he had a beer.

They arrived before noon at the modest house Monica and Four were renting. Four got out of the back seat and was silent as he walked away like a whipped dog.

Mr. Downs turned to Randy and said, "Let's go. I'll drive back to finish the hunt. I'm too mad to stay here."

Randy remained quiet regarding the previous night's antics but knew Four's behavior would eventually get back to his friend. It is hard to tell your best friend his own son is a disappointment. Randy had no children and wished so often he had a mini version of himself. But it was clear that there were no guarantees what your child would be like. Genetic lottery was a roll of the dice it seemed. Nature versus nurture. He knew his friend as a wonderful, smart man, good to his children, and Janet was a saint. What happened?

CHAPTER 11

LOURDES CAME THROUGH the side door into the kitchen at her usual time to begin her shift at the high school cafeteria. From behind a stainless wall of shelving and appliances, Charlotte smiled at Lourdes, her wig tilting toward her forehead. Lourdes went to the closet where the white aprons were hanging and picked the least stained one and lifted her hair to allow the strap over her head. She reached around behind her back and deftly tied the cotton straps the way women can do so much easier than men. She had been there a month and had her routine down.

She was proud of her negotiated arrangement that provided her lunch for a small amount of work. She liked her coworkers and they adored her. She was eager to please and a good worker. Today was roast beef day, and the cooks took pride in making the best of what they were given. She liked it when they let her help with the cooking, but most of that was done prior to when she came. So her shift was mostly spent picking up trays and cleaning tables.

She entered the cafeteria to the sound of a hundred hormone-driven teenagers laughing and shouting. There were the nerdy kids, the cool kids, the popular kids, the athletic kids, and the lonely kids. They were all thrown into the school's cafeteria in a town where they lived through no choice of their own. They were on a trip together across time and some seemed to realize the importance, while others just seemed oblivious to it all.

Lourdes began her duty by approaching the tables as the groups would finish and others took their place. She wiped them down and dried the damp surface with a dry towel. She picked up loose fallen trash off the floor and tables and placed it in the trash cans around the perimeter of the room.

She spotted the new girl from her math class with her head down sitting alone as she ate her meal from a tan plastic tray. Lourdes made her way to her table to say something to her. It broke her heart to see someone alone. Lourdes had friends and she treasured them.

"Hi, Beth! How are you today?" she approached the lone girl with a smile.

"Fine," Beth said softly without looking up.

"How did you do on the test yesterday?" Lourdes tried to engage her.

"Not sure. I think okay," Beth said trying her best to accept the kindness being offered.

"I hope I did good, but it was hard for sure. I like your shoes."

"Yes, it was hard, and thanks. My mom got them at a store in San Antonio." The shy girl smiled and looked at Lourdes.

Suddenly a loud bang from across the room alerted that someone had dropped a tray.

"Got to go! I'll see ya tomorrow," Lourdes leaned down to the girl with a smile then spun away toward the noise.

The teenage boys and girls around the scene were laughing at the boy who not only dropped the tray but slipped and fell. Lourdes knew the kid on the floor. It was Tommy Adams who was a popular, cute, funny boy. She was relieved it was him. Another person would not be as resilient in that situation.

Tommy stood up as red Jell-O clung to his white shirt pocket. He pulled it away with his hand and placed it in his mouth and chimed, "Well hello, Jell-O," in a rhyming tone.

Several kids laughed, and Tommy laughed at himself. He had turned the situation around.

"If anyone needs any help carrying their tray, I'm your man!" he exclaimed.

"Here, let me get that for you, Tommy," Lourdes said crouching down to scoop the scattered food on to the tray.

"I can help. It was my mess, not yours." Tommy was now bent over to assist Lourdes. Just as she was thinking Tommy was a great guy, her whole world changed.

"Let the dumpster baby clean it up," a girl's voice said in a condescending tone.

"Why did she call me dumpster baby? Does she think I live in a dumpster? Is this about me picking up trash?" Lourdes thoughts swirled in confusion.

"Ha! Dumpster baby!" another female voice called over the crowd.

"Dumpster baby! Dumpster baby!" a chorus now seemed to carry across the room.

"Why are you saying that?" Lourdes stood facing the chanting girls.

"Because they found you in a dumpster when you were like three years old, *moron*." The ringleader now emerged as Claudia Bergman, the doctor's daughter. Claudia was the kind of teen girl that used her wealth to separate herself from the rest. Her mother spent a fortune on clothes, and Claudia made sure everyone knew the price for anything she wore and that it was bought at some fancy store in Dallas.

A wave of shock rushed over Lourdes. She froze. Was Claudia lying to be mean or telling the truth to be even more cruel? She dropped her head as she lifted her hands to her face to cover the tears. Lourdes was mad that she was crying but she could not stop. As the mocking seemed to grow louder, she felt a strong arm around her shoulder pulling her away. She allowed herself to be guided blindly out of the room but could only cover her face in shame. She sensed the swinging door push open to the kitchen and other arms pulled her toward a large woman.

Charlotte comforted her and spoke softly, "It's okay, baby. It's okay. No one can hurt you now. I got you, baby girl. I got you now." Lourdes sobbed uncontrollably into the generous bosom.

She caught her breath and asked, "Is it true? Why would they say that, Miss Charlotte? Why would they say something like that?"

"Baby, I don't know, but you need to talk to your parents 'bout this kind of thing, not me." Charlotte was not sure what to say. She knew there had been a toddler found in a dumpster years ago but didn't know for sure it was Lourdes.

A man's voice now was heard from behind Lourdes. "Charlotte, thank you. I'll take her to my office and call her parents."

"Lourdes, honey, come with me to my office. You haven't done anything wrong. I just want you to have some privacy and we can talk," Principal Johnston calmly guided her out the side door and away from the cafeteria windows.

The principal was a kindly man in his late fifties with a big stomach that rolled over his belt and caused him to appear to be constantly leaning forward. He knew the good students and the bad ones; the average ones never crossed his desk. He knew Lourdes for the best reason. She was very smart. She was the kind of student a teacher loves to brag on at meetings or with friends.

The two walked around the exterior of the building to a side entrance then down a hall to the center of the school where the offices were located. Lourdes still had on her apron and her eyes were swollen from crying. The hallways were clear, but the bell would ring soon and students would spill out like ants from a disturbed mound. The pair entered the door to the principal's office into the empty interior office. Lourdes slumped into a leather chair in front of his desk while he sat next to her in a matching one.

"Lourdes, dear, let's call your parents. They need to come pick you up. I don't think you need to go back to class this afternoon. What's their number?" he looked at her with sincere compassion.

"They won't be home now. My mom cleans houses and my dad works at Caesar's welding shop. But . . . I don't want them coming here . . . Do you know if what they said is true?" She raised her face to the overweight man across from her.

"I don't think I should be the one that shares that with you. It should be your parents." Johnston tried his best to avoid the subject.

"If they loved me, they wouldn't have lied to me. Why would Claudia say that if it was not true? No one could make that up just to be mean." Lourdes had stopped crying and was thinking clearly and applying her logical mind to this emotional problem. It was her best defense.

"Honey, I just cannot say without your parents. It is not my place."

"So, it is true. Take me to the library," she demanded.

"Okay, why do you want to go there?"

"It would've been in the paper. We have a close date and should be able to find out the truth," she said rising from her seat. "Are you coming?"

The bell for classes had rung while they were in the office and the students had cleared the halls again. The principal led the way to the section where the local paper, *The Daily Journal*, was stored on microfilm. She wrote down a date of her birthday eleven years before. He loaded the film and began scrolling rapidly stopping occasionally to determine the date.

He slowed down and announced, "There it is."

Lourdes slid her wooden chair in front of the screen and peered carefully as if she were looking for a hidden puzzle. But the truth was not hidden. *SMALL CHILD FOUND IN DUMPSTER.* It was true. A child was found, but was she the child?

"There were no witnesses ... discovered just before the truck dumped her into the crushing ... certain death avoided ... hero saved the little Jane Doe ... who is she? ... why would someone do this?" Lourdes tried to remember the details as she read. Were they in her head somewhere?

"Wearing a pink shirt with a flower, blue shorts, no shoes, gash on her head above her right ear ... abrasions," she lifted her right hand slowly and felt for a scar, but she knew it was there. Every time her mother would comb her hair, she would avoid the area so as not to scratch her. Now she knew why.

"Can you take me home?" she turned to the principal and asked with her voice cracking.

"Of course," he answered with a little hug around her shoulders.

The ride to her house was short. She only lived a mile away and Lourdes normally walked, but today she needed someone to be nice to her—to help her. Other than Lourdes pointing the way through the old part of town to her house, nothing was said. She lived in the kind of neighborhood built for the new factory workers after World War II which once was a place of prideful new dwellings. All the homes were wood frame and some had half brick veneer fronts and single garages from a time when no one could imagine a family with two cars. She pointed to the last house on the right with the old broken-down rusty pickup in the yard. She was a bit embarrassed of her house for the first time, but it was the first time a teacher had seen it. He pulled in the driveway stopping the car.

"Thanks for the ride and the help. I don't think I can come to school anymore," Lourdes stated in a flat monotone voice, careful to not show emotion.

"I will not insult you and say I understand how you feel. I will never know how you feel at this moment. But you are very smart. God gave you something others do not have. Every teacher says you are their favorite student because you try harder than anyone. You push yourself beyond the world's expectations. I will make sure you are protected. Just give me a day and I promise, this will never, ever happen again," Mr. Johnston pleaded with the downcast girl.

"You can't promise me that and you know it, but thank you anyway," she said with surprising maturity. She opened the car door to stepped out on her piece of land. The piece of land she knew as home and her sanctuary. But what was it now?

"I'm coming to check on you tomorrow," he encouraged as she shut the car door.

Lourdes walked to the garage and found the key hidden in its normal place under the paint can with dried pink streaks on its sides. She unlocked the door and entered the little two-bedroom house. She strode into the familiar clean kitchen, through the small den, and down the hall to the bedrooms and bath. She slowly walked, carefully gazing at the few cheaply framed photos hung neatly on the hallway walls. She saw her school pictures then found the one she was searching for. She had walked past it so many times, but today was different.

She took if off the wall and carefully examined the grainy color photograph blown up to an eight by ten. It was her parents sitting on the same green sofa on which she now sat. She appeared to be around three years old wearing a blue dress with white ribbons. She wore lacy white socks and new white shoes with a strap across the top. Her little legs appeared tan in the photo, but now she noticed marks in several places. Her hair was cut short, but a large white bow hung on the right side of her head. Her mother and father were dressed as if they had been to church and there was a fourth person in the picture—a priest.

Now she knew why there were no baby pictures of her. This was the day they brought her home—her birthday or what they celebrated as her birthday. She had no brothers and sisters, and now she knew why. Danny and Maria could not have children. It all made sense to her now. Her dad had a brother with his wife and kids and her cousins were all younger than she. Her cousins didn't seem to know. No one had ever said anything. Her mother's family was in Mexico, and she never spoke of them. Her father never had any good thing to say of his wife's family. If it was something bad, she now wondered if she was the reason.

She suddenly felt exhausted. Drained from the day, she went to her room. The pink walls were too happy for her now. She lay on the twin bed with the pink and white comforter she found at a thrift store. She was still wearing her apron. She reached for the little stuffed doll that had been by her side for as long as she could remember. She pulled the doll tight to her and closed her eyes. "If I could just sleep," she thought, "when I wake up, none of this will have ever happened."

* * *

Principal Johnston walked into the cafeteria kitchen to see Charlotte and her crew busy cleaning and prepping for the next day. Charlotte spoke first, "How's that baby doing?"

"I don't know. I don't know how anyone could deal with what she's going through. But I am not letting her quit. She will come back to this school. If I have to walk beside her every damn day, I will!" Johnson said, his anger rising. "Now, I need to know what all of you know and how this started and who did what."

Charlotte started, "I was too far in the back to see. I just heard noise, but I don't know who did what. I wish I did know. All I know is Tommy Adams brought her in here away from that crowd. He was mad like I ain't never seen. That sweet baby just came into my arms and then you was here pretty quick. But you know we got them cameras."

"Yes! We had them installed this summer when we added the new security system." Johnston could not believe he had forgotten.

He spun on his heels and aimed his sizeable gut back to the offices. He was happy he could have real proof of who was there and did what. He would be calling parents today to settle this issue tonight. He entered the central part of the school passing by the receptionist. "Betty, get Officer Jim in here now. Page him."

Jim Patterson was the assigned school safety officer. He was kind of a joke with the kids as Jim was a short fellow and painfully thin. He was not very intimidating and most people called him Barney Fife behind his back. He had been to a police academy but never really worked for any police departments. He had been a volunteer deputy assistant but that was a made-up title. He had family that was in law enforcement, so when the school budgeted for a safety officer, he got the job. No one told him he was the only applicant.

Betty got on the PA system and paged Jim to the office. Jim entered the office moments later in a panic.

"What's wrong?" Jim rushed to Betty.

"Mr. J needs you in his office."

Jim entered the principal's office with his back straight and saluting as if he were reporting to a five-star general.

"Yes, sir, I'm here," Jim said out of breath.

"Why are you saluting? I just need to see the video of the cafeteria from B Lunch today. Aren't you the one who knows how that works?"

"Yes, sir!"

"Then let me see it, please . . . now!"

"Right this way, sir. The system is in my office." Jim walked out leading the way. His *office* was an old supply closet, but all the video recorders and a monitor for the six cameras were there along with his small desk and large old, cracked leather chair.

"This should be the one we need here. B Lunch . . . what are you looking for?" Jim said while pulling the tape cartridge marked *Cafeteria*.

"There was an incident. And by the way, where were you at 12:15?" Johnston just realized Jim was not there.

"I eat lunch with Mama from 12:00-12:30. Been doing that since I started," Jim replied with no apology in his tone.

He placed the tape into the VCR player and pushed rewind. He stopped occasionally to check the time which was seen clearly on the large wall clock on the monitor. There was a decent broad shot which showed most of the area on the screen, 12:04 displayed on the monitor.

"Stop here. Play now." Johnston leaned closer to the twelve-inch monitor.

He searched the scene of students and spotted Lourdes speaking with a girl sitting alone. The picture quality was not great but good enough.

"Turn it up. I can't hear anything," Johnston directed Jim.

"Not sure if that is going to help." The added volume only added to the chaotic atmosphere of a room full of teenagers all talking at the same time. Then the sound of the crash and Tommy falling.

"Stop it there. Okay, so looks like this boy drops his tray and most of the kids are staring that direction, naturally. Lourdes leans down and speaks to the girl sitting alone. I think that's the new girl that moved here recently from San Antonio. Okay, hit play."

They watched as Tommy stood and took some food off his shirt. He put it in his mouth as Lourdes walked over and began picking the mess up off the floor. Tommy could also be seen cleaning up the remnants as Lourdes looked back toward a table of some freshman girls.

"That's who starts it. Can you zoom to that table, Jim?" Johnston points to the group of girls on the screen.

"I don't think so, I never tried to do a zoom before," Jim answered with disappointment.

"It's okay; I know all of them. I can see it well enough. You can hear them all chanting, 'Dumpster baby.' Those little brats! Who else is saying that to her?" He scanned the scene for student's reactions. Several were laughing and some were staring, but most looked away in apparent disgust. He began writing names on a tablet then hit pause.

Lourdes had her hands over her face by now. Johnston wrote names while asking Jim if he knew students' names. He hit the play button again. Lourdes appeared frozen and could only stand covering her face against the brutal verbal attack. Tommy Adams rose from the floor beside her and looked with disgust at Claudia and her group. He placed his right arm around her and guided her out of the room. The voices died down at the sight of the shattered girl, blinded by sheer torment, being helped by her peer.

Johnston replayed the scene several times from the beginning to the end of B lunch looking for more clues and straining to hear more of the audio. He called two teachers in to identify a few more names and to confirm what may have been said. He had his list. Johnston returned to the office and handed the list to Betty.

"I need this typed up and every parent called today. We are having a parent and student meeting tonight with just the people on the list. Also, make sure every student on the list takes a notice home with them. Mandatory meeting tonight seven p.m. in the cafeteria."

*   *   *

Lourdes had somehow fallen asleep in her room. Her mother found her at four o'clock when she finished work. She did not wake her and she was surprised to find her asleep. She stood at the open doorway and looked at her with a sweetness reserved for mothers gazing on their dozing child. *How often she had sat and looked at her in peaceful slumber?* Then she saw the old photo on the floor next to the bed. *Why was that there?*

The loud ringing of the home phone jolted Lourdes awake, who moved quickly to answer the phone. But her mother had already picked up, and when Lourdes exited her bedroom, she heard her mother speaking.

"Hello. Yes, is she in trouble?" Maria looked at her daughter now standing in front of her with the worried demeanor of a defendant who has had no chance to tell their side to the judge.

"Yes, sir. Seven. Yes. Thank you," She stared at Lourdes and hung up the phone.

"I didn't do anything wrong, Mama," Lourdes blurted out and began to cry. "Why didn't you tell me?"

"Lourdes, what happened?" Maria looked at the girl she had raised and knew as her own with all the compassion she could bring from her soul.

"They called me dumpster baby, and they were right! I am the dumpster baby, and no one ever told me the truth! Why, Mama? Why didn't you ever say anything?" Lourdes gasped for air as she began to hyperventilate.

Maria pulled her daughter to her, held her tightly, and let her cry on her shoulder.

"I'm so sorry. I'm so sorry," She spoke softly in Lourdes' ear while painful droplets streamed down her tear streaked cheeks.

CHAPTER 12

"Line two. It's Monica," Dawn called out from her desk to Mr. Downs' office.

He looked at the phone and thought to himself, "This could be bad. She never calls the office."

"Hello, Monica," Mr. Downs tried to sound friendly even though he was busy at work.

"It's Barrett, Pop. He's in trouble at the school. Now, don't get too excited; there are a bunch of kids in the same boat. Evidently, there was some incident about name calling in the cafeteria and Principal Johnston wants the parents to be there to discuss it with the kids. I asked Barrett about it, and all he would say was he didn't do anything. But apparently a few mean girls made fun of a Mexican girl who works in the cafeteria. Four is still off somewhere; who knows where. I was hoping you could go with us."

Mr. Downs heart sank when he heard the part about a Mexican girl working in the cafeteria. He knew Lourdes was working there and was proud of her when she negotiated the deal. Anger rose in him that his son was gone again and he went into a rage.

"Of course he's gone! Why would he ever bother to be around to be a husband and father?" he ranted, but then he remembered the reason for the call and caught himself. He paused and took a breath.

"Do you know the girl's name?" he asked trying not to sound emotional.

"No," Monica lied.

"What were the kids saying?" he asked.

"They called her dumpster baby." Just saying the words broke Monica's heart. She did not tell her father-in-law she knew the child, and she wanted him there for that reason. She knew Lourdes was special and his presence could somehow resolve this terrible event.

Mr. Downs heart sank even more. His face reddened and his hands trembled. He tried his best to not let his voice betray his emotions.

"What time and where?" he managed to ask.

"The high school cafeteria at seven tonight."

"I'll meet you there," Mr. Downs said and hung up the phone.

Leaning back in his chair Mr. Downs wondered how he allowed himself to feel so much for his bright young friend. He realized how deeply she meant to him now that she had been hurt. He was surprised how he felt. How could he have allowed this girl to infiltrate his heart so much? He was never unkind toward people, but he knew he was not known for his warmth even for family. He knew he could be cold like his father was and his grandfather before him. He supposed it was a way to protect himself and not feel for the people he denied loans or repossessed cars and property. That was just the business.

He had allowed Lulu into his heart where he only allowed very few— not even all of his family. She had brought him more joy than he thought was possible. She had given him the gift of helping and teaching her. She was so smart and sweet. There was so much to hope for in that girl. His mind wandered as he imagined revenge for her. He would save her; he would punish them all for doing this to his Lulu.

Dawn came into his office, "What's wrong? You look awful."

"I'm fine. Nothing," he answered her bluntly.

She closed the door to his office and sat across the desk from him. "You can tell the rest of the world that crap, but not me. I have been with you for thirty years. We spend more time with each other than we do with our spouses. Now what the hell did Monica say?"

"There is a meeting tonight at the school. A bunch of kids made fun of Lulu. Called her dumpster kid, and I'm pretty sure she doesn't know her history. This could break her . . . and I can't let that happen." Mr. Downs glanced at Dawn trying his best not to lose control in front of her.

"Oh, I see. That is bad, very bad. If I could get my hands on those idiot juveniles, I would beat the smiles off their smug faces. I know how much she means to you . . . and me too, damn it. Anyone that knows her knows she doesn't deserve this." Dawn also had to fight back the lump in her throat.

*   *   *

The Travis City High School parking lot had only a few cars at six forty-five when Mr. Downs parked his old white Ford pickup with the dent in the tailgate. He sat waiting for Monica and Barrett to arrive so he could walk in with them. His navy-blue pinstripe suit with vest, white starched shirt, and solid red tie made him feel in uniform. It was what he was expected to wear in public. His Open Road Stetson and black alligator boots added to his persona. He was a Texas banker and statesman, a man of authority and respect.

Monica's white Chevy Suburban pulled in beside his truck. Barrett sat next to his mother with his unruly hair, so despised by his grandfather, sitting on top of his wiry body. Monica opened her door first and then Barrett opened his. He rolled out slowly. He was spineless in the way he stood, looking like a question mark with his shoulders slumped forward on his skinny body.

She was dressed impeccably as usual. Mr. Downs loved his daughter-in-law and he always had. She was the only stable force in his life lately. Janet was sick most days and unable to leave the house. His son was an alcoholic who had basically abandoned Monica and his two children. His daughter was struggling with her latest husband in California, and now his grandson was in trouble.

"Stand up straight. You look like a homeless hippie." Mr. Downs turned to his grandson with disgust.

"Yes, sir," Barrett answered meekly and stood straight.

"Before we all go in, I want to hear from you what happened. Tell me exactly and don't lie to me. It will only make it worse." The old man stood in front of his truck with his hands on his hips glaring at Barrett.

"He shouldn't even be here. He didn't do anything wrong. It was a bunch of mean girls led by Dr. Bergman's daughter, Claudia," Monica stated defending her son.

"Monica, I asked Barrett. You cannot answer for him his whole life," Mr. Downs said firmly.

"Mom's right. I told her everything. I was sitting at another table. I didn't do anything. It was Claudia and her group of girls. They must have it in for that girl because she's really smart," Barrett blurted stabbing his words like a bayonet into a stuffed dummy.

"Okay, let's go in and find out who's telling the truth. But I know that little girl didn't deserve this," Mr. Downs said and marched toward the school.

The three walked toward the main entrance of the high school. Several other groups of parents joined in looking like a migration of many different species. A total of about fifteen to twenty students and their parents. Men dressed in work boots and dirty shirts, suits and ties, or slacks and golf shirts. Women in colorful hospital scrubs, or floral dresses, and jeans, with dutiful expressions of concern. No one noticed a student in a sweatshirt with a hood over her head entering the back side of the building alone.

Mr. Downs scanned the room for familiar faces. He felt surprised at how few he knew. It was a small town, but these were not his generation and apparently no one from the bank. Monica waved at some mothers she knew and took a seat as they noticed the portly principal walking toward the end of the serving line where you would normally slide your tray to the cashier. He raised both of his hands and began.

"If I could have everyone's attention, I want to get this meeting started. First, thank you all for coming. This was short notice, so I appreciate your time. I want to say that what happened earlier today can and *should* be used as a teaching moment. A student who goes to my school was mistreated, and I personally will not stand for this type of behavior. You may not even know why you are here, and maybe your child has not told you why you were asked to come. Luckily, we installed cameras last summer to enhance our protection of the campus. Parents only; please come forward to gather around the monitor. I know it's small, but hopefully you will see what we saw."

Claudia looked at the floor and then at her two friends who had sat with her earlier that day. Her mother was beside her, but her father was absent. She had simply planned on lying her way out of any accusations and had persuaded two of her friends to lie, but now this was not going well. Her mind raced as she planned her escape.

A thirty-six-inch monitor and the attached VCR with speakers allowed for decent audio of the recording for the group. All the many different kinds of parents gathered and arranged themselves in front of the static screen. No one noticed Danny and Maria Sanchez walking in and sitting in the rear of the room.

Johnston heaved up his pants and raised his voice, "Today's situation is about how some of the kids in our school treated their fellow student, Lourdes Sanchez. Lourdes is an excellent student, maybe the best in the freshman class. She works in the cafeteria during her lunch break and trades her work for lunch payment. When the tape begins, you'll see that most of the students have received their meals on trays and are seated. Some bring their lunches, as you know. You will see Lourdes walking into the lunchroom . . . Hit play, Jim. Right here; this is the girl." Principal Johnston pointed with a wooden ruler to Lourdes on the screen.

"She walks over to this young lady—who is new to our school—and we see her speaking with her. She is actually being kind to her. Lourdes saw her sitting by herself and spoke to her. I confirmed this with the girl."

Suddenly the sound of a tray hits the floor and laughter erupts from the students in the recording.

"Now stop the tape. I want each parent to find their child sitting in the lunchroom. Just move around until you locate your child." Johnston backed away and allowed the parents a better view.

The parents crowded closer, taking turns, confirming with their son or daughter where they were sitting.

"Okay, now I'm going to turn down the sound, and we will watch together what happens. Lourdes will walk over to this table, and you will see she goes to the floor to pick up the mess from the dropped tray. Tommy Adams is the one that dropped the tray, and we see him stand first and take some food spilled on his shirt and eat it. It was some Jell-O. We see Lourdes come to help, go to the floor and began picking up the mess. Tommy also joins her."

Johnston pointed with his ruler directly at Claudia on the screen. "Now we see this student, and we think she was the one who began to taunt Miss Sanchez. We will replay this. It is difficult to hear over the noise of the room, but she calls her dumpster baby."

Johnston paused and looked at Claudia and her mother. The mother stared ahead at the monitor and Claudia hung her head.

"Stop here again, please Jim," Johnston calmly asked.

"Now, kids calling other kids names is not worth a meeting. That has gone on since the beginning of time. I believe children need to learn how to deal with the harder things in life, but this one is different. Miss Sanchez was indeed the child found in a dumpster eleven years ago. She did not know of her past until her classmates decided this was how she should learn of it. As you see, this child stands mortified with her hands over her face. I want you to see what your children are doing. We see a few chanting Dumpster Baby, some laughing, some pointing, and some disgusted at what they are witnessing. Please hit play, Jim."

The video began again and the group watched Tommy put his arm around Lourdes and guide her out of the room. The parents watched until they walked out of sight into the kitchen and the door closed behind them.

"Stop and back it up to right before the tray drops and this time turn up the sound as loud as you can," he directed Jim.

Danny Sanchez now stood, walked to the group, and watched the monitor and listened to the soundtrack. Maria could only sit with her head down aching for her child. He watched carefully and listened to the taunts and laughter and inhaled a deep breath when the video stopped. Holding his feed store cap in front of his waist, Danny walked toward the front of the crowd.

He whispered something to the principal. It was apparent only a few of the parents knew him and that he was Lourdes' father. Johnston nodded in response and waved his arm for him to step forward.

"My name is Danny Sanchez and Lourdes is my daughter. I grew up here. I went to school here and ate in this very cafeteria. I know kids can make fun of each other. I was teased by kids and I also teased others. I am no saint. But that was *my* little girl, and I want you to think how you would feel if it were your daughter or son." Danny looked up at the ceiling, breathed deeply and then lowered his head while shifting his feet. "The Bible teaches me to forgive. And I have to forgive, because I cannot keep this anger inside me or it will kill me. I'll try and teach my daughter to forgive, for her sake. But my wife will be holding this in for a long time, and I don't judge her for this. You guys have to do what you do to make sure your own kids learn something from this," he said with his voice breaking.

Mr. Johnston came up to his side and put his arm around him. "Danny, that was very kind of you. Now, does anyone else have something they want to say?"

Mr. Downs stood up and turned to his grandson seated below him. Without any warning Mr. Downs slapped the boy with an open hand across the side of his head with enough force to knock him out of his chair on to the floor. The crowd of parents and students were stunned and silent as they watched Barrett gather himself rubbing his cheek as he stood stooped over to sit back in his chair. Monica reached for him from the other side and assisted him into his seat.

"I didn't do anything," Barrett said softly under his breath defending himself.

Mr. Downs was as shocked at what he had just done as the rest of the room. The anger had risen from inside him like an oil well exploding into the air from a place far below the earth. Everyone was staring at him. He addressed his violent response.

"I am sorry for my action just now toward Barrett, but I will not stand in this place and not deliver swift punishment to my grandson. He said he didn't do anything, and that is right, but that was as bad as if he had hit her. He didn't defend her. He didn't do the right thing." Mr. Downs kept speaking, "I have known this young lady, Miss Sanchez, for four years and she is my friend. You other parents will decide how you will use this sad event to teach your own children. I want to thank Mr. Johnston for having this meeting to show all of us what happened here. But more than that, I want to say how much I admire you, Mr. Sanchez."

Pointing to the humble man, Mr. Downs continued, "I am so sorry this happened to your daughter. She is a wonderful girl and you and

Maria are the best parents I've ever known. She did not deserve this. I'm just . . . so sorry," he finished and sat down.

Lourdes sat out of sight on the floor of the kitchen. She had left before her father arrived from work and walked to the school, staying away from suspicious eyes. She was not ready to face him; she was scared and ashamed. She had been listening to the entire meeting and teared up hearing her sweet father. But she felt somehow vindicated by Mr. Downs' act. A slap felt better than forgiveness. She felt the need to leave soon, so not to be seen. She got to her feet and pulled the hood over her head.

She decided to steal a glimpse through the cracked door and spotted Claudia with her head down. Her mother stood up next to her.

"My name is Dorothy Bergman, and my daughter is Claudia. It is clear to me what I just witnessed is a terrible thing. My daughter may have been involved in this and I am sorry. Stand up, Claudia." She grabbed her daughter forcefully by her shoulder. The daughter now looked small against her mother. Mrs. Bergman was tall with long brown hair. Her hair was longer than a woman her age would normally have. She wore expensive glasses and her makeup was perfectly applied. She had sharp features that matched her voice. The room eyed the tall woman with her cowering daughter beside her.

"I will not strike my child, but I will provide a suggestion for a punishment. You mentioned earlier that this young lady was working in exchange for her lunch. I will pay her expense for her lunch for the rest of the school year," Mrs. Bergman stated to show her ability to rectify the problem with money.

"That's nice of you, Mrs. Bergman, but how does that really teach your daughter anything? It only shows you think money can buy her way out of this situation," Danny Sanchez answered for the group.

"Well, I didn't mean any disrespect," the woman answered as she turned away.

"The only one you are disrespecting is your own child," Danny pushed back with a matter-of-fact statement.

"What do you want me to do to make this right?" Mrs. Bergman pled with the father of the hurt girl.

"I have a suggestion," a voice came from the back of the room. "Why doesn't Claudia work in the cafeteria every day to pay for Lourdes' lunch?" Tommy Adams had once again come to Lourdes' defense. Applause suddenly erupted across the room.

"Okay, we don't need to point to only one child. There are others that can take some days as well," the principal interrupted. "But that to me is the best idea I've heard. I will make a work schedule and pass it out by the end of school tomorrow. If anyone else wants to say anything, see me afterward. Thank you for coming." Johnston was ending the meeting now. He had learned once there was a solution that made sense, you quit while you were ahead.

Mrs. Bergman was still standing and started to speak, but felt her daughter pulling her down to sit. She didn't need to make it worse. They left the room as quickly as possible and did not speak to any others on the way out.

Lourdes had stayed to hear Johnston's last statement but knew she should get away fast. She would have to exit and run to the other side of the parking lot to not be seen. She was running around the edge of the vehicles when she heard the crowd leaving by the front door. She spotted Mr. Downs' truck. She knew it was unlocked; it was always unlocked. The key lay visible on the driver side floor. She ran to the passenger door, pulled it open, and lay down on the floorboard. She lay still with her back against the passenger door facing the driver side. She could hear voices drawing closer. She could now hear Mr. Downs.

"Monica, I am not apologizing for a damn thing. It's over." She could hear Mr. Downs clearly, and then she heard another man's voice calling out to Mr. Downs.

"Excuse me, sir. My name is Ernest Bradshaw. I just wanted to say that was a hell of a thing you said and did in there." A man of around forty approached Mr. Downs with his hand out. A chubby teen boy pulling his too short T-shirt down over his belt trailed behind him.

"This is my son Bruce." The pudgy man with an ill-fitting dark suit pointed to his child. "I work over at Mundy-Walker Funeral Home. I've met you a few times over the years at different funerals. Anyway, I just wanted to say that was a nice thing you said about that little Mexican girl. And, uh . . . also the discipline thing . . . I, uh, well, I think more of us need to be like you."

"Thank you very much, Ernest. That girl is special to me. But we should be more like Danny Sanchez," Mr. Downs answered the man, his blunt tone ending the conversation.

While he was distracted by the funeral man, Monica and Barrett got in the Suburban and sped away. Mr. Downs watched them leave knowing she was upset. It was probably better to give her some time to cool off. As he turned to open his pickup door, Danny and Maria Sanchez came toward him.

"Mr. Downs," Maria said softly. "You are the closest thing she has to a grandfather. You know my family is in Mexico, and we haven't seen them in years. Danny's parents are both gone. So anyway, she looks up to you and thinks you are great."

Lourdes shrank smaller on the floor as she heard her mother just a few feet away.

"She thinks the world of you, and you have been very good to her is what we mean to say, and you didn't have to do what you did tonight, but I thank you, sir," Danny added feeling a bit embarrassed that his wife would imply such a personal relationship.

"I meant what I said," Mr. Downs responded. "She is a great young lady. How is she doing?"

"Not sure. I haven't seen her," Danny answered looking him in the eye. "She snuck out of the house before I got home. Maria said she was upset because we had never told her what happened about her . . . uh, beginnings. And I don't blame her. I just never wanted her to know anything but that we were her parents and loved her. It was selfish of us, I guess."

"I understand. We all do what we think is best when it comes to our children, but none of us are perfect," Mr. Downs answered reaching out to pat Danny on his shoulder. "Call me at the bank if I can help. And let me know how she's doing."

"Yes, sir, we will and thanks again. I'm sure she will be home when we get back." Danny waved as they turned and walked to their truck.

Lourdes head was on her knees while she crouched on the floor when Mr. Downs opened the door. The sunlight was fading in the western sky with orange and pink streaks lying across a blue heavenly canvas. Mr. Downs paused to admire the colorful sky, not noticing the unexpected passenger as he sat behind the wheel and closed his door with a loud slam.

"Don't tell on me, please," Lourdes entreated her mentor without trying to startle him.

"Damn! I didn't see you there. You scared me, Lulu!" Mr. Downs exclaimed while raising up in his seat.

"I needed to hide quick. I'm so sorry."

"It's okay, but you can't hide forever. Now let's get you home."

"Please, don't take me yet," She pleaded.

"Listen to me, Lulu. I am not your parent. You have a mother and father who love you, and they are good people. They are worried about you." He cranked the pickup and began driving, but she remained on the floor to not be seen.

"I don't have a mother and father! They threw me away!" Lourdes' emotions boiled over into rage. She put her head on her knees which folded up against her. She pushed her lower lip out and stuffed back the tears.

Mr. Downs kept driving slowly and never turned his head toward her. His thoughts were of anger. He hated her being hurt, and he had realized just how much she meant to him. *How did this girl worm her way into his heart? How was he so hurt and angry for her who was now huddled on the floor below him.*

"I don't blame you for being mad, but don't take it out on the people who love you the most. I don't know a better man than Danny Sanchez. He proved that tonight, and I hope you heard him speak. And your mother is a saint."

"I know they're good people, but why would they lie to me?" Lourdes responded meekly as her anger slowly subsided.

"They didn't lie to you; they just didn't tell you the whole truth. Just focus on what your father said. I was not a good person in there. I should not have lost my temper," Mr. Downs said addressing his own actions.

"Why did you? I was surprised but a little happy."

"Don't be happy at what I did. It was wrong."

"But why did you?" Lourdes pushed for an answer.

"I can't stand seeing a child hurt. I never have. It's wrong and I won't

put up with it . . . And I want the best for you. You deserve the best."
He looked down at her and stopped the truck. They were in his normal
parking place behind the bank. "Now get off the floor and sit up like a
normal person."

Lourdes pulled herself into the passenger seat pushing off the loose
dirt on her gray sweatpants. She settled into the seat, straightened her
back, and forced herself to lift her chin up as she turned to Mr. Downs.

"I'm not going back to school. I just can't do it. They are never going
to quit calling me names and making fun of me." She looked at him
with sadness in her resolve.

"That's the easy way out. Just quit because its hard and others are
mean to you? The world is divided into two types of people. Those who
take responsibility and those who blame others. Before today you were
the one who took responsibility. You were the one who tried. And now,
because some spoiled little bitch called you a name, you're quitting? I
will not allow it," Mr. Downs said firmly.

"Oh, *you* are not going to allow it? How wonderful for you. *You*
don't have to go face them!" Lourdes lashed back, surprising herself in
her anger toward him.

"No, I don't. But all of us face evil in our lives. The tormentors,
the bullies, the others who are the cause of our pain and failures. Do
not give them the power to steal your destiny. Stand up for yourself,
because you are better than any of those people. You get to decide
your own fate, not the others. It is easy to blame them, it takes
away *your* responsibility, and who *you* are," Mr. Downs lectured
his young friend. "Tomorrow morning you get to decide your path.
You get to be Lourdes "Lulu" Sanchez, and guess what? No one else
matters. In life we all get knocked down. Sometimes we are thrown
down hard, but we must get back up and keep pushing. I see more in
you than I thought was ever possible to come out of this town. You
have impressed me, and I believe in you. You have been besieged,
but I see no surrender in you." He ended with a fatherly pat on her
shoulder.

Lourdes lowered her head and thought about what he said. "Thanks,
Mr. Downs. And thanks for saying what you did in the cafeteria too. It
was very nice of you. You can take me home now. *I am determined to*

sustain myself as long as possible." The edge of a smile appeared as she quoted Travis's letter.

He cranked his pickup and the two were silent as he drove her to the little frame house with the broken-down truck in the front yard. She thought of how much he had done for her over the years, and how he had been right about so many things. He struck his own grandson in front of the town. The truck pulled in her driveway, and her mother and father were on the little front porch sitting in mismatched lawn chairs.

Mr. Downs rolled down his window as Danny walked to his door. "Hello Mr. Sanchez, I found someone you may be looking for," he said with kindness as Lourdes exited and ran toward her mother. Maria reached out with open arms and hugged her tightly.

"Thank you, Mr. Downs. I figured she was just hiding out for a while, but I was starting to worry. Her mother is upset right now, so I'll thank you for her as well."

"Well, I found her walking and knew she needed to be here," Mr. Downs answered loud enough for Lourdes to hear him.

"Hey Lulu, I want to take you somewhere special Saturday afternoon. I will call your parents and set a time."

"Thanks, Mr. Downs . . . for everything. See ya later." Lourdes waved goodbye and turned to go in with her parents.

Mr. Downs backed the truck out of the driveway waving goodbye to allow them privacy. He felt a bit strange that he was more concerned for this girl than his own family. It would quickly get around town about what he had done and said in the meeting. What would they say? *The old man is a monster, or can you believe he took up for that Mexican kid?* He thought about the backlash for himself and then pushed it aside. He didn't care what others would say. He was right in his mind.

Danny and Maria knew they had a hard conversation ahead of them. Lourdes was in an understandable state of confusion regarding the fact of who she was. It was time to sit in their little home and speak honestly. Lourdes sat on the green sofa and folded her arms in an act of defense. Danny sat in his recliner and Maria sat on the other side of her distraught child.

"I'm sorry we never told you about your past," Danny began. "You were too young at first, and then we never knew when or how to tell you the truth. I'm sorry, honey. We're both sorry." Danny spoke tenderly to the young teenager he would always consider his daughter.

"Yes, baby. We're sorry," Maria added with tears in her eyes.

"I don't know who I am! What happened to me?" Lourdes sat as anger boiled out of her. "Why did my real parents throw me away?"

"We don't have any answers. The Texas Rangers worked on your case, but they never found anything," Danny answered calmly.

"We are your real parents now; *I'm the mother who didn't throw you away*! We love you and have loved you since the first day we saw you. No one could love you more . . . Please, we just didn't know what to do," Maria said sobbing in her hands.

Lourdes stared at her mother and her heart broke. She knew Maria loved her, but the cut into her soul was new and the wound was deep.

"I know Mama; I know. I love you too." Danny joined them on the worn green sofa, and they all hugged.

Mr. Downs pulled out of the neighborhood and knew he needed to go see Monica and Barrett. There was no benefit in delaying the visit. He owed them that. His truck creaked as it pulled into the home he grew up in that now housed his son's family. He looked up at the living room window to see Monica walking toward the back door.

"Monica, we need to talk," he said as she appeared on the back porch closing the door behind her.

"Yes, we do. What the hell, Pop?" Monica crossed her arms, angry at her father-in-law for the first time.

"I guess I overreacted," Mr. Downs understated the situation.

"You think? Slapping the crap out of your grandson in front of everyone!" Monica voice was raised but clear. "I would say that was the overreaction of the year!"

Mr. Downs walked on to the porch and sat on a bench looking down at his hat in his lap. He was in an unfamiliar place and unsure how to get back. He had always been the one towering above any situation. He was not used to being the one seated and lectured like a bad child.

"Monica, I'm sorry, and I regret the severity of my actions. But I do not regret the reason behind it."

"I don't either, Pop. I couldn't stand to see her tortured. I didn't know you even knew the girl," Monica said letting her anger subside.

"Yes, she is a gifted child and a good person. I spend every morning with her and her mother at the bank before most of the world is awake. They began cleaning for us a few years ago. I found out who she was when I did a background check with local law enforcement before we hired them. Elvis told me. Did you know she is a math genius?"

"Yes, I did. It's incredible what that girl can do. I actually met her the day she was found; it broke my heart." Monica voice cracked as she recalled seeing her little shattered body.

"You're a good person, Monica. You don't deserve what I did today, and you really don't deserve the way your husband is treating you and the kids. I'm sorry for that too. Can I talk to Barrett?"

"Yes, do you want me there or do you prefer to be alone with him?"

"You should be there." Mr. Downs respected Monica as a mother. The two walked inside the kitchen and Monica walked up the stairs to retrieve Barrett from his room. Janet Ann sat at the island with a magazine opened to a car ad.

"Hi, Pop." Janet Ann wondered what was happening but figured Barrett must be in some kind of trouble. She was glad it wasn't her.

"Hi, Boopie. What are you reading?" he asked calling her by his personal nickname for her.

"Seventeen, it's my favorite magazine and check out this cool car. I'm sixteen now and getting my driver's license next week. Hint, hint." The girl smiled and batted her eyes at her grandfather.

"You've never been shy, my darlin'. You may be my favorite granddaughter," he teased back at her.

"I'm your *only* granddaughter and by far the best grandchild. Barrett is an idiot. What did he do now?"

"Sometimes it's what we don't do that gets us in trouble. Why don't you run up to your room while your Mom and I talk to your brother? What kind of car is that?"

"The cool and expensive kind. In other words, my favorite." She turned with her magazine under her arm and passed her brother with a sly look of *you are in big trouble.*

Mr. Downs walked into the den and sat in a large leather chair. Barrett and Monica sat next to him on the matching sofa.

"First, I apologize for slapping you, Barrett. I was harsh and I was angry with all those kids, so I took it out on you. But I had hoped for a higher standard from you. I hoped I would see you stand up for the girl, but you just sat there. It was hard for me to see my own flesh and blood sit there and do nothing while that girl was being humiliated by those little idiots. Do you understand that?" He looked at his grandson with kindness in his voice.

"Yes, sir. I think so," Barrett meekly answered looking at his grandfather and then glancing at his mother for support.

"You know this girl. You've been in school with her since kindergarten. Are you friends? Are you nice to her?" Monica questioned her son.

"Yeah, Mom, we're all friends at the school. But Claudia hates her. I guess because Lourdes is smarter than she is. Lourdes is smarter than most of the teachers," Barrett joked to break the tension.

"Does Lourdes have friends at school?" Mr. Downs asked.

"Yeah, everyone likes her except Claudia and her group. When someone needs a partner on a project, we all hope we get Lourdes. It means we get an automatic A. All the teachers like her too."

"I want you to promise me something." Mr. Downs looked the boy in the eye.

"Yes, sir?"

"You be nice to Lourdes. Protect her like family from now on. You stand up for her. I want her to know that you will be there for her. Do you understand me?" Mr. Downs implored the boy.

"Yes, sir. I will."

"Tomorrow I want you to find her first thing in the morning and tell her you are sorry for what happened. And if anyone teases you about me slapping you, you tell them, 'I had it coming.' Understand?" Mr. Downs sought confirmation.

"Monica, do you agree?" Mr. Downs asked her for support.

"I do. I want a son who treats all the women in his life with honor." Monica sought valor in her son, remembering when she met Four.

* * *

As usual Lourdes was spending her Friday morning at the bank cleaning before school. Maria had been given a key and her own code for entering the bank on the rare occasion Mr. Downs was out of town, but his truck was parked in his spot when they arrived. Lourdes had not slept well. Her mind had replayed the cafeteria scene over and over, but each time it ended with her standing with her hands over her face in shame. Shame was a new experience for her. It tore at her soul. It was not like any other feeling she had ever had in her life, and it was inside her now with no way to expel the awful poison.

Lourdes came into Mr. Downs' office after assisting her mother in the lobby. She needed help, but she didn't know how to ask because she never wanted to appear weak in front of him.

"Hi, Mr. Downs," she greeted him timidly as she began dusting.

"How are you this morning, Lulu?" he asked tenderly.

"I'm okay."

"You don't sound okay but that would be completely normal. You had a day that most of the world has never experienced. Most people have not been subjected to what you went through."

"I'm scared. I'm scared that it'll happen again today. I'm not strong enough to take it again." Her voice faded with her weak breath.

"Lulu, I wish I could wave a magic wand that would prevent any bad thing from ever happening to you again, but that's impossible. I can only teach you how to be strong enough to withstand the bad things that will happen to you. There is something you need to know. When I saw the tape of what happened, most of your classmates looked disgusted by the cruelty of what happened to you. But they were not brave enough to stop it. There was the exception of one boy. My point is, you have friends and supporters. You are not alone and the sooner you face this, the faster you'll heal. What was the boy's name who took you away?"

"Tommy Adams."

"Tell me about Tommy."

"He's nice and very funny but he spends too much time being the class clown. He doesn't make good grades." Suddenly she wished she had not told Mr. Downs he did not make good grades.

"He may need some help from a very smart girl." Mr. Downs sensed she liked the boy.

"Yes, sir. I'll try to do that," she answered thinking now how special Tommy was after his action in the cafeteria.

"Lourdes, it's time to go to school," Maria called from the hallway.

Maria and Lourdes were silent on the drive to the high school. The young girl stared out the window at the passing homes and businesses feeling her anxiety building as their family sedan pulled in the long line of parents dropping off kids. She felt dizzy like she was standing on a narrow board of a very tall building gazing down at the ground far below. The car crawled forward as teenagers scurried away from their chauffeurs. Lourdes knew Maria would not insist she go to school if she only asked. Her dry mouth was opening to tell her mother she couldn't go but now the car was stopped, and the passenger door opened from the outside.

"Hi, I'm Janet Ann Downs, you already know my idiot brother Barrett." Lourdes' hand instinctively reached for Janet Ann's extended hand who gently pulled her from the car.

"Hi, Mrs. Sanchez. We have her from here." Janet Ann closed the door as Lourdes found herself standing by the tall sixteen-year-old beauty dressed in a black and gold cheerleader uniform.

"Lourdes, our grandfather, Pop, came over and told baseball head . . ." Janet Ann pointed to Barrett as they walked, "to make sure you are protected at school. I was not supposed to hear all this but there was no way I was going to miss out on hearing why Pop wanted to talk to Barrett." Janet Ann spoke quickly and with an air of confidence reserved for popular girls. "Anyway, what Pop doesn't know is that I run this school. I am a junior cheerleader and date Max Harris—the greatest quarterback in Travis City history and idolized by all. From now on there is no way a bunch of freshmen are ever going to be mean to you again."

Lourdes walked with her backpack slung over her right shoulder staring at the tall girl with amazement as Barrett walked dutifully behind them like a trained puppy.

"Today I'll make sure everyone knows that Lourdes Sanchez is my friend. You let me know if anybody, and I mean anybody, even looks at you wrong. Got it?" Janet Ann stopped at her locker with her head cocked and a fake smile to ward off any onlookers.

"Yes, thank you," Lourdes mustered in response.

"Good. Barrett, walk her to first period," Janet Ann commanded. "And Barrett, don't you dare talk to me during the day. I will see you after school. I have a pep rally and the game tonight. Friday is a busy day for me. Now go, you two." Janet Ann sent them away and walked over to a group of girls dressed in the same uniform.

"Where's your first class?" Barrett asked her.

"Ms. Trammel, English. You are in the same class, Barrett," Lourdes sighed.

"Oh yeah, I forgot," Barrett said sheepishly.

The two walked down the hall together with the sound of hundreds of teenagers bouncing off the metal lockers and polished floor. She felt safe in the familiar noise and her anxiety was surprisingly gone. Five minutes with the least likely Downs family member had given her more assurance than she thought was possible. She wondered if she would tell Mr. Downs about Janet Ann's support, but she concluded no. This one belonged to Janet Ann.

After three morning classes, the bell for B lunch rang and Lourdes began her walk to the cafeteria. Tommy Adams ran up next to her, and they walked together. Tommy had thick brown hair and sparkling brown eyes. He was cute and popular. He had learned to make fun of himself to take away power from bullies but was never mean spirited in his quick wit.

"Hey, Lourdes, you okay?" he asked softly.

"I'm better than I thought I would be and thanks for yesterday. That was so nice of you," she responded with sincere appreciation.

"Sure, no big deal." He felt embarrassed. "Can you come with me to go drop this book at my locker?"

She nodded shyly and they walked back to his locker. He opened the metal locker and carelessly placed the book in and closed the door. They began strolling back toward the cafeteria, and she found herself walking slower to postpone returning to her place of torment. Tommy seemed to sense it and he slowed his pace and strategically allowed his hand to graze hers as they walked. His touch felt electric to her and her body surged with hormones. She forgot where she was as the door swung open to the cafeteria.

Both of them saw Ms. Greer, standing like a prison guard over Claudia Bergman, who was cleaning a table in a soiled apron covering a paisley blouse and designer jeans and a hair net pressed tightly over her perfect hair.

Tommy burst out laughing at the scene and immediately covered his mouth to stifle the noise. Lourdes could only stare at the hair net and Ms. Greer when she heard the first person in the room clap. It was the new girl, Beth. Lourdes stood next to Tommy as the entire room began applauding. She felt Tommy's hand in hers as he lifted up her arm like a prize fighter declaring her the winner. The room that had previously brought her such shame, had redeemed her the very next day. She felt a wave of joy wash over from the smiling students and felt her hand in Tommy's never wanting to let go.

CHAPTER 13

THE MORNING HAD been spent like most Saturdays for Mr. Downs. He drove around his property checking cattle then stopping by the ranch manager's house on the east side of the property. Dub Daniels had been working for the Downs family for forty-one years and had no desire to do anything else. He was provided a home, truck, very rarely used health insurance, and a nice retirement package. His salary and bonus structure would not be considered generous by most standards for a career which had very few vacation days, but it was his life, and he loved his job. He considered the ranch his own, so Mr. Downs knew to gently guide Dub in ways to make him feel responsible for ideas.

They discussed cattle prices and the number of fifteen-hundred-pound round bales of hay in the barn. Rainfall had been sporadic but seemed to be adequate for the year. Dub wasn't shy about bringing bad news to his boss, though he knew it was best to have a solution before bringing up a problem. This morning it was a worn-out round hay baler.

"I'm not sure how many more bales we can get out of the John Deere. I've patched and replaced almost everything, but we have over twenty thousand bales on her. She's just worn slap out. I found us a used one just like our model for sale outside of Waco. Good price, used just one season, and about five grand less than a new one. What ya think?" Dub needed an answer now. He had phoned the seller last night and promised a return call this morning.

"Good idea, Dub," Mr. Downs concurred. "Come by Monday

morning and get a check from Dawn and then go get it. I appreciate you finding us a good deal." He smiled at his manager, and they talked a few minutes more before he left.

Mr. Downs drove back through the pasture beside his house to look over the replacement heifers. These young cows were hand selected females born on the ranch which would be put in the herd the next year for breeding. He usually kept ten percent of his cow herd back each year after selling his old or barren cows and restored it with these hand selected young females. Culling and selecting the best had been done for a hundred years at the ranch. Over time, his herd improved and became perfectly adapted to that climate, grass, and terrain.

He pulled back under his carport and walked into the back door where Janet sat at the kitchen table.

"Hi, honey." He kissed her cheek. "I'm going to the skeet range this afternoon. Gonna take Lulu. She needs something completely different in her life to take her mind off things," he said in a passing manner to Janet.

"Wait, what?" Janet sounded surprised. "You think shooting shotguns will soothe the troubled soul of a fourteen-year-old girl? You can be very wrapped up in your own world sometimes, Billy. Why do you think this is a good idea?" She responded as he imagined she would. He knew her well.

"I do think it'll help her. She's not a normal teenage girl. Just let me try. If it doesn't work, we'll do something else, oh wise one," he answered with a little more sarcastic tone than he planned.

Janet shot him the look wives give when their husbands have overstepped their bounds, but it passed quickly. The message had been sent and received.

"Monica's still upset over what you did. I talked to her again this morning. I'm upset too, Billy. That was our grandson you humiliated in front of the school. I know you better than anyone, at least I hope I do, and that could have been handled better. But in fairness, I wasn't there. I know how much you think of Lulu," she conceded.

"I know, Janet. I just lost my temper, but I did apologize," Mr. Downs responded humbly.

Mr. Downs went to his back closet and pulled out his custom stainless-steel gun case and a tan canvas one. He also got a brown leather and canvas bag full of shells, shooting glasses, and ear protection. He loaded it all in his truck and headed to pick up Lourdes.

He thought about the events of the past week. The incident at the cafeteria had been on Thursday night and no talk about his actions had got back to him. Maybe it had blown over.

Right at one o'clock his old pickup groaned as he turned into the driveway of the Sanchez home. Lulu was sitting on the little porch in jeans, a white polo shirt, and flip flops.

"Good afternoon, Lulu. Are you ready to have some fun?" Mr. Downs called out from the truck.

"Yes, sir. Mom and Dad just left to go to the grocery store." Lourdes walked to his truck and got in the passenger seat.

"Where are we going?" she asked.

"Travis City Gun Club."

"I've never been there." Lourdes seemed interested. "Where is it?"

"Out Baker road five miles. Been there for thirty years or more. I was a charter member of the club. Now it's mostly a bunch of old men sitting around telling the same old stories trying to make each other laugh. It's glorious." He smiled.

"I want you to know that things worked out at school yesterday. I'm doing good. Thanks for all your help," she said almost in passing and without mentioning Janet Ann.

"Excellent news. I'm very proud of you for going back to school. I told you it would be fine," he proudly said thinking his grandson had risen to a higher standard. She just smiled at him and nodded her head.

The truck pulled off the highway east of town, and they drove south on a blacktop rural road. The range consisted of a metal clubhouse building, two skeet ranges, and two trap ranges. The building sat above the fields with a large, covered porch with donated furniture and a crude outdoor kitchen. There was almost nothing about it any woman would find appealing.

There were several vehicles in the grass parking area. Mr. Downs tried to go a couple of times a month to shoot and hear the area gossip. Travis City, as a town, had a sense of humor. It was an odd thing to say, but it was true. Laughter was heard in barber shops, cafes, and bank lobbies. Men and women were competitively funny, always trying to one up one another. Randy had pointed it out one day that the town was funnier than most places. Randy traveled a lot in his business and had been in countless towns and offices. He determined his hometown had a better sense of humor than anywhere he had been. If the town indeed had a sense of humor, then the Travis City Gun Club was the headquarters.

Only one of the skeet fields was occupied with a group of four men. Each field had a semi-circle of paved sidewalk with seven extended three foot by three-foot pads at equally measured intervals around the course. On the left side was a two-story structure with a single small window facing the field where the skeet was flung from a machine inside and on the opposite side was a shorter building with the window about waist high. Targets crossed back and forth as the men took turns attempting to hit the flying flashes of bright orange and black. The sounds of shotgun blasts were a bit startling to Lourdes when she opened the truck door.

"Take this for me, Lulu." Mr. Downs handed her the smaller canvas gun case, and he carried the larger metal one and the shell bag. They walked to the covered porch area where two men were sitting while drinking out of large white Styrofoam cups and laughing about something. Under the twenty by thirty-foot porch were six wooden picnic tables. The metal wall had a one by twelve board at the top with old caps hanging from nails. All the caps had been shot and were tattered in various stages of destruction.

"Hello, gentlemen, and I use that term loosely, this is Lourdes Lulu Sanchez," Mr. Downs announced as he sat the heavy case on one of the picnic tables. "This is her first time to shoot, so be nice," he continued.

"Well hello, Miss Sanchez. I'm Bobby and this is Charlie. How do you know this grouchy old man?" Bobby Hamm stood and took off his cap.

"She works at the bank, helps her mother. She's smart as a whip too," Mr. Downs answered for Lourdes.

"Good, I thought maybe you'd bought one of those foreign brides out of a catalogue," Charlie Knight said with a smirk.

"Damn it, Charlie! She's fourteen years old. My grandson's age," Mr. Downs said embarrassed at the behavior of his friend, but Lourdes was laughing loudly at the remark. A kid who was not easily offended was immediately welcomed.

"Why are all those caps up there? They look like someone shot them," she asked.

"That is a very good question. You see, when someone shoots their first twenty-five straight, the group shooting with that person, takes his cap and throws it in the air and blasts it. It's the law," Charlie answered for the group. "It also goes for the first fifty, the first seventy-five, and the first hundred straight."

"A hundred is very tough to do. Those caps are very few on this board," Bobby explained.

Mr. Downs opened his case and began to assemble his double barrel over and under Krieghoff K-32. It was an older model but still considered to be one of the top competitive shotguns. The value of the firearm increased with special engraving in the metal receiver and fine Turkish walnut on the stock and forearm. The fine wood with burled swirling patterns came from dug up walnut roots that were as old as fifteen hundred years. It had been sanded and polished repeatedly to create a beautiful finish. The metal was skillfully carved with gold inlay of fowl and mystical figures. This gun was jewelry for men.

"Billy, it's too bad you can't shoot as good as your gun. A man pulls out a gun like that and you don't expect him to miss. I need more excuses is the reason I shoot my cheap old Winchester 101," Bobby commented with his usual wry smile.

"I've always said, if you can't shoot at least look like you can," Mr. Downs deflected the comment.

"Open your case, Lourdes, and let's talk about safety first." Mr. Downs turned to his guest as he set his assembled gun in the wooden rack along the side of the building.

"Safety is very important. People can get killed by being stupid with a firearm. Never load your gun until you are on the station to shoot. Never point a gun at anyone and always have the breach open when you are carrying the gun. And you'll need to wear these safety glasses and put in these ear plugs. Treat every gun as if it is loaded. Got it?"

"Yes, sir." Lourdes nodded.

"You will be shooting a Remington 1100 20-gauge youth model. It doesn't kick too bad, and it's a great starter shotgun. As you can see from the group shooting now, they're shooting at eight different stations. Seven in a semi-circle and the eighth is between the high house on the left side and the low house on the right side. Each shot has different angles, and those angles effect the lead."

"What does *lead* mean?" she asked as she watched the shooters finish station six.

"Good question. The lead is how far in front of the moving target you would shoot to hit it. Think of throwing a football to a running boy. You throw it where he is going to be when the ball arrives."

"I get it." She liked the math equation aspect. "How fast are the skeet flying and how fast is the shell moving?"

"The targets are thrown at around sixty miles an hour and the shot is moving at 1200 feet per second. Regulation skeet sets the speeds. This is not a bullet. It's a shot shell composed of over 400 small pellets in a twenty-gauge skeet load of number nine size shot," Charlie answered impressed by the young lady's questions.

"So that is 88 feet per second for the target and the more perpendicular to the target the lead would increase. What is the distance of the shot?" Lourdes asked calculating the dimensions in her head.

"From each station to the center stake where the targets cross is twenty-one yards. The end of the barrel, or choke, of the gun is designed to have the perfect pattern of shot at that distance. That is, the tighter the choke, the tighter the pattern of shot. So what we call a full choke is designed for farther shots, but the skeet choke has maximum efficiency at twenty-one yards," Bobby Hamm joined in fascinated by the black-haired girl.

"How in the hell did you figure the feet per second of the target?" Charlie asked still amazed. Mr. Downs smiled, pleased his friends were impressed by Lourdes.

"You just need to know 5280 feet in a mile, 60 miles per hour, sixty minutes in an hour, sixty seconds in a minute. So that would be 88 feet per second." She smiled at the two men who were staring at her like she had snakes growing out of her head.

"Charlie, I'd appreciate if you would teach Lulu how to shoot," Mr. Downs asked knowing Charlie would jump at the chance to help her. Charlie was a Triple A shooter, former state champion, and placed high in the World Shoot held in San Antonio each September. He was now in his late fifties but enjoyed working with youth as much as competing.

Bobby joined the others as they walked to station one, and Mr. Downs shot first. He did not miss the first four shots, a high house single, a low house single then a double, where both targets are released at the same time.

Charlie placed Lourdes on the pad under the high house window. He pointed above her where the window was and then toward a stake centered in front of the range. He adjusted her feet and arms and had her bend slightly forward at her waist. She was very attentive as Charlie guided her expertly through the process. A round of skeet is twenty-five shots or a box of shells. If she hit five, Charlie would have been thrilled. She mounted the gun to her shoulder and could feel her nerves in anticipation of the kick and loud explosion.

"Say pull when you are ready to shoot," Charlie said as he gently moved her barrel to the anticipated flight of the target.

"Pull!" Lourdes saw the flying target, pulled the trigger, and felt the kick against her shoulder. The group watched the clay target explode into a hundred pieces.

"Great job!"

"Good shot, Lourdes."

"That was perfect!"

Each man was thrilled for her, and she was just as happy she hit the target. For the first time in two days, she forgot all about dumpster baby.

"How did that feel?" Charlie asked her with a big smile.

"Awesome!" Lourdes answered, surprised at how she felt.

"Good, now let's keep going. Now we are going to shoot a low one. The target will be coming from across the field from that window there. You find the target and shoot in front about a foot and a half," Charlie coached her. "You ready? Let's try another shot."

"Pull!" Lourdes called out. The target shot out of the low house window on her left and she aimed and swung the barrel and pulled the trigger. Bam! The target kept on flying.

"That was fine," Charlie said encouraging her. "You just lifted your head. You have to keep it locked down against the stock. You shot over the target."

At each of the eight stations, Mr. Downs would shoot first. He didn't miss until the sixth station, and he missed two. Lourdes listened intently to her coach and had some good shots but more misses. After her first round she had shot twelve out of twenty-five. Mr. Downs shot twenty three out of twenty-five. Charlie kept on working with Lourdes while Bobby and Mr. Downs shot on the other field. Lourdes' shoulder began hurting, but she never complained. She enjoyed the math and the hand eye coordination. She loved the sound and the feeling of accomplishment when the clay target was demolished. She had never been athletic or played sports, but she could now understand the attraction. This was fun.

The shooters finished their rounds and walked up the slight hill to the clubhouse. All three men were bragging on how great she had done, and Lourdes enthusiastically talked about specific shots she made. She was one of them. A black-haired teenage girl and three old, gray men, bonding over the fun of hitting a target. Lourdes felt different. She felt liked and none of these old men judged her. They only cared about hitting a flying piece of clay. It was how she felt when a song came on that she loved. She went to another place even if it was a brief visit.

"Lourdes, would you like a coke?" Mr. Downs asked as they put away their guns.

"Yes, sir." She reached into the pocket of her jeans for some change.

"No need for that. You are my guest. Charlie, can I talk to you a moment?"

Mr. Downs walked into the clubhouse and Charlie followed him inside.

"I want to see if this is something the girl wants to do," Mr. Downs spoke in a quiet voice. "If we don't get young people involved, the sport will die out. She seems to really like it. I want you to teach her and charge everything to me. That 1100 is fine to shoot for now, but if she gets better, maybe we can find her a better gun."

"Sure, you know how much I love helping kids. I will send you a bill if it works out. She could be very good, because she did everything I told her." Charlie seemed excited. "Most people don't listen. She does and that whole math thing is crazy."

"Thanks. Just between us, okay?"

"Of course, Billy. It would be really bad if word of you being generous got out. What would people think!" Charlie said sarcastically and laughed at his own joke.

Mr. Downs walked back to the porch where Lourdes was sitting and talking, exhibiting an unbelievable sense of comfort with Bobby and four other men. The five grown men all stared at this wonderful, smiling teen girl explaining how to convert miles per hour to feet per second.

"Okay, Lulu. We need to get you home. I promised your mother we wouldn't be late, and neither of us want your mother mad at us," Mr. Downs announced.

Charlie, Bobby, and the four other men all said goodbye, come back again, and wished Lourdes good luck, but most of all, they were dumbfounded by how brilliant she was. Lourdes pulled open the creaking door of the old truck and carefully placed the unloaded gun on the floor. Mr. Downs heaved his gun case and bag in the back, scooted behind the wheel, and cranked the old truck.

The radio was on an oldies station and *Here Comes the Sun* by the Beatles was just beginning when they pulled on to the highway. Mr. Downs absentmindedly began singing along with the song from his younger days. The windows were down as the two drove along, and Lourdes watched him intently as he looked straight ahead with his left arm playing with the wind out the window. She had never heard the song but listened to the words. *Little darling, the smiles returning to the faces.* She never knew a man like Mr. Downs could be affected by music. It didn't seem possible. She thought music was for young girls like her. The song ended and a furniture store commercial broke the spell.

"That was a pretty song, and you're not a bad singer, Mr. Downs."

"Oh, yeah? Well, I've just always thought that song was about hope. Hope is important, you know," he said feeling embarrassed.

"I liked the melody. Who sings it?" Lourdes asked innocently.

"The Beatles. They broke up way before you were born. They were really big when I was younger. Janet loves them too. I guess young people don't know who they are nowadays, but they should," he said realizing the vast separation between the two of them. "Did you enjoy shooting today?"

"Yes, sir! It really was great fun!" she answered.

"I think we should do this more, but you don't have to wait on me. Charlie said you can come anytime and he'll coach you. He thinks you have great potential."

"I'd like to, but I would need a ride. Maybe I can do some odd jobs out there to pay for it."

"Don't worry about the money. I can take care of that part. But that's a good idea. You could do some chores and I know you will. We'll get the ride part covered." He knew that she would rather work for her fun. He also knew the retired fellows would make her feel right at home there. In fact, they already had.

CHAPTER 14

Monica and Janet Downs sat at Janet's kitchen table with Janet Ann and Barrett watching television in the den. Mr. Downs had retired to his bedroom for his Sunday afternoon nap. They had finished their meal of baked chicken, green salad with home grown sliced tomatoes, steamed broccoli with melted lemon butter, and were picking at their dessert of freshly baked sugar cookies with raspberry and chocolate drizzled over vanilla ice cream.

"This is delicious, Janet. You must love to cook," Monica mused as she ate.

"I don't love to cook," Janet answered like she always did when someone complimented her food. "I love to eat good food."

"Well, it's always flawless. I know I will never live up to your standards," Monica said sincerely.

"Are you doing anything with the kids this summer?" Janet deflected the attention off herself.

"I don't have anything planned. Janet Ann is more concerned with being with her friends and getting her driver's license next week. We'll go to the beach house, I'm sure. In June, Barrett is going to a baseball camp in San Antonio and may go with Justin's family to their place in New Mexico. I would like to go to Dallas for some shopping, but that's just a day trip."

"Any word from Four? I haven't talked to him in a week or more. That usually means he's . . ." Janet did not finish but Monica knew.

"I talked to him about three days ago. He's at the beach house.

Fishing I guess." Monica tried not to escalate matters with her mother-in-law.

"It just seems that boy of mine is lost. He was doing so good for a long time, but now it feels like he has started into a slow decline. I want you to know, no one blames you." Janet looked compassionately at the daughter-in-law she adored. "My God, you have been a saint through all of this. You have your kids, but Janet Ann will be leaving for school in a couple of years and Barrett after her. Has anyone ever asked what you want to do in life?"

"I'd like to go to school," Monica answered thoughtfully.

"Then that's what you should do! I think that's an excellent idea." Janet was excited by the idea. "How can we help? Just name it. What are you interested in?"

"I'd like to get into interior design." Monica was glad to talk about anything else besides Four and being a mother.

"You should. You have a natural gift for it." Janet encouraged.

Monica did not tell her mother-in-law she was worried about Four. Four and Monica normally talked every morning, but she had not spoken with him since Thursday morning. Three days and no answer to her calls had initially incensed Monica, but now she was worried. Maybe it was something like a broken phone. But her mind moved quickly to wondering if he was dead on the side of the road or in jail. If Four did not answer tomorrow, she would call the bank and ask if he had used a credit card or maybe they could see charges that looked like it was stolen. She was not ready to alert Janet and Mr. Downs. It would just add to their worry.

*   *   *

Monday at nine a.m., Monica made a call to Four again. No answer. She remembered the message she left on Friday morning begging him to call her as soon as he got it. She was at the end of her rope. She screamed into the phone. She was done with every Downs man in her life. A worthless drunk husband, a mean father-in-law, and a useless son. She didn't mean it; she was just enraged. When was anyone going to do something nice for her!?

"Hello, this is Monica Downs," Monica spoke as professionally as possible. "May I speak with someone in the credit card department?"

"Yes, Mrs. Downs. Let me transfer you," replied the nice lady at her father-in-law's bank.

"Why are you calling about credit cards, Monica?" the familiar man's voice boomed back at her.

"Oh, Pop! I'm sorry I didn't want to disturb you." Monica was frustrated at being transferred to him.

"What's wrong?" he demanded with his voice rising in anger.

"I haven't spoken to Four in days. We usually talk every morning, but I haven't been able to reach him since Thursday morning." She tried to keep her composure.

"All right let me check. Dawn, get in here and show me how this works," Mr. Downs called out angrily.

"What is it, you cranky ass old man?" Dawn came to stand beside him at his desk.

"See if Four has used his credit card lately and pull his checking account activity too," he tried to ask nicer.

Dawn quickly returned to her office, pulled a file from a locked drawer, and returned to begin typing on Mr. Downs' computer.

"I see a charge in Victoria, Texas, at an Exxon on Thursday night at ten fifty-four. The next charge is a Houston hotel at three thirty-four early Friday morning," Dawn said knowing it was a serious situation. "No other charges for this month's statement."

"His checking account has several cash withdrawals all less than a hundred dollars and a pending check of $45,000.00 made out to Donavan House Rehabilitation." Dawn looked at her boss and understood she needed to leave and return to her office.

"Monica, did you hear Dawn?" Mr. Downs spoke solemnly.

"Yes. I've never heard him speak of that place. I have been pleading and praying with him for years to get help." Monica broke down in tears.

"Let me see what I can find out and call you back, honey," Mr. Downs comforted his daughter-in-law and felt his own anger recede to be replaced with worry.

After a few calls Mr. Downs had reached the rehab facility in Houston, Texas.

"This is Doctor James. How may I help you?" a voice with a northeast accent answered.

"Yes, my name is Downs, and I think my son is there," Mr. Downs said politely.

"Mr. Downs, I'm sure you understand that I cannot provide confidential information over the phone."

"Yes, of course. It's just that he has written a large check to your facility, and I need to verify he is actually there to allow the check to clear. I own the bank," Mr. Downs said making sure he got the doctor's attention.

"Yes, sir, I see. We do have a man named William Barrett Downs the Fourth in our facility, but I cannot discuss his condition or allow you to speak with him," the doctor responded.

"I'm fine with that, and I respect your protocol. My daughter-in-law nor anyone else knew he had checked in." Mr. Downs probed for more answers. "When would we expect his release? A few days . . . a week?"

"No, sir. It may be months. We have an extremely high success rate at our facility. We give a long-time frame because the treatment is designed to break them down and then build them back. This can be a long process." The doctor was used to concerned family members. "I show we are to contact his wife, Monica, to advise of the progress. I'm not surprised he didn't tell anyone of his plans. He has contacted us many times over the years and never shown up. This is common and most people don't tell their loved ones in case they . . . well, in case they don't show up."

"Thank you, Doctor James." Mr. Downs was grateful for the added information. "I just want my son to get better. Monica will await your call when the time is right. Thank you for your help." He hung up the phone and saw Dawn standing in front of him. As he stood up, she came around the desk and hugged him and kissed him on his cheek.

"I need to call Monica. She prayed him there and she needs to pray him back home." He picked up the phone and dialed her number as Dawn went back to her desk wiping a tear.

CHAPTER 15

2002

SIXTEEN-YEAR-OLD LOURDES STOOD holding her gun with the confidence of a seasoned shooter on station seven of Field One at the National Skeet Shooting Center in San Antonio, competing in the 4-H State Championship. It was her first big tournament, and she was leading the group of shooters heading into the last seven shots out of a hundred. Lourdes was wearing her favorite cap with the Travis City Gun Club logo in bright orange against the tan bill and crown. Her long black hair pulled into a ponytail fed through the back of the cap. She wore an olive-green short sleeved shirt with a padded shoulder on her right and the same bright orange logo stitched above her single pocket on her left. Her belt held a black shell pouch made of water buffalo hide. Her khaki shorts were neatly pressed and just above her knees. She wore flat-soled tan shoes laced tight to secure her stance. Her shooting glasses set high across her face and curved around each eye with light purple lenses to allow the most contrast against the blue sky to see the flying blaze orange and black bottomed targets. Custom fitted hot pink ear plugs protected her hearing.

For the past two years she had shot over fifty thousand targets with Charlie Knight at the Travis City Gun Club. She once spent an entire week only shooting low eight—the last shot of the round. She shot two thousand low eight shots before Charlie was happy. She once shot two hundred and thirty-one straight of just low eight before she missed. She blamed her miss on a disruption in her concentration due to the previous pull being a broken clay target. Charlie had responded, "Things will happen like this. Someone will talk, a horn will blow in the parking lot, a bird will fly in your sight, a mosquito will buzz your ear, or a target will break. Don't let it affect you. Be prepared for that to happen. Use it to your advantage. Say to yourself, 'Good! I always hit my next shot after that happens.'"

She had been using Mr. Downs' gun for the past year, and Charlie had it adjusted to fit her five-foot six height. The gun was part of her body now. Where she looked was where the pellets went. Every shot was about routine and repeating the same mechanics. Charlie had been her only coach, and he had threatened anyone if they tried to give her helpful hints or free advice. He had told her not to listen to anyone trying to change anything about her shooting. Charlie knew young and old men alike loved to impress ladies with their vast knowledge, and he would not allow amateurs to ruin his protege.

"Pull!" she called for the high house bird. The shell exploded sending the pellets speeding to the target and pulverizing its mark above her to the right.

"Pull!" The skeet flew from the window beside her upward toward the center stake, and she pulled the trigger again and watched the clay fall apart.

She loaded two shells now for doubles and stood solid on the concrete pad and called out again.

Two shots rang out in the exact cadence Charlie had taught her. Bang . . . Bang. Both targets were crushed. She walked off the station and waited for the other four competitors shooting with her. She needed to stay focused and thought only about the next target. She had not missed her first 97 targets in the round. "Concentrate on 98 and nothing else," she thought. She had completed the first three rounds of twenty-five each without a miss. Her fourth and final round was almost over.

Lourdes pushed herself to concentrate as she was taught. "You'll be nervous. Use it to your advantage," she heard Charlie in her head. She looked down when the others shot. She did not want to see their bad shots. She was the only girl left, and she had no idea who was close to her. But she knew they could not be ahead of her. The squad completed station seven and walked in a straight line in the order of shooters to the last station in the middle of the field. She would be first. High eight, pull, boom, perfect. She circled off the station and waited again for the others to complete the shot.

Low eight. She loaded two shells, set her feet, and went through her routine: pull, boom, perfect, reset.

"Pull!" she called for the final shot.

"No bird!" the official called out loudly to announce the broken clay out of the window was not to be shot.

Her mind suddenly was back home at the Travis City Gun Club with Charlie saying in her ear, "I always make the shot after a broken target." She set her feet, raised the gun, and placed her head down on the comb of the stock. She allowed her breathing to still.

"Pull!" she called out and swung the barrel with her eyes locked on the target flashing across the blue sky. She felt the curved gold trigger against her finger like it was part of her body and watched the black and orange clay target turn to black dust. Perfect.

One hundred straight! Her first time to shoot a hundred straight! She allowed herself to find her family and the old guys from the skeet club in the spectator arena and she smiled. But she respectfully waited for the four others to shoot. When all was done, the closest score to her one hundred was a ninety-seven shot by last year's champion.

The Lulu fan club rose to their feet screaming with relief and joy. Her mother raced on her short legs across the field and was the first to hug her daughter, gun and all. The other competitors mobbed her as well. This was a game where proper sportsmanship was taught, and she was an adorable winner. Mr. Downs was there with Janet in the stands, and he was happier than anyone. She felt her cap being pulled off her head and saw the four boys she had just defeated line up on station eight to load their guns. She could only watch with satisfaction as the official slung her favorite cap high in the air and watched the boys blast it to bits. It was magnificent.

Lulu's fans were all talking at once when she arrived proudly holding her tattered cap at the bleachers to greet the old men. The group circled her as Danny lifted her tattered cap in the air and Maria could not stop crying happy tears. One much younger man allowed the group to mob her first until Lulu saw him, and she raced to him and leapt in his waiting arms. Her arms and legs wrapped around the six-foot athletic body of Tommy Adams kissing him repeatedly in front of everyone. It was difficult to tell who was happier between the young couple in the celebratory embrace.

"Remind me to never make you mad. You're too good a shot!" Tommy joked.

After the awards ceremony where Lulu had stood on the highest platform to receive her medal, her fans wanted to celebrate at a restaurant. Two four-door pickups of Charlie and others from the club, Mr. Downs and Janet in her Cadillac, Danny and Maria in her Expedition, and Lulu and Tommy in his Ford Mustang bearing dealer plates headed to their favorite Mexican food restaurant.

Tommy's family owned the Ford dealership in Travis City. Tommy was the youngest and had endured the torture of having two older brothers, but the brothers were now away at college. Lourdes had been with Tommy since the day of her redemption in the cafeteria. Their relationship had blossomed during tutoring sessions to help the struggling boy in school and quickly turned into first love for them both.

Lourdes found him to be bright and quick witted even though he struggled to understand basic reading or math. When he was diagnosed with dyslexia it became clear why his grades suffered. He had hidden the learning disability with his sense of humor. Make fun of yourself first to gain power over those who seek to tease and bully. Lourdes learned that was how he dealt with the issue, and she thought it was a brilliant strategy. But then again, she thought every part of him was brilliant.

Like all teenagers, Lourdes's focus had shifted as she progressed through high school. She loved her parents and Mr. Downs, but her time now was dedicated to her friends. More than anyone else, Janet Ann had taught her how to be a powerful young woman. Lourdes was now a junior in high school with stylish long black hair and a maturing face to match her maturing body. She was beautiful and always had the beginning of a smile in her eyes. She continued to work in the cafeteria because she liked it and loved Ms. Charlotte. And she had maintained her grades, because she was not going to allow Claudia to beat her.

CHAPTER 16

2006

DANNY AND MARIA moved from the old neighborhood to their new home hidden behind the property of Danny's shop surrounded by old oaks with spreading limbs covering a green yard of Bermuda grass. The three-car garage now had a new burnt orange and white Jeep with personalized plates which read *Lulu S.* The Sanchez family had achieved the American dream through hard work and sacrifice and starting every morning at five twenty. Now two cars would leave the rock driveway to go to the bank on Main Street. Maria in her Expedition and Lourdes in her Jeep blaring Destiny's Child. Maria would not allow any of her seven employees to clean the bank, only her daughter would be by her side as she had been for the past six years.

"Get up and don't make me tell you again!" Maria called out through her daughter's bedroom door.

"Okay, I'm getting up," Lulu murmured. She was tired but knew her mother was getting angry and there was no excuse good enough to miss work. Lulu washed her face in her bathroom. Her mirror spanned the length of the wide vanity with six bright bulbs illuminating her bathroom with an ice cream parlor chair under the space right of the sink. She brushed her long hair and stared at herself in the mirror searching for any new blemishes to eliminate prior to school.

She stumbled down the long hallway dressed in an extra-large t-shirt for pajamas. Her father was his usual merry self, dancing around the expansive living room in his boxer shorts with some old dance music playing too loud for this time of day. There were no plastic framed photos on the walls any longer. Now large, framed paintings of Texas bluebonnets, cattle, and portraits of the three of them decorated the space. There was a collage of Lulu receiving awards from school and shooting tournaments and one picture of her in a long blue prom dress standing next to a smiling Tommy in a black tuxedo.

The kitchen had new stainless appliances with granite countertops and a matching island. Maria had designed the house and decorated it based on what she had seen in the nicest places where she had scrubbed toilets. The mismatched styles seemed to blend well, and she loved her dream home. Lourdes had friends coming in and out of the well-stocked kitchen constantly. Tommy was there every weekend but had been banned by Maria during the week. When Maria saw her daughter look at Tommy, she only thought of the day he would break her heart.

Lourdes entered her senior year leading the GPA race between herself and Claudia. Claudia was head cheerleader and dating Barrett who had become an incredible baseball player. Barrett played shortstop for the TCHS Defenders and had Division One schools and a few major league teams scouting his games. Tommy played defensive end for the football team, and Lourdes was captain of the Drill Team. The black, white, and gold sequined uniform with fringed skirt and vest fit her seventeen-year-old body perfectly, showing every curve and flat stomach. Her flat-topped, white cowboy hat was tilted on her head as she marched with straight arms swinging in precision and her knees high onto the field leading the other girls to the sound of the marching band behind her on Friday night. The cheerleaders would run ahead of the football team to signal the beginning of the game, as they prepared to battle. Spectacular small-town pageantry played out on Friday nights across the state.

Parents and townspeople clapped from the old bleachers as they watched their children represent the town and school. Janet was not able to attend the games as her back pain had now left her in a wheelchair. Mr. Downs would not go without her, but they would listen to the games on the local AM radio broadcast announced by extremely biased men from Travis City. The October air had finally broken the summer heat and the whole town smelled of fall. The locals cheered each great play and groaned together when the good guys faltered.

The Defenders lost on this particular night, but the score would be quickly forgotten by teenagers ready for a post-game celebration. Who would get the beer, and where would they hide from the snooping parents and local police force who were only trying to scare the wayward teens? Lourdes and Tommy, along with several others, headed to her house where Danny and Maria allowed a few kids over to listen to music and have snacks and soft drinks in the garage. Danny would do his best to hold Maria back from her inspection rounds, but he was never successful. Lourdes' group was called the goody-goody church kids by their classmates.

Claudia and Barrett were at another party held in an old farmhouse a few miles out of town. The music was louder, the crowd was bigger, and the drinks were not soft. Alcohol poured freely, young girls threw up behind cars, and boys groped with clumsy hands against schoolgirls growing up too soon. If you were cool, you were in this group. The losers were at Lourdes' house.

The truth was that both groups had members that experimented with drugs, alcohol, and sex, and both groups had members who refrained from those temptations. One group was doing their best to appear to not participate, and one was doing their best to appear as if they were.

Seniors in high school enjoy a place and time unique in their lives. They have reached the pinnacle of their association with a group of children thrown together by chance and geography. Some have been together their entire lives, sat beside each other in church nurseries, and tiny kindergarten chairs. They have watched each other grow into young men and women. Their parents look at them with amazement. *Wasn't she ten years old just last week?* Time marches slowly for children but speeds up as they age. To them, it seems as if time becomes slow motion as they reach for graduation.

*   *   *

Christmas in Travis City was a festive time when the downtown buildings were decorated with green and red ornaments and banners strung over Main Street. Local merchants bustle as the churches busy themselves with special services and choir performances. The Christmas Parade is held the Friday night school is out for the holiday break. Local organizations craft poorly decorated floats on flatbed trailers as local ranchers pull them with tractors or trucks. Pretty girls wearing sashes ride in convertibles and wave at sparse crowds lining the sidewalk. Horseback riding groups dressed in festive lights and two marching bands from the high school and junior high play brass versions of Christmas music. Mr. Downs joked, "All of our parades have way more people in them than are watching it."

Christmas Eve was Janet Down's favorite night of the year. She loved the memories of her children when they were small and then the grandchildren renewed her spirit. Daisy had come for a few days in early December and said she would be back New Year's. Daisy did not know how ill her mother was. Janet had not told anyone but Mr. Downs, she did not want anyone worrying about her. The Christmas tree was in the same corner as it always had been. The soft glow of the green and red and blue lights strung artfully around the tree lit the room in a way that felt like Christmas.

"Take me outside, Billy. I want to see the stars," Janet weakly told her husband.

Mr. Downs lay a blanket across her, put on an overcoat hanging by the back door and pushed her in the wheelchair through the French doors onto the patio. It was cold and clear with only a few wispy high clouds sailing slowly across the night sky.

"They say the light we see from a star may have come from one that died a million years ago. It takes that long for the light to reach our eyes," she mused viewing the vast glimmering sky diamonds. "I need you to let me go, honey. My light is almost gone. I'll be fine; I'm not afraid. But it's time for me to go," Janet said looking to the stars above her.

Mr. Downs could only nod in response, and he stroked her shoulders. They went back inside, and he helped her into their bed. She had slept on his right since their first night together. Each night, since their honeymoon, they said the same thing.

"I love you, Mr. Downs."

"I love you, Mrs. Downs."

"Would you sing *Silent Night* for me?" Janet asked with her eyes closed.

"I'll try." He stared at the ceiling of their bedroom and mustered his best attempt to quietly sing. "Silent night, holy night, All is calm, all is bright," he began and looked at her as she lay with her eyes closed.

. . . "Sleep in heavenly peace," Mr. Downs paused and looked at her once more. Her breathing was so shallow. "Sleep in heavenly . . . peace."

On Christmas morning, traditions played out in familiar homes. Randy and Vickie were busy with caterers and domestic help to prepare for all Vickie's siblings and children and all of Randy's sisters and husbands, kids, and grandkids. At last count, forty-one were coming. Vickie had enough tables and chairs for each person in her vast house, and she and Randy had spent most of the morning complaining about her worthless brother.

Monica and Four, always dressed in matching pajamas, were loudly singing at the bottom of the stairs. "We wish you a Merry Christmas. We wish you a Merry Christmas," to their now way too old children who stared sleepily at their weird parents from the top steps.

Danny and Maria were seated on the floor in front of the tall, decorated tree with *Joy to the World* blaring through the house awakening a smiling Lourdes.

Mr. Downs arose at his normal time and went to the kitchen for a cup of coffee and to let Janet sleep late. When he returned, he found her not breathing and cool to his touch. When he could finally speak, he said, "You made it to Christmas like you said you would, honey. I am so proud to have had you as my wife. Thank you for making me a better person." He sobbed onto her nightgown for what seemed like hours.

There were calls to be made, but they would wait. Let the world enjoy their Christmas morning a little longer. The black hearse from Mundy Walker Funeral Home pulled away a little before noon. Mr. Downs knew the process. He had dealt with his parents, but this was different.

He showered and shaved and dressed in a black suit and drove to Four and Monica's house.

Four had returned from rehab a changed man. He remained sober the past few years and worked at the ranch. He finally felt complete. He was a devoted husband and father to his children. He was a loving son who had mended his relationship with, and earned the respect of, his father. His mother had her son back, and Mr. Downs was grateful for this wound to have been healed before she died. He worried about his son more than anyone else as he drove. The overbearing weight of the news crushed him in grief. He hoped Janet's death would not send his vulnerable son back to that dark place.

As he pulled up by the back-door porch, Mr. Downs saw Monica through the living room window. The winter had browned most of the usually colorful flower beds and green lawn, but the blood red leaves of several large poinsettias filled the porch. He sat in the truck with his hat on gathering his strength. Monica appeared on the porch to greet him. She was so happy to celebrate the holiday with all of her beautiful, healthy family. She was a good mother and the best wife possible to his son.

Mr. Downs sat frozen in the seat staring blankly ahead with the deepest sorrow painted across his face. He clutched the steering wheel as if it would prevent him from falling into hell. Hearing a tap on the window, he turned to see Monica's angelic face etched with panic. He could only look at her and nod. She opened the door, reached in the truck, and put her arms around his neck. They both wept. Four stepped out of the house and saw the awful scene. He sat on the steps with his head in his hands. He knew his mother was gone.

Word spread rapidly across the town of the death of Janet Downs. She had been loved and respected by everyone since she married her Billy. The first year of their marriage had not been easy for her since she was the outsider who married the town's favorite son. But she had accepted the challenge and won the hearts of all her detractors.

Very few people knew that when Mr. Downs and Janet were first married, he had written a paper on financial principles that landed on the desk of the New York Federal Reserve president's desk. A letter arrived in Travis City requesting he and his bride come to New York

City for a visit and discuss a possible job opportunity. Mr. Down's father ran the bank at the time, and he was a junior loan officer, so this was a huge opportunity.

The young couple arrived in New York City on a Friday, and Janet was left at their room at the Plaza Hotel while Mr. Downs attended meetings. The phone rang as she was stretched out on the bed for a rest.

"Hello," Janet answered.

"Is this Mrs. Downs?" a woman's voice asked.

"Yes, it is. May I help you?" Janet replied in her slow, Texas accent.

"I'm Mrs. David Tudor. Our husbands are meeting this afternoon. I wanted to ask if I can assist you with anything while you're in New York," the woman explained.

"That is so considerate." Janet was grateful for the offer. "There is one thing I would like. I know we are all going out tomorrow night, and I would love to have my hair done. Can you recommend someone?"

"I can do better than that," Mrs. Tudor responded. "I'll send my personal hairdresser to your room. My treat. It's room 1212, correct?"

"Yes, and thank you very much. That's very kind of you." Janet was hopeful she may have made a new friend.

Mr. Downs was very busy with meetings with several people from different banks discussing his ideas, and this left Janet alone at the hotel most of Friday and Saturday. At three thirty on Saturday afternoon there was a loud knock on the door which startled her. She answered the door and before her was a woman holding a canvas bag.

"Yes?" Janet asked.

"I'm here for your hair," the woman stated sounding perturbed.

"Yes, ma'am. Please do come on in," Janet's southern drawl poured out sweetly to the woman. Janet was dressed in a simple robe and slippers.

"Why look at you! Little country girl come to town." The woman brushed past her making fun of her accent.

"We can do your hair in the bathroom. How do you want it?" the woman asked curtly.

"I like my style fine. I just need a trim, please," Janet answered trying to sound less Texan.

The woman began working on her hair, making more patronizing remarks about Janet's country accent and her plain robe. Janet sat staring at the mirror watching her work.

"Let me ask you something. If you could have anything in the world, what would it be?" Janet asked the stylist sweetly.

"A car would be nice. I have to walk or take the subway. But in the big city, cars are expensive to park," the woman responded.

"That's all?" Janet asked.

"I suppose I would like to have a house. I live in a tiny apartment now."

"What else? Remember, you can have anything," Janet prodded the woman.

"I would love to own some land." The woman was now enjoying the fantasy.

"Well, my husband and I have two cars. We have a large, beautiful home. Our ranch is five times bigger than Central Park, and I'm staying at the nicest hotel in New York City with room service attending to my every need." Janet painted a picture with her description of her life in Texas. "You are here working on a Saturday, and when you leave here, you'll return to your tiny apartment. It seems to me that this *little country girl* is doing better than you. And if I were in your business, I would learn to be nicer to your customers." Janet concluded her statement and stared at the woman in the mirror.

The woman silently finished the cut, thanked her, and left the hotel room with her bag of supplies and a lesson in manners.

That night was a wonderful dinner. Mr. Downs shone all night with powerful men and their amused wives. Janet watched her husband with pride and sorrow at the same time. She did not want to leave her home for this place.

That night in bed the young couple made love and lay their bodies against each other. Janet wanted to feel as much of her husband as possible against her bare skin.

"You could get any job you want in this city; you know that don't you?" Janet said as she lay her head on his chest.

"I have no idea, baby. Maybe. I do have offers," Mr. Downs said being modest.

"I know. I saw the way those men looked at you. I saw the way you charmed every woman at the table. You can be the most powerful man in this whole damn city. And Billy, if that's what you want, I will stand by your side," she stated doing her best to support her husband.

"I'm not sure what I want. It all seems so grand. I want to know what you think." he sincerely asked.

"Honestly, I want to go home, Billy. I hate this place and hate these people." She released her emotions.

"Thank God! Me too! I guess I just needed to know if I could actually be offered a job. Do you understand?"

"Of course, I do. I love you more than I ever thought possible." Janet snuggled in beside her husband feeling content in the life they had chosen together.

*   *   *

The funeral home was busy with visitation from five to ten p.m. Mr. Downs stood and greeted every person and sincerely listened to each one relay their personal kind words about his wife. Monica, Four, Janet Ann, Barrett, and Daisy all stood beside him dutifully shaking hands and smiled at the mourners. The line was in constant motion for five hours. The Sanchez family were there early, staying the whole time seated on a pew toward the back of the chapel.

Dawn came in and sat next to Lourdes and patted her leg. She had spent the day with her boss trying her best to console him and make him smile. She could only look at him now as he graciously greeted each person. Randy and Vickie arrived and spoke to the family and then sat alongside Dawn. Vickie wore a knee length white fur coat. She took it off and folded it neatly beside her as she sat. Lourdes was surprised when she saw her and thought Vickie had on more jewelry than she had ever seen one person wear.

"Lulu, you know Randy, but have you met his wife, Vickie?" Dawn introduced them.

"Nice to meet you. I've heard great things about you, young lady," Vickie leaned across Randy and Dawn speaking to Lourdes directly.

"I want to tell y'all my favorite story about Janet," Randy said to no one in particular. "I will tell you something not many people ever knew. Billy loved another woman before he met Janet. Her name was

Beatrice Harris, and she moved here when we were in the ninth grade. Her parents were some fancy scientists studying in Africa, and they dropped her off at her mother's sister's house. Her mother's sister was Dimple Green, the old maid teacher who lived next to the Downs house on Main Street. Dr. Bergman lives there now," Randy strayed from his original point.

"I remember Miss Green," Dawn interjected. "I had her for science in tenth grade. The personality of a screen door."

"That's her." Randy continued, "Anyway, Beatrice was crazy smart. Like learning Hebrew and Greek to do her own interpretation of the Bible, kind of intelligence. She was pretty, but not in a sexy way, more in a confident way. She was by far smarter than any of the teachers and found class boring. Most of us thought she was weird, but Billy . . . he adored her. They went to every high school function together and he did his best to keep up with her. He was smart, but not like her. She was valedictorian, of course, and got a full scholarship to Harvard. Billy and I headed to Austin to get a degree and have some fun."

"So, they broke up then?" Dawn asked.

"Sorta, he never could get over her, you know. They saw each other over summers and Christmas breaks. Well, Billy asked her to marry him our senior year in college. He had a ring and had it all set up to ask her at the church service on Christmas Eve. They were walking in late, alone in the foyer, when he dropped to a knee with his ring in his hand." Randy set the scene for the story. "She looked at him and shook her head no and told him to stand up. She says, 'Let's talk about this in the car; not here.' They get back in the car, and she told him he wasn't smart enough for her to marry. That it would ruin their relationship!" Randy began to feel angry telling the story of this woman who had hurt his friend.

"What the hell! That bitch! I hate her," Dawn said a little too loudly and everyone on the pews shot her a look.

"Now after we graduate, we go to a wedding where he met Janet and I met Vickie," Randy furthered the story. "We all start dating . . . Well . . . they started dating, and we start a lifelong argument," Randy threw a loving glance at his wife.

"That's the damn truth," Vickie agreed with a smile.

"Billy comes and tells me that he can't marry Janet. He wants to, but he feels like he would be cheating on her, because of all that crap with Beatrice," Randy remembered every detail of their youth together. "That made me so mad because, as you all know, Janet was the sweetest woman on the planet. I swung and hit Billy square on the jaw, and we went tumbling to the ground in his parent's back yard like a couple of idiots. His mother came out on the back porch and yelled at us 'till we stopped. It's the only time we fought in our lives."

"Mr. Downs was in a fist fight? That's crazy," Lourdes asked incredulously.

"Oh yes, he was. And he got plenty of licks in before we were brought to our senses," Randy laughed. "He thanked me later, and I was the best man at their wedding. So, Janet and Billy were happily married. They had a little girl and a baby boy and things are going great, when out of nowhere Beatrice shows up in town. She had been married a couple of times, never had kids, and was working on some nuclear medicine when she got cancer. Rumor was she gave it to herself to be a guinea pig for a new treatment. No one knows for sure."

"Why did she come back to Travis City?" Dawn asked.

"She came home to die. She was admitted to the hospital the second day she was in town. So Billy would leave the bank every afternoon after work, stop at the liquor store, and take her a pint of liquor to drink. He sat with her every night until she passed out from the drugs and alcohol. He was the only person she wanted to see and rejected anyone else that came to visit. She lived five days, and he was with her every night." Randy looked down.

"Now, the reason I'm telling you this is not to talk about how good Billy was, but how gracious Janet was," Randy returned the focus to Janet. "She never said a word about it. She was that good of a person. She allowed her husband to say goodbye the best way he knew to the first woman he loved. I don't know many women strong enough to do what she did." Randy folded his hands in his lap and looked up to the ceiling, and Vickie laid her head on his shoulder with tears in her eyes.

The funeral was held at the First Baptist Church. The service was filled with Janet's favorite hymns and music from the majestic new pipe organ. Flowers surrounded the sanctuary with stunning natural beauty. Everyone said that she would have loved it. Mr. Downs watched his bride be lowered into the ground with his family by his side and did his best to prepare for a life without her.

* * *

When Daisy left for California Mr. Downs was ready for her to go. She had spent the week after the funeral trying to replace her mother, but she couldn't. This was the longest he had ever gone without working. He needed to be back in the place where he could heal. Everyone but Dawn said, "Retire, don't worry about work, or take off a month or two."

Dawn called him and simply said, "Get your ass back up here. We need you." They were the kindest words she had ever said to him. She knew who he was and what he needed better than anyone.

He arrived at the office to see Maria's SUV and Lourdes's Jeep parked in the lot. It made him smile and he almost felt joy when he turned the key to unlock the door as he entered his safe place.

"Hi, Mr. Downs!" Lourdes ran to him from the other end of the long hallway and hugged him.

"It's good to be back. I missed you and this place," Mr. Downs greeted his young friend. He walked with her to the break room to get his morning coffee. Maria came from the lobby and awkwardly stood in front of him not knowing what to do or say. He looked at her with a smile and gave her a hug.

"I'm okay, really. I had a long goodbye with her. She lasted three months longer than the doctors said," he told his early morning friends. "I'm a lucky man."

"Everything is exactly like you left it. I made sure not to move a thing," Maria said trying to be consoling in the best way she knew how.

"Thanks, Maria. I knew I could count on you two." He smiled at the woman who had worked so hard for him and everyone else. She had no idea how proud he was of her business and the daughter she raised.

Around seven in the morning, Lourdes came into his office to do her usual dusting and talking.

"Mr. Scott, my history teacher, said it's not about the destination, it's about the journey. I think it is the destination. Which one do you think?" Lourdes asked.

"Let me tell you a story, and you can decide what you think afterwards, Lulu." He was happy for the return to routine and the distraction Lourdes provided. "When I was about thirteen years old there was a faded white farmhouse on the way to City Lake down on South Pecan street. There were a couple of baseball fields down there and us boys would ride our bikes to play baseball or go to the lake. It was a busy road in the summers. On the road beside the old farmhouse was a big, tin shop building. Every evening when we would go by the place, we would hear banging and see sparks flying with bigger and bigger piles of all kinds of scrap metal scattered around the tin building. This went on for years, when one day Randy asked, 'I wonder what he's making over there?' The whole town was curious, but no one bothered to ever ask the old loner. He was mean to most people—maybe because he was redheaded." Mr. Downs chuckled to himself and reached for his coffee. Lourdes stopped cleaning and sat listening intently in the wingback chair to his right.

"Well, one day we rode our bikes up there, pulled into the driveway, and sure enough we hear banging and see welding flashes. I was kinda scared but Randy stood with his bike under him and waited for the man to see him. His name was Joe Moore, and he was mean as a snake, or so we thought. Mr. Moore sees Randy standing there and I'm back a few feet in case I need to go tell the police Mr. Moore killed Randy." Lourdes was now completely lost in the story.

"He pulled off his welding mask and says to us, 'What the hell you kids want?' We both say, 'Nothin', sir,' but Randy follows up with, 'We want to know what you are making.' Now I'm ready to bolt away but Randy is holding his ground. Mr. Moore says, 'I can't tell ya yet, but it'll be really big when I'm done.'"

"What happened next?" Lourdes asked with bright eyes.

"Nothing. Nothing happened for three more years. Every evening, all year, banging, grinding, and welding. Randy and I were home from college when we heard the news that Mr. Moore was revealing his big thing on Saturday morning. It became a town event. I bet there was a hundred people there surrounding the old tin shop with Mrs. Moore standing in a house dress on her porch with her arms folded staring at her husband with a look only a disappointed wife can give. He waved at the crowd, a couple of men join him, and they push the worlds ugliest helicopter out of the shop on to the sandy field fifty yards away from the house."

"What did it look like?" she asked with a big smile.

"Near as I remember, the body was an old yellow wrecked VW with what looked like a flat head Ford engine crudely welded to the back of the bug. The large blades mounted in the center of the hood looked like they were welded together pieces of car hoods off 1950 Pontiacs. The rear blades must have been cut out of bumpers because they were chrome." Mr. Downs could vividly recall the specifics. "Mr. Moore was wearing overalls, and he put on an old-fashioned leather high school football helmet and swimming goggles. The two men who assisted him stepped back, he waved again to the crowd, got in, and cranked it. There appeared to be no muffler, so it was very loud. The whole crowd simultaneously took a step back. Mothers were putting their arms across young children and covering their ears." Mr. Downs acted out the scene.

"The motor revved louder, and we heard some grinding of gears, and the blade started spinning. It was gettin' faster and faster and the small rear blade was spinning and vibrating. Sand was flying everywhere and the VW body was violently shaking. Then to our surprise, it rose in the air. One foot, two foot, five foot. It was flying!" He shook his head as he remembered his surprise. "The crowd all burst into applause and his wife stood smiling and clapping from her porch. The helicopter reached a height of ten feet and then carefully descended back down. The engine was killed and the blades slowly came to a stop. We were all staring when Mr. Moore appeared from the helicopter, walked toward the crowd, and stood like a boxing match winner with both his hands raised with his fists clinched in victory. The crowd all clapped for him and his wife ran to her husband's side. He had done it!"

"That's a very cool story. I hope I never forget it," Lourdes said. She had been entranced by the tale.

"Now, my dear Lulu. Which was more important for Mr. Moore?

The journey or the destination?" Mr. Downs asked as she had almost forgotten about her question.

"I don't feel like I have enough information to answer. Do I?" she asked her mentor.

"Randy and I learned a bit more about Mr. Moore," Mr. Downs elaborated. "He and his wife had one daughter, and when she turned eighteen, she married a local boy who joined the army. She left her mom and dad and lived all over the place like military families do. Old Joe worked in maintenance at the air conditioning plant. We learned from the men he worked with that when his girl left, it just about killed him. He was fine at work, but when he got home, he desperately missed his daughter. So, he decided to keep busy doing a project."

"Did he ever have any experience with helicopters?" Lourdes asked.

"None that anyone ever knew," he answered her.

"Then this was obviously the journey. He challenged himself to do something he had no idea how to accomplish knowing it would take him a long time," she proudly answered.

"I agree, but he did reach his destination. If you never reached the moment of completion, then why complete anything? Just go on a journey," he challenged the young girl.

"I suppose you're right. So, it has to be both. Doesn't it?"

"Of course, it has to be both. Would you have deprived Mr. Moore of that singular moment of victory even though it was seconds compared to the years it took building his machine. You know that feeling from shooting. You practiced tens of thousands of shots to shoot that one hundred straight in San Antonio." He smiled at her.

"I did love watching that last target break." She grinned at the old man.

"We all did, Lulu. We all did."

* * *

The board meeting of Lulu Partnership was held on January 18, 2004. The stock portfolio had continued to blossom, and Lulu had been putting thousands of dollars from her savings in the fund over the past three years. The cleaning business now paid her ten dollars an hour and bonuses for extra projects.

"What stocks are we considering this year?" Mr. Downs peered over his glasses at the young lady with her hair in a bun, dressed in a gray suit, wearing fake glasses for dramatic purposes. He looked forward to this day every year and Lourdes never disappointed.

"I am thinking Amazon and Apple," she said happy with her pick.

"Neither of those stocks are making much money. I don't think Amazon has ever made money, and you know that's the whole point of this," he argued.

"Our Microsoft is doing good. You picked that one." She looked up through her clear lenses.

"All right, but I'm not strong on either of these," he reluctantly conceded.

"How much are you contributing?" he asked.

"A thousand dollars each. It was a good Christmas." She presented him with twenty, one hundred-dollar bills.

"Well, that certainly shows your commitment, so I will too. But if this gets shaky, I say we bail out, agreed?" Mr. Downs hedged his bet.

"I'm fine with that, but you will need to contact me prior to selling. It is clearly in the bylaws." Lourdes gave him a sly smile.

* * *

In early February, Dawn came into Mr. Downs office and closed the door behind her. She sat quietly in the wingback chair on his right waiting for him to talk first.

"What's up?" he asked knowing it could be good or bad.

"As you know, I'm on The Letter Committee this year, and I'm about to have a major fit on these stupid sons of bitches I have to work with. We normally have this done before Christmas and we are three weeks away and cannot agree on anyone. Any suggestions?" she asked in an exhausted voice.

"You know I hate politicians," Mr. Downs replied.

"Oh, hell no! Absolutely no politicians," she confirmed.

"Got any old teachers retiring who were loved by their students?" he asked.

"We did that last year. Mrs. Benitez retired. She was the elementary school principal."

"I forgot. What about medical people or law enforcement?"

"Nope. No one will agree, since we have a nurse and a cop on the committee." She threw up her arms.

"I have an idea. I'm thinking of a man whose family has been in this town since before it was a town. A solid citizen and successful businessman. He has contributed to youth groups and has been a loyal church member, husband and father."

"He sounds perfect. Who?"

Mr. Downs wrote the name on a paper and handed it to her.

On the morning of February 24th, a proud father and his wife and child arrived promptly at the courthouse square. He was dressed in the first proper suit he had ever owned. His wife wore a new red wool coat, and his teenage daughter wore a black fitted suit with a white fur trimmed coat and her long black hair was curled for the big day.

Danny Sanchez waved at the crowd when he walked up on the temporary stage. His brother and nieces and nephews all shouted loudly when he stood behind the microphone, and his wife and daughter were amazed at the large crowd.

"I got a call a couple of weeks ago from Dawn at the bank. She told me I was chosen to read The Letter this year. I was so surprised. I don't usually come here for this ceremony because most of the times . . . well, I was working," Danny began. "My family has been around this area for a very long time, almost two hundred years. Most of them left to go find work in bigger cities, but my little brother and I stayed. Maybe we were too scared or lazy to leave." The crowd laughed.

"I met my wife in City Bakery which we all go to today. My daughter goes to the same schools I went to, but she is way smarter than me. I eat Mexican food at El Rancho and have since I was a kid. I like the Monterey Plate." The onlookers laughed again as he rubbed his belly.

"I bought my first used truck from Mr. Adams almost forty years ago, and this year, I bought three new service trucks from his son. I started working doing whatever needed to be done at Caesar's when I was sixteen. I swept the floor and cleaned the toilets. And I still do, because it still needs to be done, and Maria likes a clean shop!" Another round of amusement rose from the crowd.

"I guess what I want to say is, I didn't start with much. But I am here because my wife never let me quit. She pushed me, and supported me, and we worked together to get where we are. And I wanted to thank her for that." He turned behind him to see his Maria smiling at him. He started clapping and the crowd increased the applause.

"Commandancy of the Alamo, February 24, 1836," Danny started to read. "To the people of Texas and All Americans in the world, Fellow citizens and compatriots,

I am besieged . . ."

*　　*　　*

The last home baseball game of the spring would decide the district champion. The Defenders were tied with their rivals from Albertville, and Barrett was at bat in the bottom of the fourth. Claudia paced back and forth in her cheerleader uniform behind the Defender's dugout. Monica and Four felt the pressure of every pitch as their son pushed his right foot into the dirt to begin his swing. Whoosh! The pitch was called a ball as it went high past him. The pitcher had a great fastball and just enough of a slider to keep the batter off stride. It was a scoreless tie with a runner on second and two outs. Ball one, no strike count. Swing, miss, strike one. Barrett dug in again and now saw exactly where the ball released from the pitcher's right hand.

Swing, ping! The metal bat crushed the ball off the wall in right field. The runner at second scored, and Barrett stood on second base smiling at his bench who were all on their feet. Claudia was cheering, Monica was standing and clapping, and Four was clapping but remained seated knowing they had more game to go. Barrett had done well, but it was not over.

In the final inning, the score remained 0-1. The Defenders made a defensive substitution in left field. A big, rangy sophomore took the field. He was very fast at six foot-two and two hundred pounds but not a good hitter. Two quick outs with one more to go for the victory and a district championship.

Barrett had signed to play baseball at Texas Christian University in Fort Worth. His Pop wanted him to be a Texas Longhorn but was still thrilled he signed with the Horned Frogs. Monica was the quintessential Texas sports mother. She never missed a game and enthusiastically rooted for her only son. Observing a mother watch her child play a sport is like viewing a Greek tragedy. Whether in the Little League World Series, college teams, or professional sports, the camera shot of the mother shows everything a viewer needs to feel the tension of the moment. The scene of a mother watching her child make the winning basket, hit the over-the-wall home run, or score the deciding touchdown is as thrilling as the play itself. But as sweet as the victory is, the heart break is just as riveting.

The batter flared a shallow fly over Barrett's head at his shortstop position, and he turned racing to the outfield. From left field, the big, athletic sophomore was also in full sprint to catch the ball. Barrett's eyes were locked on the falling ball as he called, "I got it!" He had the ball in his glove as the other boy did his best to veer away but his full weight and force collided into Barrett. The collision was loud and brutal. Barrett's entire right leg disconnected from the hip socket. His head slammed against the ground as he fell unconscious from the force and severe pain.

Barrett woke in the hospital, and the first thing he saw was his mother standing beside the bed holding a baseball and the district winning banner. He did not remember anything of the last two days. He was in Dallas Baylor Hospital and had undergone ten hours of surgery. The damage was considerable, and everyone prayed he would be able to walk again.

Barrett's pain was horrible, and Monica felt every wince of her child. Each scream sent her scrambling for more help from a nurse or doctor pleading for increased pain medication. It was terrible for her to see her athletic son laying in a bed unable to walk to the bathroom. She had not left the hospital in days, sleeping on a fold out chair that left her twisted in pain. She consoled his friends and teammates as they tried to comfort her. Janet Ann was there the first day and came every evening after class at SMU in Dallas. Her mother would push her away when she offered to stay the night. Four had been there too and offered to stay, but Monica would not leave. She was exhausted by the fourth day. She had not slept more than two hours a day. Janet Ann arrived with food her mother liked and a small overnight bag.

"Mom, this is enough," Janet Ann pleaded with her mother. "You must get some rest or you're going to die. Dad can take you back to the hotel and you can come tomorrow. I can take care of this. Please go!"

"No! I am not leaving my child like this," Monica responded sharply, her voice raspy. "He can't walk. He can barely speak. He needs me!"

"Go, Mom . . . Please go . . . I'm fine," Barrett said groggily.

"Oh, baby, I'm okay. I'll stay." She stood beside the bed holding his hand.

"No . . . Go, now." Barrett managed to be alert enough to help his mother.

Four took his wife's hand and gently pulled her away. She stumbled slowly behind him. She was asleep in the car before they were out of the parking lot. Nine hours later, Monica woke with a start in the hotel room. She showered and had room service breakfast with her husband. The doctors were hopeful Barrett would walk again but insisted sports would be impossible. The news would crush him. Baseball was the only thing at which he excelled. He was not a great student, but he loved sports.

Lourdes walked down the hallway searching for his hospital room. She was with Tommy who had been friends with Barrett since their nursery days at First Baptist Church. They found the room hoping there was a different prognosis. Word was out that Barrett would never play baseball again, but no one had told this shattering news to the crippled young man in the bed surrounded by flowers and balloons.

They pushed the door open and saw Claudia sitting on the bed. Monica sat on the other side in a fold out chair.

"Hey, buddy. How you doing?" Tommy said to the boy with the circular, steel brace screwed into his body down the length of his leg. Tommy and Lourdes did their best to not look at the sickening green, yellow, and purple bruising. Claudia got up and let Tommy stand next to the bed. She motioned for Lourdes to come out into the hallway.

The two girls sat beside each other on a small bench in the corridor. Lourdes was nervous as she waited for Claudia to begin speaking. She hoped she wasn't going to cause a scene in the hospital.

Claudia turned and looked into Lourdes's eyes. "I know you made valedictorian. It was very important to me to win, and I know it was important to you. But you were better than me, and I deserved to lose for what I did to you that day in the cafeteria. I'm sorry. I've needed to apologize for a very long time and since, well, I guess things are different now," Claudia spoke sincerely. "Barrett thinks he is going to play baseball at TCU this fall, and no one has told him he'll never play again. I'm going to California for school at USC. Everything is changing in our little world. I wish I had been a better person. I wish I would have been more like you."

Lourdes put her arm around her. "Thank you, Claudia. That was very kind of you. I spent too much of my life angry at you, but I was hurt. My dad taught me to forgive you, but that was just for me. Today I forgive you for us both."

"Thank you, Lourdes." Claudia was relieved to have her burden lifted. "I needed to clear this up before I left Travis City. I hope we are those two crazy women at the reunions who got fat and have a bunch of bratty kids. I'm going to miss you," Claudia laughed at herself, and Lourdes giggled too loudly for a hospital hallway.

CHAPTER 17

THE LAST WEEK of high school was full of parties and pictures with lifelong friends. Photographers had shoots in pastures and ball fields and in front of downtown buildings. The townspeople would honk in support at the posing teenagers. Another layer of Travis City would be peeled away to go forth into the world. Some would go to college, some would be apprentices for a trade, and some would take any job they could.

Lourdes had been confirmed she was valedictorian and Claudia was the salutatorian. The difference the between the girls' GPA was less than one percent. The amount of scholarship money, however, was much larger than one percent. Lourdes was given a full scholarship to the University of Texas Business School. Even more money flowed in from a foundation set up by Randy and Vickie which would allow her to live very well in Austin, Texas.

Graduation was held at Defender Stadium with its old PA system and uncomfortable bleachers. The class of 2003 totaled one hundred eighteen as they marched into the waning sounds of an off-key version of Pomp and Circumstance played by the combined junior high and high school bands. Finally wearing clothes which were not too tight, his cap and gown, Principal Johnston gave a short address that was appreciated by all in attendance. He finished his speech and introduced Lourdes Sanchez as the class valedictorian.

"Thank you, Mr. Johnston, and welcome, teachers, parents, family and my fellow seniors!" The students all clapped joined by the rest of the audience.

"I am honored to be your class valedictorian, and I have many to thank for my journey. First, I want to thank my parents who have always supported me and my teachers who created this great place of learning. Next, I want to thank a man whom I've known the past several years and who has taught me as well. He took me to the skeet range and made sure I had all I needed to succeed in the sport I have come to love. Mr. Downs, please stand up." The audience searched for the older man in his iconic hat and watched him stand, wave, and quickly sit back down between Monica and Four.

"Mr. Downs has taught me many lessons, but just this last week he taught me something new. When we were discussing this speech, he said, 'Don't forget a certain person. She was as important as anyone to putting you where you are. She pushed you every day, and you owe her.' Because of this reminder, I want to thank Claudia Bergman." Lourdes turned around and walked to Claudia who was seated on the stage with her salutatorian ribbon over her black gown.

Claudia stood, hugged Lourdes, and whispered, "You were always smarter than me, but I was better at cleaning tables in the cafeteria." They both laughed at the inside joke.

The crowd of people, not knowing what was said, clapped at the sight of the two former rivals embracing and laughing. The students turned to each other with smiles and applause. The competition that began in the first grade was finally over with both participants becoming better people in the end.

Lourdes returned to the podium and looked down at her notes and then up to the sky to compose herself.

"My parents and Mr. Downs have taught me about sacrifice and time, and that has been all I've known. It's all any of us need to reach our milestones. I have not regretted the time or any of the sacrifices made in order to stand here today. I had what many would consider a tough start. I was found at the age of three in the dumpster behind Don's Quick Stop." Her voice weakened and Lourdes paused. "I was hurt and could have died in that pile of trash. This town saved me."

"This town gave me wonderful friends. This town gave me great teachers. This town gave me a solid spiritual foundation. This town gave me Mr. Downs. This town gave me my loving parents, Danny and

Maria Sanchez. I couldn't have been luckier on the day I was placed in their home." She stopped and found her parents and blew them a kiss.

"To my fellow graduating seniors, many who began in Ms. Thomas's kindergarten class holding hands to stay safe together as we explored the great unknown of the playground, I hope we stay connected. I hope we stay together and safe. I hope we can lift up each other our whole lives. But I am not naïve. I know most of us will drift apart. I know that if we are lucky, a few of us will be in touch twenty years or even sixty years from now. But I hope we never forget, we marched down these corridors together for four years. I hope we can always hear laughter in the halls. I hope we can always feel the vibrations of the building when the band marches in on a fall afternoon for our pep rally. I hope we can see the school colors of black and gold on uniforms of athletes and cheerleaders representing us all with pride. I hope we can taste the cafeteria food. Well, maybe that's a bit too much. Sorry, Ms. Greer." The students and crowd laughed loudly.

"Many of us will be leaving this place. Some may never return. I'm leaving for college, but wherever I go, I'll take Travis City with me. I cannot imagine a better place to be from. Gandhi said, 'I have traveled all my life, but I only ever wanted to go home.' I understand that now because soon I will leave all I have ever known. No matter how long I live in other places, I will always say my *home* is in Travis City, Texas. Home of The Letter and home of the Defenders! Thank you," Lourdes concluded her speech.

Claudia was the first to stand with applause. Everyone else joined her as Lourdes let the thundering ovation wash over her. Only one student did not stand. Barrett was in his wheelchair, but he clapped loudly. Dr. Bergman, the president of the school board, stood on the stage and handed out the certificates and a handshake to each graduate. The top two students, Lourdes and Claudia, were the first to receive their diplomas.

When Lourdes' name was announced, she pulled up Claudia next to her so Claudia's father handed them their diplomas at the same time. He had seen the .02 percent difference in their GPA at the end of the year and knew it was kind of Lourdes to make the gesture.

The names of the remaining students were called in alphabetical order as families cheered and whooped when their sons and daughters strode across the stage waving in victory. A set of steps were at each end on the long stage, and Barrett's wheelchair sat at the bottom of the stairway as the D names were being called. Six junior boys dressed in baseball uniforms stood around the chair and lifted him as they walked in unison across the stage with Barrett giving a thumbs up to the cheering crowd. Dr. Bergman handed the diploma between the bearers and Barrett shook his hand. The group of players walked to the other end, descended carefully, and placed him on the grass.

Monica and Four greeted their son and hugged and thanked the players for what they had done. Janet Ann looked vastly more mature to the admiring boys of the team as she gave them all one of her best flirty, thank you looks.

That night there were parties all across town in restaurants and back yards and patios, but the biggest was held at the Travis City Gun Club. Cal Robinson had been manning the barbecue pit since dawn. He was a master at smoking meats for big crowds. He had fed barbecue to US senators, governors, ZZ Top concerts, and many others, but tonight he was serving one of his favorite people, Lulu. Every town in Texas has a Cal Robinson who is the unofficial king of his craft. He was big with a bushy red beard and always had a cheap motel bath towel stained with sauce over his shoulder. Cal had brought his custom twenty-foot-long cooker mounted on a trailer and parked the pit away from the crowd so the smoke was not too bad on sensitive eyes. All the other old men of the Travis City Gun Club had made their own special dishes to round out the meal.

The members had donated the money for a custom gun case with *Lulu Sanchez, Travis City, Texas*, hand painted in hot pink on the stainless case. Mr. Downs had told the members to order the case with these specifications and he would do the rest.

Over two hundred people eventually filled the grass parking lot and overflow tents were set up with tables and folding chairs. Country music filled the early June night with an occasional two-step dance breaking out under the tents. Danny stood at the first table and never tired of hearing people brag on his daughter. They loved her speech, they saw her shoot her first twenty-five straight, she was my favorite student, or she's so beautiful. Maria did not like crowds but busied herself serving and cleaning. Cal checked the tables and the line and could tell when everyone had been served. He had plenty left and he felt relieved. No one would forgive him if he ran out of food or at least that's what he always thought.

"Could I have your attention please!" a loud voice boomed over the speakers. "My name is Charlie Knight and on behalf of our little old club, welcome to our party for the smartest, and by far our best-looking member, Lourdes "Lulu" Sanchez!" He began to clap and the rest of the group joined. Lourdes was seated with her parents at the head table and Charlie stood behind them.

"This girl . . . I mean young lady, has been an inspiration to our club. She worked harder than any of you know. She was dedicated *and* listened to me." He pointed to himself as the group laughed and jeered. "She won the state championship her junior year!" Lourdes stood and did an exaggerated bow to the crowd.

"Our club all got together, and we want to give you something so you won't forget us when you go off to college." He pulled out the gun case from under the table and raised it so all could see and read the pink letters. Lourdes stood, received the gift, and leaned over to kissed Charlie on the cheek.

"Thank you, but these old guys are pretty unforgettable," Lourdes joked. "To all the ladies here tonight, if you want to feel extra special, join a skeet club. Everyone here has been so kind and gracious and never complained when I started beating them." The group laughed again.

Lourdes sat down and the members came over in groups and one by one to recount their personal story about her, congratulate her on her graduation, or just to say good luck. Mr. Downs waited for them to finish before he approached her with a proud smile.

"I have a present in my truck. Bring your case." He turned and she followed with her new gift.

"I'm doing this for selfish reasons," he said as he opened the door and handed her the large flat rectangular box. "I want my gun back."

She recognized the Krieghoff logo in the low glow of strung lightbulbs under the tents. She pulled the box from the truck, retreated to the rear of the pickup, and dropped the tailgate to provide a table. She carefully opened the box to find a new K-80 shotgun with beautiful, burled wood and an engraved nickel receiver. She had looked at this model several times in shooting magazines and knew it was well over ten thousand dollars.

"Oh, Mr. Downs, this is too much!" she said staring at the expensive gift.

"Well, it's all I could think of and you'll use it for the rest of your life."

"Can I show everyone now?" Lourdes looked at him with excitement.

"No. Please just wait. The case was designed for the gun, so I'm pretty sure the guys know. Let's keep it between us tonight." She understood his ways by now and hugged him in thanks.

"Okay, Mr. Downs. Thank you." Her heart was full as she placed her new, disassembled gun in the three black velvet custom compartments for the steel over and under barrel, the wooden forearm, and the remaining receiver and stock.

"Perfect fit." The two friends smiled at each other.

CHAPTER 18

THAT SUMMER WAS spent preparing for college, and Lourdes enjoyed her last free months with Tommy in her hometown. They shot skeet and went to City Lake for a swim on warm afternoons. They drove back roads exploring the county and hung out at the new Sonic with their classmates. Lourdes went to Austin in July for orientation and learned where her dorm was located and what to expect. Beth Davis, the shy girl from the cafeteria, was also going to the University of Texas in Austin, and they bonded over the shared new experience. In the fall Lourdes would have at least one familiar face to seek in a sea of strangers.

On the morning Lourdes left for college, she went with her mother to the bank to clean for the last time. They rode together that morning. Maria was silent on the short trip. When they arrived at the back door, Mr. Downs was waiting in the hall by the break room.

Maria held back as she watched her daughter walk ahead and embrace Mr. Downs. Lourdes held on to him and laid her head on his chest under his chin with a tear moving down her cheek. As Maria watched the scene unfold in front of her, she suddenly had no idea where to put her arms.

"I have an early appointment at seven. I'll see you after that." Mr. Downs released Lourdes desperately needing to change the subject to suppress his emotions.

Seven a.m. was her time with him. That was the time she would sit and visit. *Why did he schedule such a meeting today of all days?* Lourdes' feelings were hurt. It seemed selfish of him. Lourdes gathered her supplies with her mother and began mindlessly cleaning.

At seven she saw Mr. Downs at the rear entrance opening the door for a woman. She was plump but walked with a powerful gait. Lourdes watched as he led the lady toward his office and stopped in the doorway of Dawn's office.

"Lourdes, can you please join us in my office?" he requested formally.

Lourdes placed her cleaning items on a secretary's desk and curiously walked toward his office.

"Lourdes, I want you to meet this lady. Her name is Deborah Franks. She is here for two reasons this morning. The first is about a loan and the second is about you." The two women shook hands and sat beside each other on the sofa while Mr. Downs sat in the left wingback chair.

"Deborah has been working at the same place for many years and she has been saving money and speaking with me about buying the business. For the past four years, I've been guiding her through the process, and she has been sacrificing and preparing. Today we will finalize her loan, and I am extremely proud of what she has done." The two women sat quietly and listened.

He continued, "During our conversations last week regarding the business, I learned from Deborah something I never knew. Deborah, would you please tell Lourdes your story."

The curvy lady with a sweet smile turned to Lourdes. "Please, call me Debbie. I've been working at Don's Quick Stop for a very long time—since I was sixteen. Early one morning I was emptying trash into the dumpster behind the store. I heard a weak voice, found a little leg and pulled a toddler out of that dumpster. That baby was, of course, you." Debbie could no longer speak. Lourdes began crying and fell on the woman sobbing. When she finally raised her head, Mr. Downs was gone.

"I don't know how to thank you. You literally saved my life." Lourdes finally was able to speak.

"You don't need to thank me. I did what anyone would have done. I'm just happy with what you've done with your life." Debbie was thrilled to finally meet Lourdes. "My cousin Karla's boy is in your class. His name is David Hamm, but we all call him Bubba."

"I know David! He's a nice guy. I've known him since kindergarten." Bubba had been in the cafeteria watching the scene unfold with disgust on his face on that fateful day. He did not participate in the taunts, and his parents had not been called for the meeting.

At the doorway stood Maria and Mr. Downs. He had explained who the woman was and Maria rushed to Debbie and hugged her tightly.

"Thank you so much for saving her and giving me and my husband the greatest gift we will ever have," Maria said through her tears.

After a visit, the group exited the back door. Lourdes stood in the rear bank parking lot next to the family SUV with her mother and Mr. Downs as they waved goodbye to Debbie as she drove away.

"I can't believe I've met the person who saved my life. Thanks, Mr. Downs. That was the best gift ever." Lourdes patted him on his arm.

"Yes, Mr. Downs, that was very nice." Maria stood beside her daughter.

"Well, it's already too hot for me to stand out here in the sun. People will be arriving soon, so I better get back to work. Good luck, Lulu. You will do great."

"Thanks again, but I will be back before you know it." Lourdes knew it was difficult to say goodbye. "I found out I can't take my gun to the dorm, so I have to come back to shoot." She knew he was not wanting any more emotional fanfare.

"See you over Thanksgiving." Mr. Downs turned and went back in his sanctuary to protect himself from the pain of seeing her leave.

After a lunch of Lourdes's favorite meal of Maria's tacos, a honking car was heard. Beth was in the driveway with her compact car packed to the brim with only enough space for her to sit. The Jeep was also packed and ready to depart.

Lourdes came outside with her mother and father and hugged them one more time. The two girls pulled out of the driveway, passed the welding shop onto Main street, and then headed west on the highway out of town. Lourdes felt bittersweet as she rolled by the landmarks of her youth. The bank's glass glimmered gold when she passed, and she waved at the building. That building, at which she had spent so many mornings, was not just the setting of the beginning of her day, but the dawn of her life as she learned to think, work, and explore life with Mr.

Downs and her mother. She drove on and noticed Monica in her yard working in her flower beds to make the world a little more beautiful.

Tommy had left the day before to go to a community college outside of Houston which had a good program for dyslexic students. She still felt his last kiss on her lips as she drove past the Downs Ranch with its sprawling house and black Angus heifers grazing in the pasture.

Finally, she came to the intersection to turn south out of Travis City. Lourdes glanced to her right and saw Don's Quick Stop and the dumpster. Lourdes smiled. "Thank you, Debbie." The words softly passed her lips as she turned toward Austin.

PART II

CHAPTER 19

MR. DOWNS LEFT Dub Daniels house at ten, after their usual Saturday morning meeting and drove west to a small pasture adjacent to a catch lot used for cattle separated from the main herds. Four and Dub had bought eight yearling horned Hereford bulls from a ranch in Snyder, Texas, and had put them in the small pasture. The bulls were fourteen to sixteen months old weighing an average of a thousand pounds each. They were like teenage boys, wanting to fight and breed, but still a little too young to put in with the cattle. Mr. Downs pulled a fifty-pound sack of feed from an old barn next to the bull's pasture and put it in the back of his truck intending to inspect the animals up close and give them a treat.

He opened a metal gate and drove into the twenty-acre patch honking his horn. The honking horn alerted cattle to come for feed. Cattleman are amused by people unaccustomed to cattle who drive through a herd blowing a horn assuming it will scare away the animals, when they are actually ringing a dinner bell and the cows swarm around the vehicle looking for their supper.

The young bulls were together on the far end a few hundred yards away and responded to the horn by running toward the truck. Mr. Downs exited, opened the bag of feed, and walked away from the truck pouring the feed on the ground as he walked to allow plenty of space for the yearlings to eat. He hadn't calculated the speed and energy of the adolescent bovine and suddenly they were surrounding him, aggressively pushing each other away to consume the feed. A swinging head caught Mr. Downs against his shoulder knocking him down to the ground. He lay in the pasture with the animals' hooves stepping around his legs and extended arm.

He struggled to get on all fours to crawl away from the line of cattle standing over the emptied sack which was now blowing across the field. He managed to inch under his tailgate and sit away from the feeding animals. His right hip and shoulder were injured when he crashed to the hard ground and he could only lay on his left side unable to get up.

By twelve-fifteen Four was getting worried about his father. He was supposed to be at their house for lunch, so he called his dad's home and the bank, getting no answer. He then called Dub because he knew he would have seen him that morning. Dub had indeed seen him and told Four that Mr. Downs had gone to inspect the new bulls.

Both men knew it was unusual for Mr. Downs to be unaccounted for, and both agreed Dub should head to the pasture. By the time he spotted Mr. Downs' truck, the bulls had wandered away and were grazing down the hill.

"You okay, boss?" Dub called out to the man lying on the ground. Mr. Downs rolled back and sat up.

"Yes, I'm fine. Just can't get up. Got knocked down is all," he muttered in reply.

"Here, let me help you up." Dub leaned down reaching with an extended arm to Mr. Downs' injured side.

"Dammit! No, not that arm! Take my left arm," Mr. Downs cried out in pain and aggravation.

"Sorry, boss. Here, let's try again." From their long relationship Dub knew Mr. Downs wasn't mad at him, just aggravated to be in this situation.

He lifted him by his left arm circling behind the hurt man guiding him to his feet. Mr. Downs stood beside his truck holding on to the top of the truck bed.

"Just let me get my feet set a little better, and I'll be okay," Mr. Downs uttered in frustration.

The two men stood beside each other with Dub ready to grab him if he fell. Mr. Downs walked gingerly to the driver's door and Dub opened it for him.

"You sure you can drive? I can take you home and get a ride back. I don't mind a'tall," Dub offered.

"No. I got it." Mr. Downs turned his back to the bench seat and pushed as best he could upward onto the seat. He pulled himself around with his still strong left hand avoiding the hurt arm. He pulled his legs to the pedals and sat for a moment feeling exhausted from the simple act.

"I got it now. Y'all did good on those bulls. They look much bigger from an armadillo's point of view," Mr. Down joked though he winced while he talked.

Dub followed in his own truck as the two drove out of the pasture, and he stopped to shut the gate for his hurt friend and employer. Mr. Downs pulled into his driveway and parked in his spot to the right of Janet's Cadillac with Dub trailing behind.

"You didn't have to follow me," Mr. Downs sounded perturbed as he pushed open his truck door.

"I know, but you know how Miss Monica would have had a fit if I hadn't," Dub answered trying to switch the rebuke to a woman.

Dub held him steady easing him out of the truck while he walked him to the unlocked back door. Guiding him to his favorite chair in the den, he helped him down slowly onto the cushioned leather. When he knew Mr. Downs was comfortable, he walked to the kitchen phone and dialed.

"Yes, he got knocked down in the pasture with the new bulls . . . some, but not real bad . . . I can do that . . . See you in a little bit." He hung up the phone and met the glare of Mr. Downs.

*   *   *

The ancient dorm did not meet the standard of anyone's idea of first-class accommodations. Lourdes had received her room assignment but had no idea who her roommate would be until she appeared. She sat on the left side twin bed, the contents of her once packed Jeep stacked around where she had slept alone the night before with the unfamiliar sounds of young people running up and down the halls disturbing her sleep. The room had a composite tile floor which reminded her of an old grocery store. The walls were poorly painted a dull white with nail holes from prior occupant's attempts at decorating. Each side formed a mirror image of desk, chair, bed, chest of drawers, and closet in what originally was a lightly stained wood. The single bathroom was big enough for the toilet, one sink, and shower with walls of mauve colored tiles. A full-length mirror hung on the outside of the bathroom door. This was her and who knows who's home away from home until the end of next spring semester.

Lourdes new cell phone rang, and she retrieved it from her purse. Maria had told her to use the phone only in emergencies. It was too expensive to just talk all the time, and their plan charged ten cents a text. But she was sure this call would be acceptable.

"Hi, Mama . . . Yes, I slept good last night . . . Not yet, but I was the first one in the building yesterday when they opened . . . Hi, Daddy . . . No, I'm not scared . . . Yes, that's all . . . Yes, we kept it under a minute. Love you both." Lourdes hit the button to disconnect. These would be very short calls if they followed her mother's phone rules. Lourdes had almost finished organizing the room with only a few framed photos left to hang when the door swung open.

"Hi, I'm Maddie King! This is where they sent me." A blonde girl came in dragging a box through the door followed by a woman who looked exhausted.

"I'm her mother, Dottie," the older lady said as Lourdes stood to meet them.

"Lourdes Sanchez," she greeted them as pleasantly as possible. "Nice to meet you both. I guess we're roommates."

"When did you get here?" Maddie exclaimed in a surprised way. "You already look all organized and neat."

"I am thrilled to see you with someone who is organized," Dottie said to her daughter intended as more of an insult to Maddie than a compliment to Lourdes.

"Here we go! Been here thirty seconds, and you're already on my ass! Can we just get my stuff so you can go back to Houston?" Maddie shouted. Lourdes was shocked anyone would speak to a parent like that.

"Let me help you with the rest of your things," Lourdes interjected hoping to put the fire out.

"Okay fine! Let's go get the rest of my stuff with *super girl* here. We can get it all in one trip." Maddie pointed to Lourdes and stomped out of the room leaving her mother alone with Lourdes.

"I'm so sorry, honey. She can be a bit high strung and very rude at times." Dottie apologized for her daughter, and they walked together to the elevator to find Maddie waiting.

Maddie was five-foot five-inches tall with thin, short blonde hair. She wore little makeup but had beautiful, tanned skin yet her neck would easily turn red when she was mad. She had greenish eyes and a small mouth with thin lips. She was not a beautiful girl, but she was cute. Her body was fairly flat, but she looked athletic, like a runner.

"Sorry about that little fit, but when the beast leaves, I promise to be nicer. Is that good enough, mother?" Maddie apologized to Lourdes then turned her back on her mother as the elevator doors slid open.

The three stepped in and surprisingly were alone for such a busy day. Lourdes felt tension like she had never felt between a mother and child. This was a new experience, and she wasn't quite sure what to do or say. She couldn't stand the friction, so she had an idea to ease the situation.

"Well, this is fun," Lourdes delivered her best Dawn deadpan style.

The mother and daughter looked at the black-haired young lady and both started laughing at themselves. The sense of anxiety eased as the doors opened to the first floor. The three went to Dottie's older SUV, emptied the contents, took a trip back to the room, and then returned to Maddie's much newer Honda Civic to gather the remaining items. The next couple of hours were spent unpacking and trying to establish order.

Dottie and Maddie bickered almost continuously while deciding what went where, making Lourdes uncomfortable in the presence of such biting remarks between parent and child.

Maddie was almost finished, and her mother was moving items she had already put away when she looked at her mother and said, "Well, this is fun."

Her mother and Lourdes laughed, and Maddie allowed herself a moment of humor during the stress. Dottie walked over to her daughter who was sitting on her new bed and hugged her.

"Okay, I know I need to let you be a grown up, but this is hard for me." Dottie started crying. "I need you to be nice to me for just a little while."

"I know, Mom. I'll be fine. You got me here and now Lourdes is here to take over." Maddie smiled at her mother and Lourdes.

Maddie walked her mother to her car, they hugged once more, and the daughter waved goodbye as long as she could see the vehicle driving away. All Maddie had hoped for now lay before her, and for the first time in her life, she was unfettered.

Lourdes and Maddie spent the rest of the day sitting in their room telling each other about their lives. They had one thing in common; they were both very smart and extremely competitive. Maddie wanted to be an environmental lawyer and Lourdes was a math major focusing on finance. Both were idealistic, yet at opposite spectrums of the world—at least in Maddie's mind.

"How can you want to work for *The Man* like some corporate pawn making money for rich people?" Maddie asked pointedly.

"How can you want to make up reasons to sue companies that are baseless shams designed to steal from people who work for a living?" Lourdes was not one to back away from a fight.

Maddie stared at her in disbelief. In Maddie's world no one ever argued with her and prevailed.

"What did you just say?" Maddie spat out her question. "Are you one of *those* people?"

"If you mean, one of those people who don't buy into your propaganda and actually look at both sides of a debate, then yes, I suppose I am," Lourdes answered.

"There are *not* two sides to this. Manmade global warming will destroy our world in just a few years if we don't take serious action now!" Maddie defended her position.

"Let me ask you just one question. Who benefits from global warming?" Lourdes calmly asked.

"Are you kidding me? There are no benefits at all! Everyone knows that!"

"Everyone? Or everyone who's marketing fear? It seems that a normal person would look for benefits if this is supposed to definitely happen."

"What possible good can come of global warming?"

"Maybe a huge increase in lands that are not used for agriculture crops."

"But everyone would be dead. That's just stupid! You're an idiot," Maddie was reduced to mocking.

"Ah, name calling. The last thing a good environmental lawyer would do. So, we now know you cannot accomplish winning a simple argument." Lourdes folded her arms. "What's wrong, Maddie? Not used to losing because no one ever pushed back? You picked some made up cause you thought would make your life easier and you could look righteous in front of your weak-minded peers," Lourdes said evenly.

"You are a selfish, horrible person!" Maddie yelled and rolled over on her side facing away from her.

"Okay, I'm sorry you got your feelings hurt so easily." Lourdes finished. "I guess we can blame global warming for that too."

CHAPTER 20

B ARRETT TRIED TO climb the stairs to his room but could not
bear to put pressure on his injured leg which left him stranded
on the first floor. Therapy was slow; his pain unrelenting.
With encouragement and love, Monica tried her best to prevent the
depression that had clearly penetrated his soul. Most of his friends had
gone off to college, and the extent of his devastating injury had finally
become clear. He lay in the den on his makeshift bed with the drapes
drawn tight.

"Mom! I need some pain pills and something to eat," He bellowed
hatefully at the person who loved him more than anyone else.

"Okay, I will have lunch ready soon, but you had some pain pills two
hours ago. We have to wait another hour," Monica answered back from
the kitchen which was open to the den.

"That's just wonderful. You get to walk around with nothing wrong
with you! Meanwhile your child is in pain and needs relief. But *no*! He
has to wait another hour!"

"Stop that! Those are the rules and you know it." Monica had
reached her breaking point. "I'm sorry for what's happened, but it is
not my fault or anyone else's. It was an accident—a terrible accident.
We're going to do exactly what the doctors say, and you are going to be
walking soon. But taking this out on the one person in this world who
is doing her best to get you well, is not helping."

Barrett lay sullen and quiet. His life had taken a severe turn. He was
still unable to safely walk up the stairs. He could walk on flat ground
with a single crutch. Four had some carpenters build a ramp to ease

going in and out of the house. He and Monica talked about getting him a place to force him into some independence now that he was able to do some walking but had not discussed it with their son. Based on what he had learned in rehab years before, Four was very careful to watch for any sign of a dependence on pain medication.

Monica called for Barrett to come eat lunch at the kitchen table. He reluctantly got out of the bed and ambled over stiffly swinging the one leg. He sat with no assistance, and Monica served him a plate of chicken fried steak and mashed potatoes covered with her homemade gravy.

"Thanks, Mom." He began to quietly eat.

Four had located a small rent house a couple of miles from town for Barrett. He felt it would push his son into helping himself to get well. He needed support but not babying. Four knew too well the path of least resistance and how it caused him a life that was unfulfilled for too many years. He furnished the house with some used furniture and Monica put in the finishing touches. The baby bird needed to leave the nest even if the new nest was in the same tree.

A couple of weeks passed, and Barrett began driving and was able to walk with a cane. Four and Monica asked him to go for a ride and they all got into her Suburban.

"Where are we going?" Barrett asked his father.

"A surprise, son, but you'll like it."

Soon they were pulling into the driveway and parking under the single carport of a small, green frame house with a tiny porch.

"What's this?" Barrett asked.

Monica got out of the back seat and opened the door for Barrett.

"This is your new home," Four announced.

"What does that mean?" Barrett was bewildered. "My home? I thought I lived with y'all."

"Just come in and see." Four stepped up to unlock the door.

Using his cane, Barrett made his way to the open door with his mother behind him. He walked through the brown painted wooden door into a little living room with a kitchen to his right and a hall straight ahead. The carpet was freshly vacuumed, and the white painted walls were clean. The kitchen counters and sink smelled of bleach and cleanliness. Barrett walked down the short hall to find one bathroom on his left and one bedroom straight ahead with a queen-sized bed with a new comforter, a nightstand and dresser. There was a small closet in the far corner. The other bedroom across from the bathroom had only a twin bed and nightstand with the same size closet.

"What do you think?" Monica said with excitement.

"I guess it's pretty good, but why are you doing this?" Barrett was still confused.

"You need your own place," Four said with authority that was final. "You need to experience life away from Mom and Dad."

"Okay, I'll try." Barrett thought living alone could be fun. No job or school. Just a constant party in his future.

"Next semester you'll start online classes, and if all goes well, you'll be in school somewhere next fall. Your Father and I are in full agreement. And as a matter of fact, I'm going to take some classes too." Monica's statement suddenly crushed Barrett's fantasy of partying all the time.

The rest of the day was spent taking boxes from his old room and grocery trips. It appeared he would be eating a steady diet of sandwiches, but he had to start somewhere.

Barrett spent his first night in his new home hosting a small celebration with some baseball players and a few old friends. The alcohol flowed freely. When he awoke the next morning, the nice tidy little house was a wreck. The kitchen table lay broken on the floor. The single living room chair had been thrown out in the front yard. The smell of stale beer on the carpet permeated the atmosphere. Food stains on the used furniture topped off the disastrous look.

CHAPTER 21

MR. DOWNS STRUGGLED to get out of bed and make it to the bathroom the morning after the bull incident. There were very few places on his body that were not sore and bruised. He felt like he had been in a bar fight and lost. Four had come over the day before when he got the call from Dub and spent the night in his old bedroom. He tried in vain to get his father to go to the hospital. In the morning light, Mr. Downs wished he had gone.

"Dad, how are you feeling?" Four greeted his father. The battered man stood in his bathroom holding on to the vanity.

"Not so good. There aren't many places that don't hurt. But if I can get a shower, I can go to church and be fine for work Monday," Mr. Downs said to his son's image in the mirror. He was wearing only his boxer shorts which revealed his bruised body. Hoof marks where the bulls stepped on him were seen clearly on his back and hip. On his right shoulder, a large purple bruise made from the swinging head and blunted horn of a bull indicated the force of the blow.

"Dad, you're really hurt. Let me take you to the hospital," Four said tenderly.

"What the hell are they going to do? Tell me I'm beat up? I already know that! Nothing is broken. I just need some aspirin and time. I'll be fine," he stubbornly stated with his voice rising.

Four just stood there. He knew he would not win this argument. Mr. Downs gingerly walked down the hall, sliding his left hand along the side of the wall as he slowly stepped. Four made coffee and called Monica with an update. Mr. Downs sat in his leather chair in the den and looked out over the heifer pasture. A heavy dew glistened on the grass left thin by the dry August and September. It would hit a hundred degrees by noon, but the early morning was pleasant.

"You and Dub picked some good bulls. Were they from the Dover Ranch?" Mr. Downs asked as he took a cup of black coffee from his son.

"Yes, sir. Howard Dover called me last week about a set of yearlings he had that would work good on our black Angus cattle." Four knew his father wanted to change the subject.

"Is Howard Jimmy's son?"

"Yes, sir. I met him when he came to Mom's funeral with his family."

"Oh, that's right; they did come. It was a hectic day. Sure was a lot of folks there." Mr. Downs spoke to the glass door as much as to his son. "Your mother would have loved the flowers. Gina at the flower shop told me it was the most she had ever delivered to a funeral." His mind wandered to memories of Janet whenever someone spoke of her. He would lose himself for a brief moment recalling a time and place spent with her.

"Mom would have wanted you to go to the hospital. You know that," Four took his shot. "And you would have if she were here."

"Well, *she's not here*," he answered bluntly.

"Why don't you at least stay home from church? Monica and I will let people know what happened." Four knew he had carried the argument as far as he could.

"I can do that." Mr. Downs surprised his son with the answer.

"We'll bring you some food from that new place you like, Ward's Café."

"Yeah, that'd be good. Anything is fine and get some peach cobbler."

Four left his bruised father and drove the few miles back home. He and Monica would go to Sunday school and let people know Mr. Downs was unable to come. He was a man who was never sick and rigid in his routine. Janet's death had been the first time he missed over a week of work in forty years. He did not take vacations. He always said going home to the ranch was a vacation.

At twelve-thirty, Four and Monica showed up at Mr. Downs' with enough food to last a couple of days. Monica sorted the food and set the table for the three of them. Mr. Downs struggled to stand but made it to the kitchen table where he sat in his usual place. Four sat where he sat as a child and Monica sat in Daisy's spot. Janet's space remained empty.

"Pop, I know you're going to say no, but I really want you to do this for me." Monica knew how to work the old man as well as anyone. "I want you to get a cell phone."

"I have two phones already. Here and the office and that's where I am ninety nine percent of the time," argued Mr. Downs.

"Yes, I know that, but you've taught me to protect against the one percent chance of disaster like with insurance. And I need you to do it for me for that one percent of the time you aren't at home or the office," Monica pushed. "We worry about you. Yesterday you could have been seriously hurt and a cell phone would've helped."

"I am fine. Been around cattle all my life. Just an accident is all," he obstinately responded.

"That's true but this is how people communicate now. They text. You can learn to text and keep up with the kids and even Lourdes." She was hitting him in his most vulnerable spot. Mr. Downs looked at her and then Four who was pointedly not joining the argument.

Monica pulled her Blackberry out of her purse. "This is my phone and it's like carrying a compact computer with me everywhere I go. It makes everyone's life easier. You see here is a small keyboard for typing." She showed him her device as he glanced at it and then back to her.

"No, I'm too old to learn anything new." Weak as it was, it was his best excuse.

"I'll get it set up with Dawn, and she can show you how it works. She's younger than you." Monica ended their discussion by simply ignoring his hard headed answer.

* * *

Lourdes and Maddie had reached somewhat of a detente regarding their argument on the first night. They were both an only child, but that is where the similarities ended. Maddie was the daughter of a single mother, and she had no relationship with her absent father. She called him the sperm donor. He had very little involvement in her life, but he did make a few attempts at paying child support. Dottie tried to be her friend more than her mother and this led to discipline issues from the beginning. She had dedicated all her resources to Maddie using the proceeds from her career at an insurance company in Houston.

Dottie was an attractive woman who had completely placed her life on hold for her cherished child who was born on her twentieth birthday. Mother and daughter celebrated their birthday each January 30, but there were never any gifts for mother. She was the oldest of four and overshadowed by three brothers who took most of her parent's time with sports and outdoor ventures with their dad. Her father was a dedicated outdoorsman and not so much a dedicated provider. Her unplanned pregnancy gave him an excuse to dismiss her from his life and Dottie's mother was too weak or just too tired to fight him.

At thirty-eight years old, Dottie King was free to date and finally allow herself some joy which was not related to her daughter. A nice-looking man from the building where she worked, had been flirting with her for months and she enjoyed it. He was divorced with two kids, the oldest of which was Maddie's age. Dottie and he had gone out a few times but only if Maddie had plans of her own. He had gone through the parent guilt after his divorce but realized that never helped the kids. Dottie was trying to let go of her only child, but old habits die hard. He tried to support her and give her strength to change, but she still felt a little giddy when Maddie called her.

"Mom, you may need to come get me," Maddie said in a quivering voice.

"Oh, Maddie, what's wrong?!"

"I'm not as smart as I thought I was. This is hard and Lourdes made me cry." Maddie had been in college for nine days.

Dottie took a deep breath. This was a critical moment and she had prepared for it.

"Maddie, you are not quitting. I'm sure Lourdes didn't mean to make you cry. I love you but I'm hanging up now. Figure it out." And Dottie hung up the phone.

Maddie stared for a moment at her cell phone in disbelief. Figure it out? Dammit, Mom! The dorm room door opened, and Lourdes walked in with her backpack and laid it on the floor at the foot of her bed.

"Well, you look like crap. What's wrong?" Lourdes asked her roommate.

"My mother just told me she hates me."

"Really? That's what she said? *I hate you,*" Lourdes said sarcastically looking at the girl seated on her unmade bed.

"Well, not those exact words. She said, 'Figure it out.'" Maddie made air quotes with her fingers.

"That's not even close to I hate you. Sounds like you need to *figure it out* to me."

"You would say that. You and my mom have some plan to destroy me." Maddie was now angry.

"Oh yea, crazy. You figured it out. Our vast detailed secret plan to take you down. Maybe it's a worldwide conspiracy." Lourdes matched Maddie's anger with a biting finish.

Maddie did not fight back and silently turned her body toward the wall. Lourdes had gone too far, and now she just felt sorry for the girl lying on her bed.

"I'm sorry, Maddie. We need to get along, and I don't want to keep fighting and trying to one up each other," Lourdes said kindly.

"There are so many people against me—pushing me down," Maddie whined.

"A man I know once told me there are two kinds of people in the world. Those who take responsibility and those who blame others. Blaming others is not a good look on you." Lourdes tried to push Maddie out of her mood.

"What does that really mean? You know people can cause you pain and people can push you down. It's others that cause it all."

"I didn't say other people don't cause you pain. What I mean is, it's up to you to deal with it. You're smart or you wouldn't be here," Lourdes said to her sweetly but firmly.

"I guess. It's just more convenient to blame someone else." Maddie smiled.

"Let's go eat supper. I'm starving . . . loser," Lourdes said and playfully slapped her slouching friend on the shoulder.

Maddie laughed as she got up from her bed and looked briefly at herself in the mirror on the way out of the room and smiled. The two took the four flight of stairs and walked to the closest cafeteria without talking until a boy ran past them going in their same direction.

"That was spikey haired boy number one," Maddie said to Lourdes as they walked.

"Who?"

"Spikey haired boy number one. I don't know his name yet, so I go with that. And he is really cute." Maddie answered.

"Is there a number two?" Lourdes asked.

"Well, of course there is, and he is even cuter, but not a three . . . yet." Both girls laughed.

It was funny how a few minutes prior, Maddie was down, yet now she was laughing. But Lourdes was glad her new friend was happy again. Two young ladies strolling together on a campus of close to fifty thousand students were not easily noticed. If they failed, someone would gladly take their place. They were a small part of the great machine that is the education business which generates a piece of paper representing one hundred and thirty-two hours of credits and the hope of a better life. A diploma hanging in your home or office tells all who enter that you went to a school and learned something. And although you had many experiences along the way, you received a printed destination.

CHAPTER 22

D AWN WALKED INTO Mr. Downs office a few days after the cattle
incident which she now called the "Battle of the Bulls." Mr.
Downs had indeed gone to the doctor on Monday and was
sent straight to the hospital for X-Rays that found some cracked ribs.
Nothing can be done about this injury except pray you never sneeze. It
was the following Thursday, and he was getting around better but still
not back to his old self.

"I need to take off tomorrow," she told her boss nonchalantly.

"Why?" He looked over his glasses more curious than anything else.

"Gettin' married," she answered with the same even tone.

"What! Really? Again?"

"Now, let me explain . . ."

"Who is it this time?" Mr. Downs wanted to know.

"Paul."

"Your first husband, Paul?"

"Yes, that Paul. You know we have the girls together, and we've been
seeing each other at the kid's stuff and the grandkids' birthdays. He
never remarried, but who could after you've had this?" Dawn ran her
hand flowing downward from her breasts.

"Oh, don't get me wrong, I always liked Paul," Mr. Downs said
nodding in approval. "And the kids and grandkids thing make sense."

"And to be honest," Dawn said, "I'm too damn old for anyone new
seeing me naked. Everything I got needs ironing."

Mr. Downs laughed at his work wife's unique sense of humor.

"Stop it. It hurts too bad to laugh." He laughed, wincing at the same time.

"Serves you right for being mean to me." She pointed at him.

"I wasn't mean to you. I've been nicer to you than anyone."

"I know. I'm just kidding. Do you want to come to the wedding?"

"Sure. When and where?"

"My house, Friday at six. Bring a bottle of wine. Paul's gonna need it." She sashayed out of the room swinging her rear in an exaggerated fashion.

*   *   *

Martha Stall entered the small examination room to find a young man lying on his side on the metal frame bed. He was pale and thin wearing old jeans that looked like they had never been cleaned. He had on a dingy white t-shirt under a long-sleeve plaid shirt even though it was a ninety-five-degree day. His hair was dirty and long. His beard was thin with facial sores indicative of meth abuse.

"Hello, I'm Martha Stall. You are in bad shape, young man. I need you to tell me exactly what drugs you have taken and how much. And I don't care where you got them." Martha stood and looked at the twenty-two-year-old boy coming down from a drug overdose. The local police had found him on the ground outside a convenience store in town. No one knew him and he had no identification. He had been in the clinic for several hours.

"You have to drink and eat or you will die. I don't like people dying on my watch, so don't make me look bad." Martha tried to gain the young man's trust.

He did not respond. He only lay there silently in a fetal position holding his stomach. Martha slid a blood pressure cuff over his weak arm and began pumping the bulb to create the pressure around his spindly arm. She did her best not to be judgmental but all she could see was a wasted life caused by a series of poor choices. She had seen this too often. Travis City was not immune to the drug problem. It was a difficult balance of care and punishment. If you provide too much care and services for the people affected, then you begin to attract this element to your town.

Travis City's city council had the hard conversations about what they could do about the drug problem and had studied other communities' responses and the real outcomes. The results were not surprising, the more help you offered the bigger drug problem you had in your town. The drug community flocked to areas that showed compassion by helping them get clean and stay that way. It worked for some but not for the majority.

Health officials and law enforcement did their best, but they knew making it easier to be a junkie was not the answer, although it sounded like the right thing to do. It was the compassionate thing to do. It was the kind thing. But in the end, it was not the best thing for Travis City and the people of the community.

The police chief of Travis City was Darrell Roberts. He had joined the department after receiving an associate degree, making his way up the ladder over thirty years while earning everyone's respect. He was tough on his officers, but extremely fair. Chief Roberts was black and was the first to defend a white officer being accused of racism. He instituted cameras on the dash of every patrol car and made sure any incident was looked at in its entirety. Two young black officers were fired when they beat a very drunk white man stumbling down a street. They had beaten the man so severely he could barely stand.

Chief Roberts asked them one question. "Would you have done this if the drunk man had been black?" There was no news story about this, and few people knew why the men were fired, but the police force of twelve other black, white, and Hispanic men and women knew and agreed with the decision. Abusing their power was not acceptable. Chief Roberts had known these type men through the years, and they were the most dangerous police officers on the force—regardless of race.

Chief Roberts walked into Dawn's office in his dark blue uniform and his hat tucked under his left arm.

"May I see Mr. Downs?" he politely asked.

"Come on in, Chief. Good to have you here." Mr. Downs had recognized his voice.

"Thank you, sir. Do you want the door closed?"

"If you think so, then yes." Mr. Downs now knew this was a personal matter for one of them.

Mr. Downs slowly walked around his desk and sat on the left wingback chair and pointed to the other for the policeman to sit.

"How can I help you, Chief Roberts?"

"A couple of things. First, I heard you had a fight with some bulls. You okay?"

"I'm fine, just sore." Mr. Downs tried to downplay his health to get back to the reason the man in blue was coming to see him.

Roberts got down to business. "I guess I'm here for something I heard about your grandson, Barrett."

"Oh hell, what did he do?"

"Nothing really, but I just wanted your permission to kind of scare him. He's had a couple of parties at his little rent house out on Pine Street that got bigger than they should, but no complaints were filed."

"Monica told me she and Four were trying to get him out of the house and push him to be more responsible. They probably didn't think this through very well. What'd ya have in mind?" Mr. Downs was very fond of Chief Roberts and had a great deal of respect for his tactics.

"I have a cousin who lives out that way on past Barrett's house. It's at the edge of the city limits. He's going to call me next time he sees a bunch of cars at the rent house. I may just make a surprise visit. Give them all a good scare."

"That sounds good to me," Mr. Downs approved. "Did you talk to his parents?"

"No, but I will if you want me to," the officer responded respectfully.

"I think we can keep this between us. Mothers don't understand this kind of thing," Mr. Downs concluded.

"By the way, I was really moved when your grandfather read The Letter." Mr. Downs shook hands as Darrell prepared to leave.

"And thank you for coming to his funeral," Chief Roberts responded. "He always liked you."

"Well, I tell ya, this whole town liked Mr. Sookie Burns."

"One more thing," Chief Roberts added. "We're seeing an uptick in drug use in town. Mostly meth but pain killers are being found too. Call me if you have a loan concern about anyone. Drugs can ruin all kind of families. Even the best people in town." The officer opened the door and nodded to Dawn as he left.

Dawn immediately walked into Mr. Downs' office.

"What did Darrell want?" she asked in a whisper.

"Nothing really. It's just Barrett being a young idiot like most of us were. Darrell is a smart fellow. He'll stay on top of this."

* * *

Martha held the limp hand of the nameless young man as they quickly pushed the gurney out the doors of the clinic to the waiting ambulance. He wouldn't make it through the night. An overdose of a cocktail of drugs were found in his system including OxyContin. He was losing the battle to hold on to his fragile life as his body's systems began to fail. No one knew him. No one claimed him. And there was no identification found. Some mother somewhere had lost her son. Maybe she already knew he was gone. Maybe she had done her best to save him. Maybe she had been the reason his life was over so soon. Maybe he had turned things around and was clean but one last time was the one that killed him. In the end, it was a series of his own tragic choices that ended his life.

Men and women in medical services and law enforcement see the worst of people. The lost souls and the tragic wastes of precious lives. They also see the broad spectrum of families affected. No town is immune to addiction or free from the individuals that try to escape their realities through drugs and alcohol no matter the costs.

CHAPTER 23

MARIA AND DANNY missed their daughter more than they wanted to admit, but it was Danny who felt her absence more keenly. He missed the early morning complaining from his teenage daughter, he missed her quick wit, and he missed how she could push her mother's buttons. They were both very busy at their jobs which kept them sane. It was the evenings and early mornings that were hard to endure.

"Did you talk to Lourdes today?" Danny asked Maria while eating his supper.

"No, and you've asked me twice already," Maria answered with a smile.

"We should call her after we eat. Just check on her." Danny waved his fork around his plate.

"Sure, but you know it is expensive to talk to her so often."

"Why should we work so hard if we can't spend a little money on hearing our only child's voice?" he argued.

"Okay, after you clean up the kitchen, we'll call her." Maria knew how to bargain.

They both laughed and finished their meal and rapidly cleared the remnants of the evening meal and called Lourdes' dorm room. It rang several times and the answering machine picked up with Lourdes and Maddie stating they were, "Not here because we are studying," the two girls giggled, and the beep sounded to leave a message.

"Hi, baby girl. We miss you and you can call us tonight when you get home if it's not too late," Danny said with a touch of disappointment in his tone as they disconnected the call.

"We can call her cell phone. She may just be at a friend's room," Maria said, punching in the phone number.

"Hello," Lourdes answered with loud noises in the background.

"Hi, baby! It's Mommy and Daddy. Where are you?" Danny and Maria both pressed their ears to the receiver.

"I know it's you. My phone has caller ID. I'm at an outdoor concert place. Let me walk away so I can hear you better." Lourdes left her seat next to Maddie and some girls from the dorm and retreated behind a walled area leading to the restrooms of the small outdoor venue.

"Okay, I should be able to hear much better now," Lourdes spoke into her new Nokia cell phone.

"Why are you at a band place on a Thursday night? This a school night," Maria projected the authority and concern of an only child's mother.

"It's just a local Texas singer one of the girls in the dorm likes. It was free for ladies, so we came. It's fun," Lourdes defended herself.

"You should have fun, but not at the expense of your grades. You are in college to get the degree, not have party time," Maria lectured.

"Maria, let the girl have some fun. We know nothing about college. Our daughter is very smart, and she will make good grades." Danny took up for his adventurous daughter. "Lourdes, you have fun too!"

"So, when she gets kicked out of school because she's a pregnant party girl, don't blame me." Maria was getting mad.

"Mom, I'm sure you're the only person in the world to coin the phrase 'pregnant party girl,' and please don't worry about me so much. I'm doing good in all my classes, and I'm making friends and having fun. I love you both, and I'll see you in a few weeks."

"Goodbye, baby girl, you know we'll always worry about you. When you're a parent, you'll understand," Danny said.

"Love you and be good!" Maria finished and they hung up.

Lourdes returned to her seat and listened to acoustic guitar original ballads about highways, trucks, and barbecue performed by a lone young man in a worn straw cowboy hat. A cute boy with sandy blonde hair wearing shorts and a faded blue t-shirt was looking at her and smiling each time Lourdes looked his way.

The boy with the sandy blonde hair appeared beside her as her group exited the venue around eleven that night. Lourdes was wearing a burnt orange cap with a Longhorn logo, her long black hair pulled through the back of the cap. She had on her best fitting jeans and a baggy sweatshirt.

"Did you enjoy the show?" The boy asked Lourdes in a forced nonchalant manner which made it more awkward.

"Sure." Lourdes looked at him and nervously smiled.

"I'm Chase." The boy extended his hand to her as they walked down the sidewalk along with the crowd.

"Lourdes." She shook his hand.

"I've seen you in the cafeteria. Can I come talk to you sometime?" he asked.

"Sure. I got to go this way now, Chase, but see you around." Lourdes took a sharp right, leaving him walking straight on with his friends.

Lourdes caught up to Maddie who was about to burst with curiosity.

"Well, he's cute! Are you going to have a thousand of his babies?" Maddie started walking backwards to face the blushing Lourdes.

"You idiot! He was just trying to flirt with me, and it appears we're both really bad at it!" Lourdes laughed. "And besides I still have a boyfriend."

"Well, he's in Houston a million miles away, and you are all alone in Austin surrounded by hot college boys. I didn't hear you tell the new guy you have a boyfriend!"

"It didn't come up in our ten second conversation. Should I wear a name tag that says, 'I'm Lourdes and I have a boyfriend from high school'?"

The group laughed and teased each other as they walked back to the dorm in the early October night. An enjoyable evening of listening to music, getting beer with fake IDs, and immersing themselves in their great adventure. College was going to be fun.

*   *   *

Beth had remained a true friend after their memorable meeting in the cafeteria, and she and Lourdes met once a week on Monday evening to study and stay connected. Beth lived with her aunt and uncle in south Austin, so she wasn't as involved with the campus life and had not met many people, so Lourdes was her lifeline. They both loved having the connection to someone from home.

Tommy was coming Friday for the weekend. It was his first trip to see her, and he was staying at his parents' friend's lake house on Lake Austin just below the dam of beautiful Lake Travis. The Colorado River ran through Austin and there were a series of dams used to control flooding that created a string of lakes. Lady Bird Lake was located in the city limits of Austin and lined with jogging trails and people kayaking in the clear water. Lake Austin was above that and the Mansfield Dam cut into the rocky hills and created Lake Travis, the largest of the chain.

Saturday was college football day and Lourdes and Tommy had tickets to see the Longhorns play the Baylor Bears. Lourdes was amazed at the spectacle of it all. Tailgating, the seriousness of the fans' sports talk and seeing the athletes on campus was like spotting a Hollywood celebrity. High school football was big in Texas, but college ball was on a level all its own. She and Mr. Downs had talked about the Longhorns and the Travis City Defenders every fall. Danny was a big Dallas Cowboys fan and the old guys at the skeet range were always talking sports of every kind. *How is the team gonna be this year? Who are the stars and the coaches? What are the sports radio and television people saying about their chances?* Sports permeated every corner of the state.

Texas had many college teams to choose from, so there was no dominant state team like Nebraska or Louisiana State University. The fans of Texas A&M were as rabid as Baylor or Texas Christian University or Texas Tech. Southern Methodist University was up there too, until the NCAA issued them the death penalty for being too blatant in their cheating, which meant they were severely punished for their actions. The University of Texas had prior National Championships and it was hard to beat the iconic Longhorn Bevo surrounded by his exclusive team of Cowboys taking care of his every need, standing behind the end zone for the games.

Lourdes got the text from Tommy she had been waiting for at four Friday afternoon. He was downstairs waiting for her. She was so excited at just seeing his name on her phone, and now she would see him and feel his embrace. She exclaimed to Maddie, "He's here!" and ran toward the stairway, jumping down three steps at a time to see her first love. She had carefully selected her clothes and makeup and spent the past two hours doing her hair to look her very best when she emerged from the dorm and saw him at the bottom of the short steps.

He saw her before she noticed him, and he began walking to her. She ran and leapt in his arms like she did that day at the skeet championship. She didn't care if it made her look vulnerable. She genuinely loved him.

"I missed you so much!" she said after she finished kissing him.

"I can see that! I missed you too," he said with a big grin.

"Come on up! You have to meet Maddie." Lourdes grabbed his hand and started dragging him behind her.

The young couple found the elevator door open, pressed Maddie's and her floor number, and waited for the doors to close. As soon as they slowly slid shut, they began kissing passionately.

The doors opened and they reluctantly separated from their bond. Lourdes pulled Tommy down the hallway passing rooms with the sounds of Friday night. Loud music and laughter and screaming about some crazy event. They reached her room and pushed through the doorway.

"Maddie, this is my Tommy!" Lourdes squealed like the excited young girl she was.

"Hi, 'My Tommy,' I'm Maddie." She stood and hugged him.

"I feel like I already know you since she talks about you constantly, even in her sleep." Maddie tried to embarrass Lourdes with her teasing comment.

"You should hear what I sing in the shower about you!" Lourdes joined in the game.

Tommy laughed at the two girls as he sat on the bed next to Lourdes holding her hand.

"What are we doing tonight?" Lourdes asked Tommy.

"Hey, this is your town, so you tell me," he answered.

"Where are you staying because this is not a place suited for guests?" Maddie indicated the tiny room.

"Lake Austin. Go up Bee Caves Road to 620, go right, and turn right again at the water tower that looks like a golf ball," Tommy said based on memorizing the verbal directions. "I thought we could go there tonight and come back here for tailgating and then the two o'clock game."

Lourdes looked at him and nodded her head. "That sounds perfect. Let me pack a small bag. Maddie, if my parents call, you know I am at the library."

"Of course, *the library*. Studying anatomy!" Maddie cracked up at her own joke.

Tommy and Lourdes left campus in his car dealer plated F-150 pickup trying to follow the map Lourdes had printed before they left. They found the water tower and turned on the gravel road past a couple of old farms which were positioned to become prime real estate. The final descent to the ancient riverbed, or Lake Austin, was a steep decline that teed into a road that went right and left to a handful of scattered lake houses. A few were big and new, but their destination looked like a late nineteen-fifties house with a middle section and two wings extended at an angle facing the water. There were ancient pecan trees surrounding the structure with a flagstone walk that curved around the terrain about fifty yards to a wooden dock with a boat lift.

Gazing at the magnificent setting, Lourdes was amazed at how beautiful it was. The owners lived in Houston and were car dealer friends of Tommy's family. Tommy had been there several times and was thrilled that his dad's friends allowed him to stay there. The interior matched the retro style exterior with orange sofas and star shaped wall décor. The appliances were all original with yellow tile countertops. The living area had a glass wall to allow a clear view of the pecan trees and the glimmering water and the open land across the lake. The wildlife added to the ambience as there were deer in the yard that didn't seem to be bothered by their presence.

They stocked the refrigerator with beer, soft drinks and some sandwich meat. They had chips and a loaf of bread on the counter with a package of Tommy's favorite cookies. They grabbed a couple of beers and walked down to the dock. It was early October and the nights were cool. Tommy found a couple of folding chairs in a little storage building, and they sat on the dock as the sun was starting to set behind them. A wave of slight chill was felt with shade now spreading in front of them.

"How do you like your school?" Lourdes asked.

"It's good, but I had hoped they would fix my problem immediately," Tommy spoke of his dyslexia. "But I guess that's not reasonable."

"You'll get there; I know you will."

"How are your classes?" he asked.

"It's just basic stuff right now, so not much to talk about. It's just so big. There'll be more people in that stadium tomorrow than I have ever seen in my whole life. I get overwhelmed with how huge it all is, but I don't let anyone know." It felt good to open up to someone about her experience. "It gets easier every day. You just have to do it."

"I know the feeling. Houston is like sixty miles across. Going anywhere seems like it takes at least an hour. Every time I leave campus, the drivers act like they're in an apocalyptic movie, Death Race 2004. But I'm like you, I tell everyone it's great. It's what we do, but at least we can be honest with each other." Tommy reached for Lourdes' hand.

"Do you remember the first time you held my hand?" she queried as she twirled her fingers against his.

"Yes, the day we walked into the cafeteria and saw Claudia cleaning tables and wearing that awful hairnet." Tommy smiled at her.

"I loved you the moment you lifted my hand up. I went from the lowest I had ever been in my life to the highest, all because of you. I never properly thanked you for taking me out of that room." She leaned over and kissed him as the sun had disappeared behind them and the stars began to emerge in the darkening sky.

"I've loved you since the first day of kindergarten when you were already smarter than the teacher and prettier than anyone I had ever known in my whole five years on the earth." He stood and they walked together up the curving trail into the lake house and closed the door.

The next day was filled with crowds and music and food and drink. The game was glorious, and the Longhorns beat the Baylor Bears to remain undefeated.

Tommy waited as long as he could to drive away from Lourdes on Sunday. They had spent the weekend at the lake house alone and for the first time awoke in each other's arms. It was painful to be separated again, but they would see each other at Thanksgiving, at home in Travis City.

* * *

Lourdes became bored when she discovered she had too much free time. She had been working since she was ten years old and needed a job at least a few hours a week. It was strange how free hours had made her wasteful. The busier she was the more focused she became, and she understood this about herself.

She read the posted jobs at the university. They were mostly minimum wage clerical positions which did not appeal to her. There was a maximum earning potential issue she did not like. She was taking eighteen hours of her basics with not much of a challenge for her academically. She felt like she could devote twenty hours weekly to work, and then she got an idea.

Lourdes drove up Interstate 35 to a group of car dealerships. She wore a professional blouse, black slacks, and black pumps. She styled her hair to make her appear more mature. She walked into the showroom of a Toyota dealership and was immediately approached by a young man standing on the showroom floor.

"Hi, I'm Adam. Can I help you with anything?" A young man handed her a business card.

"Hello, Adam. May I speak with the manager please?" Lourdes smiled and politely made her request.

"We have different ones. Which manager are you needing?"

"I would like to speak to someone about a sales job."

"Then that would be Derrick. Follow me please." Adam led her to a group of glass front offices facing the showroom, pausing at the largest one. A man of about forty sat speaking on the phone. Adam pointed to Lourdes and back to Derrick indicating she wanted to speak to him. Derrick waved to a chair where Lourdes sat. Adam returned to his post, and Derrick continued his conversation.

Lourdes sat patiently as the man relayed a series of numbers associated with a car sale into the phone. The numbers of course piqued her interest, and she mentally began playing with them in her head to keep occupied while she waited. The sales manager was punching his adding machine as he talked and paused to view the calculations. He stated a final number and ended the exchange.

"Hi, I'm Derrick Sanders, sales manager. How can I assist you, miss?" He stood and handed her a card in what seemed to be a theme.

"My name is Lourdes Sanchez; I wanted to speak with you about a part time sales position," Lourdes spoke with authority.

"We don't have any part time salesmen. Its a full-time job only," Derrick responded dismissively.

"I understand that is your policy, but I am seeking a commission only job. Should it matter how many hours I work?"

"No one has ever offered that, so I need to think about it. Have you ever sold cars before?"

"No."

"Have you ever had any job before?" he continued to inquire.

"I've been working since I was ten."

"How old are you now?"

"Eighteen."

"You go to school?"

"Freshman in mathematics at UT."

"That's interesting. You're good at math?"

"People seem to think so. Actually, I think you missed a number when you were on the phone," she said looking straight into his eyes.

"What do you mean, you think?"

"I can only do in my head what you were saying, so if you said it incorrectly, then I could not be sure," she answered him honestly.

He picked up a document with several handwritten numbers that were related to the call.

"What was wrong?" He held the paper close to him where she could not see.

"You miscalculated the sales tax. You said $1,243.97 and based on the total and the proper percentage of tax applied, it should have been $1,421.88 which in turn changed the total by the difference of $177.91. That makes the correct total number $28,455.66. You lost $177.91."

Derrick stared at her and began recalculating immediately. He finished and did it again and compared the numbers on the tape to those on the sales slip. He looked at her with amazement.

"When can you start?" astonished he stood and extended his hand.

CHAPTER 24

THE POLICE CRUISER slowed as the officer saw scattered cars parked around Barrett's rent house on a Friday night around ten. Chief Roberts was alone but not concerned about violence or needing backup as he pulled into the yard and hit his emergency lights and siren. He later described it as if he kicked over an ant mound. Kids began pouring out of the house tossing beer cans and cigarettes as they scattered running in all directions. He just let them go. He was only there to get some attention and it was working. He then got on his loudspeaker and ordered all of them to line up in the bright headlights of his car or he was releasing the dogs.

No one responded to his command, so he turned off the siren and placed a CD in his player and soon the sound of multiple vicious snarling and barking dogs were heard blaring through the loudspeaker. The dispersed teenagers came running back to the front yard and stood in the blinding lights searching for the pack of dogs. Chief Roberts had captured the entire group with a recording. He stopped the CD player and got out of his car.

"All of you sit down on the ground right now!" he ordered the crowd of around twenty teens.

"Barrett Downs, come get in my back seat. Now!" he shouted.

Barrett made his way through the group and opened the back door of the cruiser and got in. The others sat orderly on the ground. Some still nervously looking for the invisible dogs.

"Everyone else is free to go home. If you have been drinking, I should warn you there are several police officers on the road back to town, and they all have the description of your vehicles and license plates. If you are stopped and you are drunk, you will go to jail. Up to you. Or you can call a parent and they can come get you. You can come get the car tomorrow." Darrell finished his speech and could hear the whispering among the partygoers.

He opened the driver door and sat behind the wheel. His headlights remained on, but he turned off the emergency flashers.

"You sure been having a lot of parties, boy. I think this may be the fourth or fifth one this month." The chief looked at Barrett in his rearview mirror as he spoke. "You see, my cousin lives past you down the road a piece, and he's been telling me all about these gatherings. He works evenings and drives by here between ten and twelve most nights, so I know every time you decide to have a party."

"This is not my fault. People just show up and pretty soon it gets out of hand." Barrett lamely tried to excuse his behavior.

"Not my fault, you say. I wonder who you could call if people started gathering and playing loud music and drinking against your will? Do you know anyone who could stop these people from trespassing and breaking the law on your property?" Chief Roberts asked sarcastically.

"The police," Barrett meekly answered.

"Yes, the police, me. I will come, turn on my lights, and play a CD of dogs barking and get them to leave . . . Well, that only works once. I would need real dogs next time. Listen to me, Barrett. I know your mom and dad and I know your grandfather. They are good folks, and you need to remember this is a small town. You cannot do anything without it getting back to me, understand?"

"Yes, sir."

"So what are we going to do after tonight? I'll tell ya," Chief Roberts said with the full authority he held in his position. "You're out of the party business. I will put a damn police car in your driveway every night if I have to. Understand?"

"Yes, sir," Barrett said submissively.

* * *

Lourdes and Derrick had worked out a schedule at the dealership which worked with her classes but still gave her time to study. She had not told anyone but Maddie and Tommy what she was doing, because she wanted to conduct an experiment. Car salespeople were consistently rated low on trustworthiness, just slightly ahead of politicians. She wondered why and what better way to learn than be one. Her first shift was spent filling out paperwork and background checks and training. The training consisted of a two-hour video on how to sell a car which she found hilariously full of clichés and of poor quality.

She was given the only available office next to the hallway near the service garage. She was taken around the dealership to meet the service people, the parts manager, and the other salesmen. She was the only female salesperson. There were women in accounting and one ditzy girl with a large chest who answered the phone at a desk on the showroom floor. She was nice to Lourdes, but she did not make a great first impression.

"Hello, I'm Lourdes Sanchez, the new salesgirl."

"Hey, I'm Tiffany Box." The buxom girl barely acknowledged her.

Lourdes restrained laughter at the cartoonish nature of her name and matching appearance but was nice to the young lady.

"How long have you worked here, Tiffany?" Lourdes asked in an attempt to be gracious.

"I don't know. Maybe two years. Listen, I know you're just being nice, but you need to know something." Tiffany looked at her with her head tilted. "The men at this place are pigs, and no one is going to be nice to you for at least a month. People like you come and go real quick. So why bother? You will be gone in a month."

"Thank for being honest, Tiffany. That was very kind of you," Lourdes responded.

"Sure, no problema, Lormas." As she picked up the ringing phone she chirped, "Austin Toyota—How can I direct your call?"

There were ten men of varying ages working as salesmen. The oldest of the group was over sixty with sloping shoulders and thick black and gray hair parted to one side. He wore gray slacks and a white dress shirt with a pen and business cards in his shirt pocket. Lourdes had watched him with an older couple asking about a used Camry sedan. He held his hands behind his back and leaned forward as they spoke.

He quickly answered each question about the car features, but Lourdes knew most of his answers were not quite correct based on her review of the vehicles. The buyers would just nod, and he would nod, and soon they were in his office buying a new SUV that was completely different than what they said they wanted.

A young couple walked in and she watched another salesman approach them with his card in hand. She listened as the young couple stated they were needing more room for a new baby and the husband was looking for a job. The salesman deftly asked what payment method they preferred. Cash or financing? They said finance but had little money for a down payment and he responded with, "Let's get a finance report going first to give you the best deal on an interest rate."

The salesman walked the sheet of information to the finance man who ran their credit. The finance man waved the salesman back in his office and she could not hear what was said but it appeared to be bad. The salesman walked back to the young couple with a smile and informed them what he could do for them. They would not qualify for the best program, but if they could put down fifteen hundred dollars, he could get them a really nice used car that would perfectly fit their needs. The couple looked despondent at the news, but Lourdes naively wondered why they were not aware of their credit situation. Surely, they did not expect a miracle. And why did they have a new baby and not have fifteen hundred dollars saved?

Each Thursday morning the salesmen met at seven in the conference room to discuss upcoming promotions and their total sales from the previous week. Each salesman's name was on a big whiteboard with total units sold for the month and total earned commissions. Lourdes arrived early and sat in the room with Derrick at the front writing updates across the black squares. Lastly, he penned her name at the bottom of the list.

"Yesterday you had a chance to go around and meet most everyone, but today will be your first day of real work. Don't worry about these bastards you are working with. Just do what I tell you and you'll be fine. I know you have classes until two, but you'll be back this afternoon. Today I want you to sell a car," Derrick said as if he were demanding rather than hoping she would sell a car.

"Yes, sir," she answered enthusiastically.

The salesmen started to drift in a little after seven with coffee in hand, grabbing donuts from the box Derrick had brought. Derrick stood at the front by the whiteboard waiting for everyone to get seated and stop their morning banter.

"I think most of you have met Lourdes Sanchez. She's a student at UT—something none of you idiots were able to accomplish. She is going to be selling cars and working part time. I know we've never had a part time salesman, but I want to give her a chance while she's going to school." He indicated the only girl in the room. "Lourdes, stand up and tell everyone a little something about yourself."

"Sure, I'm Lourdes Sanchez. I'm from Travis City, Texas. I'm studying finance and math and I like skeet shooting. I look forward to learning from all of you, and I'll appreciate any pointers from you guys to help me sell some cars." She sat back down not knowing if what she said was enough or too much.

"Thanks, Lourdes. By the way, let me explain why she's here," Derrick elaborated. "First, because she convinced me she could do this job. Second, she's smoking hot. And last, and more importantly, she's smart. Marcus, give me the year you were born."

"The year I was born?" Marcus asked confused.

"Damn, Marcus! It shouldn't be that hard even for your dumb ass," Derrick teased.

"1969?"

"Are you seriously asking me?" Derrick asked in disbelief.

"No, it is 1969."

"Carson, what year were you born, and please don't make this hard," Derrick pleaded.

"1964. No doubt," Carson joked and the others laughed.

"Lourdes, what is 1969 times 1964?" Derrick quickly turned toward Lourdes.

"3,867,116," She quickly responded and the group all stared in amazement.

"How do we know she's right?" Derrick held up his calculator. "Check her. You'll be shocked."

"Thank you, Lourdes. Now if any of you sons of bitches come to

me whining about having a part time young lady salesperson, you now
know that she is smarter than any of you will ever be. And another
thing—I know you all too well—I better not see any of you betting with
people about what she can do with math in her head. She is not here
for your entertainment. I want all of you to help her with any questions
and be nice! Got it?" When Derrick finished, the group of men were all
nodding.

"Good, so let's start with Bradley. You really suck, Bradley. What
the hell are you doing? You have sold only four units so far for the
month. I'm going to need you to step it up or you're fired . . . Next,
Carl. Wow, are you getting lessons from Bradley on how *not* to sell?
You are pitiful."

Lourdes was shocked at the brutal remarks directed to the first two
on the list. Was this what it would be like all the time? She looked at
Carl and Bradley expecting to see them near tears, but only saw them
grinning at the others.

"Duane. Hey, Duane! You alive? I need you to at least pretend you
want this job. Barney, if you walked any slower to greet a customer,
they would think you are doing some slo-mo dance. Act like you're
excited every once in a while . . . Marcus, what can I say? Do you want
me to sprinkle some *be back powder* on all your customers? Everyone
of your customers tells you they'll *be back*. Franklin, you actually did
a good job last week. I know; I was shocked. And I'm sure the whole
group agrees that a blind squirrel finds an acorn every once in a while."

Lourdes did her best to watch the faces as Derrick ranted and saw
mostly smiles.

"And finally, King David, the old wise man of Austin. We bow
before you yet again. If you can sell two more today, you can beat
your own record. Let's all give the king a round of applause." Derrick
and the group clapped loudly for the older man with salt and pepper
hair.

"I want to thank all my minions for making me the leader once
again. If Derrick ever hired anyone but idiots, I may be worried. No
offense, young lady." David waved his hand toward Lourdes.

"None taken," she said with a smile. "I just hope one day I beat you."

"Bold! A *Young Lass* has arrived to take down the *Old One*," Derrick said in an English accent. "Will she do it? I say, nay, because she is only part time."

"Aye, what if we prorate my hours against his? Would that be considered fair play in this kingdom?" Lourdes also responded in an English accent to join the fun.

"An excellent idea and we shall return to this place on the first day of December to see who shall proclaim the victory!" Derrick said shouting to the applauding group.

Lourdes stood and greeted the salesmen and lastly David who smiled at her and said, "You may do it, but I will always do my best to win."

"I would expect nothing less from such a nobleman as you." Lourdes smiled and they walked out together.

CHAPTER 25

DAWN CALLED OUT to Mr. Downs from her desk, "Line three . . . Randy."

"Hey, sum bitch. What's up?" Mr. Downs' mood always improved when his friend called.

"Hey, sum bitch. Got some unreal news a few minutes ago. Dr. Fowler from Austin called me and said the governor had me on the short list for the Board of Regents for UT," Randy announced.

"Wow! That's really something. I guess you and Vickie finally donated enough money to make the list," Mr. Downs joked.

"Vickie loves having her picture made with governors and presidents more than anyone I know. I got the nod because she never went to UT and I did. For that matter, she never went anywhere but cosmetology school. But she never lets on to anyone about that little morsel of information."

"I do hope you get selected. They need you on the board. We got way too many idiots down there in my opinion," Mr. Downs was proud of his friend.

"The term would start next January and last three years. I'm not sure if I can actually sit and listen to people saying nothing for hours at a time, but the regents get the best football seats. It may be worth it just for that."

"When do you find out?"

"Around Thanksgiving. I'll tell you when I see you. We're planning to come to Travis City this year. My sister Emily wants to do it at mom and dad's like when we were kids. I asked if I could eat at the grownups' table."

"Ha, if you make the board, you can sit at the head of the grownups table from now on," Mr. Downs laughed.

* * *

Lourdes drove into her parents' driveway late Wednesday night before Thanksgiving. She had worked at the dealership until six when they closed for the holiday. Her sales were good, and in fact, she had calculated she was in the lead by a single car. She had straight A's this far into the semester, and she and Maddie had become close friends. She continued to see Beth regularly, and she was also doing well in school.

The garage light came on and she saw the figure of her mother walking toward her.

"Hi, Mama. I'm home," she said with a happy tired voice.

"Oh baby, I've missed you so much," Maria said as they hugged. "Your daddy fell asleep on the couch watching some football game. Come on in and let me help you carry some things." Maria grabbed a couple of plastic bags stuffed with dirty clothes while Lourdes rolled a large suitcase across the drive.

When they entered the kitchen from the garage, the familiar smell washed over her. Danny lay in his boxer shorts snoring on the couch oblivious of his daughter standing a few feet away.

"Danny! Wake up! Lourdes is here!" Maria startled her sleeping husband awake.

Danny quickly lifted himself up and smiled through sleepy eyes at his daughter.

"My baby girl is finally home!" He stood to embrace his daughter.

"Glad to be here, Daddy."

"You're making the good grades, I hope," he said.

"Yes, I am. All A's so far."

"I saw Tommy today at his dad's dealership. He said he got in yesterday. Looked good. You still like him?" Danny teased her.

"Of course I do! What's not to like? He's just like you—handsome and smart and he loves me! What are the plans for Thanksgiving this year?" she asked her parents.

"Dinner and watching football here tomorrow with your Uncle Jack's family," Maria said. "No real plans after that, but we don't want you being gone the whole time you're here. We would like to spend time with you. I want to hear all about this new job. I could never do that. Try to sell something."

"It's a challenge because you deal with all kinds of people. I've learned there are tons of people who don't have any money saved. It's just amazing. They all want new cars but have no money for a down payment and they owe more on the car they're driving than it's worth. It's called being upside down. Everybody wants things right now. Nobody wants to save for anything." Lourdes shared her new knowledge.

"I see that all the time here in Travis City. Drive around and see new cars parked in front of shacks, or even new houses with mom, dad, and kids with new cars and a boat. All I see are payments adding up to every penny they make. And if one bad thing comes around, like a lost job or illness, poof there they go down the drain." Danny joined in.

"And think of all the people that have owed us money and next time you see them they're driving a brand new car." Maria knew the game some of her customers played all too well.

"The key to it, baby girl, that your mother and I know, is some people will not pay you. You cover that by having as many customers as possible to even things out. We get our money from lots of different people and businesses, so a few bad ones don't take us down," Danny said to Lourdes who was now snacking in the kitchen.

"The law of large numbers is what Mr. Downs calls it. A spread of risk. Mom, how is he doing?" Lourdes asked.

"Good, he got beat up by some bulls a while back, but he was back to normal in a few days. He asks about you every day. You need to go see him. He'll be there Friday," Maria responded. "I've been sending Doris to clean the bank, but I go by most days and check on how she is doing, and he and I talk for a few minutes."

The next morning Lourdes woke to the comfortable smells of her mother's kitchen and the sound of her father's music. She had slept well, although being alone in a quiet place felt strange after being with Maddie surrounded by the sounds of the dorm. She brushed her teeth and her hair and smiled at the sight of her Dad dancing in his boxers around her busy mother in the kitchen while she playfully shooed him away. She smiled and wondered if she would be that happy after thirty-five years with anyone.

Thanksgiving was a grand success especially since the Cowboys beat the Bears in the late game. Danny struggled to stay awake watching the game. All the guests had left, and Lourdes helped her mother put away the leftovers in the kitchen.

"Tommy is coming over in a few minutes. We may go do something," she said to her mother.

"Okay, I know you want to see your friends, but please don't be out too late. We're going to the bank in the morning," Maria reminded her.

"Do we have to go at the crack of dawn?"

"No, we can go around eight," Maria conceded.

Lourdes went back to her room and freshened her makeup and changed to a warmer sweater as the nights were cooler this close to December. She put on the jeans she wore to the lake house which Tommy had complimented. But she was pretty sure she could have worn a sack and he would still flatter her. When she heard his voice from the den, she skipped down the hall to greet him.

"Tommy!" she ran to him and squeezed him, embarrassing her mother to see such a display of affection.

"Hey! You look awesome as always." He stood back and admired her.

"You two behave yourselves tonight and be back by ten . . . Okay, eleven." Maria smiled at the young couple.

Lourdes gave a quick hug to her mother, waved at her snoozing father, and they walked out through the garage door to the driveway where Tommy was parked in a new two door pickup.

"I never know what you'll be driving. I guess that's something I need to get used to, dealer man," she said and got in the passenger side. He got in the driver side where she immediately slid over on the bench seat to be right beside him.

"This truck does have its benefits." He kissed her.

"Where we going?" she asked as he turned around the truck in the driveway and started driving toward the highway.

"Barrett's having a small gathering at his house," Tommy said as he drove with her hand on his thigh.

"Will his parents be there?"

"No, I mean, he has his own house. He said they moved him out to make him grow up, but it doesn't seem to be working all that well. He's still a jerk about some things."

"How's his leg? I haven't heard and really haven't asked? I know I should have."

"He has a limp and says he's still has pain. I haven't talked to him much, but the latest gossip is he hangs out with kind of a druggy crowd."

"I don't want to go if it's going to be a drug party. My parents would kill me."

"It's just going to be our class friends there. Claudia's in town. She'll be there. I heard she and Barrett broke up but are trying the friend thing. We'll leave if it's bad. Let's go see. But I promise, when you want to go, we'll go."

*   *   *

Mr. Downs turned into his long drive and felt the familiar rumble of the tires over the cattle guard. The garage light was on making it easier to park Janet's car in her spot. The luxury car had a heater that worked and better headlights for night driving, but it was hard getting in and out of it since the bull fight. He opened the heavy door and swung his left leg out. He steadied himself a moment then lifted his right leg with both hands and placed it on the garage floor.

He took his grandfather's wooden cane from the passenger side and pushed it against the cement floor to help him rise. He grunted at the effort but was soon standing. He hoped no one knew how hard this was for him. So far, he had hidden his injuries pretty well.

He allowed a few more moments to gather his strength then began to walk to the back door. He opened it and ambled through the house to the master bedroom closet. He placed the heel of his right boot inside the curved boot jack and lifted his leg while stepping on the other side and then repeating the process for the left side. He disrobed, carefully folding his pants back on the hanger and his suit jacket on the same wooden hanger. The starched shirt went in the cleaner's basket and his tie on the tie rack.

He retrieved his red and black plaid pajamas he wore in the winter from their place on the top right-hand side of the chest of drawers and put them on with his robe over his shoulders. He slipped his bare feet into his slippers and walked back to the kitchen. He stood at the open door of the fridge staring blankly at the contents. He was not hungry; it was just a habit. He poured a glass of tap water and took his nighttime medications.

The night air was cool and clear. He opened the door to the patio and looked up at the moonlit sky.

"Well Janet, my girl. We had our first Thanksgiving without you. The food was not as good as yours and the laughter not as merry," Mr. Downs mused to his beloved wife in heaven. "Monica did her very best to make everything the same. And she was the perfect hostess. Janet Ann is becoming quite the young lady, becoming more like a young you. She is dating a boy she seems to like, and I would not be surprised if she married him the way she goes on about him. Four was upset like we all were, this being the first Thanksgiving without you, but otherwise he's doing good. Daisy stayed in California, and to be honest, I was happy about it. Her helping most times is far worse than doing nothing. I wind up helping her after a couple of hours. I don't know, honey; we just do the best we can. Barrett moved out. Four and Monica rented a little place for him to do some growing up—learn some responsibility. It might be a good idea, but the police chief has been watching for trouble. Seems he has a party almost every weekend. I worry about that boy. Lulu is doing great at UT, and Randy just heard he's on the board of regents for my alma mater. He's going to do them a great job. I'm sure proud of him. Dawn married Paul again, but I think I already told you that." He pulled his robe across his chest tighter to ward off the cold.

"I'm doing pretty good. I get so lonely, Janet, when I come home to this empty house. I keep thinking you are in another room and I call your name, but you never answer. I wish you had never fallen off that damn ladder. When I found you crumpled on the ground beside the barn, I first thought you were dead. When the doctor said you broke your back, I thought you were paralyzed for sure, but you were tougher than us all. I know you were in pain for over twenty years, but you never complained. I saw you when you were in bed for days because you couldn't move. I watched you go through five operations that gave you some small relief, but never healed you. We were together on this patio when you asked me to let you go. I guess I haven't let you go yet. I miss you, but I know you are in a better place. Good night, Mrs. Downs."

The old man turned and went inside out of the cold air and back down the hall to their bedroom. Most nights it seemed he would lie awake for hours before he would drift off but tonight slumber came quickly, and he slept to his normal four-thirty.

* * *

Barrett's house was much more crowded inside than the number of cars parked in the front indicated. Lourdes and Tommy knew almost everyone there and loud music and laughter filled the little house. As usual Claudia arrived late, dressed in shimmering blue low rider pants and a white fuzzy sweater, looking like a model.

"Wow, look at you fashion queen!" Lourdes shouted above the music to her old adversary.

"You too, babe! How's Austin?" Claudia responded with a genuine grin.

"Fun! How's LA?"

"Crazy! I see so many stars . . . like all the time."

"That sounds awesome. I want to come and see you sometime."

"Totally, you have to. We would own that town if you and I were together." Claudia sounded fake to Lourdes.

She felt Tommy's hand in hers pulling her away.

"Excuse us, Claudia." Tommy stuck his head between them and guided Lourdes to the front door and outside.

"What's wrong?" she asked seeing concern on his face.

"We need to go. I'll explain in the truck."

They got in his pickup and he quickly backed out on the road and headed to town driving the speed limit.

"What's happening?" Lourdes wanted to know.

"Cops are on the way. There's a guy back there named Kenny who used to work for my dad. We fired him because of drug use. Turns out most of his family are dealers in this area. Grass and prescription drugs mostly. Like Oxy."

"I didn't smell any weed. Did you see him selling or something?"

"Yes, I did. Barrett was buying Oxycontin and one of the guys there told me Barrett is hooked on painkillers like really bad. There are a few of the guys in the class below us that got in the painkiller thing. I don't care if somebody wants to use grass. Hell, I've tried it, but that Oxy is bad stuff, Lourdes."

"When did you smoke weed?"

"Once when I was a junior and more when I was a senior and a couple of times at parties this fall in Houston," Tommy admitted.

"What?" Lourdes was shocked. "You could get in so much trouble!"

"I know. I'm so stupid but cops around here don't care if you smoke grass, but they'll haul your ass to jail in a minute if you're caught with pills."

On the horizon the sight of two police cars rapidly approached them.

"I have to tell Claudia," Lourdes said in a panic. "She could get kicked out of school!" She began texting her friend in all caps. *LEAVE THE PARTY NOW RUN COPS ARE COMING.*

"How did you know they were coming?" Lourdes realized she missed that piece of information.

"My oldest brother. He's friends with one of the new cops. They were just talking in the Sonic parking lot when he heard the dispatcher say Barrett Downs. He knew I was going there tonight, so he texted me. We were lucky."

CHAPTER 26

Mr. Downs heard that familiar voice he had been missing coming from Dawn's office.

"Lulu, come in here and tell me how the University of Texas is treating you!" He stood as Lourdes circled behind the desk to hug him.

"Don't she look smarter?" Dawn said enjoying the reunion.

"I don't know about smarter, but I'm really having a great adventure. My grades are good, and I got a new job. I'm selling cars. Toyotas to be exact." Dawn and Mr. Downs both hung on her every word.

"That's a surprise! I've never thought of you as a salesman type, but I'm sure you're good at it. You'd do good at anything you set your mind to," Mr. Downs commented.

Dawn's desk phone rang and she went back to her office closing the door behind her to allow the two friends to catch up.

"Tell me what you like about the job and what you've learned," he asked with bright eyes.

"Well, one thing I've learned is the many bad decisions people make. It's shocking to me so many grown people have no savings."

"Tragic. I see it all the time."

"But credit seems to be available to most of these people," she said in amazement.

"Credit score valuations. The predictive number based on historical action. The score says you have this percentage of debt and that payment history, and somehow it magically tells us what that person will do in the future," he sounded frustrated.

"Yes! How does that work? You taught me that no one knows the future. I watched a young couple with a baby trade in a car they owed more money on than it was worth, to go in debt for six years on another car to look cool, I guess. Who's raising these people?" Lourdes marveled.

"Not Danny and Maria Sanchez!" Mr. Downs responded. "I hope you realize how very blessed you are to have them. The good Lord placed you with them, and they've been a shining example for you every day of your life. Now tell me about fun things in school. Tell me about going to the football games."

"I've been to three games. It's so much fun. Just that one loss to OU, or we would be playing for the national championship. I'm becoming a huge fan, and everyone says we should be just as good next year. It's a great time to be a Longhorn," Lourdes said with the hook 'em horns sign.

"It is never a bad time to be a Longhorn, darlin'. What else have you done for fun?" he asked his exuberant friend.

"I love the live music. I've gone a few times to some concerts with friends."

"And you like your classes?"

"Yes, but they're mostly the first-year basics taught by grad students it seems. There is one weird thing I have noticed, though. Evidently, they think I need special assistance because I'm Mexican. The black kids need the most help, but so do the Mexicans according to the way teachers act. The Asians need no help neither do the Indians or Middle Eastern students. The white kids seem to not need any help either, or I should say, none is offered."

"What do you mean? Give me an example?"

"I don't know . . . Like the midterm test I had in English. The teacher came to me and asked if I needed extra time since English is not my native language. I don't even speak Spanish. She didn't ask the Asian students in the class. It is very offensive because the teacher assumed I needed help. On the other hand, the teacher didn't offer to help the white girl in the class who *is* having a hard time. They just assume I need extra everything because I'm Hispanic. I must need more time or more help in some way. Like 'this brown girl must not be smart enough.' Do you get what I'm saying? The fact that the teacher thinks she is helping, is in fact, making it worse."

"I'm sorry you are not being judged equally on an individual basis," Mr. Downs tried to comfort her. "That's not your fault. That's the system's fault."

"It's even worse for the black kids. The teachers are always acting like it is a miracle they made it to college. There are two black girls on my same dorm floor. One is the daughter of some fancy attorney and the other has a doctor for a dad. They are both wonderful and smart, and they get treated like they are from the ghetto all the time. My roommate Maddie is very intelligent—she's white. Her mother raised her alone, and they didn't have much growing up. She has no dad in her life and her single mother struggled but she did what she had to do for her child. There is no *special* treatment for Maddie. It seems wrong," Lourdes confided to her mentor.

"Another thing, I get asked what I am. Am I Hispanic, Indian, Middle Eastern, Native American? I guess the black hair and the darker skin creates this guessing game."

"You're a very clever young lady, and I'm truly sorry that you are learning about the world away from home. We are not perfect by any means, but I've always been proud of this community and the treatment of all based on their individuality. If people ask what you are, just answer you are a Texan. "

"It's so big. There are tens of thousands of people and Austin traffic is awful, but all in all, I love it. I just feel lost some days."

"That's a by-product of becoming anonymous, my dear. A dangerous thing, anonymity. You know when you walk into mass with your mother, and Maria knows everyone because there's not many people there. When you miss church and there's only forty members, people notice when you're gone. Someone calls her after church and checks on her. When you were in school, the teachers knew the names of their students and the principal knew you all. You were not anonymous in that school. No one was. Anonymity is the enemy of accountability. People who've never lived in a small town make fun of them, but those people can't disappear. It's easier to make poor choices or be a criminal in the big city than here. The news of a local crime spreads fast and if you don't know the person that committed the crime, you probably know someone in his family."

"I understand that now," Lourdes said as the door opened.

"Hate to interrupt," Dawn said. "Four is trying to reach you since you don't turn on your cell phone. He is on line one. Doesn't sound good."

Lourdes stood and mouthed she was going to the kitchen and would be back. Mr. Downs nodded.

"What is it, son?" he asked with a grimace on his face.

*   *   *

Barrett Downs sat in the small jail cell listening to the familiar sound of his father's voice coming from down the hall. He thought to himself, "It's about time someone came to get me out of here." He had been arrested for possession of illegal drugs and disturbing the peace the night before. He was the only one taken to jail, but others were ticketed for minor in possession of alcohol. Barrett had been in jail since midnight and sat alone with OxyContin still in his bloodstream.

"William Barrett Downs the Fifth, you have made bail," the potbellied jailer announced as he unlocked the cell.

"Follow me, and I would stay quiet if I was you. You still got trouble coming," the guard said as they walked to the end of the hall through the final door.

"Come on, son. Let's go home. You and I have to talk, but I don't want to hear one word from you until we get there," Four said sternly and somberly signed the paperwork. He grabbed Barrett's arm as they exited the city police office and jail.

Four got in his F-250 work truck and started the engine as Barrett crawled in the passenger side, slumping down in his seat.

"Put on your damn seat belt," Four ordered as he put on his own.

Barrett complied slowly and began to speak but stopped himself. The ride to Four and Monica's was quiet between father and son. Both knew a single word could release the anger boiling beneath the pair and neither one was ready for the fight to begin. Pop's old truck was in the driveway when they arrived, and Barrett knew things had just gotten worse for him.

Monica stood with her arms crossed at the window with Janet Ann alongside her mother mirroring her stance. Mr. Downs was seated in the den in a leather easy chair when his son and grandson walked in the room with the mother and sister circling behind like a pride of lions about to attack their prey.

"What the hell happened?" Mr. Downs started the inquisition. "I thought you knew the consequences for this."

"I didn't mean for it to happen," Barrett began with his usual lack of accountability. "It's just that everybody was in town for Thanksgiving and word got out real fast that I have a house now and it just spiraled out of control." Barrett tried to block the next verbal blow.

"The party is bad, but what they found at your house, in your pocket, and I bet in your blood right now is the drugs!" Four exploded at his son.

"Hey! Yelling is not going to solve anything. This can be fixed. We just have to get Barrett some help and you are definitely moving back in with us. This little independence experiment was a giant failure." Monica looked at her son.

"Pills? Really, Barrett? Oxy? You are dumber than I thought," Janet Ann piled on.

"I'm the only one here that almost lost a leg!" Barrett was deep in self-pity. "I'm in pain every hour of every day! My whole life went in the toilet when I got hurt. None of you know what I'm going through," Barrett lashed out.

"You're right. None of us know. But is this your solution? Is this how you see handling the problem? Just throw your life away?" Mr. Downs joined in the shouting match.

"Okay, okay. Let's settle down." Four took control of the conversation. "We know a really good treatment facility in Houston. I went there years ago. The truth is, I do know some things about addiction. Mine was alcohol and your mother kept believing in me when most people would have quit. We are not quitting on you, son. But you have to go and get treated, or it will take over your life," Four said tenderly.

Janet Ann was the first to hug her brother, and then all the family members surrounded Barrett in a physical symbol of support. Arrangements were made and Four dropped him off the following Monday at Donavan House Rehabilitation in Houston, Texas.

CHAPTER 27

AUTO SALES THE last day of November were steady at the dealership and Derrick had told Lourdes she was narrowly in the lead. Lourdes had been calculating matters in her head and knew with only six hours to go, all she had to do was leave work to guarantee a win. King David would have to sell two cars if she quit now. There was nothing in the rules about what hours she worked, just how they were prorated. She was competitive but winning on a technicality was not worth violating the fairness rule.

David had a slender cowboy in his office, and Lourdes knew he was a good candidate. He was an oil field hand by the look of his steel toed boots and the items in his truck. He had a duffle bag big enough for a two-week hitch in the back seat of his worn-out pickup. He had a parking sticker for a lot in Sabine Pass on the coast, so he worked offshore. He made good money and if he had been working for a few months, he would have job stability and enough income. She was upset she missed him; she'd have him driving a new Tundra.

She peered out over the lot and saw another cowboy looking guy, casually searching some used vehicles. She thought, "Here I go. We'll see what this brings."

"Hello, I'm Lourdes Sanchez. May I assist you in buying a new vehicle today?" she said with a smile and extended her card to the tall, rough young man.

"Naw, I'm okay. I guess," he shyly responded.

"What are you driving now?" Lourdes asked using her feminine skills to keep the conversation going.

"That old truck there." He nodded to the truck with the sticker.

"Oh, I thought that was your buddy's truck."

"Nope, she's mine. He rode over with me. I live down in San Marcus. We grew up together."

"What's your name?"

"John."

"Hi, John. I see that sticker on your truck. Who do you work for offshore?"

"Rowan—offshore drilling."

"Good outfit, I've heard. How long you been with them?"

"Five years." John was warming up to Lourdes. "Made driller last month."

"Oh, that's great. I see you may be interested in this four-wheel drive Chevy. The keys are right here. Do you want to take it for a drive? I need to get away from this place anyway. There's been a guy following me, and I'm a little scared."

"What guy?" John looked around.

"If he saw me leaving with you, I'm sure he wouldn't bother me."

"Sure, I wanted to drive it anyway."

The duo got in the two-year-old, fully loaded Chevy 2500 Silverado. Lourdes deftly directed him through the normal route they took for test drives.

"I must say, you look good in this truck, John," she said as he parked it back at the dealership next to his truck.

"Did you want to keep your truck or trade it in?"

"Trade it," John found himself answering.

"Let's go on in and get everything started. You are smart to get a used one with such low miles. Follow me, please." Lourdes walked through the showroom past David's office with the young man obediently following.

"Sit right here and let me get some very basic information. Being a driller on a Rowan rig, did you want to pay cash or finance?" She smiled at him.

"Cash," he simply replied.

"That's great! Now let me get that trade-in price for you. Have you already tried to sell it, and do you have a price in mind?"

"A guy on the rig offered me five grand, but I told him no way." He snickered.

"Well, let's see what we can do." Lourdes left the office with a wave.

"Derrick, I need a trade-in on the truck parked over there, please." She pointed to John's old truck parked in front of the showroom. "I need it to be over five thousand for the Chevy 2500. Cash price. No financing."

"Good job. By the way, David's guy blew up. Credit score of four-five-o, and that means N-O," Derrick said letting her know she would win with this sale as the day was almost over.

Lourdes returned with two cold bottles of water and handed one to John. "Cheers," she toasted the grinning young man.

"You married, John?" she asked.

"Nope, I guess I work all the time. And besides, I've seen how some women take all the money from hard working men. My mama and me had it rough when my daddy left us, and I make sure she gets taken care of, you know. I live with her and help pay the bills."

"You're a good son, John. There needs to be more sons like you. And you're right, women can be awful tricky. I was a little bit that way to you, and I owe you an apology." Lourdes felt a wave of remorse.

"Oh, I knew you was letting on some back there, but it's okay. I liked it mostly." He blushed.

Her phone rang and she answered Derrick, "We'll be right there. Come on, John. Let's get this deal done and you home to mama."

CHAPTER 28

2005

LOURDES WAS NOW in her sophomore year and classes were beginning to challenge her. Over the summer she had moved into an apartment with Maddie and taken twelve hours while working selling cars. Maddie was waitressing on weekends and some weeknights at a couple of different trendy places owned by a man that liked smart ass women. And Maddie certainly fit the bill. The fall began very hopeful that Texas would have have a great football team and both girls looked forward to going to games.

Lourdes and Tommy still talked, but the relationship was slowly fading. New guys were constantly hitting on her at work, and boys in her classes often looked her way. The sandy haired boy was usually in the cafeteria when she was there, and he would sit with her and awkwardly flirt. She went home about every six weeks to spend the weekend with her parents and old friends.

She would text Mr. Downs and show her friends how he would write a text back like a formal letter. She actually found it very sweet and would never make fun of him. She would usually get texts from him at five-thirty in the morning when he apparently thought she was awake.

She was making money at the dealership and the crew had learned to respect her after she won the contest. She worked deals with her sales friends to split commissions when she had class and one of her customers asked for her. She was generous and the other salesmen were very fair. The sales banter on Thursday mornings had made her one of the boys which she cherished. A new salesman would come and be gone in a few weeks, just like Tiffany said. She was still answering the phone and rumors swirled that the owner's worthless son, who had hired her, was also entertaining Tiffany in the evenings when his wife was away.

Fall was a busy time. Lourdes attended four home games with bad seats and cheered the Longhorns as loud as anyone. The Halloween parties at the frat houses were a rite of passage for all aspiring attractive women. When she was a freshman, she did not venture away from the campus, but this year she and Maddie were going to make the full party circuit.

Maddie worked until ten and Lourdes planned to meet her at work, then they'd hit the various events. Lourdes had gone to a thrift store and found a boy scout shirt and she put her hair in braided pigtails, wore olive cargo shorts with high brown socks and tennis shoes. She thought she looked cute as she left her apartment for the drive over to pick up Maddie.

As she drove through the south side of campus, she saw parades of students in crazy outfits and found herself laughing at the creativity of some of the costumes. Maddie was just finishing counting out her tips for the night when Lourdes came in the door.

"Don't go too crazy there, Boy Scout!" Maddie teased her.

"What are you supposed to be?" she looked at Maddie who had a white round cutout poster about two feet around that covered her chest and back completely.

"I'm an aspirin," Maddie explained pointing to the word Bayer written across the front. "Like everyone will need me tomorrow morning. It's the perfect pickup line. Get it? Take me with you because you will need me in the morning!" She laughed.

"You're hilarious. I spent three dollars on my outfit. Should be great people watching, if nothing else," Lourdes said as they walked to her Jeep. The evening weather was perfect, cool but not cold. The two drove to the fraternity houses first. The streets were busy with monsters and zombies, but no parking places. Lourdes luckily saw a car leaving and she quickly took its place. The two girls got out of the vehicle and walked toward the first house decorated in fake cobwebs with cardboard caskets in the yard.

The two-story house was vibrating with a heavy bass rap beat and every room was crowded with hormones. Maddie was the first to spot a group of freshman girls wearing skimpy lingerie and angel wings.

"What the hell? Victoria Secret models!" Maddie screamed over the music to Lourdes.

"Dang, they're half naked. In public!" Lourdes shouted in Maddie's ear.

A large group of frat boys circled the scantily dressed girls making sure they had plenty to drink to fuel more poor decisions later in the night. Lourdes and Maddie pushed through the crowd to the back yard where the bar was set up and each got a red Solo cup of beer.

"I saw Jackie and Hillary over by the back fence," Maddie shouted.

"I saw Ellie too. She dates one of these guys." They were in a refrigerator box together with a door and windows drawn on the side and Lourdes approached the girl she knew from the dorm.

"Hey Ellie, what are you guys?" Lourdes asked as Maddie stood beside her looking around.

"Trailer trash!" Ellie answered. Her hair was a mess along with heavy blue eye shadow and one costume makeup black eye.

"This is Tristan. This is Lourdes and Maddie." She introduced her date over the music.

"Great costume! Very original," Maddie said.

"What are you?" Tristan asked Maddie.

"Oh, I'm an aspirin!" she responded.

"Very good! There is a guy here named Jamie who's a bottle of red wine. You should meet him. He's my roommate."

Maddie smiled and nodded.

Lourdes and Maddie walked through the expansive first floor of the house and found the composite pictures of members dating back to the nineteen fifties. They were laughing at the hairstyles of the young men when she spotted the photo of a young William Barrett Downs III. She was seeing him at the same age she was now, and it seemed strange to her. She put her finger on the picture and then found the name of Randy Weyers on the bottom row.

Would the two old men ever imagine a party like this in their fraternity house with half naked girls and people packed together listening to loud rap music? She smiled to herself and could not wait to tell him she saw his and Randy's picture.

CHAPTER 29

BARRETT SEEMED TO be doing well following two months at the rehab center. He had started school in a community college in Fort Worth. It was not the glamorous life of a spoiled college athlete he had anticipated but at least he was away from his parents and he tried to pass a few classes. His limp was not as obvious any longer, but he did have nagging pain. This could be managed with over-the-counter medication, but he occasionally craved the high he once had from OxyContin. The rehab staff had warned him this would happen, and he had a phone number to call if he needed help getting past the deep-seated desires.

He was only taking three classes in the fall semester and he wasn't working. This left him with too much time to waste away on video games and alcohol. Barrett was a handsome young man and retained his athletic physique making it easy for him to meet women.

He lived alone in an upscale apartment close to the school in south Fort Worth. There were strip malls full of restaurants and taverns. He found a sports bar that accepted his fake driver's license, and he became a regular. A group of girls showed up one night for a bachelorette party, and Barrett met Darcy. Darcy McKnight was loud and fun and the life of the party wherever she went. That night she and some friends were hosting a bachelorette party for a bride-to-be.

Barrett sat at the bar and watched the show of girls wearing matching t-shirts bearing the soon to be bride's picture of her standing on a ski boat in a bikini downing a longneck beer. The caption read, "We'll miss you!"

Other regulars were watching a Thursday night NFL game and yelling at the television. Barrett had a four-day thick beard and was wearing a Texas Rangers baseball cap and a long-sleeved polo shirt and jeans with boots when he felt her standing next to him talking to the bartender.

"Hey! Tell the waitress we need another round of shots and this guy is buying." Darcy placed her hand on Barrett's shoulder.

He looked at her and smiled. "Yeah, I'll do that for such a beautiful girl."

"Woo-hoo! I told you bitches I could get us another round!" She turned back to the cheering drunk girls.

"Thanks. Tell me your name so I can fantasize about you tonight when I'm alone in my bed," she whispered to him.

"Barrett. And you are? "

"Darcy McKnight, otherwise known as the future Mrs. Barrett." She leaned in and kissed him.

The two embraced for a moment as the girls at the table cheered again. Darcy was five-eight with a nice figure and long brown hair. She wore her t-shirt with tight jeans and high heels that made her appear six-feet tall. Her face was naturally pretty with deep brown eyes and a cute button nose and small mouth that did not match her brash personality.

Barrett watched her walk away to the bridal party in amazement. He had never met anyone like her. The girls finished their last round, and each came to Barrett under Darcy's orders and kissed his cheek for the drinks. As they were leaving Darcy asked the bartender for a pen and paper. She wrote her name and number and handed it to Barrett. She kissed him on the cheek and ran after the group of girls. Barrett smiled at the note embellished with a little heart.

*   *   *

On Christmas morning across Travis City, traditional celebrations played out with young children running into decorated living rooms to find presents from Santa and colorfully wrapped gifts. For parents and grandparents, it was just as joyful watching the children open them, as it was for the children who received them.

Lourdes had come in two days prior to help her mother prepare for hosting the family Christmas. She had bought her parents a few gifts, mostly clothes, since they never shopped for themselves. She had seen Tommy with a new girlfriend in town while shopping. Lourdes was surprised how much it hurt her to see him with someone else. She had enjoyed a few dates, but none generated any spark. Maybe she was expecting too much from men who were not named Tommy Adams.

On Christmas morning Danny was playing Christmas music extra loud and dancing around like always, and her mother was fussing at him for not helping when there was a knock on the front door. Maria looked outside and saw a black Cadillac.

"Mr. Downs is here. Get the door, Lourdes, while your Daddy puts some clothes on," Maria ordered.

"Hi, Mr. Downs! Merry Christmas, please come in," she greeted the man in the suit and hat.

"Merry Christmas to all of you, too. I won't be long, but I could not wait to give Lulu her gift." Mr. Downs grinned.

Lourdes noticed he was not carrying a package, and he had never before given them anything for Christmas except a bonus and her mother had received that check earlier in the week.

"Come, please and sit down. Would you like some coffee?" Lourdes ushered him to the sofa.

Danny came in from the master bedroom buttoning his shirt. "Hi, Mr. Downs. Merry Christmas."

"Merry Christmas, I have a very special gift for Lulu," Mr. Downs said, and Lourdes looked confused.

"I went to see my friend Randy in Dallas this week and he handed me something that half of Texas would love to have." He pulled an envelope from his jacket. Lourdes stared at the plain white paper as he withdrew two items from inside.

"I have two tickets to the Rose Bowl for the National Championship—UT's playing USC. I want Lulu to go with me." He handed her one of the tickets.

"Oh my God! I cannot believe this!" Lourdes began jumping up and down and screaming with stunned joy. Danny was laughing and slapping his knee, but poor Maria had no idea why they were all so happy.

"Randy's on the Board of Regents now and he got four tickets to the game. He gave me two of them and said I could invite whomever I wanted. And they're great seats! It's going to be fantastic. Janet and I used to go to games before she got hurt, but I haven't been in many years. I thought you would enjoy them more than anyone I know. There is one catch though, we have to go in a private jet and come back the same day," Mr. Downs said happier than anyone.

"Did you say *private jet*? This just keeps getting better! This may be my best Christmas ever!" Lourdes saw her mother's face of confusion. "Well, second-best Christmas. The year I got the Barbie Mansion was the best." Maria smiled and they all laughed.

*   *   *

Monica always had a place in her heart for the underprivileged because of her own background but she had difficulty warming to Darcy. Barrett had brought her home for Christmas saying she had nowhere to go for the holidays. Four tried to pretend he was happy, but he thought this girl would be nothing but trouble. Janet Ann was embarrassed her boyfriend would have to see Darcy the first time he met her family.

"Mother, you have to do something. I don't trust her to be around our family. She's trash," Janet Ann whispered to her mother while they stood at the window watching Darcy and Barrett bring luggage in from his truck on Christmas morning. They had arrived late the night before and stayed in Barrett's old bedroom. Barrett had not told anyone he was bringing her. Maybe he didn't know until the last minute, but now Darcy was there.

Breakfast was very uncomfortable. Darcy was dressed in nothing but a thin men's tank top over a thong when she walked into the kitchen with the shirt barely covering her butt. Barrett knew this was unacceptable, but it seemed they both liked the shock effect. Monica had simply gone to her bedroom, retrieved a robe and draped it over Darcy without saying a word as the two young people snickered.

Barrett seemed to be hoping for a reaction from his family that would punish them all for his accident and subsequent drug problem. He liked Darcy. She was a free spirit and not a snob like his family. She had moved in with Barrett three days after they first met. She was fun and strangely maternal with him. She did his laundry and cooked for him and he felt loved.

Darcy went into Barrett's bathroom and Janet Ann heard the shower, so she peeked in to see her brother alone in his room.

"Listen, you spoiled little dumb ass, this Darcy stunt is over. You need to take her back to the trailer park where you found her. I will not have you drag this family into the garbage dump. I can get past the fact she's not educated and poor. That's not it. If she was sweet and tried to follow the rules of society, I could get to like her. But this behavior is not going to work for me or anyone else in this family. She stole my bracelet!" Janet Ann let her brother have it.

"You don't know if she stole anything. You don't like her because she is different from your snotty sorority friends," Barrett defended his girlfriend.

Janet Ann went to the old piece of luggage with Darcy's clothes and started rifling through the compartments as Barrett tried to wrestle her away.

"And look what I found!" Janet Ann raised the gold band above her head as the door opened and Darcy stood staring at the two siblings.

"You need to pack your things and leave now. I can take you to the bus station and I'll pay for a ticket." Janet Ann showed the evidence in her hand.

"Barrett said I could have it. Didn't you, sugar?" Darcy quickly said.

"Sure, I gave it to her. I knew you wouldn't care. You have like ten bracelets just like that one," Barrett said supporting Darcy.

"Well, I don't have ten of them. Nanny gave me this and it was never yours to give. Even if that *was* the truth," Janet Ann sneered at her brother.

"What's going on? Why are y'all yelling?" Four came into Barrett's bedroom.

"She stole the bracelet Nanny gave me and then lied about it!" Janet Ann pointed to Darcy.

"I gave it to her Dad. She didn't steal it," Barrett quickly responded.

"Where did you find the bracelet, Barrett?" Four asked as Monica came to stand beside her husband.

"I don't know. I don't remember."

"It had to be this morning so that makes no sense," Four pressed his son.

"You said you found it on . . ." Darcy began speaking.

"Not another word, Darcy," Janet Ann interrupted.

"Where was it, Barrett?" Four pushed his now panicked son.

"It doesn't matter. We're leaving. Janet Ann can keep her stupid bracelet! Come on, Darcy. Let's go back where we're not hated."

Four and Monica stood at the bottom of the stairs and watched their son and Darcy leave in silence. Janet Ann marched behind them like a bouncer throwing them out of a bar.

Monica began to cry as she stood on the porch and watched them drive away wondering if she would ever see her son again. A few minutes after they drove away, Mr. Downs pulled in the driveway dressed for Christmas lunch wearing a big smile still thinking of how happy Lourdes was about the game.

Barrett was cussing his family as he sped away west on Main Street when he realized he may not make it without his generous allowance. It was one thing to be principled and another to be broke. He turned around in the highway and went back toward downtown to the bank ATM.

"Why are we coming here?" Darcy asked.

"Getting some money," he answered and drove up to the keypad and slid his bank card in and began the withdrawal process. He knew he could not be overdrawn because he had heard his father say Pop covered the family if they were overdrawn. Barrett entered his pin number and the amount of a thousand dollars. The machine whirled and began rapidly dispensing twenties.

Darcy looked over as he stuffed the cash in his front pocket. Barrett drove off heading west again back to the highway, but he had one more stop. He turned on his blinker and turned left into his grandfather's drive.

"Who lives here?" Darcy was amazed at the estate.

"My grandad. He's gone and we're just going to borrow a couple things. Come on."

Barrett went through the unlocked garage door into the kitchen and through the den to the bedrooms. Darcy followed observing the paintings and beautiful furnishings. He returned from the master bedroom with a frown on his face.

"What are you looking for?" she asked.

"I know where it is." Barrett walked back outside to the old truck. He opened the unlocked door and pushed the button to open the glove compartment and took his grandfather's pistol in the leather holster.

CHAPTER 30

LOURDES SAT IN the passenger seat while Mr. Downs drove down the highway east of Travis City to the small county airport. He had picked her up in his car at her parent's at seven a.m. on January 4, 2006. The plane should be there by seven-thirty if the weather held clear. Mr. Downs parked the car and got out wearing his hat, a camel-hair blazer, burnt orange button down shirt with a white longhorn emblem on the pocket. Lourdes had a new leather fringe western jacket and jeans with a white long-sleeved t-shirt with University of Texas across her chest. Her jeans were tucked in her cowboy boots with UT in white across the front of the tall shafts above the instep. There would be no doubt who they were rooting for when they walked into the stadium later that day.

Mr. Downs checked his watch and looked in the morning sky for their plane. Lourdes paced trying to release her nervous energy. She was sure the next few hours would be remembered her whole life. Mr. Downs seemed perturbed at the plane not being there, but they were early.

"Did you bring binoculars?" he asked while his eyes were fixed on the horizon.

"In my bag. I also have a small blanket and a thermos. I have room if you want to add something."

"Okay, put my binoculars in your bag. They're on the back seat. The plane should be here," he sounded agitated.

Soon a tiny moving dot appeared in the northern sky and quickly took on the unmistakable outline of a small jet plane. The noise came next as the sleek Cessna Citation jet landed and turned back to taxi to the only two people standing on the tarmac.

"Here we go!" Mr. Downs said with the excitement of a child on a carnival ride.

The plane stopped and the door opened. Stairs folded down in front of the old man and young lady. A man of about forty dressed in navy slacks and a short sleeved white shirt with gold epaulets on his shoulders came down the stairs and over the sound of the twin mounted jet engines introduced himself as one of the pilots. The pilot took Lourdes' bag and followed them inside the cabin.

There were six comfortable cabin chairs available as they walked bent over to reach their chosen seats on either side of the center aisle. The pilot took her bag to a storage locker in the rear of the plane and returned to find the two passengers adjusting their seatbelts.

"There's a cooler with water and soft drinks in the back and a very small restroom. We expect to be at Bob Hope airport in about three and half hours. In case you couldn't hear me outside, my name is Lloyd, and our captain is Mickey. Once we are in the air you can come up to the cockpit if you need anything. Now, if you're ready, let's go to the Rose Bowl."

The plane taxied to the end of the runway. The nose was positioned straight forward. Lourdes could feel the plane vibrate and heard the engines revving but they remained still. She turned to her right seeing no concern on Mr. Downs' face which gave her comfort. Suddenly the brakes were released, and the jet lurched forward and began to speed down the runway. She watched through the cockpit window and could see the oak trees on the horizon getting closer. She looked out her window and saw the ground go by in a blur of speed when she started to hear a different sound and feel the plane lifting in the air. She watched as the trees now were below her, and she could see the skeet range from the air and a little further away, her hometown.

The plane banked a hard right placing her in position to briefly see her Daddy's shop and her house before the plane leveled out and she remembered to breathe.

"I cannot believe we are in a private jet," she declared as much to herself as well as to her host.

"How much is this going to cost?" she blurted out.

"More money than you need to know about, but I'm going to spend some of my kid's inheritance," Mr. Downs joked.

"Have you heard anything around town about Barrett?" he asked.

"Just that he came into town with some new girl but went back to Fort Worth," she answered knowing more but not wanting to continue.

"If you know that, then you know why I'm willing to spend a little money on some diversion. But I'm not going to let that bother me on this day. This is my treat to myself, thanks to Randy and you. Even I need some fun every twenty years or so!" His smile said it all.

The flight was incredibly enjoyable for Lourdes. She went to the cockpit and asked questions. She kept her head turned looking out the window watching the brown and red landscape below her across the desert southwest. She thrilled at the sight of the Grand Canyon from twenty thousand feet. Mr. Downs had leaned back and slept a couple of hours to pass the time and was asleep when Lourdes gently shook his arm.

"We're here, Mr. Downs. Flying over Los Angeles now. Lloyd said we should land in less than ten minutes."

After landing, Lourdes was amazed to see the rows of private jets lined up bringing well-to-do fans to watch the game. They taxied to an area especially zoned for smaller planes not far from various limousines ferrying the passengers away into the vast city.

"Randy said to look for a white Rolls Royce," Mr. Downs read a text on his phone.

"There it is!" Lourdes shouted as she saw a white Rolls with a chauffeur holding a sign that simply read DOWNS. Lloyd came back through the cockpit and turned the locked pressurized door and unfolded the steps.

"Watch your step, sir," he said as the older man picked his way down the stairs into the sixty-eight degree sunshine followed by the overwhelmed young lady doing her best to act like this was normal.

"We'll be here after the game. Just remember to look for the number on the plane. I have it written on this card. Have fun and hook 'em horns!" Lloyd shook Mr. Downs' hand.

The pair walked to the gleaming white car. The chauffeur shook Mr.

Downs hand, opened the back door, and took the bag from Lourdes then placed it in the opened trunk.

"Welcome to Los Angeles. We're about ten miles from the Rose Bowl and my instructions are to take you to Mr. and Mrs. Weyers' house for a meal before the game this evening. I'll also be returning you to the airport," the man in the black uniform said in a professional manner.

"What's your name?" Lourdes asked.

"It's Thomas, miss."

"Thank you, Thomas. You own a beautiful car. My name is Lourdes Sanchez, and this is Mr. Downs. We are from Travis City, Texas," Lourdes bubbled over with sweet excitement.

"Well, thank you for saying so but it's not my car. It belongs to the service I work for," he replied smiling at her innocence and thought how this lecherous old man was taking advantage of a naïve girl. But then again, he saw it too often in this city.

"Well, it sure is nice," Lourdes said to the man in the rearview mirror.

"I just let Randy know we are on our way. I'm sure glad you came along with me, Lulu. This'll be a story you can tell all your friends back in Austin." He smiled at the young woman who kept her eyes peeled for a celebrity and foolishly thought she might see Claudia. Lourdes laughed at herself. She was not on Main Street in Travis City; she was in the second biggest city in the country.

She had experienced traffic in Austin and occasionally on trips to Dallas, but LA was on a different level. The ten-mile distance took over an hour before the Rolls pulled into the curved entrance of a tile roofed residence in Pasadena with the top rows of the Rose Bowl visible a few hundred yards away.

"Mr. Downs, thank you again. This is the nicest thing ever. You've been so good to me and my family since I was a child. I can never repay you."

"You've already repaid me by being the class valedictorian and representing our little town with such grace and intelligence at UT. I just wanted to express my thanks to you in a way you would never forget." Mr. Downs loved spoiling his grateful friend.

The driver pulled under the porte cochere then rushed to open Lourdes' door first and then Mr. Downs'. He retrieved the bag from the trunk and handed a card with his cell phone to Mr. Downs.

"I will be monitoring the game, and I'll be back at this address immediately after. The traffic will be bad, but I do know a couple of detours." He smiled and felt different about the old man and the young beauty. Maybe there were good people left in the world.

Lourdes let her eyes search the horizon of the neighborhood with the huge stadium looming to her west. Mr. Downs was about to knock on the door when it opened to his lifelong friend greeting him with open arms.

"Hey sum bitch! Welcome to beautiful California!" Randy greeted his old friend with a hug.

"Hey sum bitch!" Mr. Downs responded in kind.

"Well, look at little Lourdes all grown up and pretty as a newborn calf." Randy hugged the girl he had known since she was ten.

"When I handed those tickets to this old man the very first thing he said was, 'I'm gonna take Lulu!' And here you both are. Vickie's in the kitchen on the phone. Oh hell, she's always on the phone. Did Billy tell you why I gave him the tickets?" Randy asked as they walked through the massive living room to the sound of Vickie talking loudly.

"You see I got these two extra tickets and I told Vickie and she said she wanted to invite some rich customer of hers, and I told her there's no way I'm gonna sit with some pretentious SOB watching the game of the year. So I said Billy should get them and she was teetering, but then Billy said he wanted to invite you and she smiled so big it may have busted through her Botox." Randy laughed as they arrived in the kitchen just in time to hear Vickie end her call.

"How did you get this house right next to the stadium?" Mr. Downs asked.

"We bought it last year before we came out for the game against Michigan. We just got lucky that Texas is right back out here this year. We could be at the hotel with the team and the board, but this is way better," Vickie answered.

"It's just so beautiful," Lourdes said thinking how great it was to know rich and powerful people.

"Honey, I love that outfit. You look like a real Texas girl," Vickie complimented the young woman.

"Thanks, I got the jacket at the store you told me about. I spent a whole commission check on it, but I do love it." Lourdes twirled around letting the leather fringe dance in the air.

"The caterers are in traffic, but they should be here soon. We'll eat and walk over to the stadium at five, so plenty of time for a nap for you two old men," Vickie teased.

*   *   *

Janet Ann and Monica sat in the den with a piece of warm pound cake on dessert plates of the family china positioned in their laps. Monica had taken Janet Ann through the process that allowed the cake to be baked to the proper density with a brown crust.

"This is really good, Mom, if I do say so myself," Janet Ann complimented her own baking although Monica guided her through each detail.

"It's a simple recipe, but I love the way Nanny made it. She always used brown eggs to get a golden color." Monica slowly placed the warm cake in her mouth and let the flavor and aroma flow through her senses.

"Have you heard from Barrett?" Janet Ann finally broached the sensitive subject.

"No." Monica could hardly talk about her son.

"I'm sorry, Mom. It's like he has to learn everything the hardest way possible, but he'll be back." She tried to comfort her mother.

"I know. I just hope he stays away from the drugs that sent him down this path. You need to pray for him. He is your brother."

"I do, Mom, but he sure makes it hard."

"What do you think of Ben?" Janet Ann asked her mother about the boy who came for a couple of days to meet Four and Monica.

"He was delightful, sweetie. So smart and appears to be ambitious according to your dad. Do you feel in your deepest soul he's the one?" Monica asked her daughter already knowing the answer.

"I do, Mama. He loves me, too."

"Tell me one thing that he did or said that made you know."

"There was this girl drunk at a party making a real fool of herself. You see it all the time in college. I barely knew her, but apparently she had a big fight with her boyfriend and was falling all over a couple guys for attention. Ben said we needed to get her home. He didn't know her at all, but he saw the danger she could be in. We walked over, I told her who I was, and we gently guided her away and left the party and took her to her apartment. Her roommate thanked us for getting her there safely. When we got back in the car, I asked Ben why he had helped her and he simply said it was the right thing to do."

"I get that. A moral compass is important," Monica said softly. "Your father and grandfather have that compass. I just hope your brother has it planted somewhere deep in his soul."

The two were silent as the television presented sports' anchors talking about the game that night in Pasadena. The sound was turned low when Monica noticed the iconic Open Road Stetson hat worn by her father-in-law as he stepped off a private jet with Lourdes behind him.

"Look!" Monica pointed to the television and turned it up to hear what the announcer was saying.

"Big rich Texans have been arriving in private jets all day for this evening's big game." The camera panned the row of jets and limousines taking in the sight of Mr. Downs and Lourdes getting in the white Rolls Royce.

"Oh my gosh, I can't believe they're on TV! Look at Pop. The dapper old man and Lourdes with her cool leather jacket. Oh crap, I hope no one thinks he's with some young thing! She's almost family. I was so thrilled to hear they were going, but this kind of looks bad," Janet Ann commented.

"No it doesn't! No one in their right mind would think that." Monica assured her.

"I hope you are right, but it's a creepy world we live in these days," Janet Ann replied.

*   *   *

The undefeated, number one ranked team in the country, the USC Trojans, were seven-point favorites over the undefeated number two Texas Longhorns at kick off. Lourdes sat twenty rows up on the forty-five-yard line. Vickie sat on her right and the mother of one of the players to her left. Lourdes asked which player was her son, and the large woman pointed out one of the offensive linemen, her pride overflowing. "There he is. Right there," spoken with a love only a mother can declare.

The game raged back and forth. Lourdes stood and cheered when the Longhorns scored then bit her fingernails when the Trojans roared back. The game had historic swings of momentum for each team and the cheering never stopped. The game came down to one dramatic play with the Horns trailing by five with just twenty-six seconds to go. Fourth and five from the Trojan nine-yard line. Many have called it the greatest college game of all time.

There was no script, no author's imagination, only the primeval desire of highly trained young men at the height of their physical abilities going to war on a field of grass on a January night in Southern California. The mother next to Lourdes watched her son, the big offensive tackle, execute a perfect block while everyone else watched the quarterback race to the corner and score. Lourdes leaped in the air and bounced up and down with Vickie and the player's mom as all the fans around her were elevated to be the best team in the nation. The Longhorn fans couldn't tell you how long they stayed in the stadium that night. No one except Trojan fans wanted to leave. The emotion of the game was overwhelming to the fans with cameras going off constantly in the crowd. Randy finally led them to the exit and across the parking lot to their home. The white Rolls sat in front with the driver seated behind the wheel. He saw his passengers approaching and exited to stand waiting by his car.

"Congratulations! That was the best game I've ever heard on the radio, even though I could also hear the crowd and the public announcer at the same time," Thomas greeted them with his own excitement.

"Thank you, Thomas! *It was so great!*" Lourdes was the only one left with sufficient energy to speak but her voice was very hoarse.

"Please allow us a few minutes to freshen up and we'll be right back," Mr. Downs said as they walked past the car to go inside.

"Very good, sir." Thomas nodded.

"Would you like a soft drink or do you need to use the restroom?" Lourdes asked.

"That would be very nice. miss. Thank you." Thomas thought to himself, "That young lady is one of the nicest people. I wonder if all young Texans are like her. "

The plane did not land until six-thirty a.m. Texas time and both passengers were jolted awake by the landing. Lloyd opened the door to the chilly January morning, and they walked slowly down the steps to the parked car. Lourdes watched Mr. Downs open the driver side and she opened her side and sat on the cold leather seats. The keys were where he left them on the floorboard under his seat.

"You left the keys in the car the whole time?" she asked confused.

"Why would I want to take keys with me on the trip. Keys are something you lose and then we would be in a big mess. If I always leave the keys in the car, I know where they are," he said having clearly thought this through before.

"But someone could steal the car," Lourdes responded logically as he pulled away from the airport.

"I am nearly seventy years old and not once has anyone stolen my car. I've never spent one second looking for keys because I know where they are. How many hours have you spent searching for keys in your young life?"

"I don't know, but I live in Austin now and not Travis City, so I have to lock everything," Lourdes said.

"True, but why would you want to live anywhere that you needed to lock your car, if you didn't have to." Mr. Downs drove into her parent's driveway and saw the light come on in the living room.

CHAPTER 31

MONICA SAT ALONE in her bedroom in the empty house. Barrett was not responding to any calls or texts and she was worried. Earlier in the week, Four had driven to the rented apartment in Fort Worth to find it empty. The manager said Barrett had moved out a week before and rent was unpaid. The credit card showed use for gasoline and food in the same area so that was a good sign. He had not gone far.

Janet Ann had returned to Dallas to complete her junior year at SMU but checked on her distraught mother regularly. She was angry with her brother for what he was doing to the family. Barrett had never been bright, but at least he had never been a criminal. This new girl could lead him down a path of no return, and they all knew how much danger Darcy represented. He was easily manipulated by the opposite sex, and Darcy obviously knew how to exploit his vulnerabilities.

Monica had grown obsessed with having her phone close by to make sure she did not miss a call or text from her son. Mr. Downs had called Four to tell him his pistol was stolen but there did not appear to be anything else missing. Monica and Janet Ann were not told about the gun. It would make them both more worried.

* * *

"Can you get any more cash? We're gonna need more money pretty soon," Darcy asked Barrett. They had rented a travel trailer in a RV park.

"I don't know. I thought you were making good money at the club," he responded not wanting to let her know he had already attempted a withdrawal that had been rejected.

"I do, but I'm not supporting you," Darcy declared. "I've seen two of the most expensive houses I have ever been in. You're rich, so my dancing money is mine!" She worked occasionally at a seedy strip club next to a truck stop. A busy night could bring her four to five hundred bucks, and she usually worked ten shifts a month.

"All that nice stuff you saw, I don't want! And I won't be getting anything from them unless I live the way they want me to. My grandfather is the tightest old bastard in the world. He never spends any money. He sure as hell isn't going to hand out any money to me. My mom grew up poor and now she acts all high and mighty. My dad was a drunk when I was younger, and now he gets all preachy to me. And my sister, you already know, has it out for us both. The whole bunch takes my sister's side on everything!" Barrett argued.

"Well, at least get some kind of job. What *can* you do?" she asked.

"I've never had to work, but I'm sure I can get something," he stated.

"Good. We'll be fine," she assured him.

"I don't even know how to find a job. How do you?" Barrett was beginning to realize how unprepared he was for the real world.

*   *   *

When Lourdes returned to Austin for the spring semester, she rather unexpectedly found herself a minor celebrity. The school newspaper, The Daily Texan, had published a series of three photos of Lourdes shot during the winning play on a half-page spread. The first one was a picture of pure anxiety showing her clinched right fist pushed to her lips, the second was her eyes widening at the sight of the play unfolding and her hands willing the player to run, and the third epitomized the pure joy of the winning play. The caption read, "This beautiful Texas co-ed tells you all you need to know about the greatest game ever played." The issue printed the most copies ever in the history of the school and every student saved a copy in their dorm or apartment.

Lourdes was not aware of the photo until she got a call from her friend Beth.

"Have you seen it?" Beth questioned with excitement.

"Seen what?" Lourdes asked as she walked out of her apartment heading to her first class of the spring semester.

"Lourdes, you are a star! Your picture, or I should say three pictures, are in The Daily Texan from the game."

"What? Three pictures? Who am I with?"

"Just you!"

"Wow, I can't wait to see it! Thanks for calling," Lourdes was always happy to hear from her friend.

Lourdes cranked her Jeep and drove to her first class on the cool January morning. She realized she was wearing the same jacket she wore on the night of the game and wondered if anyone would notice. She parked in the student lot and began the half mile walk across the expansive campus to her first class, Economics 211.

Her long black hair was gleaming in the morning sunshine, her olive skin glowed, and her dark eyes stared ahead through the meandering students when she heard the first comment.

"That's her. Man! She's even hotter in person."

"She's wearing that same jacket. It looks expensive."

"She looks like a rich snob."

Lourdes tried not to turn to see who the comments were coming from and suddenly felt uncomfortable. She saw a metal rack with the papers stacked and a line of kids getting their copy of The Daily Texan. She stood behind a couple of guys talking about the game and they grabbed a copy each. Lourdes took the top paper off the dwindling stack not wanting to look through it in public.

"Would you sign my copy?" a younger looking boy asked appearing to her right.

"Mine too? Wow, you're even prettier in person," a girl from the growing crowd spoke.

Soon a group of twenty or so classmates were requesting her to sign their paper. She did not want to be rude, but she felt very nervous at the attention. Last semester she would have been just another girl walking to class with the occasional look from a boy, but today she was elevated to celebrity status over three pictures she had no idea were taken.

Lourdes took the pen someone handed her and began signing her name and even personalizing, "To Jerry, Lourdes Sanchez." The crowd of curious undergraduates grew larger, and soon she was needing to get to her class and was not quite sure what to do.

"Thank you very much, but I have to get to class," she demurely stated.

A collective sigh of disappointment came across the remaining group as she trotted away toward her Monday morning class. She found the lecture room number and was just in time to take a seat.

"I am Doctor Riesling. This is Econ 211 so if you are in the wrong class, now would be a good time to move along. You miss, I recognize you as a model for our school paper, so I'm not sure you need to be here." He stared at Lourdes as he spoke, and she was embarrassed to be singled out.

"No sir, this is my class," she answered politely.

"My fault, we don't usually have models in this class," he said sarcastically and the class laughed.

"I'm not a model, sir. I was at the game and my picture was taken by someone at The Daily Texan. I wasn't even aware of it until this morning." She remained polite.

"But to make sure everyone noticed you, I see you are wearing the same jacket."

"That was a coincidence. As I said, I wasn't aware of it until this morning, and I wore it because it was cold." Now Lourdes was defending herself.

"All right, we have spent entirely too much time on this subject, so let's discuss why the university pays me. There is a syllabus of required reading and test dates for you, so please pretend you care and take one before you leave."

Professor Edward Riesling was in his mid to late thirties. He wore his usual attire of navy blazer, khaki pants, and worn brown leather loafers. He was handsome in a confident way with a neatly trimmed, full beard. His hair was over his ears and collar but looked styled. He thought very highly of himself. As he lectured, he paced back and forth, arrogantly authoritative in his delivery.

Lourdes had read the entire textbook over Christmas as she was warned of this professor's high standards. She preferred to hand write notes while other students used their laptops. Her retention was excellent on anything she wrote compared to typing. She listened intently as the professor delivered his opinions on market forces and analytics. The topics were very interesting to Lourdes. She had been challenged over the years in discussions with Mr. Downs which usually ended with him encouraging her to dig deeper.

The bell rang and signaled the class was over, and she waited in line behind the other students to pick up the syllabus. A student behind her asked about the game and another told her he had a friend who went to the game.

"I expect you to not be a disturbance in this class from now on, miss," Professor Riesling half smiled at her. "I'm the only star in this room."

"Yes, sir," was all Lourdes replied and then left the room only to find another group of students waiting on her with outstretched newspapers in the hall.

*   *   *

The conference room at the bank was stuffy from the heater, not to mention the nine people gathered for the annual board meeting on the last Friday in January. Three presentations were given by the officers on the economic environment of the city and possible expansion on the horizon. The bank's chief financial officer made a dry but pleasing account of the 2005 Annual Report showing a nine percent profit for the year. An investment banking consultant made an hour-long presentation regarding predictive analytics of the financial sector showing great optimism from the stock market experts.

Mr. Downs owned ninety percent of the outstanding bank stock. This had been accumulated over the past forty years primarily from distant cousins who fell on hard times or bad decisions. The other ten percent was held by four board members and two percent to the employees. The board was comprised of citizens of the community who were elected by unanimous vote thirty years prior when Mr. Downs became president. He sold each of the four board members two percent each at a discounted price with the caveat they had a lifetime obligation to serve on the board. They officially met once a year and meetings were called for emergencies throughout the year.

At this particular meeting, Mr. Downs talked of the big championship football game and even the rival Aggies in the room had to admit the game had been very entertaining. The board was now comprised of all old people and for the first time, it was painfully obvious.

One old rancher named Wilburn "Buck" Horn was now on a walker. Ms. Ovie Williams, who owned the furniture store, was in a wheelchair. Cab Morris, a retired paving contractor couldn't hear thunder, and Hubert "Hubie" Little, the oil driller, thought he was in Saudi Arabia half the time. Dawn, who had served as the corporate secretary for the last twenty-five years, was sitting in the corner fanning her cleavage.

"Thanks for the reports from all three of you. I now would ask you to leave us so the board, along with Dawn, can have our closed session," Mr. Downs announced.

"Cab! Cab, you stay here with us." Mr. Downs stopped the old man from leaving with the rest while Dawn suppressed a laugh. The room was now just the four-elderly board of directors, Mr. Downs, and Dawn.

"What the hell happened to us?" Mr. Downs exclaimed as the door closed.

"We got old," Buck stated the obvious. "Hell, I'm lucky to be here. I was in the hospital yesterday."

"I know. I know we've all gotten old. I want every one of us, including me, to figure out what the future holds for this bank. Buck, who could you recommend to replace you?"

"I got a nephew, Merle's boy. He's smart as he can be. Maybe him."

"You mean Donnie? Oh, hell no! We ain't putting no funny boy on the board," Hubie disagreed.

"He's not a funny boy. Just hasn't found the right girl yet," Buck defended his nephew.

"He's fifty!" Hubie hollered back at Buck. "When do you think that's gonna happen, Buck?"

"Stop it! Donnie is fine. He's an attorney, and we could use a good lawyer on the board. I'm sure you are not his type, Hubie." Mr. Downs quashed the discussion about Donnie.

"Ms. Ovie, who are you thinking about?" Mr. Downs asked.

"My daughter, Susie. She's been running the store with her husband Larry for the last few years since they moved back from Oklahoma City."

"I think she would be wonderful. Came back to be home. That's noble of her," Mr. Downs said.

"And her husband finally got out of the pen," Hubie said under his breath.

"He did not go to the pen, Hubie! It was community service. He was sitting in his parked car drinking, and they called it a DUI. Besides, I'm not nominating Larry anyway," Ms. Ovie was annoyed with Hubie's negativity.

"Cab, who do you have in mind?" Mr. Downs raised his voice so the man could hear better.

"For what?" Cab asked, and Dawn lost it and began to laugh hysterically.

"The board. Who would you like to replace you?" Mr. Downs asked again, waving at Dawn to hush.

"Oh, I guess since I don't have any family, I think Ms. Flores at City Bakery would be good."

"The cook?" Hubie asked.

"She owns the bakery. Bought it five years ago. Billy loaned her the money. She sees everyone in this town at least once a week. The fatter folks three or four times a week." Cab laughed at his own joke. "She knows everyone and knows the ones that treat her nice and the ones that don't. For me, anybody that treats her bad, don't deserve a loan from us," Cab endorsed his choice.

"Cab, that was very thoughtful and I understand your choice." Mr. Downs nodded at his old friend.

"Okay, Hubie. This better be a saint because you have belittled everyone else's nominée," Mr. Downs asked the old man.

"George Douglas."

"The horseshoe guy?" Buck asked.

"No, his son the veterinarian. He's like Ms. Flores and Susie, seeing people in the community every day. That's what made us all work so good on the board. We knew what was happening in our town. Ovie stopped us from loaning to that con man she sniffed out, and he took

Albertville for close to a million I heard. Cab was the one who got that developer who was turned down by some other outfit, but we did great with him here. The secret is all of us love our town and we want to keep it thriving. Well, I guess everyone we talked about would do great too . . . even the attorney."

"Thank you all. I think it's important for us to begin the transition as soon as possible. Please notify your recommended member and have them contact Dawn, and she'll get the paperwork started. I've been very proud to have had you all in this room with me for a generation. We've done well because of your guidance and passion. Meeting adjourned."

CHAPTER 32

LOURDES WOKE EARLY on Easter morning to the sounds of her mother cooking and her dad's music. She smiled from her bed at the sweet memories of her youth. She remembered a sunrise service at age twelve when she had a brand-new dress and some days she longed for those innocent times. Back then they lived in the old home and there was no gourmet kitchen and no built-in speakers. It was just a tiny galley and a boom box on the floor beside the old green sofa. She thought of the photograph of herself with her parents and the priest. That photo was so bittersweet for her. Who was she the day before? Did her real mother throw her away? As confident and smart and loved as she was, there was still that scar on her heart.

"You better be getting up, Lourdes. I have your dress ironed and ready." Maria stuck her head in the bedroom.

"Okay, Mama. I'm up." She slowly got up and immediately began making the bed. It was a habit that never changed; dorm room, apartment, lake houses with Tommy, she always made the bed. She got in the shower and washed her long hair. She finished and brushed out the tangles and walked to breakfast with her robe warmly wrapped around her.

She had been a coffee drinker for a few years now, but always wanted cream and sugar. She sat at her spot and her mother presented her with two slices of thick cut bacon, two scrambled eggs, a large flour tortilla fresh from a seasoned black iron skillet and Maria's homemade salsa. Danny sat with his black coffee and just looked at his daughter seeing the subtle changes of her maturing. Maria sat with her plate full and began to eat and noticed her husband looking at their daughter.

"What are you thinking, Danny?" Maria asked.

"I was thinking I wish she was a little girl again," Danny said in a melancholy tone.

"Sorry, Daddy. I can't go back. You're stuck with this version for now." Lourdes looked at her father and saw the sweetness in his eyes.

"Oh, I love all the versions of you, but I can still miss the little one." Danny smiled at his blessing.

The Sanchez family finished their breakfast and prepared for two services. Danny went to sunrise mass with Maria and Lourdes each year as a family tradition. They drove together in the predawn darkness. The service attendance had dwindled lately. Maybe it was the hour or just the reduced membership. They parked and walked to the benches set up facing the east. The original Catholic church was built on this location in 1858. The Easter service placed benches where the original pews had been in honor of the original, humble church that had burned down in 1910. The state had placed a historical marker at the site.

Maria spoke to the other parishioners as they walked in from the parking area. The sun was making its presence known with the first weak light fading the stars on the horizon. The minutes before dawn are the coldest of the day and a quiet chill fell over the whispering worshippers.

The bright orb rose against the eastern skyline and they all sang Christ the Lord is Risen Today. The priest read John 20: 1-9 where Mary of Magdala discovers the empty tomb. Lourdes sat between her parents on the simple bench and felt the old familiar comfort from her childhood. The group stood and listened to the final prayer on the cool morning.

As they drove home, Lourdes gazed out the backseat window and saw the faded old farmhouse and tin building. It was rusted and falling down, and she thought of the builder of the world's ugliest helicopter. Was it the journey or destination? Her life was mostly journey now.

She would be in school for a couple more years and then where would the next expedition begin? Lost in her thoughts, they were soon home again to await the next service.

Danny and Lourdes left at ten thirty as Maria said she would prepare lunch and see them after their Baptist service. Danny loved the time he had alone with Lourdes. He could tease and embarrass her, but she was getting too old for that now. They were mostly silent on the way to church, and Danny parked in a place in the back. The two walked into the morning service with women in colorful dresses and men in suits and bright ties. Danny and Lourdes saw a young father with a little girl all dressed up in a pale blue and white dress topped off with a white bonnet.

"She's adorable," Danny said to the proud daddy.

"Thank you. She's a handful sometimes." The man lifted his toddler into his arms to speed up the pace.

"Enjoy it, because in the blink of an eye they're grown." Danny nodded knowingly at Lourdes.

Lourdes waved at the little girl and playfully made faces to make the child smile. The father turned to take the child to the nursery, and Lourdes and Danny went to the sanctuary. They entered the church by a side door, and Lourdes scanned the auditorium for familiar faces. She spotted Janet Ann walking in with Monica and Four. Barrett was not with them. She knew he'd been a problem lately. Small town gossip easily reached her in Austin.

She saw Mr. Downs seated alone with his balding head looking down at the program awaiting his son's family. He never wore his hat in church. That would be disrespectful, he would say. The organ music began signaling the start of the service, and Lourdes sat beside her father on his favorite pew.

The minister of music stood behind the pulpit. "All rise and join me in singing all four verses of hymn 414, Crown Him with Many Crowns." Lourdes and Danny joined the rest of the church in standing. The pipe organ and the piano joined with the choir and the congregation as every voice sang the familiar hymn. Lourdes sang too but loved to hear her father sing loudly and poorly. She smiled every time at how joyfully he sang but he was always off key. She teased him once and he simply said, "I am not singing for man. I am singing for God."

After a prayer, some announcements, and another hymn, an older man in the community came forward for a solo of The Old Rugged Cross. He carried an acoustic guitar with him and simply smiled and began playing the melody.

His voice was raspy and deep but very reverent. The guitar played with no fanfare but matched his melodic expression. The congregation sat in silence as they were collectively entranced by the man and the immense passion in his delivery. Lourdes had no idea the man singing had been there the day she was found in the dumpster. She had joined the Baptist church when she was eleven even though her mother wanted her to be Catholic. The sound of The Old Rugged Cross brought her back to feeling closer to God. She had not attended a single church service in Austin and now felt a pang of guilt as the last of the song was finished and a rare round of applause filled the sanctuary.

"Thank you, Mr. Ray! That was beautiful. God gave you a wonderful talent," the pastor complimented him. Mr. Ray smiled and humbly bowed as he walked to his pew.

"Does God have a plan for you? Today is a sacred day in the church, we celebrate the resurrection of Jesus Christ our Lord from the grave after he died for the sins of all mankind. The tomb could not hold Him for God had other plans. Just as God has plans for you. Don't let your *tomb* keep you from being the best you can be. God has a plan for each of us. Do you know what God has planned for you? Make your life count. Don't waste the fact that God sent His Son for you! Turn to the Word and pray. Study God's Word and talk with the Almighty. You can be in the biggest congregation or sitting alone in your car but speak to him. Say, 'Lord I need to talk.' Isn't that amazing? We can speak to the Creator of everything!"

Lourdes felt like the pastor was speaking directly to her. How did he know the message was what she needed? The song brought her to a place she needed to be, and the words of the pastor filled her needs. She was not evil. She had few sins to confess, but she had an empty place in her heart because she didn't know who she was. She was Lourdes Sanchez, daughter of Danny and Maria, ninety nine percent of the time, but that one percent created so much consternation. Today she wondered if her dumpster was the tomb she overcame. Maybe there was some reason she was spared. She closed her eyes and prayed in her mind, "God, please give me guidance and peace. Your will be done. Amen."

The hymn of invitation was starting, and she stood with her daddy and sang Just As I Am. The benediction was given, and the pipe organ filled the sanctuary with a processional hymn. Danny and Lourdes walked to the left side of the church to speak to the Downs family who were standing.

"Hi, Mr. Downs. Happy Easter," she greeted him.

"Happy Easter." He looked up with a big smile. Mr. Downs shook Danny's hand. "Mr. Sanchez, happy Easter to you and your family."

Lourdes felt an arm around her and saw it was Janet Ann. She whispered to Lourdes, "Barrett's in jail."

*　*　*

Easter Sunday was no different to the prisoners and the jailers at the Tarrant County Jail. It was just another day with the same routine. Barrett walked in his orange coveralls to the open area and found a seat alone. He was scared and angry. When he called four days ago, his father had simply said he needed to stay in jail awhile to learn a lesson. The only lesson he was learning is that he had no family anymore. Who allows a twenty-year-old to be left alone in a jail for justly defending his girl?

He had been arrested three nights prior at the trailer park. A customer from the strip club followed Darcy home. She was usually careful when leaving but did not notice the black pickup pulling in behind her at the RV Park. Darcy had put a t-shirt and jean shorts over her skimpy club outfit to save time and parked next to Barrett's pickup in front of the trailer. The truck driver had turned off his headlights, so she didn't notice him until he parked blocking her exit.

The only things she knew about him was his name, Rick, and she had taken him for a couple hundred in cash the past two nights. All he knew was her name was Shelby and she was a nursing student. She was just playing a role to make a living, but he was in love. He was no different than the others. She pretended to be fond of him to get his money, but for some reason he had it in his mind she needed him to rescue her. In his fantasy, if she saw him away from the club, she would fall into his arms.

"What the hell are you doing here?" she demanded startled at the sight of the man she had left behind at the club.

"I just think that we have a real connection, and I can help you get out of that club," Rick stammered and walked between Darcy and the door to the trailer.

"Rick, this is my house and you need to leave now." Darcy had not dealt with these situations before, but she knew it could escalate. She was firm and she also knew Barrett was inside.

"I didn't mean to bother you, but you can't tell me how much you like me then turn me down like this."

"You need to leave now!" she yelled in his face.

The man was over six-foot and stocky. He grabbed her by her arm and began dragging her to his truck, his rough left hand covering her face. She kicked and twisted, but he was too strong. He was at the driver's door of his truck when Barrett opened the door of the trailer. Darcy could see an outline of his body and his outstretched arms pointing her direction.

"Let her go! I will shoot your ass if you don't let her go!" Barrett screamed. Lights started coming on in neighboring trailers, blinds were pulled to the side as people were looking at the incident playing out in the early morning darkness.

Looking back into the flood light over the door, Rick could not see anything but a man's outline. Darcy took advantage of the distraction and pulled away but fell on the gravel in front of Rick's truck. Barrett rushed to her with his grandfather's pistol in his right hand. Rick could now see the pistol clearly and leapt over Darcy and onto Barrett's shoulders as he bent over Darcy.

Bam! The pistol rang out a shot in the dark. *Bam!* A second shot and the two men rolled together on the ground while Darcy crawled away toward the trailer. A siren could be heard in the distance and almost immediately red and blue flashing lights filled the darkness. The police car slid to a stop almost hitting the two men.

"Drop your weapon!" The first policeman ordered standing only a couple of feet away from the men on the ground. Barrett rolled away, tossing the gun toward the other side of the road. A second officer rushed to pick it up.

"Spread out on the ground, both of you. Let me see your hands!" the closest policemen shouted. Both men complied and lay still as the two officers searched them for weapons. Barrett was wearing only a pair of boxer shorts and the gravel had torn his knees and elbows during the scuffle. He suddenly realized he may be shot or he may have injured the other man.

He felt the cop pull his hands together and snapping the handcuffs tightly on his wrists and ordered him to get on his feet. He saw the other man standing with no obvious gunshot wounds.

"I heard two shots, bang! Then a couple seconds later another bang. Bullets must have gone into the dirt," a neighbor lady with a long cigarette hanging from her mouth was talking to a third officer across the street.

Barrett turned to see Darcy sitting on the steps of the porch with a policewoman interviewing her. His mind swirled at how fast it all happened. What was the lady with the cigarette saying? He had been taught by Chief Roberts back home to always do what the police tell you and always be truthful. Fight your battle at the station or court and not with the police officers at the scene.

Soon he felt a tug on his arm guiding him to the back of a patrol car. The other man was led to another cruiser and not an ambulance. "Good," Barrett thought. "He was not shot. Was anyone shot? Where did the bullets go?"

He looked around and saw several neighbors in various stages of undress trying to see what happened. This was sadly not an uncommon event for the local law enforcement at this park. Once every four to six months, police cars were seen parked in front of one of the thirty trailers. Tonight's episode was more exciting because of the gun, and the crowd seemed morosely disappointed no one was shot.

Darcy came to the backseat window and asked, "What do you want me to do?"

"Call my mother. She's under Mom in my phone." Whether you have a skinned knee or are sitting in the back of a police car, every troubled child wants their mother.

CHAPTER 33

THE CLASSROOM FOR Economics 211 became less crowded after the last exam. Half of the students had dropped the class rather than try to bring up their plunging grades. Lourdes had surprised Dr. Riesling by doing well on the one hundred question multiple choice test. Lourdes was in fact leading the class with a ninety-one average even without the class curve he had instituted when he incorrectly assumed no one would have an A average.

"I see we're down to the predictable group of nerds who make up the winners in my class. I too was like you in my youth, an outcast of society, criticized for my superior intellect." He strolled back and forth in front of the remaining thirty students like a hyena sizing up his prey but not allowing himself to look directly at Lourdes.

"From now until the end of the year, I will occasionally stray from the syllabus to issue a pop quiz. The real world does not have a rigid structure. You'll need to learn to react properly to sudden changes or you will fail. Today is one of those days, and I want you to come to the front and take a paper from the stack on the desk. The questions are random and variable in their difficulty. Some will get an easy test, some will get a more complex one, and Lourdes, our very own supermodel, will get one specifically for pretty girls from small towns." He stared at her as she felt the whole class's eyes on her.

"You'll have five minutes to hand write an answer to the question presented and return it to me. I will read and assess your answers in front of the class. Now come quickly and let's get started."

The students rushed and received their tests. The professor handed

Lourdes her test separated from the pile of the other tests. She looked at him trying not to show her disgust. She and the other students settled into their desks and Professor Riesling announced the start.

Lourdes read her question carefully. Name an influential economist who changed the course of the United States and for a bonus, add any quotes attributed to this person.

Lourdes wrote her answer quickly and turned over her paper. She noticed many of the other students that were finished were grinning as if they were sure they would get a good grade.

"Time! Please bring your completed papers to me now."

The students all talked quietly among themselves as Dr. Riesling sorted through the stacked papers and pulled a single one to the side.

"Okay, let us begin. The first one is Mr. Johnson. His question, who teaches this class? Surprisingly he got it right." The class laughed.

"Next question, what is the name of this class? Economics 211, from Mr. Lufang. Econ 211 would have also been acceptable."

The rest of the twenty-six students had similar questions, and he quickly confirmed they were all correct. Lourdes now understood what the other students were smiling about.

Lourdes knew he was making an example out of her, but she sat still with a blank expression on her face as he picked up her test.

"Name an influential economist who changed the course of the United States and for a bonus, any quotes attributed to this person. So, this was a question that may have challenged even her. Let's see what little Lourdes Sanchez said." Dr. Riesling began to read, "'An influential economist who changed the course of the United States was Adam Smith. His book *Wealth of Nations* laid the groundwork for the capitalistic system that guided the USA to become the leading economy in the world. He is best known for his quote, *It is not from the benevolence of the butcher, the brewer, or the baker that we expect our dinner, but from their regard to their own self-interest.*'"

The class applauded Lourdes' answer and she smiled, but Riesling did not. He stood in front of his students and glared at Lourdes. She had received applause in his classroom and the class had never clapped for his genius.

"Wrong! Do not give her praise for ignorance. The correct answer is John Maynard Keynes, and the proper quote, *The political problem of mankind is to combine three things: economic efficiency, social justice and individual liberty.*" He glared at Lourdes in rage. The class looked at her and back at the professor. Lourdes met his stare and did not waver as she formulated her response.

"Your question was name *an* influential economist, and I believe I correctly answered within the parameters you supplied me. For you to announce my answer as wrong seems to be based on bias and not proper methodology," she stated firmly but evenly.

The entire class listened to her argument and were on her side. The professor had overstepped a sense of fairness outside the bounds of the student teacher environment.

"If you disagree with me, you can see me in my office. Everyone makes an A, but Lourdes, you failed the exam. Class dismissed." Dr. Riesling grabbed his leather briefcase with the tests leaving ahead of his students.

"What the hell was that? You were right and he knows it." The first classmate came to Lourdes as the others gathered around her.

"What a pretentious stunt," another boy stated.

Soon all the class had circled her in support. "If you need a witness . . . He needs to be fired . . . What a little Hitler." Lourdes appreciated the encouragement, but she knew this was a personal battle. She needed to be brave and confront him immediately. She would not escalate the situation, but she would try to defend her position. She walked to his office door and lightly knocked.

"May we discuss this, please?" she asked as she looked around his cluttered office full of books and framed degrees and a few mounted photos. One in particular caught her eye.

"What is there to discuss? I am the one who holds the power," Professor Riesling said looking up at her from behind his desk.

"I want to apologize for anything I have done to offend you, and yes, you are the one who holds the power. I have learned a lot in your class, and I want to continue to gain from your knowledge." Lourdes knew how to flatter the pompous instructor.

"You don't have any grounds to have your grade overturned," Dr.

Riesling dug into his stance. "You will have to accept my authority in the classroom. You don't know as much as you think you do."

"Ok, I guess I still have more to learn," Lourdes pretended to yield the argument as she glanced around the room. "I see you shoot guns. Is that some type of sport?" She pointed to a photo of Dr. Riesling holding an over and under shotgun gun and a small trophy.

He turned to confirm she was viewing one of his favorite pictures.

"That's skeet shooting." Professor Riesling was easily distracted when talking about himself. "I was club champ in my class last year. I'm pretty good, but it's a very difficult sport to master."

"Oh, I'm sure it is," Lourdes replied stroking his ego. "Would you consider shooting with me?"

"Sure," Dr. Riesling's self-absorption overshadowed any common sense a teacher should have possessed. "I shoot on Sunday afternoons with a regular group, but I'm sure they wouldn't mind having a pretty girl take me away from beating them."

"You must be very good," she said pretending to admire the photo.

"I score in the mid-nineties. That is four rounds of twenty-five each. The best is a hundred." He was engaged with impressing her and momentarily forgot his resentment. "Here's the address of the range. I'll make sure we have a field reserved for just us, so you won't be embarrassed. Two o'clock okay with you?"

"Perfect. Thank you for allowing me to go with you." Lourdes turned to leave, her pleasing face becoming a mirror of disgust when he could no longer see her.

*   *   *

The financial consultant's market projections created a telling smile on Mr. Downs face as he read the detailed forecast. The educated young man who came to make the presentation to the board of directors was sincere. It created great concern for a man of Mr. Downs' age when someone tried to predict any market. The only thing certain to Mr. Downs was uncertainty. Optimism in the crowds was always a sign of possible doom as far has he was concerned. His bank based its loans on the individual and average economic conditions. Not groups of people, and surely not on seemingly excellent conditions and sophisticated models. The latest financial instruments were derivatives that seemed too hard to explain. If a salesman could not clearly and easily define what he was selling, Mr. Downs was not buying.

There were tech stocks in Mr. Downs' portfolio that were profitable, but he could understand Microsoft and Apple. Coca-Cola he very much understood. Sugar water made for less than 5 cents then sold for ten times the amount, was going to make money. Walmart he understood. Open a big store and sell to the masses common household items for as cheap as possible. Made sense to him. The same went for Home Depot.

Banking and insurance were his comfort zone, but the stock market offered a long-term play for him. Pick as best you can then let it ride was his philosophy, but there were ways to make money even in a down market. Shorting the market allowed traders a way to make big profits by betting the market would drop. Mr. Downs used this as an insurance policy of sorts. If you bought a future position for a much lower price, it could be very cheap, but also very unlikely to happen. A tip that a stock would drop in a month from $100 per share to $95 per share, would cost much more than saying the stock would drop to $50 six months from now. If the market was trending upward, the cost for the *put* position would be extremely cheap, because the odds were like a lottery ticket. It was very unlikely it would drop.

Mr. Downs would buy these puts on the extreme fringe as protection. This strategy had cost him an average of two percent of his portfolio a year. But about every ten years, he would make more than fifty percent when an unpredictable crash occurred in the market. He became concerned when the so-called experts predicted good things, as was happening now in the financial markets. It triggered him to enhance put bets.

In spite of Excel and new software which created beautiful charts and spreadsheets, Mr. Downs used hand-drawn charts to get the feel of the market. He knew the younger employees called him a relic, but this is what he understood. He took his ruler and pencil and manually plotted the stock price to evaluate the trends. It was painstakingly slow and meticulous—everything he enjoyed.

His phone alerted him he had received a text from Four. "Barrett's home. Charges were dropped."

Mr. Downs read the brief message and sighed. Last week he had called an old attorney friend he had known since college who was a senior partner in a huge litigation firm in Fort Worth. They had an elite division of attorneys set aside for wealthy clients who ran afoul of the law. Internally it was called the Dad's Got a Mistress and the Kids Are On Drugs Bunch. Many young attorneys made their mark with wealthy clients to land lucrative in-house jobs for companies held by top-tier customers.

Barbara Vincent was smart, tough, excellent in the courtroom, and even better in halls of the court. When she appeared alongside Barrett for his arraignment the Monday morning after Easter, the case was over before it began. The judge learned Barbara had all she needed to have her client exonerated when she stood beside the young man. The judge simply nodded, after Barrett plead not guilty.

Barbara had spent a full evening interviewing the trailer park witnesses convincing them they would not have to come to court, if they recounted to her what happened into her hand-held video camera. If they were reluctant, she would recite some of their own transgressions with the law. She did her homework and was prepared with past discrepancies and suddenly, the neighbors were on Barrett's side.

The final interview was of a more delicate nature. "Miss Darcy McKnight or should I call you by your birth name, Darlene Hopper?" Barbara asked while seated in the surprisingly neat little travel trailer.

"I prefer Darcy and how'd you know about Hopper?" Darcy stared at the woman wearing a plain black pantsuit. Barbara was no one's idea of feminine or pretty. She had cropped brown hair and wore little makeup with the exception of an abundant amount of blue eye shadow. Barbara made three hundred dollars an hour with a ten thousand dollar minimum but had no idea how to dress or apply makeup. No one had the nerve to tell her.

"Don't worry about how I know things. I just do. Your boy Barrett is getting out Monday morning."

"Good." Darcy perked up. "When should I pick him up?"

"That is none of your concern. You have no future with young Mr. Downs."

"What does that mean?" Darcy demanded.

"I'll tell you what it means," Barbara said evenly. "There's a van that will be arriving in a few minutes. You and the two men in the van will be loading these wonderful items you have collected over the years." She waved her hands over the meager contents in the tiny space.

"Your car will be driven by one of my associates, and you will ride with the other gentleman to your brand-new dwelling in beautiful Amarillo, Texas. Your sister Pamela will be so thrilled to see you back home and doing so well. She's been struggling on the small salary she gets at her job as the Church of the Living God youth director, so this will be a great blessing. We have taken the liberty to let her know you are coming, and she wants you two to live together. There's a furnished apartment that has been paid for the next twelve months that you and sweet Pammy can enjoy. I am also handing you this magic credit card that will be preloaded with a thousand dollars each month for the next year."

"What if I say no?" Darcy asked calculating what she could do to increase her offer.

"Door number two is this warrant from Kansas City and that sure sounds like a bad door for you." Barbara smirked as she held up a folder. "This is a great deal for you and you know it. I fought hard for you to get this and I can assure you, it's the best you'll get. This is the price for you to go away. My clients don't care either way if you disappear from Barrett's life in comfort or if you go to jail in Kansas City."

"Okay," Darcy managed to say.

The sound of the van was heard outside the door. Two men in black t-shirts, jeans, and plain black caps entered the trailer. They started throwing clothes and other soft items in large black garbage bags.

"Darlene, you do have a good sister who sounded very excited to see you. She has no idea where you work or the life you have lived the past three years. Use this as a chance for a better life," Barbara said kindly.

Darcy finished packing her clothes, boxed up a few kitchen items, and walked out to the van. Her dented Honda Civic with the red clear plastic tape over the right rear brake light looked rough but started up and sounded solid.

"One more thing, hand me your phone." Barbara reached out to accept Darcy's phone.

Barbara opened the device and began deftly pressing buttons and pulled a new phone from her purse and handed it to her.

"Here's your brand-new phone with only one number in it—your sister's. I have also spoken with your former employer at the club. He and I have worked together before. He knows all about your sudden departure with a rich client to Mexico. Go be free and enjoy your new life."

CHAPTER 34

THE AUSTIN SKEET Club was a few miles from the rapidly growing city and looked similar to Lourdes' club in Travis City. Maddie sat next to Lourdes holding the new digital video camera Lourdes had provided her roommate who was going to serve as her witness and protector. The gun and case she received for graduation sat on the floor in the rear of the Jeep next to her shooting bag and was out of sight when she pulled into a parking space.

Lourdes tried to shoot each time she went home to keep herself sharp and to see her old friends at the club. Charlie would watch for any glitches in her routine, and Lourdes did her best to stay confident.

"Are you ready, my dear Maddie?"

"Always," She responded with a military salute.

Lourdes walked toward the red painted wooden clubhouse. She wore shorts and a V-neck t-shirt that fit her figure tightly revealing more cleavage than she would normally allow. Her black hair was pulled into a long ponytail. The familiar cadence of the loud shooting had no effect on her as she walked.

"Hello, over here!" Professor Riesling waved from a wooden bench behind station four on the first of three fields. She turned toward him with a forced smile and strolled to her host.

"I'm glad you're here and on time. I like people to be on time. I need to go over the safety rules first." Dr. Riesling lightly guided her with his hand on her shoulder toward the empty middle field. Lourdes tried her best not to cringe when his hand touched her body but walked toward the vacated field. Maddie positioned herself near station one as Lourdes instructed.

"This is my friend, Maddie. She just wanted to watch, if that's okay," Lourdes introduced Maddie to Dr. Riesling.

"Of course, but please stand where I tell you to," he said with obvious disappointment he was not alone with Lourdes.

Lourdes listened to the safety rules noting he never asked her an important question. "Have you ever done this before?" He handed her a decent Remington 1100 similar to the one she shot the first time with Mr. Downs eight years prior. He guided her on to station one standing very close as he spewed his knowledge of the sport.

"This is your gun. Nobody shoots my Beretta." He handed her the Remington as he showed her his nicer weapon.

"I watched a video and read the rules before I came, so I feel comfortable. Will we be shooting four rounds? That takes four boxes of shells and a hundred shots, correct?" Lourdes turned to find him breathing over her shoulder.

"Well, aren't you little miss perfect. You watched a video and read something so now you think you can do this." He laughed at the black-haired beauty looking back at him with a slight grin.

"I think I can do as well as you," she said with a taunting tone.

"Alright. Tell you what we'll do. Let's make a wager, and one of us will learn a very hard lesson in humility." He handed her a box of shells.

"Okay, if I win, you change my grade to an A like it should have been for my answer of Adam Smith. Will you give me any free shots?" she said with a flirty smile.

"I'll give you ten shots and agree to your demand. If by some miracle, you pull this off. In fact, you will get an A in my class and never have to see me again. If I win, you stand before the class and admit you were incorrect and accept the F. Agreed?" they shook hands sealing the bet.

"Agreed," Lourdes replied. "Although it should be noted, I have *earned* an A in your class." Lourdes couldn't help but make her point with the haughty professor. She turned to her friend. "Maddie, would you do me a big favor? Would you get my case and bag from the Jeep?"

"What kind of case?" Dr. Riesling felt the blood leaving his face.

Lourdes didn't respond as Maddie brought the stainless case and leather bag and set them on a tall table by station one. A group of shooters finishing their round noticed the hot pink lettering on the gun case and wandered over to see. Lourdes opened the bag and pulled out her favorite shooting cap. She put on her black belt and pouch around her trim waist. Next, she put on her nine-hundred-dollar custom shooting glasses. The foursome of shooters intently watched her open the case to reveal the beautifully engraved K-80 which Mr. Downs had given her for graduation.

"Whoa! That's a twenty-thousand-dollar gun. Very nice, young lady," one of the men said.

"When you see a gun like that being pulled out, it usually means someone is about to get their butt kicked," another shooter joked. "Good luck, Eddie." The men laughed.

Dr. Riesling tried to stay composed. One member of the foursome volunteered to pull the targets for the pair, and another said he would keep score. Maddie sat on the little bench behind the rear center station four with the other two men who treated her like a queen.

"Pull!" and *bang!* were followed by the scorer calling out hit or miss. Lourdes did not miss the first two twenty-five shot rounds and after each round the growing crowd applauded. The score was fifty to forty-four.

Professor Riesling could not say anything in front of his peers as they were clearly enamored with the skilled young lady wielding the impressive gun. The fourth round began with Lourdes missing not a single target. Riesling had missed two more. The score was now seventy-five to sixty-seven and the defeated, arrogant professor felt the anger of humiliation by this pretty girl who seemed able to do anything.

"I'm fine with quitting now. You win," he said quietly when only Lourdes could hear him.

"The rules are a hundred and that's the bet. Besides, I have a growing fan base to shoot for." Lourdes nodded to the group of twenty people watching her instead of shooting themselves.

"You lied to me," he muttered.

"I would not go down that road if I were you," Lourdes sternly stated. "Now let's both do our best to show the people what good sports we are." She walked to station one and promptly called, "Pull!"

Lourdes missed a shot on low six when a sudden gust of wind knocked the target below the projected flight. She watched the target fly to the ground and shook her head but behind her heard a round of applause. She turned and waved at the onlookers and said to herself, "I always hit the next target when that happens."

She finished with a ninety-nine. Riesling ended up with ninety-one. The puller and the scorer both shook her hand first and then Riesling's. The crowd of people drifted her way and asked how long she had been shooting, and everyone admired her gun.

Riesling slipped away and put his two-thousand-dollar gun back in the leather case, emptied the spent shotgun hulls in the trash bin, and began slithering away when he heard a girl's voice calling his name. He turned to see Maddie.

"Because you are a known power-hungry liar, I recorded the terms of the bet. Would you like to watch it?" Maddie waved the camera in his face as she hit play.

"Alright, I'll tell you what we do. Let's make a wager, and one of us will learn a very hard lesson in humility." Dr. Riesling heard his own voice thrown back at him.

He stared at Maddie and the evidence as his face fell. He was beaten, and he knew it was because of his own arrogance.

CHAPTER 35

BARRETT'S CHILDHOOD BEDROOM had changed little since he had left. It just felt silly to him now. He had tried to call Darcy, but the phone was no longer in service. The only thing his parents told him was that they were not aware of her whereabouts since the night he was arrested. But he was sure they did know. He rode home with his mother from the courthouse as his father drove his pickup back to Travis City. According to his mother, there would be no more freedom for him until he proved himself. He had allowed himself to be in a dangerous situation and he was lucky it was not worse.

"Come downstairs." Monica stuck her head into his upstairs bedroom. "Pop's here."

Barrett stood and joined his mother as they came down the long curved wooden stairs to the living room where Mr. Downs was seated with Four waiting for the youngest William Barrett Downs to join them.

"Hi, Pop," Barrett barely mustered a greeting for his grandfather.

"Sit down." Mr. Downs ushered the boy across from him to a wooden armchair which was original to the 1921 home.

"This is not a meeting to discuss the past. That's behind us," Mr. Downs spoke with calm clarity. "This is a meeting to discuss the future—your future. As you have clearly demonstrated to this family, you will require rigid guidance in your immediate future."

"None of this is my fault!" Barrett immediately defended his actions in his usual manner.

"All of this is your fault!" Four responded aggressively.

"Stop it! Both of you!" Monica joined in as Mr. Downs sat quietly with his hands folded in his lap. Despite being inside the home, he was wearing his customary Stetson as he peered at his grandson from under the brim.

"All of you stop talking now!" Mr. Downs voice boomed with authority. The three turned to see his reddened face and quickly obeyed.

"Barrett, you'll have a very short, sad life if you continue to blame others for all that's wrong in your world. You have been blessed to have the resources available for you to succeed, but you need to learn bad things happen to all of us. You need to deal with them correctly. This girl Darcy was not good for you. It does not mean she's evil, but she had you on a bad path. I hope she finds a way to lift herself up above her circumstances, and I genuinely pray she does." Mr. Downs looked directly in his grandson's eyes. "But now we are talking about you. What can you do to contribute to society?"

"I had a job doing emergency cleanup for water and smoke damages. I had only worked there a few weeks but I kind of liked it," Barrett answered.

"Good. That's a very good start," Four encouraged him.

"I agree. It is a good start. There are a couple of those type companies who have accounts at the bank. Let me look into it and see if we can get you back on a good path. We want you to succeed, son. All of us. But we're going to need you to put in the same effort you put into baseball into work. Put in the work and succeed. Understand?" Mr. Downs turned to Barrett and both of his parents.

"Yes, sir. I understand." Barrett reluctantly nodded.

* * *

Economics 211 class grades were posted in the hallway at the end of the semester. Only two of Riesling's students had an A average. One was proudly reading the results and the other was a sharp young lady who had not been to class in weeks. Lourdes may not have attended every lecture, but she had more than earned her A. She knew the material and could hold her own in any economics discussion. She had done very well in her first two years at college and looked forward to a light schedule for the summer of 2006.

Business in the counselors' office was slow when Lourdes stopped by. She had finished her basic requirements and now her classes would shift to focus on math and finance. There were specialty classes that were only offered once a year and she wanted to ensure proper planning to allow her to graduate on time.

"Hello, Miss Sanchez. How may I help you?" an energetic young man asked having met her before.

"I want to confirm the required classes I should take to receive a double major in math and finance." Lourdes set her backpack on the floor beside her.

"There's something new being offered the coming fall that would be very helpful before we take a look at the classes. It's an internship with the PUF here in Austin. You really should apply." He hoped he was impressing the attractive young lady.

"What's a PUF?" she asked.

"Permanent University Fund. It's been around since 1876. It's very cool. The Texas legislature gave some land for the proceeds to go to college education way back in the eighteen-hundreds. And now with oil and gas revenue over the years, it's valued in the billions. Hard to believe politicians did something that smart, but the fund is protected like an endowment," he said.

"I can't believe the politicians haven't spent it on themselves." Lourdes found herself sounding like the old guys at the Travis City skeet club.

"It's a really big deal to be accepted. The big New York money managers look at these interns and feel like they could hire them right out of college. You know, if you did good and the markets don't crash," he joked as she smiled and accepted the application.

"I see your grades reflect you having a good chance. You even have an A in Riesling's class—very impressive. There are not many who even pass his class, much less do as well as you. I need to know your secret to help some other students," the young man marveled.

"Just gave it my best shot," Lourdes replied with an ironic smile.

*   *   *

The morning drive to the office was suddenly disrupted by a deer leaping across the road and colliding with Mr. Downs' truck damaging the front grill and hood of the old pickup. Mr. Downs was not injured, and he was able to drive to the bank. He would drop off the truck later at Adams Ford, and then have Dawn pick him up and take him to get Janet's old car. He arrived late due to the incident and was happy to see Maria's SUV parked in the rear parking lot. She had been sending one of her employees since Lourdes left for school, but some days she would fill in and they both enjoyed those days.

"Good morning, Maria," Mr. Downs loudly announced walking in the locked back door.

"I'm in the lobby. I'll come back there," she responded.

Mr. Downs sat in the kitchen waiting for the coffee to brew, and Maria sat with him at the table.

"You want some coffee?" he asked.

"No thank you, sir," she answered.

"How's Lulu doing?"

"I think good. She don't call me much. All she wants to do is text. I don't like the text."

"I understand. Maybe it's just a fad," Mr. Downs sympathized with a smile.

"Oh no, it's here to stay. Now she does the Mine Spaces and a new thing called Facing Book. She speaks in this strange language I don't understand with all the technology things."

"When did you start here at the bank, Maria? About ten years ago?"

"Yes, sir. Lourdes was ten and she is twenty now."

"I want you to know something, Maria. I consider you one of my heroes. Coming from where you started in life compared to where you are now is remarkable. You provided Lulu a perfect home. I wish I was as good a parent as you. Lourdes is proof of what a perfect, loving mother can do in this world."

Maria sat silently at the compliment. She wasn't being rude. She just felt awkward at his sweet sincerity. She knew if she spoke, she would cry. All she could do was smile at him and hope her eyes would somehow say what she desired. She wanted to hug him and say thank you, but she sat frozen in her shyness and moist eyes. He knew her well and did not require a verbal response from her and gave her a way out of her anxiety.

"I need to get to work." He stood and took his coffee to his office.

By 8:30 Dawn was in his office displaying her usual upbeat mood.

"Nice truck you're driving, old man. Who'd ya run over this morning? Somebody who owed you four dollars?" she quipped.

"Not unless a white-tailed deer owes me. I need you to follow me to Adams Ford to drop off the truck and take me home to get Janet's car." He looked up at her from behind his desk.

"It's a miracle! W.B.D. 3 is getting a new truck! I will let the staff know to see who won the pool for closest date you'd buy a new truck," she said with her best sarcasm.

"Very funny. And I am not buying a new truck. They can fix this one."

"They'll have to hire some old man to come out of retirement to work on that antique. Younger men won't have any idea what to do."

"Okay, you've had your fun. Just meet me there," he said exiting his office with his hat on.

"Hello, Mr. Downs. I see you have a little problem with your old truck," Freddy the service manager greeted him as he pulled under the canopy by the service door.

"Hit a deer a mile east of my driveway. Dang deer must not read well since the deer crossing sign is on the west side of my drive," Mr. Downs joked.

"I never understood that clueless piece of brain power from the state highway boys in putting up those signs," Freddy stated as he circled the truck with a clip board. "You need a ride back to the bank?"

"No, Dawn's coming." As soon as the words were out of his mouth, Mr. Downs recalled Freddy was one of her ex-husbands.

Freddy did not respond but appeared engaged in his evaluation of the damage. Soon Dawn drove up and parked in a space behind the damaged truck but stayed in her car a few yards away with her window down.

"I'll talk to Sean in the body shop, but the truck is old and parts are worn out. May take some time . . ."

"I don't want a new one," Mr. Downs knew where Freddy was going with his comments. "This is what I want. I would like this one done up like new. All new paint and I need new interior. Same colors, just new. Keys are in it. You call me when you have a good price to do it all. And I need a new bumper on the back and tailgate. Another thing, that radio hasn't worked in six months, so fix that too. Also, I want you to go through the engine and transmission. Oh, and the air conditioner and the heater aren't so good either."

"How's the steering wheel?" Freddy jibed.

"It's fine."

"So basically, everything but the steering wheel?" Freddy smiled.

"And the horn. It still blows."

"Yes, sir, we should have this done easy in time for next year's Christmas Parade," Freddy teased.

"Just call me when it's ready." Mr. Downs crossed over to Dawn's car to see her scowling at her ex-husband.

"What'd he say about me?" she asked crossly as he got in her sedan.

"Nothing."

"I heard him saying something about me being old and worn out," she said backing out.

"What the hell is wrong with you? He was talking about the truck! I swear. Settle down, crazy."

"Don't call me crazy! What if God decided to turn up your thermostat? It feels like someone is shoveling hot coal on my chest. I got to take my nut pills, so I don't kill you most days."

"What are nut pills?"

"Hormones, idiot! Good Lord, Janet was the greatest saint to ever live in this town."

The two argued like they had been married all their lives as Dawn drove too fast back to the ranch. She pulled under the carport next to Janet's old car.

"Come in. I got to find the keys. For some reason I took them out of the car, and then we'll see if it starts," Mr. Downs said calmly as if they had never argued.

Dawn and Mr. Downs walked inside where he searched for the keys to the Cadillac mad at himself for not leaving them in the car. Dawn wandered around the large living room admiring the paintings and window treatments—things Janet had done only a few weeks before she died. Dawn sat on the large sofa and gazed through the wall of windows out to the rolling pasture and thought of when she was last in this home after Janet's death. She saw framed pictures of Janet with her children when they were young and then Janet as a grandmother with Janet Ann and Barrett as smiling toddlers. There was another candid photo of Monica and Janet with their mouths open wide in laughter at Four and Monica's wedding.

"She was the glue, you know," Mr. Downs said when he walked in the room and saw her holding a picture of Janet in her kitchen full of pots and pans. "She held us all together. I'm not sure how to do it without her."

"I know, Billy. I'm sorry."

"I have you though. And through it all, you've been there for me."

Dawn walked over and hugged him and wiped the tear away from his cheek with her thumb.

"Let's get out of here before my jealous husband comes in and shoots us," she joked, breaking the sad remembrance as she wiped away her own tear with the back of her hand.

When they returned to the bank Mr. Downs asked the bank's vice president to join him in his office. Josh Simmons began his career at a bank in his hometown of Houston, but married a local girl named Penny Morris. Penny told him the position at the bank was available seven years prior, and he adored the small town and gladly accepted the job. Mr. Downs had tutored him in the banking business over the years, and by his own good graces, he soon became the front man in the community for all charitable events. He was an excellent public speaker and very polished in Mr. Downs' opinion. He and Penny had three girls who were all redheaded like their mother.

"Josh, please have a seat." Mr. Downs joined him in the opposite wing-back chair.

"What can I do for you, sir?" Josh asked in his always professional demeanor.

"I'll be making an announcement soon, and I need your permission before I do. I want to name you as President and CEO of the bank. I'll be stepping aside to serve as Chairman. This is, of course, if you are in agreement."

"Of course I am!" Josh was humbled by the opportunity bestowed upon him by the man whom he greatly respected. "This is a great honor. I will make you proud, Mr. Downs. Thank you so much. I'll prove to you that you made the right decision." He stood and firmly shook his boss' hand with an appreciative smile.

"You and I both know you've been running the day to day for quite some time and the employees have responded well to your leadership. I'll still come in and work every day. I don't know what else I could be doing, but I've called the board and they were all in agreement. They'll be your board. Let them help you. Would you like to know if you are getting more money to go with this new title?" Mr. Downs chuckled.

"Yes, sir. That would be nice."

"We voted to double your salary. The new board pointed out to me that you have been grossly underpaid. You have three daughters, so you are going to need it." Mr. Downs laughed and patted Josh on his shoulder and opened the door to Dawn's office.

"Honey, meet the new president." He motioned toward Josh.

"I don't think you should call him honey. And everybody already knows I run this place." Dawn laughed at her own comedy, and Josh stood frozen trying to navigate the office humor.

"Be nice, Dawn. He's going to be everyone's new boss. Even you."

After the bank doors were closed for the day, Mr. Downs walked with Josh into the lobby to personally make the announcement of a new era and the passing of the baton.

CHAPTER 36

Summer 2007

THE FIRST BAPTIST Church sanctuary was filled with friends and families attending the wedding of Janet Ann and Ben Jordan. Bouquets of assorted white flowers decorated the end of each pew and filled the front of the choir loft. The fragrance of summer magnolia blossoms filled the room. Mr. Downs walked down the long center aisle alone wearing a classic black tuxedo, and Ben's parents, also formally dressed, followed. Monica, wearing a pale pink suit and matching heels, was ushered in by Barrett, and he looked fit and handsome to onlookers who had heard rumors of his decline.

The pastor led the groom and groomsmen into the sanctuary to take their places, and the bridesmaids began their procession. Lourdes Sanchez, holding white tulips, was the first down the aisle in a strapless peach colored, floor length dress with a small white orchid in her styled hair. The organ softly played Ode to Joy as she turned side to side with her eyes to meet the approving faces watching her glide past them to stand in her place on the platform. Janet Ann had called her months ago with the surprising request saying, "I want you to be a bridesmaid. You know I don't like that many people, and I've always felt close to you."

The rest of the bridesmaids flowed down the aisle wearing the same dress, but to Tommy Adams, none were as beautiful as Lourdes. He sat with his newest girlfriend, Trish. He had been dating her for a few months, but Tommy was young, and commitment was not on his mind. If Trish knew what he was thinking about a lake house weekend with Lourdes, he would have suddenly been sitting alone.

Danny and Maria sat toward the front on the same side as Lourdes, worshipfully admiring their daughter as if she were royalty. A blast from the pipe organ heralded Mendelssohn's Wedding March, and Monica stood with the rest of the crowd rising at her cue. The doors were opened by two ushers and every eye was on Janet Ann and Four walking through the doors.

As they walked down the aisle, Dawn tried to hold back tears as she began sniffling.

"Are you crying?" Paul asked.

"Yes, I cry at all weddings. I'd cry if Lizzie Borden married Charles Manson."

"You didn't cry at either of ours."

"I cried on the honeymoons." Dawn grinned through her tears.

"You did do that. Both times." Paul nodded as the father and daughter walked past them.

The bride wore the same dress her mother had worn when she married her father. She smiled as she tried to keep her emotions in check, gripping her father's arm as they moved slowly down the rich red carpeted aisle. Four clinched his teeth in a smile as his friends and family watched his beautiful daughter being taken from one home and given to another in a tradition enjoyed across all cultures.

Verses were quoted, vows were exchanged, and prayers were made as all the attendees listened approvingly. The pastor declared, "You may kiss your bride!" And then he happily announced, "Ladies and gentlemen, Mr. and Mrs. Ben Jordan." The organ music swelled, and the smiling bride and groom quickly strolled to exit the church amidst the sound of the applauding guests. The groomsmen followed escorting the bridesmaids down the aisle, and the young man who escorted Lourdes thought he had hit the lottery with his pairing.

The reception was at the Downs ranch. A huge tent overflowed with three hundred people eating from a side of beef cooked over a spit with dozens of attendants serving ten different side dishes and five desserts. Daisy was there alone while pretending to help Monica with the details and taking care of her father. There was a dance floor in front of the bride and groom's table. A live band played various tunes for all generations and little children playfully ran around pretending they could dance.

Four danced with his lovely daughter as the entire crowd looked on and Monica dreamed of grandchildren. Mr. Downs, as was rehearsed, tapped his son on the shoulder before the end of the song and finished the dance with his granddaughter.

"I'm very happy for you, Boopie. I knew you'd find someone with high standards. You always knew more than anyone what you wanted, and you never compromised. I hope he knows what he has in you," Mr. Downs said tenderly as they danced.

"Thanks, Pop. He reminds me of you and that's the nicest thing I can say about anyone." Janet Ann tried to hold back tears. "I just wish Nanny was here. She would have loved everything."

"Oh yes. She would have loved all of this." Mr. Downs smiled broadly thinking about what Janet would have said to make him happy.

The young man sitting with Lourdes was doing his best to impress her, but he noticed she seemed to be looking at a tall fellow sitting with a pleasant young lady. Lourdes excused herself and walked to greet her parents, because she knew her mother was ready to leave. Her Dad would stay and dance all night if Maria would let him.

"Hi, Mama, you look so beautiful in your dress. And Dad, you look very handsome."

"My little girl! The most beautiful one here!" Danny exclaimed with his arms wide.

"Hush, Daddy!" Lourdes admonished him with a smile. "I think the bride is by far the most beautiful one here. You're prejudiced."

"There's someone behind you, Lourdes." Maria lifted her hand.

"Hi, Lourdes," Tommy said looking in her eyes. "I agree with you, Mr. Sanchez. You are the most beautiful one here."

"Can we talk somewhere private? I promise it'll be quick. Excuse us, Mr. and Mrs. Sanchez," Tommy pleaded.

"Sure, let's go around to the patio." Lourdes walked toward the rear exit of the tent.

Tommy delayed for a moment to pull two beers from an open bar cooler.

"Why are you doing this?" She asked gazing down as she accepted the bottle of beer.

"Doing what?"

"Making me miss you," Lourdes was tired of playing games and ready to be vulnerable. "I can go so long without you, and then I'm right back where we left off as soon as I see you. And you're with another girl."

"And you seem to be having a good time at the head table yourself."

"Oh, please," Lourdes rolled her eyes. "He's trying way too hard, and he's not very good at it."

Tommy pressed against her and she looked into his eyes and kissed him. It felt like the first time she held his hand. The noise of the party was only a few feet from them, but she always felt like she was on the other side of the moon when she was in his arms. She didn't allow herself to be swept off her feet, however, and she pushed him away.

"I'm never going to be the other woman, Tommy. It's been hard having to let you go, but you need to return to your date, and I need to return to my duties." Lourdes turned her back on him and walked back to the tent.

Tommy wiped the lipstick from his mouth and sauntered back to the tent through another entrance. The party went into the night and two photographers captured happy moments between the newlyweds and their guests. No one noticed when Barrett left with a cute girl from the catering staff.

CHAPTER 37

THE THURSDAY MORNING sales meeting was full of the usual politically incorrect banter between the car salesmen. Lourdes had asked Derrick in advance for a moment to make an announcement. Only five of the original group remained from when she started. She remembered Tiffany saying most of them don't last, and she was right. Success in this environment required thick skin and results. The weak were culled quickly.

"As you see on the chart of shame, we're doing very well so far this month, but do not slow down. Keep your foot on their neck and keep selling. Now I want to turn the meeting over to the only person in this room who anyone cares about, our own princess, Lourdes Sanchez!" Derrick began applauding loudly as the others joined in a standing ovation.

"Thank you all, but I'll not be tipping anyone for clapping, so please sit down," Lourdes teased them and they began booing and laughing at themselves. "Thank you again. Please just be quiet so I can say something." She waved her hands up and down.

"Saturday will be my last day. I've accepted an internship and my senior year is going to be very busy with some really hard classes. But I learned so much from all of you guys, and I want to thank you for showing me a world I would have never known if you had not shown me." Lourdes sat down to another round of applause.

"Lourdes, dear, you'll be missed." Derrick would certainly miss one of his top sales personnel. "Now I will have to put up with these beasts alone because we are losing our beauty."

"Derrick, that was the cheesiest crap I've ever heard," Lourdes quickly responded and the whole room roared with laughter, but no one louder than Derrick.

The salesmen broke from the meeting still enjoying the fun afterglow of the morning gathering as they returned to their offices. Lourdes followed Derrick into his office for a quick debriefing.

"I have three deals working, and I'll give you the files if I can't get them closed before I leave. There are four sales on the last pay period. Just let me know when I can come pick up the check. It's been fun. I did learn a lot from you. Thanks for treating me like one of the guys. That was important to me." She smiled at her boss.

"Every person should be a waiter or a salesman at some time in life. You really learn about people and how to deal with them. The game we play is all in the customer's heads— making them feel good about buying from us," Derrick spoke honestly. "I have worked at Ford, Chevy, Lexus, Toyota and the selling is all the same. We work here with these Toyotas every day, and I bet not one of the salesmen drive one. That's because it doesn't matter. It only matters what the buyer thinks. You did good at this job because you let people talk themselves into buying a car. Most salesmen talk too much, and then say one wrong thing that triggers the buyer, and boom, they lose the sale."

"I get that," Lourdes nodded. "I learned it from David."

"Oh, he's the best I've ever worked with at saying nothing. It's brilliant. Keeps it all very simple and the buyer winds up selling him on taking their money. It's a beautiful thing to watch."

"Thanks again." Lourdes was sincere in her gratitude.

"One more thing," Derrick finished. "What you got on this job was earned. You were tough. That was my favorite thing about you. Most young girls would have folded quickly. Heck, most grown men quit. Too thin skinned and worried about their feelings. No place I ever worked worried about my feelings, but this is a business and feelings don't pay the bills. You must have grown up with a bunch of roughhousing brothers."

"No, only child," she answered. "I just have really good parents."

"Yes, they are." Derrick had learned more from his time with Lourdes than he was willing to let on.

Lourdes had three days left to make money for the fall. Her scholarship and the additional money from Randy and Vickie would be gone next May. She calculated from the current market pricing of her portfolio with Mr. Downs she should be fine, but the markets change unexpectedly, and Mr. Downs was not liking what he was hearing from his trusted sources of old men at the Fed and Wall Street.

She was thinking of her new internship and the financial market when a young man stood in her doorway.

"Hello, how may I assist you?" She could now say these words in her sleep.

"I wanted to ask about a new car—a Corolla." The man appeared to be in his early twenties.

"Sure, I can help you," she said and began walking with him to the outdoor lot. "I'm Lourdes. What's your name?" She handed him her card.

"Pete." He shook her hand.

"What do you do, Pete?"

"I just graduated this summer from UT."

"Excellent! What did you study?"

"Art history."

"That sounds interesting." Lourdes was genuinely interested in all subjects. "Where will you work?"

"Not sure, trying some museums but I just started looking." They stopped in front of a row of new cars.

With a sharp eye and even sharper mind, Lourdes came to a quick assessment of the buyer's potential. He had driven up in an older Chevy sedan with cracked green vinyl seats and a collection of student parking stickers on the windshield. It was late August, and he had the windows down meaning his car had no working air conditioner. He had no job and had not started looking until he graduated in a field with very little demand.

"This whole row is brand new. Let's walk and talk some more." She smiled and waved him to stroll past the forty cars in ninety-degree heat at 8:40 in the morning.

"Where are you from?" she inquired.

"Illinois," he replied

"Why did you come all the way to Austin to go to school?"

"Just heard it was good, and easy to get student loans."

"How long have you been here?"

"Six years total."

"You work anywhere while going to school?"

"No, wanted to make sure I did good on grades."

Lourdes stopped and turned him back toward the showroom. She needed to end this debacle gently. She led him back to her office where she asked Pete to close the door behind him.

"Pete, how much do you owe in student loans?"

"Not really sure," he responded. "I haven't paid any because I've been in school."

"Did your family pay a portion of your education or were there any scholarships?"

"Yes, I got a hundred-dollar scholarship when I graduated high school."

Lourdes looked down and tried to think how she was going to tell him his predicament.

"How were you planning on paying for this new car?" she asked preparing him for the coming lecture.

"I got this in the mail." He handed her an envelope. The return address proclaimed it was from a well-known credit card company.

She pulled the letter and attached check from the envelope, and carefully read the offer and saw the check in the amount of fifteen thousand dollars.

"It says I can just put that check in my bank, and then I can buy a car." Pete proudly pointed to the check portion of the offer.

"I see that, Pete, but I need to understand how this happened. You have no job and have not worked in years. Your only source of money has been student loans, which I am assuming are now far in excess of a hundred thousand dollars. This company blindly sent you a check for fifteen thousand dollars for a noncollateralized loan with a very enticing 19.99 percent interest rate. That may increase per the fine print here to 28.99 percent if you are five days late on any of your payments." Lourdes was shocked at the absurdity of the offer.

"I got two or three of them when I graduated," Pete said with a misplaced sense of pride.

"I'm unsure what to do here, Pete," Lourdes wanted to help him. "You could clearly use a new car because you may be living in it very soon. If this credit card company is stupid enough to throw away all this money, they should be punished. But a part of me wants me to tell you to get in your old car and return to your parents as quickly as you can. Find any job possible—maybe two or three jobs and start paying off your student loans."

"I don't understand what do you want me to do? It was so easy to sign up and I just kept doing it. Everyone else does it." Pete was clearly confused.

"Pete, I am not upset at you, but this is really bad. You have a degree that may never work out for you and you have high debt. I cannot sell you a car. I just can't do it but thank you for this. I have learned something I never would have known without you." She stood and shook his hand.

"What do I do now?" he asked with a puzzled look.

"Just hope that car of yours makes it back to Illinois."

Pete left the dealership, but Lourdes kept the credit card offer and called Mr. Downs to tell him the story in detail.

* * *

Danny lay next to Maria in their bedroom in the early evening. Both were early risers and by nine p.m. they were usually asleep. This time relaxing in bed was when they discussed the events of the day.

"Do you still love me?" Maria asked looking at the ceiling. The question was seemingly out of the blue, but as all couples know, these types of inquiries often find their way into a marriage.

"Of course, I do. Why would you ask me that?" Danny answered in genuine affection toward his wife.

"I am old and fat and not pretty anymore," Maria replied exposing her own insecurities.

"So am I," Danny reassured his wife. "Don't be silly, Maria."

"I'm not being silly. Don't say that." Maria needed more than platitudes. "It's true. I know I've aged."

"Listen to me, Maria. You made me who I am. You made us who we are. You are the reason we have anything." Danny was serious in his devotion to Maria. "I was just an average guy living day to day, but you saw the future. You were the one who had us prepared when the welding shop came available. I see poor men all the time working hard, but their wives spend every dollar they bring in. They have nothing. I see wives trying to make a life and their husbands squander their money on selfish things. Would I trade you for some younger, thinner woman? Never. I'm sorry if I've ever made you doubt for one minute that you are perfect in my eyes."

Maria rolled over to face her husband and kissed him.

"Thank you, Danny," His words were exactly what she needed to hear. "We made this life together."

That night they made love and held one another close until they drifted to sleep. Both reflected on their years of marriage and on their daughter away at college.

CHAPTER 38

THE AUGUST HEAT was stifling the morning a service crew van pulled up to a Fort Worth house. A kitchen fire had started from an unattended cast iron skillet of frying fish when the elderly owner visited with a neighbor in the backyard. Barrett led the crew into the house and reassured the woman they were there to help her, and he would work with her insurance company to resolve the issues. He could be charming and kind to the clients. He had been working for a few weeks at a local emergency repair services company in Fort Worth. He had earned some respect from his family for holding down a job, and they even considered purchasing a mitigation company if a deal was available. But Barrett knew he would need to stay employed and learn the business for a decent time frame.

He was doing drugs again, but he rationalized his use as only recreational like a functioning alcoholic, and his family did not seem to notice any behavior issues. He dated a few girls who came in his line of sight and enjoyed sex as much as drugs. None of the girls kept his interest for long. He moved into a duplex on the south side of Fort Worth in a family neighborhood. On the surface, he appeared to be an industrious young man.

"We'll get these items packed and inventoried for you. We have a cleaning service that will restore most of the items. We'll need to replace these kitchen cabinets and the ceiling insulation. All of this room will need a complete gut job and the flooring stripped. It will take us about

eight to ten weeks to get things done. Do you have any questions?"
Barrett had moved up to a supervisor position and was enjoying the
role.

"How much is all this going to cost?" The lady was visibly concerned.

"I will work it all out with your adjuster. We've done quite a bit of
work with your insurance company. You'll only owe a thousand dollars
which is probably your deductible." He smiled to soothe her.

"Thank you. You've made all of this very easy. I can't believe I nearly
burned down my house."

"Thank goodness you weren't injured." Barrett gently patted her
shoulder. "Just know we're here to put you back to good as new."

*　*　*

"Did you ask your family about those credit cards offers in the mail?"
Mr. Downs asked Dawn.

"Yes, they all get the same offers, and I do too. I just throw them
away, but I've been getting them for years," Dawn called back to him
from her desk.

"Unbelievable. I thought the reason I was getting them was because
of my high credit score and assets, but apparently everyone receives
these offers in the mail." He walked into her office with his hat in hand.
"I want to go for a ride. You drive."

"Sure, I like adventure driving." Dawn grabbed her purse, and they
both walked out to her car and got in the vehicle.

"I want to go to that new neighborhood east of Baker Road . . . Whew!
Set that air conditioner on snow. It's hot in this car." Dawn cranked the
car to begin the battle with the September heat.

"No problem," Dawn agreed. "My car is always set on snow. Even in
winter. Why are we going there?"

"I want to see how many houses are for sale. Then I want to drive
over to Albertville and check a couple of developments there."

Dawn drove through the streets lined with new brick houses and
dirt yards in various stages of stalled construction. There were no
workmen to be seen and realtor signs were found in the individual
yards. It appeared there were a total of fifty houses and approximately
forty were for sale or under construction. Mr. Downs did not know the

contractor but knew the family who had sold the land for a hefty price the previous year.

The same scene repeated itself in the rival neighboring town with even more houses for sale. He had been watching the housing market foreclosure numbers start to rise. Although they were not always empirically correct, he usually liked to see things for himself.

He and Dawn returned to the bank, and Mr. Downs entered his brokerage account information on the computer. The market was skittish but holding on despite conflicting news stories. As he contemplated the future, his cell phone dinged indicating a text message.

It was from Lulu. "I started my internship; we need to talk tonight. I'll be home at six. I can call you then."

At exactly six, his cell phone rang while he sat in his den with a plate of leftovers on the coffee table.

"Hello," he answered.

"Hi, Mr. Downs! How are you?" Lulu began with pleasantries.

"I'm fine. What did you find out?" Mr. Downs never had time for small talk.

"I can't be sure, but I think they're deeply invested in financials like big banks," Lourdes answered her mentor.

Lourdes had begun her internship at the Permanent University Fund (PUF) and was tasked by Mr. Downs, by way of Randy, to see how well the fund was managed. Randy had tried to find out as a member of the Board of Regents, but it was not technically under the University's purview even though it created massive influence over their budget.

"Can you get more details? There should be a public report. I've looked for one but couldn't find it." Mr. Downs needed a young person who could do online research.

"I found a financial report, but it's from two years ago. I don't know what they are invested in now. This is a big organization, Mr. Downs, with an overabundance of moving parts," Lourdes was enjoying being a sleuth.

"What are you seeing in the housing market?"

"Austin has a boom mentality. It's as if they think nothing bad will ever happen. There are housing developments everywhere you look," she answered him honestly.

"Lulu, I don't like the feel of this. Would you mind selling most of our partnership stock? We can get back in after this housing bubble is over. We'll just leave the fund in cash and buy some short positions." He cautioned his young protégé with sage advice built over a lifetime of experience.

"Mr. Downs, you know more than I will ever know, so I agree. But not our Apple stock." Lourdes also had opinions of her own. "The new iPhone came out a week after Janet Ann's wedding and it is huge. It has been our best growth stock and should not be affected in the long run. I'll try to get a clear answer about mortgage-backed derivatives, if I can. I'll be home Thanksgiving. We'll meet then."

"I agree on the Apple, because that was your pick. Call me if you find out anything else."

"I sure will, Mr. Downs. Bye."

CHAPTER 39

T HE TABLE WAS set with the best family china and silver the Wednesday afternoon before Thanksgiving and Monica was admiring her table. Janet Ann was coming home from Dallas tonight with her new husband, and Barrett promised he would be there as well, even though he was on call for emergencies. The menu was planned down to the tiniest detail and each recipe had been carefully followed. Monica enjoyed her title as family matriarch but would have much preferred to have Janet by her side on this of all holiday meals.

Down the street at the bank Mr. Downs was meeting with Lourdes who was home from "The University" as the University of Texas was referred to by alumni.

"Not one person out of all these very smart people I have talked to can easily explain what these derivatives are or, more importantly, properly value them. Most of these men dismiss me as a "pretty young thing" who doesn't know how this business works," Lourdes began with her research into the PUF.

"How much do they have in the market?" Mr. Downs asked.

"That's another big issue. No one seems knows how to answer that since they are buried in funds across the entire market."

"Thanks for asking around." Mr. Downs was proud of Lourdes' interest in the subject. "I know I'm a very little fish in the ocean, but this bank must survive to make sure my town survives. We're in good shape and our loan defaults are minimal. Can you ask the PUF market manager to hedge their position by buying short positions, like I taught you, like an insurance policy?"

"I can try."

Lourdes left the bank stopping at the grocery store for her mother who was preparing for Thanksgiving with Uncle Jack and his family. During the holidays Maria felt a pang of sorrow for her own family. She had two brothers out there somewhere and probably lots of nieces and nephews. She fantasized about the two older boys seeing her beautiful house and her successful life. But those daydreams were quickly erased by conflicting thoughts of her family being bad people who might be jealous and steal everything from her.

Lourdes loved being home and away from Austin for the break. She had invited Maddie to come this year, since her mom, Dottie, was spending the holiday with her new husband in Cozumel. Maddie was invited to go with them but declined knowing her mother needed to have some fun, and she had no desire to see her mother and stepdad playing grab ass with each other. She was working the lunch shift and would be in Travis City by seven.

Maddie's text said, "Leaving now," and Lourdes smiled. She thought how much each of them had changed since that first day of college. They would both be graduating with honors in just a few months, and it seemed to have gone by so fast. Maddie had abandoned her idealistic environmental lawyer ideas and found her niche in computer science. She had the kind of brain that could knock out coding with ease. She took an entry level class her sophomore year and it all clicked for her. It was Maddie in the middle of five hundred geeky young men, and she loved being the hottest girl in every class.

The two girls would stay up late talking for hours about every detail of their lives. Lourdes told Maddie about her adoption and parents and how her history stirred complicated emotions in her. Maddie wondered what having a father would mean to her life, and she admitted she sought the attention of men just to feel loved. They would fight like the competitive girls they were but loved each other like sisters. Lourdes said God knew what they both needed, and He put them together.

When the headlights of Maddie's car pierced the living room window, Lourdes jumped up and ran to the garage door to greet her.

"I made it!" Maddie announced as she exited her car.

"I'm so happy you came." Lourdes hugged her friend.

"Welcome to Casa de Sanchez."

"It's exactly how you described the place. I'm very impressed!" Maddie said as they walked through the garage and into the kitchen.

"Mom and Dad, this is the girl who has been taking care of your daughter the past few years, Maddie King."

Maria was in her kitchen and Danny was watching a football game in the large open den.

"Well, it is a great honor meeting you, Miss Maddie. Thanks for taking such good care of our little girl." Danny stood as he greeted her.

"Nice to meet you." Maria shyly smiled nodding toward the guest.

"I have heard so many nice things about you both, but *Lourdes* has been taking care of *me*. She's the adult. I'm still a child." Maddie laughed and they all joined in.

That night was spent helping Maria prepare for the next day's feast of traditional American food along with added Mexican dishes. Maddie had been working in restaurants for years and naturally loved learning about Maria's cooking methods. She enjoyed the wholesome atmosphere and being with her best friend's family.

The next day after the two o'clock meal and cleaning up the kitchen, Lourdes and Maddie drove around Travis City to see the landmarks of her youth.

"That's my school." Lourdes waved toward the huddled buildings of Travis City's schools.

"Which school? Elementary, middle school, or high school?"

"All of them," Lourdes laughed.

"That is the elementary and middle and high school?"

"Yep, all of them." Lourdes grinned.

"I think my kindergarten was bigger," Maddie jested.

"There's Mom's Catholic Church and up there is Dad's Baptist Church. I go with my mother to mass and then walk to meet my dad for his service."

"No wonder you are such a good girl. You got a double whammy of religion." Maddie wished someone had introduced her to religion when she was young.

"I enjoyed it, and I miss church when I don't attend. It grounds me, I think," Lourdes had grown in her faith as she matured and was making it a personal choice rather than something only for her parents. "Okay, that's City Bakery and I would weigh five hundred pounds if I worked there. It's that good. It's also where my parents met . . . Here is Mr. Downs' bank."

"I *have* to meet him while I'm here. You've talked about him so much." Maddie enjoyed touring Lourdes' hometown life.

"That's a good idea. He asks about you all the time. That's his son's house there. They have a son my age named Barrett, and a daughter who is two years older. I was in her wedding this summer."

"Yeah, you told me all about that wedding. So, where does Tommy live?"

"We are not driving by his house like we're in high school, Maddie." Lourdes still felt the emotions of what happened at Janet Ann's reception.

"Okay, didn't know you were so sensitive about it. Give me a break." Maddie smiled at her friend.

"Shut up," Lourdes responded playfully.

"Mr. Downs' ranch starts here on the left. That house is Dub Daniel's, the ranch manager."

"It is a beautiful place. I lived in apartments my whole life. It doesn't seem real that someone would have this much space around them." Maddie observed the continuous open space of pastures with occasional scattered oaks and black cows grazing on the remaining fall grass. Barbed wire fences enclosed the large spaces and six-foot round bales of hay were seen stacked three high in open sided barns. From one end of the ranch to the other was four miles.

The ranch house entrance was on their left. Lourdes pulled her Jeep into the driveway and parked to the right of Mr. Downs' restored pickup with its glistening new paint and shining chrome bumpers and trim.

"Wow, that old truck looks brand new," Maddie said noticing the gleaming vehicle.

"That's his baby. He just had it restored." Lourdes walked to the back door and knocked.

The two girls stood dressed in jeans and sweatshirts in the cool afternoon waiting for the door to open.

"Lulu, Happy Thanksgiving! So happy to see you!" Mr. Downs beamed at his young friend.

"Hello, Mr. Downs!" Lourdes was just as happy to see him. "I wanted to stop by and introduce you to my roommate, Maddie King. Maddie, this is *the* Mr. Downs." The two shook hands already knowing so much about each other through their mutual acquaintance.

"What an honor to finally meet you." Maddie looked at the old man with a feeling of fondness. "I feel like I've known you forever."

"And I feel the same about you," he said sincerely.

The three went to the den and Mr. Downs related to Maddie how he and Lourdes first met and how she got the nickname Lulu after she bested him in a math challenge. Lourdes told the story of the cafeteria and how she hid in the very same, now restored, truck. Maddie recounted from her point of view all the details of the skeet shoot against Dr. Riesling. Mr. Downs howled at her story even though he had already heard it from Lulu. Then he told about Lourdes winning the skeet state championship in San Antonio. When Maddie asked about his cows, he offered a tour of the ranch and the three got in the pickup with Lourdes in the middle.

After seeing the heifer pasture, they drove to the back of the ranch and saw the clear flowing water of a creek over the limestone rocks as they drove across a concrete dam. A herd of deer scampered away from the truck with their signature white tails flagging as they scurried for cover in the back brush. To Maddie's surprise, a flock of wild turkeys trotted across the crude pasture road in front of them. Cows were gathered in a large pasture east of the crumbling remnants of a cabin surrounded by tall cedar trees. Lourdes had never seen it before. It was in a forlorn condition, looking neglected for a hundred years.

"That house was where my great, great, grandparents lived over a hundred twenty years ago," Mr. Downs related his history. "I wanted to preserve it, but it was too far gone. They're the ones who built this ranch and made me who I am. I owe Robert and Molly Downs for their bravery and sacrifices."

Staring at the long-abandoned cabin, Maddie was overwhelmed

by the humble origin of all she had seen driving through Mr. Downs' ranch.

"I don't have anyone like that in my family," Maddie sadly stated.

"Then you be the one in your family who starts something big," Mr. Downs encouraged the young blonde.

"She will be, Mr. Downs. She will be." Lourdes was sincerely confident in her friend.

"Sure! Why not me? It has to start somewhere," Maddie cheered herself.

"Sacrifice and time. That's what he's taught me," Lourdes said looking at Mr. Downs.

Returning to the ranch house, they said their goodbyes and for the first time in Lourdes' life, Mr. Downs began to look old to her. He walked slower and his face had aged. But despite these outward signs, there remained a sparkle in his eyes that still let her see him as she did when she was ten years old.

CHAPTER 40

THE VICE PRESIDENT of investments for PUF had received the email from an intern named Lourdes Sanchez outlining her thoughts on market conditions and probable dangers in housing and mortgage-backed derivatives which no one seemed to understand how to value as a bundled product. Dr. Victor Anders read through her analysis and her remedy with surprise and even amusement. She had requested an appointment to discuss the matter, and he was just curious enough to meet this audacious young woman.

He found her file and intern application and researched her background. Each solicited professor had praised her for her brilliance and demeanor, except one. Edward Riesling had written, "She is smart but dangerous." Anders checked her grade in his class and was surprised to see an A. Why would he use the word dangerous for a girl with such an otherwise spotless resume? This caused even more curiosity and he emailed her to meet him in his office at three the next afternoon.

Dr. Anders' office was on the top floor of the downtown PUF building where he was considered the lead investor for the fund. He was arrogant and dismissive toward everyone beneath him. He was a fan of the predictive analytical research that had been gaining power since the 1999 tech bubble burst the market. He came from Yale, Wharton, and Columbia and made sure anyone he met was informed of his pedigree. He would point out how under his leadership the fund consistently made great strides, but statistically he had never beaten the S&P broad index of funds.

An attractive woman sat at her desk guarding Anders' office and kindly greeted the young lady with long black hair who was dressed smartly in a navy pinstripe jacket and skirt.

"Hello, Lourdes Sanchez to see Dr. Anders. I have a three o'clock appointment." Lourdes announced her presence with authority but politeness.

"Please have a seat, Miss Sanchez," the assistant said professionally. "I'll let him know you're here."

She picked up her phone, "Your three o'clock is here ... Yes, sir." He asked you to please wait, and he'll be with you shortly," the secretary said knowing how this scene would typically play out. Dr. Anders would pretend to be very busy and make people wait as a power play. The secretary looked at the young lady and thought, "You're being tossed to the wolves."

Lourdes checked her watch; it was three o'clock exactly. She decided to only wait seven minutes as that was her way of telling him she would not be mistreated. Lourdes sat with her legs crossed with the folder of her research on her lap. She made no small talk and casually checked her watch. Three more minutes to wait. She glanced through a copy of The Daily Texan on a table next to her chair. Her stomach was churning in anticipation of the waiting game. Randy had coached her over the phone how to deal with Dr. Anders. Randy did his research too, and he was a master businessman.

When seven minutes passed, Lourdes stood, and smiled at the assistant. "Tell Dr. Anders I was here on time. I expect him to promptly keep his appointments with me, and I look forward to hearing from him to reschedule." She turned and walked out of the office as the assistant sat stunned and smiled to herself.

Dr. Anders appeared in the outer office eight minutes later with a confused look.

"Where is my three o'clock?" he asked.

"Oh, she said she was here on time. Since you kept her waiting, she left," the assistant was pleased to pass on the message.

"Why didn't you call me?" Dr. Anders angrily demanded.

"I guess I thought it would be fun to see your face. And I quit. I have watched you keep people waiting just to be rude long enough. I can't work for you anymore." The woman walked away from her desk clutching her purse and paused at the door.

"You need to email her to reschedule; I won't be doing that any longer." She walked down the hall to the elevators leaving Dr. Anders standing speechless in the empty office.

Lourdes sat in the first-floor lobby texting Randy, when the lady came walking toward her.

"Are you looking for me?" Lourdes asked.

"Not really. I just quit," Dr. Anders' former assistant said with the adrenaline still racing inside her. "But I did want to thank you. That was the best thing I have seen in a long time. He makes everyone wait, and I loved it when you stood up and left. That SOB will now be looking for his third assistant in two years. "

Good for you"," Lourdes praised her. "It takes guts to stand up to a man like that." Sensing an opportunity, she continued, "I don't want to ask you to do something illegal, but do you know what Anders invests for the PUF?"

"Yes, I have my own user IDs and passwords for all of the accounts. Anders wanted me to be able to access them to provide reports, but I cannot place orders."

"Where are the user IDs and passwords?"

"Right here." She pulled a small black book from her purse.

"Would you mind if we go somewhere to talk?" Lourdes asked.

"I could use a drink, and I know a good bar close by."

"Lourdes." She stuck out her hand.

"Amy. Nice to meet you."

* * *

On the days Barrett was busy with jobs, he did well. The days off were his problem. He sought women and spent time in bars and strip clubs. He managed to stay out of serious trouble and went back home enough to keep his family content that he was keeping clean. He did have pride in having his own paychecks and rarely used the family credit card. He thought of himself as his own man now, and conveniently ignored that the truck he drove and the duplex he lived in were paid for by his family. His insurance was on their dime as well, but he felt he was starting to make it on his own.

The owner of the emergency management company, Ken Oliver, liked Barrett and tried to teach him the business and give him more responsibility. Ken had been to prison for drugs in his younger years and spotted familiar patterns in Barrett.

"I want you to know I see good things for you if you don't screw it up," Ken said as he and Barrett sat in a small office of the warehouse.

"Thanks." Barrett needed compliments and liked having Ken as a boss.

"I also know you have a problem with drugs." Ken continued and Barrett looked surprised. "I know you do, so don't try to lie your way out of it. I've been there, boy. Went to the pen for five years for losing control. I was like you. Thought no one would know, and it worked for a long while. Until it didn't."

"Yes, sir," Barrett said with surprising honesty. "Why aren't you firing me?"

"I will if you keep going with the drugs. Let's make a deal." Ken was serious but kind. "You be honest with me and I will help you. An ex-con helped me when I got out and taught me this business, but it took me a few years to build it up. You know Sammy who runs the drywall team? He's an addict like us, but he has kids now, and having a family and a life is more important than getting high."

"I do better when I'm busy on projects, and I'm pretty good at my parents' house," Barrett confided in his boss. "It's the days off that I have the problems."

"That makes sense. Let's try and make work your new fix. I just worked all the time when I had the chance and all that time sweating and earning money took me away from wanting that life again. If I tested you now, what would show up?"

"Hydrocodone and some weed and four beers. That was last night." Barrett was honest.

"Good start, boy," Ken appreciated his frankness. "I believe you. Now next time I ask, what will your answer be?"

"Three beers?" Barrett laughed. Ken joined him with a chuckle but both knew addiction was not a laughing matter.

CHAPTER 41

THE CONFERENCE ROOM still showed remnants of the Christmas party as Randy, Lourdes, and Mr. Downs sat with a pile of papers to sort through. Lourdes had used the information from Amy to download the multibillion-dollar fund information and printed the reports. After careful examination, Lourdes and Mr. Downs were sure Anders had the fund in a precarious position. After Mr. Downs recommendation, Randy was able to get his own access to the accounts after an audit from the oversight committee.

"What do we do now?" Randy asked.

"With your new password, we can take a short position that will protect us against what I think will be a big drop. The profits from a bet of only three percent of this total fund will make money despite the market all going to hell." Mr. Downs said.

"Why wouldn't Anders do that to protect the PUF?" Randy asked.

"Because he would be betting against the companies who are feeding him information. He came from Wall Street and now they are all sucking up to him because of his access to this huge sum of money," Mr. Downs answered.

"How do you understand and see all this from little 'ole Travis City and the smartest people in the world of finance not see it?"

"Some do see it. And the old men I know are worried." Mr. Downs had been watching the market his whole life and talking to trusted people for months. "We need to get that order in today, and we should know if we are right in a few months. It might even be a few weeks, for all we know."

"I can do it from here—right now." Lourdes removed her laptop from her backpack and the men watched her place a three hundred-million-dollar order that had the potential to be worth thirty times that in just a few months. Lourdes felt no worries since this was under Randy's name and authority and she had his personal instruction to take the action.

Dr. Anders was taking off a month for Christmas vacation and gave strict orders to his new assistant to not concern him with anything while he was in the Caribbean with no access to the internet. He had set all his market positions based on sophisticated proprietary algorithms prior to leaving. The data was always right.

*   *   *

2008

Reading The Letter on a frigid day in February was Debbie Franks. Her two children and proud husband were seated on the makeshift stage behind her, and a nice crowd of townspeople stood cheering as Debbie blushed and smiled and waited for the noise to die down.

"That's enough! I'm not Brittney Spears." The crowd laughed as Debbie responded to the attention in her usual manner.

"Thank all of you who came here today. And thanks to the committee who must have run out of people before asking me to read The Letter." More laughter came from the audience.

"I'm a girl who grew up in Hardy Trailer Park. I watched important people stand up on this very spot to read The Letter. They would give a nice speech, but I never thought I would be the one reading it. I got a job at Don's Quick Stop at sixteen where I was paid minimum wage, but I was thrilled because I knew it was a good job. I know everyone here—maybe not by name—but by what you buy. Hi, Dr Pepper in the can, and Snickers bar sitting there, and Marlboro Reds over there. I have spent thousands of hours in that store and now I own it. We remodeled and added on a few years ago and thank you, Mr. Downs, for guiding me through the process. I promise I'll pay you back!" She gestured to the man in the hat who nodded at her with a smile.

"I'm evidence that anyone can be whatever they want. This once poor girl is living proof that anyone who works hard can rise above."

"To the people of Texas and all Americans in the world,

Fellow citizens and compatriots-

I am besieged . . . "

* * *

The PUF oversight committee sat in its designated conference room with Dr. Victor Anders facing them. Chairman Randy Weyers had begun the proceedings a week prior to spring graduation.

"Thank you for coming, Dr. Anders. I believe when we met a year ago you told us your analytics were signaling an excellent future for 2007 through 2009. Do you still hold that position?"

"No one could have predicted the harsh market forces that we've seen the past few months," Dr. Anders answered smugly. "None of the leading economists had this correct, so it would have been impossible to have reacted properly."

"So which one is it? You can predict the market, or you can't predict the market? You were very sure of yourself until you were wrong." Randy was not a man to take double talk.

"I did take a position that protects the fund even in this down market," Dr. Anders evaded the direct question. "I've put the fund in a position to make money."

"That's very impressive, Dr. Anders," another board member interjected.

"That sure is very impressive," Randy began to setup the fund manager. "When exactly did you take this brilliant action? It appears it was done December 20, 2007."

"That's correct," Dr. Anders said. "The order was placed on that date. It just came to me to do this, even though it may have angered some of the Wall Street boys. But I'm my own man," he concluded by leaning forward to Randy.

"Did you place the order from your office here in Austin?" Randy peered over his glasses at the pompous man.

"I suppose so."

"You suppose so? In fact, Dr. Anders, you were in the Caribbean at that time, and you had no internet access until you returned. You told your office staff this information yourself. Our auditor found no emails or any notes of your involvement in this trade at all."

"I don't know how I did it or remember exactly," Dr. Anders started stumbling over his words. "But I'm the only one with the credentials to make the order, so I had to have been the one who . . ."

"That's a fascinating testimony. Have you ever in your entire career predicted anything correctly to indicate you have taken similar actions before?" Randy pressed him.

"I'm sure there are multiple times I've been correct," Dr. Anders defended himself.

"We looked into that. Since you have served as the lead investor for this fund you have ranked in the bottom ten percent of other people in your position. I have a friend who has relationships with real traders in New York. They usually laugh at intellectual fancy boys like you. Do you know people laugh at you?" Randy twisted the knife and the tension soared.

"I have a world-class education and consider your insults an ignorant attempt to rattle me," Dr. Anders would not go without a fight. "I was hired by this prestigious institution to manage the fund for the betterment of all." His face was now reddening.

"All that education and no one bothered to teach you not to lie? I hereby recommend the committee fire your sorry ass," Randy posed a motion.

"For what? You have no proof of any misconduct," Dr. Anders demanded.

"Lourdes and Amy, please come in," Randy called to the outer office.

The members of the room turned to see Amy Dempsey and Lourdes Sanchez walk through the door and sit at the table to Anders' right.

"Amy, thank you for coming. I understand you worked for Dr. Anders as his assistant for a few months, correct?" Randy asked as the fund manager and the committee all stared.

"Correct," Amy answered.

"What were you told by Dr. Anders when you took the position?"

"I worked seven years as a broker in New York. He told me he would make sure I would only be his assistant for a short time, and he would bring me in as a consultant because of my experience."

"Did that happen?"

"No, sir. He treated me like a secretary and never attempted to promote me within the organization."

"So you quit," Randy led the questioning while Dr. Anders seethed in his chair. "Why?"

"I had been asking him for weeks when he was going to move me. I have never been a secretary in my life. My dad was a trader for forty years and I learned from him. I went to a community college, so I was viewed as unqualified by Dr. Anders, but he also never gave me a chance. Then he had an appointment with Miss Sanchez," Amy continued. "She showed up on time and he did his usual rude, make her wait to see the all-powerful Oz Anders." She pointed her thumb at her former boss.

"I did not do that!" he blurted out.

"Yes, he did. Miss Sanchez waited for seven minutes exactly, stood, and told me to tell him to reschedule. I thought it was the finest thing I'd ever seen." Amy turned to the red-faced man. "If you didn't do that, then why was she gone when you finally walked out?"

"Miss Sanchez, is that correct?" Randy pretended he didn't know Lourdes.

"Yes, sir."

"Why were you there to see Dr. Anders?" Randy asked Lourdes.

"I had researched the market conditions and consulted with some contacts I have regarding derivatives and the actions of the financial companies. I emailed him an outline of my research along with a plan that would protect the PUF by purchasing puts as insurance against a severe drop," Lourdes replied.

"Was what you proposed done?" Randy asked knowing the answer.

"As far as I know, it was done exactly as I recommended," she responded only looking at Randy.

"Thank you. No further questions. We have proof he's a liar and proof he's not good at his job. That's enough for me," Randy concluded. "Now regarding my motion. Can I get a second in dismissing Dr. Anders from his position?"

The seven members were unanimous in firing Victor Anders. Dr. Anders thought of Professor Riesling's one curious word—dangerous— as he watched Lourdes shake hands with Randy.

* * *

Graduation day was overwhelming for Maria as she made her first trip to Austin to witness her daughter march across the stage and receive the coveted diploma. Danny kept his bride close and held her trembling hand through the large crowds to sit and hear their baby's name called. When Maria heard it, she stood and unexpectedly yelled, "I love you, Lourdes!"

Maddie walked across the stage in long, athletic strides and held up a victorious fist after shaking the chancellor's hand. She was going to stay in Austin to work in the software business on a new program for smartphones called apps.

Lourdes had three offers from Wall Street which was amazing since most companies were laying off. But her interviews were strong, and a small bidding war allowed her to receive an unexpectedly large salary in the depressed economy.

Lourdes only had a few days at home before leaving for New York. Her new firm had a realtor locating a one-bedroom apartment close to Wall Street. She realized she would need to make much more money to afford anything to rent in New York. She finally agreed on a one bedroom which was thirty percent of her salary. In Austin it would have been five percent. In Travis City it would have been one percent.

Lourdes had been told to ship most of her things to the apartment and just take a couple of suitcases on her flight. She was almost packed and standing in her childhood bedroom when her father walked in.

"Let's go for a ride," he said in a surprisingly solemn tone.

"Okay, Daddy. Where we going?"

"You'll see. Just a short drive."

They got in his truck and pulled out of the driveway and drove passed Danny's shop where a new building was being added. They drove in silence on the sunny June day. He turned on the street entering the old neighborhood and parked in front of the little wood frame house he and Maria brought Lourdes home to twenty years before. It needed paint and the tiny front porch roof was leaning now. There were children's toys strewn about and an old minivan missing two hubcaps was parked in the driveway. An aluminum folding chair with worn plaid strips lay folded on the ground. A Styrofoam cooler sat in the garage along with a tall toolbox with scattered wrenches on a scratched steel top.

"I want you to take a good look at this house." Danny turned to face his daughter. "This place formed you into the person you are. I was the proudest man in this town when your mother and I bought this house. We worked on it all the time to make it better. Your mom put in a nursery the first week we moved in and she painted it pink. She was positive we would soon have a little girl. We tried so hard, but it looked like we were not going to be parents. Your mother prayed every day for you. She never lost her faith and never blamed God." Danny shook his head remembering his wife's belief.

"We were both thirty-six years old when Father Michael called telling us our prayers had been answered. The hand of God has been on you from that day. I don't know why you were in that dumpster, but I know with all my heart, your mother prayed you out of there and into this little house. I want you to remember this place; no matter where you go in this world. Your mama and I have known for a long time that you need to be in a bigger place than this town. But you must never forget where you started and never ever forget your mother has been praying you home years before you were born."

"I'll never forget, Daddy." Lourdes leaned over and kissed her father's cheek.

The next day Danny and Maria drove Lourdes to the DFW airport and said goodbye to their daughter who was flying off to begin her career. Maria sat in the front seat of her SUV while Danny retrieved the two bags from the back and set them on the curb. Busy passengers rushed about and gave little notice to the beautiful, young woman hugging the graying older man and the lady sitting in the front seat sobbing into her cupped hands.

"Tell your mother goodbye, baby, and tell her you love her too. This is very hard for both of us." Danny hugged his daughter one more time and got back into the vehicle.

Lourdes spoke as she opened the passenger door, "Mama, I love you and promise I won't be a pregnant party girl." She tried her best to lessen her mother's sadness in their parting.

Maria could only look at her only child through her tears and forced a smile which looked more like a grimace, but she could not manage to say a word.

As Lourdes turned toward the bustling airport, her fathers' words about her past echoed in her ears. Danny, Maria, Mr. Downs, and Travis City itself had prepared her for this moment. She realized she had never even navigated an airport much less a life in a huge city. While she wasn't sure what lay ahead for her, she was confident Travis City and its people had laid a foundation within her which would serve her well as she took these steps into her future. That place would continue to reside within Lourdes as she moved to New York City.

Lourdes walked into the busy airport pulling her bags and realized she had never done this before. The only time she had flown was on the private jet to the game with Mr. Downs. She looked at the hundreds of people walking all directions and thought, "If all these people can do it, I can figure this out."

"Excuse me, miss? Can you help me?" she asked a woman about her age pulling a small, rolling bag and shouldering a large purse.

"Of course. What do you need?"

"How do you do this?"

"Do what?"

"All of it!" Lourdes laughed at herself.

PART III

CHAPTER 42

Summer 2008

THE SOUND OF the city that never sleeps was the biggest revelation to the young woman from Texas. When she arrived at the apartment building, she paid the taxi driver and rolled her large suitcase to the entrance where a uniformed doorman opened the door and offered to take her bag. She said no thank you, but at his insistence, she allowed him to walk her into the art deco lobby of her new thirty-story residence.

The doorman placed her luggage in front of his station asking, "Whose apartment?"

"Mine actually, but this is my first time here," Lourdes replied. "What's your name?"

"It's Stan, miss," said the athletically built man of around forty with a thick black trimmed beard and salt and pepper hair which was carefully groomed.

"Hi, Stan. Lourdes Sanchez." She extended her hand.

"Nice to meet you, Miss Sanchez. There are packages for you behind the desk."

He went behind the concierge desk into a locked closet and came back with a dolly stacked with numerous boxes. There was an envelope on top addressed to Lourdes which he handed to her.

"Oh great, here are my keys. It says I'm in 24B," she said after opening the envelope.

"Very good, let me carry this for you, and I'll show you your new apartment."

The elevator ride was slower than she expected, but the building had been built in the nineteen twenties. The elevator doors parted, and the door attendant allowed her to exit first and pointed to the right. The hallway was elegant, painted a creamy white with thick wooden doors adorned with brass hardware on either side of the corridor. They walked to the end of the hall on the right where Lourdes took the key and turned the deadbolt. She had seen photos prior to agreeing to the one-year lease, but it was surprisingly small.

Stan carefully stacked the boxes in the living area and stood by the door awaiting a tip.

"Stan, thank you so much. You were very sweet to help me."

He stood for a moment and bowed as he left but smiled knowing she had no clue what to do. He wasn't upset; her innocence was refreshing, and her genuine kindness was better than a monetary tip.

Lourdes noticed there were two boxes that were not part of the consignment she had shipped from Texas. She curiously opened one of these, a brown and white printed box with Stetson Hat Company boldly printed on the top. Inside was an Open Road Stetson just like Mr. Downs'. She smiled, placed it on her head, and found a mirror in the small bathroom where she playfully posed with her new hat. The handwritten note in the box simply said, "You will always be a Texan! WBD 3."

Next, she opened the long, narrow box to find a free-standing dark wood hat rack with another card, "He forgot you needed a way to hang it up. Love, Dawn."

Lourdes spent the rest of the day organizing her new home and making a list of all the things she needed. She followed up by texting Dawn and Mr. Downs a quick thank you, even though she would also mail them a proper thank you card. She called her mother next to let her know she was safe in her small apartment and to tell her dad she missed them already. She would start her new job in three days. Maybe she would explore and be a tourist for a while.

*   *   *

Ken Oliver had changed Barrett's life by succeeding in making the young man responsible when all other people and programs had failed. Barrett had his phone put in his own name. He called the family insurance agent and had his truck and homeowner policies transferred to his name and set up a draft to make sure it was paid. He was clean of drugs and alcohol, healthy, and loved his job. He relished the feeling of accomplishment in a job well done. He learned how to do drywall and paint and flooring from the guys in the company. Now he was the first one to arrive at work and the last to leave.

Ken and his wife Kelly had two girls in high school named Kerrie and Kendra. Kelly kept the books for the company, but she needed help in their growing enterprise. Ken hired more men as the business grew and gave Barrett more responsibilities. Maybe he really was a Downs like his Pop and would be a huge success and respected by everyone.

Ken had a mitigation firm for emergency services, a construction company for repairs and remodels, and had started a roofing division when he saw the need after a hailstorm. There were now forty men working in the field and four people in the office. Barrett became a trusted person to handle problems with customers. He was not excitable and remained calm when a customer was upset or making unreasonable demands. He allowed them to vent without interruption, and then identified their main concern to provide a solution. To watch him in action, he made it look easy, but Ken knew he had a gift.

2010

The work environment was aggressive and brutal on Wall Street, but the training at the car dealership fully prepared Lourdes for the testosterone filled environment full of sexist and demeaning remarks. She deflected the barrage with ease and gained respect quickly, because her coworkers found she was tough. Her work ethic and intellect shone brightly, and soon she was given more opportunities.

The firm had promoted Lourdes twice in her first two years. First, she worked as a quantitative analyst, or quant as they were called in the financial sector. She worked on trend analysis but eventually moved into IPO pricing. Initial Public Offerings are offered to new companies that had accomplished a proven business plan through organic growth, usually with the assistance of venture capitalists seeking a big payoff. These corporations are introduced to the financial markets giving investors an opportunity to spend money on the hope the company would soar in size and value. Lourdes' job was to assign a proper value for the debut stock. This value was never based on the current profit and loss like normal businesses are valued. The initial IPO was what it *could* become some arbitrary day in the future.

All prices are set by buyers and sellers reaching a mutual agreement in an open market. The price may have nothing to do with current profitability, but rather based on the *hope* of profitability. There is a vast separation between what the rules are on Main Street as opposed to what they are on Wall Street. Surviving for a small business requires real money to be earned, but public companies can lose millions and survive because their stock can create a capital cushion. Fundamentally it should matter that the public company makes money, or it will lose the support of the public, however many are able to survive hardships much longer than the small local businesses.

Lourdes made friends and dated ambitious young men who loved to discuss their dreams, but none of those dreams ever appealed to her. She loved the restaurants and bars and even had become almost accustomed to not having a car.

She had been home a few times since moving to New York, enthralling the small-town folks with tales of the big city, but each time she was sad to leave Travis City. With her salary and bonus, she earned more money than anyone back home, but in New York she was just a tiny drop in a big bucket. She fantasized of making one big deal and having enough money to start her own business or simply to move back home and leave the fast-paced, cutthroat world behind to again join the cleaning business with her mother.

"Sanchez, I need you to revise this number for the LSS IPO," her boss ordered as Lourdes stared at her two computer monitors.

"Why? Those numbers are correct," she retorted.

"I didn't say they're incorrect. But I need them to be higher by about fifty percent." He stood over her desk with his hands on his hips.

"That's a ridiculous number," she answered him as she stood.

"Listen, just tweak the math thing and make the number go from $10 per share to $15 per share." He shrugged.

"I cannot in good conscience just change the number. It would be cheating." Others were beginning to notice the confrontation.

"Calm down, little miss perfect. This is how all of us get paid. Your bonus at $15 per share will be three million. Mine will be five million, and so it goes all the way to the top. If you keep the stock at $10, maybe you make a million and maybe I make two, but the firm needs you to step up and deliver us that $15 per share." He turned and left Lourdes standing with thirty people watching. In the group was a man from a local business news network who began winding his way through the cubicles.

"Javier Lewis." He extended his hand appearing out of nowhere as soon as the boss left.

"Lourdes Sanchez," she responded curtly, still fuming.

"I will soon be asked to leave this building for speaking with you without permission, but here is my card. I am a producer with Wall Street Morning. Call me, please." Swiftly the man glided to the exit.

*   *   *

The kitchen was dark in the predawn morning as Mr. Downs tried to remember what day it was. Was it Saturday or Friday? Why was he in the kitchen? He stood alone for several moments, his mind unable to clearly determine the simple answers. "I guess I am getting old and losing my mind," he thought and then remembered it was Thursday, and he was going to scramble a couple of eggs and make coffee. He chuckled at his own confusion.

Mr. Downs now spent most days at the ranch. He enjoyed mowing the pastures and his yard in the spring and summer months. It was odd to see the old man wearing a stained straw hat mowing his own yard. The passersby thought he could afford to have people do the work for him, and he obviously could. The feeling of immediate reward from mowing is what he relished. He would sit on his zero-turn lawn mower and breeze back and forth while his mind wandered. For the pastures he had an air-conditioned cab tractor, and he would spend hours mowing pastures looking back to see the clean results with satisfaction.

Dawn worked part time and assisted Mr. Downs with his sparse appearances, but he made sure she was paid the same salary. She traveled with Paul, but they both preferred spending time with their five grandchildren. Josh Simmons was doing well at the bank but would call Mr. Downs asking him to come in to discuss a problem. Mr. Downs knew he didn't need him but was appreciative of the kind gesture.

Randy and Mr. Downs always looked forward to the annual dove hunting trip in September. Both spent less time hunting and more time reminiscing when they went to the annual event. The hunting was just an excuse to be together and each year, one or two less members were unable to attend due to health reasons or had passed away. The two friends traveled together in Randy's SUV and made the hunt for the fiftieth time. Their eyes were weaker, the shots seemed harder, but the sounds of the dove hunt were as comforting as a mother's arms to a returning soldier.

*   *   *

Lourdes's apartment was like a hotel room. It was nice but not really home. She never quite grew accustomed to the tiny space and no jeep in a driveway. It was the first thing she wanted to do when she landed at the airport on her trips back to Texas—drive the open roads. She missed home and wondered about her future the longer she was away in this foreign land. The string of men who sought her attention were mostly nice, but she never felt a connection.

She would lay awake in her apartment fantasizing of being married to a wonderful man who adored her and made her laugh. She never saw children in her dreams. Did she fear she would become like her birth mother and throw her child in a dumpster? She could not risk that. While she didn't allow herself to even form the thought, part of her felt she could never bear a child.

Lourdes sat with her laptop at the small dining room table, and the business card in her hand made her feel nervous. There were repercussions at her firm for speaking with the press. They had specialists handling the media, and Lourdes was not on the approved list. Despite her concerns, she composed a brief email to the television producer, Javier Lewis. She had verified he was who he said he was because she had learned New York men were very creative with their stories to impress attractive young ladies with Texas accents.

Dear Mr. Lewis,

Thank you for your kind interest but I do not feel this is a proper time for me to call.

Best regards,

Lourdes Sanchez

She sent the email and immediately called his cell number.

"Javier Lewis," he answered announcing his name.

"Hi, this is Lourdes Sanchez, we met briefly. I just sent you an email. I apologize for the confusion, but emails are easier to find than phone records and this is my private cell."

"You are clever, and you should be concerned. Companies can be severe in their treatment of honest people." The journalist was pleased to hear from Lourdes. "I heard most of the conversation with your boss and this is a big story. Not that falsifying values aren't happening, but it seems you have morals which we don't often see, and I wanted to thank you. I would love to have you on our morning show as a guest. Honest, beautiful, smart women are the unicorns we all want to find in my business." He rattled off words so fast she wondered if it was English.

"First, thank you, I would be honored. But if I do this, I will lose my job," she stated as a matter of fact and not of fear.

"I get it, but what do you want to do?" Javier knew he already had her on the hook. "Really want to do?"

Lourdes paused because the past two years had been all work with significant pay, but not much else. However, per usual, she did have a plan.

"I need to think about that." She had been saving and preparing for opportunities and maybe this was her chance.

"I will tell you this," Javier continued to press her. "If you come on this show, you will go from an anonymous smart girl in a cubicle on Wall Street to a known personality. People will know your name in the business and that can be very powerful."

Lourdes had been quietly designing how she could start her own investment fund. Over the past few months, she had spent time internally strategizing about managing her own fund. Now she had a catalyst.

Making up her mind she said, "I'll do it, but I need to leave my current job first and properly prepare. I would also need assurances you put me on the show, and I need that in writing."

"I can do that, but breaking news may bump you," he cautioned.

"Then we will reschedule."

"Of course. I also want you to know I asked around your firm about you, and you are highly thought of by everyone. I wouldn't be sticking my neck out for you if I hadn't checked," Javier said as a way to give himself more credibility and simultaneously compliment her.

Lourdes immediately began planning exiting her job and even from New York for that matter. If she could raise fifty million seed money, she felt secure in her ability to make her investors' money without throwing her morals out the window. She had saved diligently and lived frugally since coming to New York and was now financially prepared to launch her new venture.

She emailed Maddie and got a recommendation for a website developer in Austin. She hired a phone answering firm to ensure all calls did not go just to her cell phone. Next, she needed to find an office, so she placed a call to another trusted friend.

"Janet Ann, it's Lourdes. Can we visit for a few moments?"

"Of course, how are you?" Janet Ann responded, happy to hear her voice.

"I'm well, thanks," Lourdes replied. "I'm about to make a big move, and I know you're doing real estate in Dallas and working for Vickie. I need a favor. I need an office."

"Anything for you." Janet Ann was good at her job thanks to Vickie's training. "I can think of a few options right off the top of my head."

"I kind of need it to be furnished and look impressive. I'm hoping to start my own business if all goes well," Lourdes explained.

"That's great news, and I have the perfect idea. Let me take care of everything." Janet Ann sounded excited.

"I can pay whatever you need. I don't need charity, but a good deal would be nice," Lourdes laughed. "Also, don't tell anyone yet."

"I can keep a secret."

"Thanks, Janet Ann. I knew I could count on you."

CHAPTER 43

TWO FIRETRUCKS AND an ambulance were parked in front of a nice suburban home in south Fort Worth when Barrett arrived at midnight. An insurance agent called him to consult on fire damage restoration. Ken and Barrett had created an extensive network of agencies who called them when emergency claims occurred. They assisted their customers quickly and had developed an excellent reputation for customer service.

"What do we have? A kitchen fire?" Barrett was dressed in a company shirt and addressed a fireman walking back to his truck.

"Electrical, probably. Two dead." The fireman shook his head.

"Oh no, that's awful." Barrett had not experienced a fatality with any of his fire claims. "Who died?"

"Parents of the young woman sitting on the porch. They died in their beds of heat and smoke inhalation, looks like. I think she lives here too. It's a bad deal."

Barrett saw an attractive young woman dressed in jeans and a Texas Rangers baseball jersey and briefly thought under different circumstances, he would have asked her out. Unsure how to approach her and not wanting to disturb, he decided he would just hand her a card and express his sympathies.

"Miss, I'm from Fort Worth Fire and Water Services. I was sent by your insurance agent. I'm so sorry for your loss. Here's my card. Just let me know if there's something I can do for you. And again, I am so sorry." Barrett did his best to tactfully handle the situation.

"I don't know what to do. Can you help me?" The young woman of about twenty-five looked up at him with her face strangely blank.

"Miss, all I can do is put the house back together," he said softly.

"My name is Whitney Gains. This is my parents' house, and I just moved back in with them a few months ago. I don't have anyone else. The rest of the family is gone. I used to have a cat. My dad had a pistol, but I'm scared to stay here by myself," she rambled disjointedly about her situation.

"Miss Gains, you can't stay here tonight. Can I take you to a hotel or call a friend for you?"

"I don't really know anybody. I was staying here until I got my own place. I haven't found a job yet, even though my parents asked me every day if I had a job," her voice trailed away.

Barrett looked at her with sympathy. He wanted to put his arm around her and let her know he would take care of her.

"Would you take me to a hotel?" she gazed plaintively up at him from the steps of the porch.

"I would be glad to help."

Whitney rose slowly and went back into the fire damaged house. Barrett followed with a bright flashlight he had pulled from his pants pocket. The fire appeared to have involved only the side of the house where the master bedroom was located. The master was on the right side of the home as you entered, between the garage and kitchen. The other two bedrooms and a hall bath were on the left side, down a hall from the living area, with only smoke damage.

He shined his light for Whitney as she went to her bedroom and packed a small bag of clothes and overnight needs. She took Barrett's arm as they walked out of the house and got into his truck.

"I know of a hotel nearby, and I can take you there," Barrett reassured her. "Do you have a phone with you?"

"Yes, I have my cell." She seemed less in shock now she was away from the grim scene.

"Are you hungry?" he asked.

"Sure, anything is fine."

"Tacos?"

"Sure." She smiled oddly at him like they were on a first date.

Barrett went through the drive through of a 24-hour taco place for their meal, then pulled up to the hotel around 2 a.m. He went to the front desk with her to check in and she stood waiting for him to pay, which he didn't mind.

"The insurance company will pay for what is called your additional living expenses like hotels and meals. I'll get this tonight for you and let the adjuster know. Call me in the morning and I will come get you and we'll meet with the adjuster. You have a good insurance company, and I have worked with them before. Here's my card with my cell number. Call me when you're ready in the morning," he said comforting her as best he could.

"Thank you, you're my gallant hero." Whitney hugged him and crossed the lobby toward her room as Barrett walked back to his truck.

*   *   *

Lourdes emailed a report to her boss with one last chance for him to do the right thing. She had not changed the number for the IPO, as demanded and was aware he would fire her as she sat in her cubicle. She patiently awaited his call or for him to appear over her shoulder. Her desk phone rang, and she could see it was her boss's extension.

"Yes, sir," she answered with her voice firm but even. "No, I will not change it. I am sure there are others that will, but I will not . . . I understand, but I have read my contract and my bonus remains at $850,000 for the correct evaluation and due diligence . . . If you want to fire me, then that will be my severance demand . . . I understand . . . I expect payment in fifteen days . . . It will not be necessary for you to send anyone to escort me out of the building." Lourdes hung up the phone pleased with the exchange.

A person prepared to quit rather than suddenly being fired has a huge advantage in preparation. Lourdes had seen others fired and others who had quit with a plan in place. She had activated her new company website and agreed to appear on the TV show in two days. The producer had asked her to speak on IPO valuation and the corruption associated with altered modeling.

Lourdes had first seen Wall Street Morning when she started cleaning the bank. Mr. Downs would have it showing on the kitchen television. The brilliant and highly regarded, Sherry Halverson hosted the show. Lourdes looked up to her as a role model and a true American success story. Sherry was born in Queens and had clawed her way up to have her own show after years of proving herself in her field. She was tough but fair to the most powerful men and women in business and was universally well respected.

Lourdes checked her watch once more as she left her apartment at four thirty in the morning. For her plan to prosper, she had to make a powerful impact on the audience and on Sherry. Her segment would be the first one after the seven a.m. break. As she checked her outfit, hair, and makeup once more in the full-length mirror, she got an idea. She was happy with her gray suit jacket and matching skirt, but black cowboy boots with her Stetson hat would pull it together to make an unforgettable impression.

Clutching a small black purse under her arm, she strode down the hall to the elevator with the confidence of a matador going into battle with a charging bull. When she appeared on the street, she saw the car Sherry had sent was waiting for her. She opened the door and got in the back seat while the driver nodded with a big smile. There was little traffic at the early hour and soon the car parked in front of their destination. A production assistant greeted Lourdes as she walked into the studio's lobby.

"That is an awesome outfit. We don't get many people dressed like you for the show," the assistant complimented Lourdes.

"My cowgirl princess has arrived at the ball wearing her crown, I see," Javier greeted her with a big smile as she walked into the studio. "Come meet Sherry. The show starts in ten minutes. I am so glad you are here. You are going to be fantastic." Javier spoke in his typical fast-paced manner. He led Lourdes to Sherry Halverson who was seated in the anchor chair reading notes.

"Miss Lourdes Sanchez, meet the boss, Sherry Halverson," Javier proudly presented his find.

"Why look at you!" Sherry exclaimed. "I love the boots and that hat."

"Thank you, it's a real honor to be here and to meet you." Lourdes felt starstruck.

"And that Texas accent! My audience is going to love you!" Sherry knew Lourdes would be a good interview.

"I'll do my best."

"Javier has briefed me, and he will let you know what questions I will be asking. Just be yourself, be honest, and have fun," Sherry coached.

Feeling more comfortable, Lourdes followed Javier to the green room. There she was introduced to the other people scheduled to be on the show that morning. An economist from The University of Chicago who was older but very charming, a tech billionaire from California who was complaining about the food the show served while they waited not being organic *enough*, and a married attorney who specialized in ethics who promptly tried to hit on her.

Others came and went for the next two hours and most of them were pleasant enough people who asked about Lourdes' hat and why she was there.

"I'm speaking on mathematical formulations that are designed to determine stock valuations," she would say, and they would nod and go back to what they were doing.

"I need you to come on and get seated during the break," Javier hurriedly ordered. "Let's make sure we have the lighting adjusted for your hat."

Lourdes Sanchez from tiny Travis City, Texas, was now seated at a curved, acrylic desk beside the most powerful woman in business news. She fought nerves and used her energy to focus like when she was shooting skeet. Sherry was reading and having her hair and makeup touched up when a woman appeared in Lourdes' face and began applying makeup. A grip was checking the lighting when a red light suddenly started flashing prompting the makeup lady to quickly step out of the frame. A microphone was hurriedly attached to Lourdes' jacket lapel, and she was told to not pay any attention to the cameras and just have a natural conversation with Sherry.

"And we are back! Good morning again," Sherry began. "Today we have a young lady with us, and I will let you guess from where she hails. Thank you for coming, Lourdes Sanchez."

"Thank you, Ms. Halverson," Lourdes tried to steady her voice. "I'm honored to be here."

Danny, Maria, Dawn, and Mr. Downs were watching from the Sanchez's living room when the camera panned to Lourdes. The group cheered in unison.

"She's wearing your hat!" Dawn hollered.

"Hush! Listen," Mr. Downs insisted.

"Tell us, Lourdes. What does a beautiful young woman from Texas do on Wall Street?" Sherry asked.

"I'm a quant," Lourdes explained. "Basically, I design mathematic formulations to value IPOs."

"You *do not* look like the math geeks I've met," Sherry joked.

"Thank you, but I've always felt at home in roles primarily taken by men. Not sure why though," Lourdes was beginning to feel more comfortable.

"Let me ask you, do you feel this algorithmic takeover of Wall Street is legitimate? There are buildings filled with whiz kids like you from all over the world. Why is this happening?"

"Where there are trillions of dollars at stake, this will naturally attract the smartest and most ambitious people to get paid. Just like the best athletes play in the major leagues. The very best get paid ridiculous amounts. There is a difference, however, in that the athlete's money is directly based on performance. Or should I say *past* performance and proven abilities, whereas algorithms are based on mathematically designed shots in the dark. In my experience, statistically, we are all guessing. These sophisticated *models* are no different than having a vote of a thousand random people decide an outcome."

"Then why would they spend all the money to do it? Investment banks and brokerage firms spend a ton of money to gain an edge. Are you saying they are worthless?" Sherry focused intently on her guest.

"They spend the money to make them *feel* they are right. When they are correct, about fifty percent of the time, they walk around like a bunch of peacocks pretending they can predict the future. When they are wrong, they hide like the losers they are or far worse, they blame their losses as 'unpredictable.'" Lourdes let her frustration flow freely.

"Lourdes, I must say my producer swore I would love you and I am beginning to see why." Sherry was pleased with Lourdes' camera presence. "What is your answer to the issue you are describing?"

"The same answer that has worked for centuries. An open market with transparent information for all. It can be very messy and volatile, but in the end, the market decides value when buyers and sellers come to an agreement. The rest is just so much fluff and rooster crowing."

"Impressive," Sherry laughed. "You must know a thing or two about roosters being from Texas! Tell us, what are you doing these days?"

"I've launched a fund called The Letter. I have been in the market since I was ten years old. I can make you money by investing in solid companies but keep your money safe by also having some insurance on the side. It's no different than you would treat your own home just in case there is a fire," Lourdes said confidently.

"Tell us, how did you get to be who you are?" Sherry had plainly fallen under Lourdes' spell like everyone who ever met her.

"My parents Danny and Maria Sanchez taught me hard work, honesty, and love. Mr. William Barrett Downs the Third, my hometown's banker and my mentor, taught me the business, and Ms. Dawn Monroe taught me to say what I think. I'm here this morning because people like them encouraged me and believed in me. I just never wanted to disappoint them."

"I wouldn't think they have ever been disappointed in you. It isn't possible. Would you come back and see us sometime?" Sherry smiled invitingly. "We don't have many guests as candid and honest as you."

"Sure, anytime." Lourdes' eyes sparkled.

"The fund is called The Letter, and is managed by Lourdes Sanchez, superstar. She has a website and phone on the screen below me, so check it out. We will be right back after this break."

Javier rushed to Lourdes' side as the camera light went off and disconnected the microphone clipped to her jacket. Sherry stood and hugged Lourdes.

"When you started punishing those arrogant SOBs, I wanted to cheer. You were fantastic! Stay in touch. I mean it! Javier, give her my private contact information. Lourdes, whenever you have a rant or see an injustice, let me know. Good luck with The Letter. By the way, how did you come up with that name?" Sherry asked as she turned to walk away.

"It's a hometown thing and *thank you again!*" Lourdes called over her shoulder as Javier whisked her back to his office.

"I am so glad you had a website and phone to give out, the switchboard has been very busy. I knew you would do great and good luck to you. A car will take you back to your apartment." He showed her to the lobby exit then rushed back to the set.

Lourdes strode purposefully in her boots into the bustling, New York morning. She removed her hat and held it in her hands as she reviewed the whirlwind events in her mind. She hoped she had made her family proud.

In the car, she stretched out her arms and legs and exhaled a huge breath of relief. She remembered her phone was on silent and pulled it out. There was an absurd number of text messages and voice mails. She called her mother first.

"My baby, the movie star!" her daddy excitedly announced on the speaker phone.

"You were perfect!" Mr. Downs was next.

"I cried like a baby," Dawn said proudly.

"What was it like?" Maria asked in an awed voice.

"It was very cool. They were all so nice, and everyone loved the hat, Mr. Downs." Lourdes said through her broad smile.

"You looked like you had been on television your whole life. Were you nervous?" her dad asked.

"I was before, when I was sitting there waiting for it to begin, but as soon as she started talking to me, I was fine." Five calls had beeped in since she started the conversation. "Thanks all of you! I have to return some calls. I love you all!" She pressed the button to disconnect.

Her answering service had called several times with messages, and there were more texts from old coworkers than she could respond to. As she scrolled through her phone, she thought she would need to get organized at her apartment before attempting to go through all the messages, and then Tommy's name caught her eye.

"I saw you this morning, and I was not surprised you did so well. I'm in Dallas now at a new job. I'm sure you're very busy but call me some time. I miss you." He seemed happy for her.

The car service stopped in front of her apartment building and Stan was there all broad shoulders and big grin.

"We watched you this morning. I've never seen the take no prisoners Lourdes before. That hat and boots made you look like a true Texas character!"

"Thanks, Stan! It was fun, and I might get to do it again." Lourdes skipped through the lobby like a little girl.

Her apartment became her temporary headquarters until she could get to Dallas. The lease was up in two weeks, so the timing was perfect. She sat her laptop on the small kitchen table and navigated to The Letter Fund website. She was amazed to see 3,567 visits in the past hour. Her new work email had received 654 inquiry requests for information.

Lourdes searched for her name on the web, and when she saw her picture, she admitted the hat was indeed an image maker. She needed to get to Dallas and start hiring people now.

CHAPTER 44

BARRETT'S TRUCK PULLED in front of the hotel at ten the next morning to pick up Whitney Gains. She had texted him to let him know she was ready. Barrett was taking her to meet with the adjuster and help her find a place to live for the next two or three months it would take for repairs to be completed.

"Good morning." She opened the passenger door.

"Good morning. Did you sleep okay?" he greeted the young lady.

"Not really. I guess I'm still in shock." she said even though she appeared refreshed, and her brown highlighted hair was neatly styled. She wore red shorts and a pink sleeveless cotton blouse. Her makeup was pretty, and Barrett thought she looked like a whole new person.

"You look very nice this morning," he said as he viewed her tan legs and arms.

"Thank you. What happens now?" she was not oblivious to his overtures.

"We try to put your house back together," Barrett said as he drove.

"Can you put *me* back together?" she asked pitifully.

"I'll do my best," he said tenderly, and she smiled at him.

They arrived at Whitney's parents' house to find Barrett's crew had done a significant amount of work in cleaning and restoring everything in front of the master bedroom which was behind the crime scene tape and remained sealed away pending the fire marshal investigation. The stench of smoke was still strong and reminded Whitney of the previous evening causing her emotions to overflow.

The adjuster was present and taking photos and measurements as he assessed the damage.

"Barrett Downs." Barrett approached the adjuster with his hand extended. "We worked together a few months ago on that Jackson claim—the attic fire."

"Yeah, how you doin'?" Mike Thompson responded with a handshake. He was stocky with a bass voice that carried across any room he was in.

"Good," Barrett replied. "This is Whitney Gains, the daughter of the insureds and the victims. She will be the contact on the claim, and she has hired us through the agent to take care of the damage."

"I am so very sorry for your loss. Miss Gains. I know there's no good time to ask you a few questions, but if we could go sit in my car, I need to take a recorded statement," the adjuster respectfully proposed.

"Okay, I don't know what I can tell you, though," Whitney seemed reluctant to discuss the previous night.

"I'm sure it's standard things, Whitney," Barrett comforted her. "Mike just needs to check the boxes."

Mike and Whitney walked to his car, and she sat in the front passenger seat. Barrett went to assist the crew in tearing out the water and smoked damaged carpet. The fire department had doused the fire with hundreds of gallons of water. What wasn't burned was wet, and Barrett's experienced eye told him the removed debris was exposing additional damage and cost. Barrett surveyed the worst areas and peeked through the burned wall to see the remaining metal bedsprings lying on the floor.

Next to the bed was a scorched metal cylinder, an oxygen tank by the markings. There was a nightstand with several melted appliances on and around the charred remains with a clock radio, lamp, a space heater, a computer and monitor, and the twisted remains of a power strip. It appeared to Barrett the combination of pure oxygen and too many devices plugged into the power strip had caused of the fire.

The rear exterior wall was burned out to the brick veneer and the ceiling was completely gone from the fire and water pressure. The roof decking was charred black along with the rafters and when Barrett circled the exterior, he saw holes chopped in the roof by the fire department to vent the fire. The glass was broken out in the master bedroom's lone window caused maybe by fire or, more than likely, a fireman.

"I'm back." Whitney tapped his shoulder.

"Good, is there anything else I can do for you?" Barrett asked as they met in the driveway.

"Mike's getting me set up in a condo not far from here, but all my clothes need cleaning.

What I'm wearing stinks too. I have this little car, but Mom and Dad's car keys were in the bedroom so I have no idea when I will deal with that. Anyway, Mike said I could take my clothes and get them cleaned. He gave me a check for five thousand dollars to get what I needed. He said I should just keep all the receipts. I could use some help, and I have some money." She looked at him with pleading eyes.

Barrett was a sucker for a pretty girl he could rescue, and while he went to several other jobs during the next couple of weeks, he was drawn to Whitney's condo each evening to check on her. Finally, one night, he spent the night.

"Hi, Mom." Barrett answered his cell as he was working at Whitney's house on a hot summer morning.

"Can you take off for the Fourth of July to come to the beach house?" Monica implored her son to come to the family event. "Janet Ann and Ben are coming, and we never see you anymore."

"I might come. Can I bring a girl?"

"Who is this girl? You haven't mentioned anyone new," Monica asked needing more information.

"I met her at a house fire." Barrett understood he would have to ease his mother's fears. "Her parents died in the fire. I think she needs to get away."

"Oh, that's horrible. Of course, she can come. We would like to meet her." Monica desperately hoped this girl would be good for her son.

* * *

The report was finished, and a feeling of accomplishment fell over Barbara Vincent. Darlene "Darcy" Hopper was doing remarkably well. The influence of her sister with financial help from the Downs' family had led to a fundamental change for the former exotic dancer and drug user. Barbara checked in on her every six months and reported on her progress to Mr. Downs. Darlene was now married to a young man who worked in the tire shop at Walmart, and she was the lunch waitress supervisor at a big steak house which sold a giant steak as a promotion. If you could eat all 72 ounces plus the trimmings, it was free.

When Barbara asked her if she ever thought of going back to stripping because of the easy money, she responded, "I did, but I would have to move somewhere else. I can't see me dancing naked in front of boys I went to middle school with."

Barbara mused, not all payoffs to people like Darlene make them go away quietly and turn their lives around. Many go right back to bad choices or try to extort the client for more money.

*   *   *

Seven people were waiting in the foyer of Lourdes' new office for interviews. She had hundreds of inquiries to respond to, and she had four people assigned to that job. Mr. Downs had recommended a friend in Dallas to help her get organized, and she was a nervous wreck that she was not doing as much as she should to get things right. As she entered the waiting area to call the next interview, she saw a familiar tall, handsome man standing in the door dressed in a black suit, white shirt, and pink tie.

"Hi, Lourdes," Tommy said with a little wave.

"Hi, Tommy," She was so busy her mind was thrown by him standing there. "I, uh . . . I have so much . . . I . . . Can you come back later? Wait, no stay."

"That was clear as mud," Tommy liked the obvious influence he still held over Lourdes. "Why don't I come back after five, and we can talk then?" He smiled.

"Perfect. I do want to see you, but I have all these people . . . you get it," Lourdes desperately tried to regain her composure. "See you after five."

Lourdes took the next candidate to be interviewed, and by five p.m., she had hired four new employees. She needed warm bodies; soon enough she would see who rose to the top and who failed. Her first hire was her friend from high school and college, Beth Davis. Beth was the shy girl in the cafeteria those many years before who had remained loyal to Lourdes since that day. She carried with her an accounting degree and had recently passed her CPA exam, but most of all, Lourdes could trust her unequivocally.

Though Beth and Lourdes were constantly on the same page, she also needed other people with different skills. She needed a balance of personalities. She thought of Dawn and Mr. Downs. Complete opposites in many ways but an unbeatable team. They were in Lourdes' office recapping the day when Tommy's voice was heard calling from the foyer.

"Hello?"

"Back here!" Lourdes shouted, and Beth grinned at her.

"Tommy, you remember Beth Davis?" Lourdes said to Tommy when he walked into the sparsely appointed office. "She's my accountant and my everything else, for that matter."

"Of course I know her. We spent all of high school together. You look great, Beth," Tommy complimented his old classmate.

"Good to see you, but if you'll please excuse me, I have an enormous stack of work to do," Beth said as she left the office.

"You look nice. You wear a suit at your new job?" Lourdes sat behind her desk as a barrier of protection. Tommy was so handsome and in excellent shape.

"I sell boxes. Nice boss, and I like talking, so it works for me." He comfortably sat in a chair across from her desk. "Everybody needs a box. I don't wear the suit often, but we had a meeting so . . . What are you doing for the Fourth of July?" he casually asked.

"Work, I have so much to do," she answered sounding exhausted. "I've been here eighteen hours a day so has Beth. It seems we never get close to break even."

"I know you pretty well, and I know you will stay here until it gets done, but you could use a couple of hours away. Why don't we go eat somewhere and watch the fireworks?"

"What about your girlfriend?" she said in the rehearsed manner she practiced for months on the off chance she saw him.

"Hasn't been any of those for a year or more. What about all those rich men you met in New York?" he retaliated in an equally measured way.

"Too many to count, but none of them Longhorn fans or skeet shooters." She grinned. "That's kind of a deal breaker for me."

"So, Thursday night at seven? I can pick you up here." Tommy raised his eyebrows hopefully.

"Since I'm practically living here now, yes, pick me up here."

CHAPTER 45

D ALLAS' LOVE FIELD was buried in summer holiday travelers the afternoon of July 3, 2010, and Barrett held Whitney's hand as they pulled their overnight bags through the terminal to gate 44 for the flight to Corpus Christi.

"Hi, baby brother!" Janet Ann greeted her brother and Whitney.

"Sis, meet Whitney Gains; this is my sister Janet Ann and her husband on the phone over there is Ben Jordan." Ben waved and Janet Ann greeted them with a hug.

"You look darling in that blue seersucker sundress, Whitney. Way to go, Barrett." She nodded approval to her younger sibling.

"Thank you very much and you look like a model in those white pants and red, white, and blue top. Very patriotic," Whitney responded with a smile.

The two attractive couples boarded the flight bound for the Gulf of Mexico for a four-day weekend. Whitney had been coached by Barrett for the past week as to what to wear and say to forge a successful relationship with his family. He explained his father was nice enough but a recovering alcoholic; and his mother was sweet but liked everything to be perfect. Ben worked in hospital administration and was busy all the time. And Janet Ann would by far be Whitney's toughest critic.

Barrett showed Whitney pictures from the wedding and other family events to see what Janet Ann was wearing after Whitney insisted on properly investigating for the trip to meet the family. Barrett was thrilled she was so interested in making a good impression. During the flight Janet Ann had subtly interrogated Whitney and she seemed to pass the test.

Monica was behind the wheel of a red Cadillac Escalade at the arrival's lane of the Corpus Christi airport and waved like an excited kid at the sight of her children.

"Hi, Mom! Meet Whitney." Barrett opened the front passenger door and pulled his new girl close.

"Nice to meet you! Hi, baby girl," Monica turned to the back seat to say hello to Janet Ann.

"Where's Ben?" Monica asked.

"He is getting a rent car just in case we need another car or if he needs to leave early for work," Janet Ann replied.

Barrett sat in the front and the two young ladies in the back. The drive to the island required a ferry ride with a long wait due to the holiday. Whitney looked out her window at the sights and echoes of the island with gulls swooping around, fisherman wading in the bay as the car inched forward to drive on to the ferry. Monica recalled trips to the beach house with the kids when they were small and teased Barrett for always taking off his clothes at the beach when he was little, making them all laugh.

The family beach house had been painted and remodeled a year prior and looked new to Whitney who began to add up the dollar signs. Considering the Escalade, house, and Monica and Janet Ann's jewelry, it appeared to her to be close to a million dollars. When they arrived, Four was under the raised two-story home standing by a large custom grill with smoke rising, being swept away from the constant ocean breeze. Ben pulled in behind them and the party began.

Under the house there was a concrete floor, a large, enclosed garage with bathroom, a refrigerator stocked with soft drinks and beer, and Four had installed a sound system. Two long picnic tables provided seating for all after they stowed their belongings in the bedrooms upstairs. The crashing surf was thirty yards in front of the house with a wooden walkway over the protective sand dunes to the white beach. Ben and Four talked of fishing the next morning, and Monica helped with the food preparation and tried to get to know Whitney better.

"Have you been to the beach often?" Monica asked Whitney.

"No, this is my first time. Not many beaches in Arizona," Whitney joked.

"The boys like to take the boat in the bay and fish. Do you like to fish?" Monica asked.

"Again, not much fishing in the desert, but I would love to try," Whitney responded openly.

Barrett interjected, "Sure, we can do that. Dad likes to be on the water at dawn." Whitney frowned slightly.

"But we can go in the afternoon, too," Barrett quickly inserted.

"Yeah, we can go early then meet you at the marina at eleven, and you can take her out. You know where to go," Ben tried to solve the issue, really not wanting her on the boat because he was a serious fisherman.

"That would be much better. We'll go for a boat ride and hit a few spots. Janet Ann, you want to come?" Barrett asked.

"No, thanks," she replied. "You two have fun."

That night the family dined on grilled steaks and boiled shrimp. Whitney found herself being careful to watch Monica and Janet Ann for any cues in manners while mostly staying quiet throughout the evening. When Janet Ann cleared the plates after the meal with her mother, Whitney joined in to help. She tended to Barrett like a loving wife, and he responded in kind.

The next day while Barrett and Whitney were on their afternoon fishing trip, the family gathered to eat lunch and to discuss Whitney's pros and cons like a grading system.

"I like her," Four began. "She's pretty and seems very nice—A minus."

"She's all right. So much better than most of what he's been with lately—B plus," Ben voted.

"Yes, I suppose we're all so thrilled she's not a stripper. The bar is very low, but I like her. She helped clean up and that is a huge bonus. Most people who come here act like we are their servants, even my friends," Monica added and then all eyes were on Janet Ann.

"There seems to be a few holes in her story, but we will fill them in over time. I give her a weak B but need much more information for an accurate grade," Janet Ann gave her assessment.

"Wait! Did y'all have this discussion about me?" Ben asked.

"Honestly, no," Four laughed. "If you were able to get past Janet Ann, you were good enough for the rest of us!" Janet Ann crossed her arms in a mocking frown then joined the laughter.

CHAPTER 46

2011

THE VICTORIAN HOME on Main Street which had been in the Downs family for ninety years was undergoing a complete restoration. Monica had thrown herself into the project with the full energy of an empty nester. Modern wiring, plumbing, flooring, exterior paint, interior paint, fresh wallpaper, and a new roof. Monica spent all her time meeting with the general contractor and a designer friend who was painstakingly assisting her in choosing the perfect colors and fabrics.

Monica and Four had moved in with Mr. Downs at the ranch during the extensive project, and they were all enjoying being together. Monica doted on her father-in-law, cooking his favorite dishes from Janet's cookbooks.

"Pop, when I get done with our house, we can do this one," Monica mused over dinner one night.

"Please don't worry about that; I need it to stay the same. It wouldn't seem right to change the way Janet had it, but that's very sweet of you," Mr. Downs said not wanting to hurt her feelings.

"Don't worry, Dad. She just needs a grandchild, and all of this decorating will stop," Four teased.

"I deserve a grandbaby," Monica responded. "Since Janet Ann is not helping me with one yet, and Barrett is not married, it seems I have to wait."

"What does being married have to do with anything these days?" Mr. Downs said.

"I know, but still. I want grandchildren so bad!" Monica stated.

"I must admit, you will make the most beautiful granny in town," Four rushed to compliment his wife hoping to dispel her frustration.

*   *   *

To anyone who had ever met Lourdes Sanchez, it was no surprise that The Letter Financial Services was a success. The fund now had four hundred million dollars under management, and Lourdes was a regular on-air contributor to Sherry Halverson's show. Lourdes would go to the local Dallas affiliate studio to be patched in live whenever Sherry asked for her to appear for commentary. Each time she wore her hat and boots, although no one ever saw her boots on air. Even if only subliminally, the boots were still part of the image.

Janet Ann found a modern condo close to The Letter's office, and Lourdes purchased it as the very first place of her own. The drive to Travis City took about two hours with no traffic, and she visited often unless Tommy whisked her away for a weekend. Their relationship had quickly become what she dreamed it would be when she had practiced signing "Lourdes Adams" in her notebook at fourteen years old.

Tommy asked her to marry him at the lake house in Austin under the spreading ancient pecan trees on the manicured slope down to the lake. They bought the property when it came available but had no plans to change a thing about the older place. Lourdes called it a fifty-thousand-dollar house on a million-dollar lot with priceless memories.

There was talk of a huge Dallas society wedding by her employees or a destination wedding in the Caribbean or even a hometown event that would be the biggest ever seen in Travis City. The actual wedding was in the chapel of the First Baptist Church with reception following in her parent's backyard with just family and a few friends, including Mr. Downs and Dawn, the rest of the Down's family, Maddie, and of course, the Adams family.

A proud Danny Sanchez emerged from the rear of the sanctuary escorting his only child on his arm to the sound of a single violin playing Pachelbel's Canon in D. Lourdes found a wedding dress on sale at a bridal store because she could not bring herself to spend that much money on a dress she would wear once. In spite of her budget, she could not have looked more beautiful. Dawn cried when Maria stood to signal the entrance of her daughter on her beaming husband's arm.

The traditional vows were said in soft tones through nervous smiles and after it was complete the pastor said, "You may kiss your bride." Lourdes rose to meet her tall husband's lips and he bent down for a quick, innocent kiss.

The families cheered when the couple turned to face their loved ones, and the old preacher raised his arms and unexpectedly said, "Y'all can kiss better than that. I think *even I* could kiss better than that!"

The small crowd erupted in laughter, and the couple embraced again for a much more passionate kiss with loud applause filling the church. The beaming couple turned to the guests, and Tommy raised her hand like he did that day in the cafeteria so many years ago—the day Lourdes fell in love with him.

Lourdes and Tommy spent the evening receiving congratulations from the guests and eating dishes prepared by Maria and Monica who served as caterers. A plywood dance floor had been built for the occasion, and Danny danced with his daughter first and then every woman there until Maria said it was time to stop. The newlyweds drove to a hotel on the way to Austin that night, there was no lavish honeymoon on an exotic island. They then spent the next few days at the lake house feeling as much in love as when they were fourteen years old.

CHAPTER 47

BARRETT AND THE owner of the restoration company, Ken Oliver, met early every Monday morning to discuss projects and the week ahead.

"I am very proud of you, Barrett," Ken praised the younger man. "You have kept your nose down at work and stayed clean and sober."

"I owe it to you, man. I never knew how good it felt to actually work. It's like when I played shortstop and would go deep in the hole and come up firing to first to get that out. When I lost baseball, I didn't think there would be anything else for me. I came from a pretty rich family and just didn't think I would ever have to work."

"You are doing great; keep it up. What about this new girl you were talking about?" Ken asked.

"Mostly just talking and texting now. She lives in California. We dated in high school, and her name is Claudia. She's pretty and very smart—too smart for me."

"You still seeing that crazy girl, Whitney?"

"Oh no, man she was just too intense for me. I've been trying to stay away. It was great for a while, but I can only do crazy for so long. I took her to our family beach house last July, and she started planning our wedding as soon as we got home!"

"Oh, I bet! She saw the money and she was off to the races," Ken teased.

"I don't tell most people my financial background. It affects them, you know?" Barrett confided.

"If you had told me you were from money, I probably wouldn't have hired you. Money changes people."

"Money doesn't change people; it reveals people. That's how my grandfather says it." Barrett was reminded of Mr. Downs lessons.

"And speaking of the devil, just got a text from Whitney. *Need to talk, very important.* Everything is very important. It's always high drama with her," Barrett vented.

"Well, good luck with all that," Ken joked.

Barrett texted Whitney saying he was busy, but he would call her after work. It did not seem to appease her, since she texted him constantly throughout the day and called several times which only angered Barrett. When he was alone in his truck at the end of the day, the phone rang again, and he answered in frustration.

"What the hell, Whitney! I have a job. I can't spend all day dealing with you. I said I would call you after work. What is so important? Did you break a nail or have a bad hair day?" He intentionally let his annoyance take over.

"Well, if you're going to act like that, then I am not telling you," Whitney pouted.

"Take the thirteen-year-old girl approach. Every man loves that!" Barrett was approaching rage.

"Just come to my house. I have to tell you in person, and I will call every thirty seconds if you don't!" She hung up.

Barrett knew she was not bluffing about the repeated calling. This would be a good time to finally break it off completely. No more after work or late-night trysts; he would end this mess tonight. Things with Claudia were getting interesting as she was considering moving back to Texas and wanting to reconnect. She clearly saw his newfound work ethic and maturity as attractive.

Barrett pulled his bright yellow painted, graphic wrapped truck into the driveway behind a new silver SUV parked in the clean garage. Whitney had settled with the insurance company and started a job at a copier company as a customer service representative. Most of the day she worked seated in a cubicle listening to her coworkers complain about their jobs between calls.

He knocked on the front door and saw through the narrow window beside the door the silhouette of Whitney coming to the door.

"Come in, sweetie. I'm so happy to see you," she crooned as if the screaming earlier that day had never happened.

"I want to keep this brief, Whitney." He stood just inside the door as she closed it behind him. "What is so important you could not tell me on the phone?"

"Just follow me. I have it in my bathroom," she ordered as she turned toward the master bathroom.

Barrett threw up his hands in aggravation and followed her thinking how trivial this was going to be. In the bathroom she picked up a small item off the vanity and spun around holding it up in in his face.

"I'm pregnant!" she announced triumphantly holding a pregnancy test.

"Is it mine?" Barrett stammered.

"Of course, it's yours! I'm not cheating on you!" Whitney could go from elation to rage in no time at all.

"Settle down; I'm sorry. It's just a big shock. When . . . like when is it coming?" Barrett tried to calm her down and come to terms with his own surprise.

"Next January is the best guess. So, five more months. Now what are you going to do about this?" she demanded.

"Whitney, I'm not going to abandon my responsibility, but I don't see you and me together in the future."

"We are *together* from now on, Mister Downs! You will never disrespect me again. Never!" she shouted throwing the test at his back as he walked away down the hall to the front door.

"I'm not staying here tonight listening to you have a fit. When you're ready to discuss this rationally in a couple of days, I will call you," he said, his mind swirling.

The screaming was not going to stop tonight. He knew her well enough to know her wrath could last for hours. Besides he needed counsel before he said the wrong thing. He left the hysterical woman behind him and got in his truck leaving her standing at the front door yelling obscenities at him. He drove away quickly but stopped in the parking lot at a corner store at the edge of her neighborhood to make a call.

"Dad, we need to talk. Do you have the contact information for the lawyer lady we used for Darcy? We need her again. Whitney says she is pregnant . . . Yes, it could be mine . . . I know Dad. I'm sorry. She always said she was on the pill . . . Thanks . . . I love you, too."

CHAPTER 48

THE OFFICE OF Barbara Vincent was chaotic, reminiscent of the crimes scenes where she spent her days and nights. The cleaning staff were not allowed to move the slightest scrap of paper in her workspace. She kept boxes on the floor crammed with notes of former cases and contacts. With her photographic memory she could scan the piles in her office and somehow recall the one thing she needed to solve her problems. Baby mamas of the wealthy were common and took advantage of rich young men who were thinking with the wrong head as Barbara often said. They were not all gold diggers. Some were genuinely in love with the young man. Sometimes the man was enamored with the woman, but it was never the baby's fault in Barbara's point of view. She tried to only focus on the child and the DNA test. Barbara had found the test eliminated about forty percent of claims since it became the definitive answer. It also caused a few surprises in the modern era by revealing old secrets.

She interviewed Barrett Downs for an hour and found him to be a changed person since her last dealings with him. He was honest and admitted his unfortunate involvement was possible, but understood he needed to step away and let Barbara handle Whitney. He explained how they met at a fire where her parents were tragically killed. Barbara had a virtual PhD in the ways of psychotic women and had her plans laid out for Whitney if a few leads came in, but she had time. The wildcard was Barrett's mother who was in a panic that the baby would not be properly cared for, and Barbara could lose her bargaining ability if Whitney somehow got to Monica. Monica would do anything for that child, and while noble, it could be very bad for negotiations.

*　*　*

The ranch was suffering from a summer drought that also affected the entire state, and water levels in area lakes were dropping to all-time lows. Cattle were being sold off by the hundreds of thousands, and there were not many sources for hay except from some of the southeast states that had normal rainfall. Dub and Mr. Downs stood under the carport and discussed strategies to address the dire conditions.

"What do you want to do, Dub. We can't sell out at a known loss," Mr. Downs began the discussion. "We kept three hundred round bales back from last year, and we got a decent first cutting of hay before it decided to stop raining."

"But without rain we'll be out of grazing in a month. We would have to start feedin' 'em three months early to hold the herd together. And prices are awful low. It's just a bad deal all the way around." Dub rubbed the gray stubble on his chin as he spoke while leaning his wiry body against his truck.

"We are in the cattle business, Dub. The way I see it, the price is bound to come back way higher, and cows will be sky high next year. We culled heavy last year and got rid of the old and barren cows, so we got a solid herd for the future. I say we hold what we got and try to buy fifty truckloads of hay from where we can and lose money until it turns around. If we sell the herd now, we will be selling in the lowest market. Then we will have to buy back when they turn higher."

"Thanks, Billy. Sounds good and if we get some rain, we'll make it for sure," Dub said watching Four drive up in the driveway and get out of his truck.

"What y'all decide?" Four asked knowing what the planned discussion was about.

"Holding pat," Mr. Downs confirmed. "If we are going to be in the cattle business, got to take the good and the bad."

"Well, I got to get that fence fixed where them bulls were fightin' like a bunch of drunks at a rodeo. I'll see y'all later." Dub left in his company truck as the father and son watched him drive away.

"Tell me the latest on Barrett." Mr. Downs beckoned his son inside to escape the late summer heat.

"Barbara Vincent is staying on top of this Whitney girl and keeping everyone else away. Monica just wants the baby to be safe and healthy."

"We all want that for an innocent child. I swear, that boy cannot keep his mind off sex for ten straight minutes. So, we all wait until January and see if this is his baby then hope for the best after that. At least Janet is not here to fret over this mess." Mr. Downs sounded tired of it all.

CHAPTER 49

2012

THE HEALTHY CRY of a newborn baby was strong in the delivery room early on January 4, 2012. Whitney lay with her tiny son on her bare chest as she held him for the first time in the delivery suite. There were no family present to share the exciting news, only a woman in a black pantsuit with blue shaded eyes staring intently through a crack in the door. A nurse swabbed the infant's mouth, placed the sample in a sealed tube then handed it to Barbara Vincent without Whitney ever knowing.

"What are you naming your son?" the delivery nurse asked as much out of habit as genuine interest.

"William Barrett Downs the Sixth," Whitney said with conviction.

"That is one fanciful name. Got five ahead of him. I don't hear that very often. In fact, I've never heard of a sixth before."

Barbara forwarded the baby's sample to the same private service for DNA testing she had previously sent Barrett's test. The DNA service did not publish results in any public register as her clients preferred this for obvious reasons. She would learn in a few days if he was the father.

Whitney had been relatively cooperative throughout the pregnancy, and Barbara had kept the Downs family away to prevent any interference. Barbara did not trust Whitney, feeling she was capable of anything. Her investigation revealed Whitney had anger issues since middle school. While most of the records were expunged, Barbara was able to track down some former teachers and classmates in Phoenix where she grew up who had confirmed a past with occasional violent outbursts.

Her parents were described as having been kind of weird by people who had known them. There were rumors Whitney's father was physically and mentally abusive to his wife and daughter but no known sexual abuse or police reports. Her mother smoked for years and suffered from emphysema requiring oxygen. The family had moved to Fort Worth for Mr. Gains' state job in the highway department just after Whitney graduated high school. Whitney drifted to different community colleges and odd jobs for a while before moving back in with her parents. She'd had no known friends.

Whitney went for a walk after ten each night. She had stated she was on her walk when the fire occurred. A convenience store camera supported her alibi as she could be seen strolling by the store at ten thirty. Barbara had interviewed the store owner and clerk who were working the night of the fire, and the clerk stated he saw the girl walking most nights. Whitney had not entered the store the night of the fire per the clerk and it was confirmed by the digital security camera showing her walking past the store but not entering.

The fire marshal later ruled the fire accidental with electrical malfunction being the likely cause based on what was found at the scene with the overloaded power strip. The oxygen tank's plastic hose had burned through releasing pure oxygen creating a very hot fire that ignited the bedding and overwhelmed the sleeping couple. There was no evidence of incendiary fluids like gasoline, but products like lighter fluid left little to no residual evidence. There was some life insurance money, a hundred thousand dollars, of which Whitney was the sole beneficiary, but there was not enough evidence to support any real suspicion. Yet Barbara just knew there was something here that pointed to Whitney. Her gut was telling her that Whitney Gains had killed her parents and she had gotten away with it.

*   *   *

Randy and Vickie were the first guests to arrive at the Downs' home on Main Street for Mr. Downs' seventy-fifth birthday party. Monica had been preparing the celebration for weeks to keep her mind off the possibility she had a grandson she might never see.

"Hey, sum bitch. How you doing old man?" Randy greeted his lifelong buddy.

"Hey sum bitch to you, and I may add that you are six weeks older than me, old man." They laughed at the same joke, told for fifty years.

The guests drifted in over the next hour. Friends from the bank, church, skeet club, and cattle sale barn. Janet Ann and Ben were there with Barrett and Claudia Bergman. Claudia had made the move back to Texas after suffering through a harsh relationship in California. She desperately needed to mend, and Barrett had now become the man to heal her. Lourdes and Tommy came along with Danny and Maria who brought some of her homemade salsa which Mr. Downs loved. People were strictly told not to bring any gifts, but Janet Ann announced she had a present for her grandfather.

"Attention, everyone!" Janet Ann called out loudly across the crowd standing on the hearth of the old fireplace.

"I know we were all told not to bring any gifts, but I had no choice. I had to bring just one. You see my gift is inside me. I'm pregnant!" she announced with great joy.

The entire group looked toward the glowing mother to be, except Monica who was so overcome she slowly sank to the floor and sat stunned. Four saw her and went to lift her up in an embrace. The burden of not knowing the fate of Whitney's baby was momentarily eased. Monica was thrilled for her daughter, son-in-law, and herself.

"You okay, Mama? I didn't mean to knock you off your feet." Janet Ann hugged her mother.

"When?" Monica could only muster.

"June thirteenth, but we don't know for sure."

"We'll be firmer on the date in a couple of months. I'm sorry I didn't tell you sooner, but we wanted to wait to be sure and then this party fell right in place, so . . ."

Lourdes was happy for Janet Ann but dreaded the eventual pressure of answering when she would join the mother club. She always answered the question saying she was focusing on her career for now.

"Claudia, when did you get back from California?" Lourdes asked to get off the subject of babies.

"Maybe a couple of weeks ago. I can't tell you how much I love being home. I miss the weather in LA, but that's the only good thing I can say about that place."

"I know what you mean, New York had some wonderful parts, but this is home. Where are you living now?" Lourdes asked.

"I moved in with Barrett for now. He's turned into a really good guy. It's been nice," Claudia lowered her voice, "but we're dealing with some drama."

"I've heard some things," Lourdes sympathized. "I hope it all works out, and I was happy to hear Janet Ann's news."

"I will tell you more later, away from here. When are you and Tommy going to add to the population of the planet?" Claudia teased.

"Why don't you and Barrett go first, then you can tell me all about it," Lourdes jested.

Mr. Downs was standing next to a tall leather chair and using the back to steady himself, he looked fragile to Lourdes. She waited for Daisy and Four to leave his side, and then she pushed forward and gently took his arm.

"Why don't you have a seat, Mr. Downs." She guided him into the seat of the chair.

"Thanks, Lulu. I guess I've been standing for a long time." He sounded tired.

"Sit here on my right side," he invited her to sit on the arm of his chair.

"Can I bring you anything?" she asked.

"No, honey. I'm fine, just tired. Been a long day." He gazed out the bay window and began a story.

"I saw something today that I found interesting. On the drive over, I saw a boy, maybe eight or ten, on a bicycle peddling down the sidewalk. Now that in itself is unremarkable, but it was what he was wearing that caught my eye. This boy had on a helmet, elbow pads, and knee pads as if he was heading into battle. Now I know that parents and society are trying to safeguard the kid from getting hurt, but it gives the child a false sense of protection. With *no* protection he will have some injuries, but they will be based on risks taken and a skinned knee or two to punish mistakes. By placing padding to eliminate the bumps and bruises, it fosters a false sense of bravado that eventually will allow a much more severe injury."

He turned to Lulu, "Watch out for the companies that are padded too much. They will be the ones that fall the hardest. Understand? Works for people, too. I trust people with skinned knees more, because they risked something and learned a lesson."

Lourdes nodded with a knowing smile. She appreciated his lessons now more than ever.

They sat quietly and watched most of the guests slowly drift away. Tommy visited with Barrett and Ben in the kitchen while Janet Ann and Claudia caught up in the den. Monica and Four were thanking Danny and Maria as Dawn and Paul were waving their goodbyes. Randy and Vickie left early in the evening, arguing about how old they were when they bought their first house.

"This has been a good party but time for me to get on home," Mr. Downs said and rose from his chair.

"Happy birthday, Mr. Downs," Lourdes said to him once more.

"Have you seen Janet? We need to get on home," he called out rather loudly. Everyone in the room heard him and saw him look around in confusion.

Four quickly stepped to his father's side with a comforting expression on his face.

"Dad, why don't you let me help you to your truck." He began leading his father slowly away while glancing back at Lourdes with a slight shake of his head as if to plead for her to not say anything.

Lourdes and the rest of the small group remaining in the house stood silently and watched the old man get in his truck and nod to his son as Four waved goodbye from the driveway.

The quiet group was jolted back from what just happened when Monica announced, "There have been a few episodes like this. Not many, but all of you need to be aware. Pop is not well."

"Has he been to a doctor?" Janet Ann shakily asked as a tear appeared on her cheek.

"Yes, he's been diagnosed with Alzheimer's. He may stay like this for years or it may get much worse and that could happen quickly. It was the reason we wanted to have this party," Monica said lovingly as Four returned from outside and stood beside her.

"Listen, I know that this is a shock. Monica and I wanted to tell you all, but we wanted to wait until after the party." Four supportively put his arm around Monica.

Lourdes suffered in a state of disbelief like the rest of the family. The thought of her mentor being robbed of his great mind seemed cruel beyond belief. He had always been there for everyone in the room. The one constant in all their lives was now being taken down by a merciless disease.

"Is he okay to drive?" Ben asked bringing up what should have been obvious to the remaining group.

"Yes, and who here is going to tell him he can't drive that old truck anymore?" Four answered. "That day is going to be very hard on everyone."

Inside Tommy's truck on the way home, Lourdes despondently laid her head against the interior passenger door staring blankly toward the unknown future. She would need to tell her parents about Mr. Downs, but not yet. She needed time to absorb the solemn news. She relied on him so much for investment ideas, and she wondered if she had trusted him too much lately. But she could not think of any incident indicating the slightest confusion. For the first time in her life, she could not blindly trust the word of Mr. Downs, and she fell into a deep state of hopelessness.

Tommy could see her pain but had no idea what he could do or say to help her. It was as if she just watched her favorite pet get run over by a car. She was in a profound state of depression.

"Why bother with any of this? All the hard work and time, just to have it snatched away like a thief in the night," Lourdes' thoughts began falling out of her. "His mind is being stolen, Tommy. Not just a normal mind either; the brightest man I have ever known. He was so much smarter than any professor or New York boss I ever had. Wisdom is rare, you know. He wanted every person he ever met to succeed."

"I'm sorry, baby. I'm so sorry," Tommy empathized with his wife as they drove home to face the new reality.

CHAPTER 50

THE DNA RESULTS were in. Barbara Vincent opened the email attachment to read the report from her office. Barrett had a ninety-nine percent chance of being the father. It was time to implement Barbara's plan, but she had one more troubling item to double check. She left her office and drove to the convenience store where Whitney had been observed on the outside camera the night of the fire.

She pulled into the store parking lot and met the manager. They walked to the back to review the camera images from another date—the day before the fire. At ten thirty p.m. the image of Whitney Gains appeared in front of the store camera, but this time she turned and walked into the store. Barbara asked who the clerk was as Whitney came through the door.

"He worked part time for a while, mostly on Sunday nights. This was on a Sunday. The fire was on Monday." The manager realized it was a different clerk after they checked when they looked on both days.

They followed the three cameras and watched Whitney reach for an item on a shelf hidden from the clerk and put the small item about four inches by three inches in her pocket. She then walked back in sight of the cashier and purchased a pack of chewing gum.

"What did she steal? What's on that shelf?" Barbara quickly pointed to the monitor.

The two came from the back room and went to the same shelf and found what she had stolen. Barbara's plans for Whitney changed. She had the digital video sent to her email and raced back to the office to gather the evidence for the police.

*   *   *

Claudia teased Barrett about his work truck with its bright yellow paint and printed flames and ocean waves crashing on the sides making them look like a rolling billboard for the restoration company.

"I like my truck like it is. Everyone knows it's me going down the road," he said as they headed to a late lunch on a Friday afternoon in Fort Worth, a few days after Mr. Downs' birthday party.

"Any more news on your grandfather?" Claudia asked as they drove over to his favorite Mexican food place.

"Nothing new. It doesn't seem possible he could be sick." He didn't notice the SUV making a U turn to follow him on the busy four lane street.

"What about Whitney? What's happening there?"

"Just stay away is all the attorney says. Apparently, she's home with the baby, and the little fellow is healthy." Barrett pulled into the restaurant's large lot, parking his truck across from the building. Getting out of the truck he noticed a car to his right backing out of a space, and he watched it to make sure the driver didn't bump his truck. Claudia paused to check her makeup and was just getting out of the passenger side when the car began to drive past.

Barrett caught a faint impression of a familiar image in his peripheral vision to his left as he stood in the open space between the two rows of parking spaces, when he heard the sudden revving of an engine and saw the silver SUV heading directly for him and Claudia. He spun back and pushed Claudia away toward his truck, but it was too late. The front of the accelerating vehicle hit Barrett squarely on his hip, and he immediately crumpled under the charging SUV. Claudia was clipped by the right side of the bumper sending her spinning to the ground landing partially under Barrett's truck.

Screams rose from startled patrons in the parking lot who began fleeing in all directions to escape the crazed driver of the SUV with an infant in a car seat in the back. A city police officer had followed the SUV when it committed the illegal U turn, but he had been caught at a red light and arrived late on the scene. The officer had seen the offending vehicle turn into the parking lot of the popular café and knew there was only one way in or out.

Barrett lay broken under the vehicle with the heat of the exhaust pipe burning his back. He was suddenly jerked backwards underneath the moving car and then launched forward when his head was twisted under the tire and crushed. He died instantly.

The vehicle stopped and Whitney launched herself out the car brandishing her father's pistol. She came to the front of her SUV and looked underneath to see the trickle of blood coming from Barrett's head pooling around his motionless body pressed into the gray pavement.

Despite her fractured leg, Claudia desperately tried to crawl away from the horror a few feet away from her. She heard Whitney's voice and looked up to see her standing in front of the damaged car and Barrett's lifeless body. She was pointing the pistol directly at Claudia.

"You think you're better than *me*? I had his baby. He loves me not *you!*" Whitney screamed in an otherworldly voice.

Claudia heard a shot and flinched as she covered her face with her hands. She lay alone on the ground waiting to die.

"Miss, are you okay?" the policeman asked in an apprehensive tone as he knelt beside Claudia. Whitney lay behind him, killed by a single shot to the head.

Sounds of fading sirens filled the air as Claudia lay on the stretcher inside the ambulance. Barbara Vincent stood beside the SUV that remained on top of her client's body. Barbara did not lose often but she was too late on this one by a few, deadly minutes. She had been on her way to meet Whitney with the photo of her stealing the lighter fluid she used to set the fire. Barbara had turned over all the evidence to the fire marshal and police. The police would have been arresting Whitney for the murder of her parents if she had not seen Barrett's truck and followed him into the parking lot.

Barrett's healthy, baby boy was transferred in his car seat to Barbara's car along with his diaper bag. She made all the statements needed and watched the ambulance take Claudia to a local hospital. Now she had to make a painful phone call and deliver precious cargo to Travis City, Texas.

*   *   *

William Barrett Downs the Fifth was buried in the family plot close to his grandmother. The family asked for privacy and only held a graveside service allowing very few people to attend. Monica sat under the green canopy with her grandson on her lap in front of the hole her son would soon be lowered into. Four sat quietly and motionless next to her. She was numb as the preacher tried to offer some solace to the grieving people before him. The service concluded with a lone bagpipe playing the mournful tune of Amazing Grace.

Four stood and went to thank the preacher on the other side of the casket. Mr. Downs rose. Seeing the sorrow around him, he sat next to Monica and put his arm around her as she stared at the little infant's face.

"It is said that the loss of a child is the hardest thing anyone can endure. It would be easy for us to collapse under the weight of all this injustice. I spent many years preparing to bury my own son for the choices he was making, but you pulled him back from a certain death. I don't know if I ever thanked you enough for saving my son." Monica lifted her eyes and looked at Mr. Downs with immeasurable sadness.

"Monica, what if God said to you, 'I am going to bless you with a son, but you can only have him for twenty-six years.' Would you take that deal? Would you rather have none of the countless joyful moments with Barrett to erase this unfair ending?"

"No," Monica answered weakly.

"I know you wouldn't. I hate this for all of us, but I want to remember the good days and thank God for those times. I want to appreciate my grandson's life."

"I know, Pop, but it's so hard." Monica could not imagine life without her son. The baby cooed in her lap.

"Janet said to me one day, 'Monica loves children more than anyone I have ever known. We could not have found a better mother for our grandchildren.' Now you have a whole new baby to raise and love. I cannot think of a better way to help us all recover than to watch you love this child."

Monica took Mr. Downs' old hand and placed the aged fingers against the baby's tiny hand. Mr. Downs felt the little one grip his own. He smiled at the child with so much hope ahead for his young life. The few gathered in the city cemetery disbanded unhurriedly to return to their lives and allow their anguish to slowly dimenish over time.

2016

"What's this for?" Lourdes asked Tommy looking at the strange, small box on the kitchen counter as she walked in from work to their Dallas condo.

"That is a DNA kit. Remember we talked about it one night, and I said you should try to find out about your past. You said, sure," he recalled the vaguely remembered conversation.

"Well, now I don't want to do it." Lourdes stared at the box.

"Okay, then don't do it. I just thought you might learn something. I didn't mean to sound like I was insisting you do anything," Tommy sounded frustrated.

"I'm afraid, baby. I don't know why," Lourdes tried to explain. "I'm just afraid I'll find out something bad."

"I get that, but nothing will make me love you less, and I couldn't possibly love anyone more than I love you."

"Okay, but I make all the decisions on how we use the information. Agreed?" She looked at her loving husband.

"Agreed." He nodded pleased with her conclusion.

"Anyway, it'll take a few weeks. They mail you the results," he added.

The weeks passed and the results arrived. Lourdes placed the envelope on the dining room table and stared at it. Not today she thought, and the envelope remained unopened.

After getting a call from Dawn, Lourdes left Dallas by herself for Travis City the next Friday morning. Dawn wanted her to come to the bank and assist in deciphering some accounts. Dawn had retired but remained the board of directors' link to Mr. Downs since his health decline over the past few years. For the last six months, he recognized fewer people and sat in his home with full-time nursing care.

Dawn and Lourdes sat together in the bank's board room with files scattered across the large conference room table. There was a corporation Mr. Downs used exclusively for anonymous charitable donations from himself and Janet. One file was titled Lulu Partnership, and Lourdes was shocked to see the total at the bottom of the last report from a month ago. It was one thousand times larger than she had calculated on her own. All the statements had been placed in multiple files by Dawn, but she needed to make sure someone else knew where they were. Dawn asked if Lourdes would take over managing the account as she had staff to handle the complicated ventures for the family, when Mr. Downs left this earth. Lourdes accepted and was honored to help the Downs family.

Janet Ann was in town visiting her parents with her two children, and Lourdes stopped by to see them. Monica greeted her at the back-door porch where a shy four-year-old boy peered from around her legs as Lourdes climbed the steps.

"Who's this big boy?" Lourdes asked in a childlike voice.

"Tell her your name," Monica encouraged her grandson.

"Willie," he said shyly.

"Hi, Willie. You are a cutie."

"Get over here, Lourdes. Come brag on my kids, now!" Janet Ann called toward the door, sitting on the floor with her four-year-old son, Robert, and her two-year-old daughter, Molly.

"Hello, you smart and beautiful children!" Lourdes threw open her arms to greet them all.

Monica and Lourdes sat next to each other on the sofa watching the kids run around the den filled with toys and games. They happily visited about their busy lives, sharing stories of work and social events. Monica remained a beautiful woman, maintaining her shape with diligent exercise, which she needed now to keep up with the active grandson she was raising.

Lourdes noticed a photo book on the coffee table and opened it to find Janet Ann and Ben's wedding album. She began leafing through the photos, prompting recollections of that special evening.

"Did you know that was Mom's dress?" Janet Ann said pointing to a photo of her dancing with Four.

"It was really cool to use it and maybe little Molly will use the same dress. I don't think I've ever seen Mom's album, just the framed picture Dad has on his nightstand. Oh, look there we are. Dang, we look hot!" Janet Ann laughed at a photo of herself and Lourdes together at the reception.

"Hey Mom, go find your wedding album, please. We want to see it, so we can find out who wore the dress better," Janet Ann asked as Monica began searching in a cabinet.

"Here it is, found it." Monica placed the heavy, ornately decorated volume in her lap, sitting between Lourdes and Janet Ann to show them the photos. "I bet I haven't seen this in thirty years," she said as she opened the volume.

"Wow, you were so beautiful! I mean you still are, but wow. I guess I never thought of you being a young bride." Lourdes said staring at the image of the stunning woman of so long ago.

"You made that dress look better than I did!" Janet Ann bragged on her mom. She turned the pages and stopped at a photo of a young, dark woman with long black hair and a huge smile wearing a flowing bridesmaid dress standing next to Monica.

Lourdes stared at the image and felt a strange sensation as she heard Monica's voice say. "That's Anika Laghari from India. She was my bridesmaid. We met in college and she was my best friend back then. I don't know what ever happened to her. She just disappeared one day." Monica was still as she and Lourdes stared at the picture.

"I never noticed before," Monica mused. "but you look so much like her, Lourdes."

CHAPTER 51

Lourdes could not erase the image of Monica's bridesmaid, Anika, from her mind. On the drive back from Travis City she was filled with an overwhelming desire to solve this mystery. Why had Anika disappeared from Monica's life all those years ago? Lourdes arrived at her Dallas condo and parked her car in the enclosed garage and waited for the door to fully close behind her before exiting the car.

She came in the through the kitchen door, entering the sleek modern glass and metal interior that Tommy referred to as the "operating room." On the dining room table was the envelope she had been ignoring for the past couple of months—the results of her DNA test. She glanced at the white and blue lettering as she walked to the bedroom to change clothes. She placed the black dress in the dry-cleaning pile and put the shoes in the correct hutch. She took off her bra and pulled on some baggy shorts and a t-shirt and went to the kitchen for a bottle of water.

With a mounting fear she had never known before, she stood by the table and stared at the paper that might completely change her life. She carefully lifted the envelope like it was a poisonous snake and sat on the sofa with the paper in her lap. She turned on the lamp beside her and used her fingernail to push along the edge of the flap. She peeked at the inside first as if she were checking for a bomb, and then withdrew and unfolded the document.

Country of origin 43 % Northern India. 41 % England, 5% Scotland, 5% Southern India.

A map of close DNA matches revealed one in Harlingen, Texas, with shared DNA 55%, possible aunt or cousin named Nandini Chanda.

Lourdes began shaking as she reread the report for every morsel of detail. She wasn't Mexican; she never had been. She was apparently half white and half Indian. A sudden thought struck her; Anika could be her mother! Lourdes stood and drank some water as her mouth immediately went dry. She paced around her living room trying to decide what her plan should be. How do you find out who you are at age thirty? She screamed at the wall. Who the hell is Nandini? Does she even know I'm alive?

She sat again on the sofa and held a throw pillow for comfort. Would she tell her parents? What would that do to them if she found her real parents? Were they the ones who threw her away? Monica said she hadn't heard from Anika in over thirty years. Was she dead? Was she killed the night she was thrown away? And if so, by whom?

Lourdes went to her laptop and searched the name, Nandini Chanda, Harlingen, Texas. A sparse record appeared, but there was a phone number. Lourdes jotted it down on a pad and began formulating her strategy to contact Nandini. She just wanted to meet her to see if she knew anything that could be helpful, but she did not want to frighten her.

She dialed the phone number.

"Hello, Sundown Motel. How can I help you?" a young woman's voice answered in an Indian accent.

"I was given this phone number for a Nandini Chanda. Does she live there?" Lourdes asked doing her best to speak calmly.

"No, she does not live here anymore. Why are you calling her?" the voice from the motel responded. Lourdes heart sank. She was no longer there.

"It's business, there is some money owed her that I am trying to send her. But she has to sign for it in person," Lourdes said to the young woman desperately hoping for some new clue. "I just need to meet her personally. It will only take two minutes."

"She is home all-day Tuesdays, but she doesn't come to work much anymore. She owns the motel. Tuesday is when her maid comes, and she thinks she is stealing from her, so she won't leave that day. I can give you the address."

"Please," Lourdes said hopefully. "That would be wonderful."

"She lives on 811 24th Street, Harlingen, Texas. Don't tell her I gave you the address," the young woman cautioned. "She is private. Even with someone trying to give her money. Her home number is just one digit different than the hotel. It ends with a six and not a seven."

"This has been very helpful and thank you. I'll keep this our secret." Lourdes pushed the red button of her cell phone and began breathing again. She scrolled through the phone and pressed Hubby.

"Baby, I opened the envelope. I have to take a trip to the Valley Tuesday . . . Yes, day after tomorrow . . . No, I have to go by myself. I'll tell you everything I know tonight . . . I'm fine, I promise. Love you." She hung up and was suddenly exhausted.

Lourdes booked the earliest flight from Dallas Love Field on Southwest to Harlingen and rented a car. The return flight was scheduled for the last flight back that night. She would have ten hours to find Nandini and learn what she could.

Tommy held his wife against him in their bed that night as she lay her head on his chest. She told him the whole story of the Anika picture and the DNA results. It was so incredible and seemed unreal.

"So, I don't have a hot Mexican wife. I have a new, hot Indian wife. I feel like I'm cheating on you with you." He tried to make her laugh.

"Do you want me to go with you, baby? I can take off," he asked.

"No. I have to do this alone. I don't know why for sure, but I really don't want to scare this woman. I may only get one chance."

"I get that. You know I'll be praying for you." He caressed her hair and they fell asleep in each other's arms.

The plane was crowded as all flights on Southwest seemed to be. It was the reason she bought their stock. She looked around at the vast majority of the passengers who appeared to be Hispanic, except her— the newly minted half Indian woman dressed in tan slacks and cream blouse. The plane landed after only an hour and half flight over South Padre Island and the Gulf of Mexico, its inviting blue water passing on her left.

The car rental counter was efficient, and she got into the white rental car and headed to Nandini's address. Her stomach was churning like the day when she went back to school after the cafeteria incident. Just keep going she thought. The GPS on her phone said ten minutes away when she spotted a McDonalds. She pulled through the drive through, buying a coffee and some biscuits with butter and jelly to offer Nandini.

The old neighborhood was neatly kept, but the houses appeared newer as she searched for the address. Patio homes that mostly looked alike with minimum yard space and elderly people out for morning walks with tiny dogs on leashes. She saw 801, 807, and there was 811. An older car was parked in the driveway, but there was room for her rental car to park along side. She parked her car with a quiet hope and said a quick prayer.

She sat in her car still preparing her speech when the front door opened and a woman of maybe sixty in a pink and light green traditional sari walked out on the little porch. Lourdes opened her door and approached the lady slowly without speaking but kindly waving when suddenly the older lady screamed and fell to the ground sobbing. Lourdes rushed to the kneeling woman and reached out to pat her shoulders.

"A ghost! Who are you?" Nandini cried out as the cleaning lady appeared behind her with astonishment.

"Anika's daughter!" Lourdes blurted out not knowing for sure, but the words tumbled out of her. "Are you related to Anika?"

"I'm her sister and I failed her." The woman was completely on the ground sobbing in convulsions as Lourdes dropped down next to her.

Lourdes held Nandini as the older woman attempted to overcome her shock. The two women were eventually helped to their feet by the young maid and went into the house where they sat on the sofa beside each other.

"Thank you, Marta. We need to be alone. I will pay you for a full day. Hand me my purse." The young woman handed Nandini a large green bag, and she pulled out sixty dollars in cash. The maid took the money and with an inquisitive glance over her shoulder, left her boss with the stranger.

"I have some coffee and some biscuits in my car. Let me go get them and we'll talk. I have as much time as you can give me." Lourdes left returning with the sack and coffee cup.

"What do you know?" Nandini asked quietly.

"I only know I was found twenty-seven years ago in a dumpster outside Travis City, Texas, with a head wound and no one ever claimed me. I was adopted by a loving couple named Maria and Danny Sanchez. Until a couple of days ago I thought I was Mexican."

"How did you find out about my sister and find me?" Nandini asked earnestly.

"I saw a picture of Anika a few days ago. She was in a wedding album of a lady named Monica Downs; Anika was a bridesmaid. A DNA test showed me to be half white and half Indian, and your name came up as a possible matching relative," Lourdes answered her.

"Do you know anything about your father?"

"Nothing, and there were no matches that showed up but you. I guess you did the DNA thing too."

"Yes, I had to for a crime a few months ago at the motel. All the employees had to do it to eliminate us as suspects. I never knew it would put us together. I don't know who your father is either, but that was the reason for everything that happened."

"Do you know where I was born?"

"I do know that, because Anika called me to come. You were born here in Harlingen where she could hide from our father and use me for some protection."

"Protection from what?"

"Our father and his brother. Anika brought disgrace to the family by her disobedience. She would not marry the man my father had arranged for her, and then she had baby out of wedlock." Nandini paused as she revisited the past. "Are you familiar with the term 'honor killing'?"

"No, but that sounds horrible. What happened?" Lourdes yearned to hear the truth.

"I will tell you all I know. In my culture, if a girl disobeys a family, then the men can punish her. They can even go as far as killing the woman by saying they are defending the family honor. It is barbaric," she spat the last words in disgust. "My uncle and his son, my cousin, found you and Anika hiding in a rent house north of Austin. Anika had dyed her hair blonde as best she could and was trying to survive by doing remote computer work from home. I think she was doing things like engineering. She was very smart." Nandini had a look of pride on her face as she remembered her sister. "I think that's how they found her though, because our father worked in that industry. He called his brother, my uncle, and my cousin and they went to her house late one night."

"My poor mother." Lourdes teared up.

"The only way I know what happened next is from what my cousin, Kazi told me. He confessed it all, and it is horrible. Are you sure you want to know the details?" Nandini cautioned her newfound niece.

"Yes, I need to know." Lourdes nodded keeping her eyes on the woman's face as she returned back to that time so long ago.

1985

Nandini was twelve years older than Anika, and they were never very close. Their mother died when Anika was in college, and Nandini had tried to fill that role as best she could. Nandini had moved with the family to the United States when she was fifteen, where she underwent a severe culture shock. There were not many Indians in the Corpus Christi schools and she was teased for her accent. But Anika was so much younger and grew up American with no accent at all, plus she excelled in school.

It had been arranged for Nandini to marry Sudhir, who was much older than she, but he was buying a motel and could provide for her. Anika was only nine when her sister left to marry. Nandini believed in duty to family and honoring traditions and had read the romantic stories of meeting the love of your life on the day of your marriage. The brutal truth differed greatly from the fantasy. She became a motel maid and personal sex worker for her husband.

Anika had finished her degree in mechanical engineering and had been working at a plastics manufacturing plant north of Corpus Christi for the past few years. She had her own small apartment and had repaid her father for all his assistance for her education. She was now making more money than he, but she dared not tell him.

One day Anika arrived at her father's for a family party unsure why her father had insisted she attend. She planned on staying a short while to fulfill her family obligation, then leave early. There were a couple of unknown cars parked in front of the middle-class neighborhood home. She also recognized her sister and brother-in-law's car along with her uncle's older sedan.

Anika parked her car and approached her father's house wearing jeans, a yellow blouse, and tennis shoes. Her sister ran to meet her, dressed in a traditional Indian sari.

"We need to talk now. Do you know why you are here?" Nandini asked in a panic.

"No, why are you acting so crazy? Where is Sudhir?" Anika stopped before they got to the driveway.

"Sudhir is working. I didn't think you knew," the older sister exclaimed in a whisper. "Dad has arranged you to marry a man and he and his family are here!"

"What the hell is he thinking?" Anika asked stunned to hear the news.

A man's voice could now be heard calling from the driveway.

"My daughters, please come now to assist me in hosting our fine guests."

Anika walked toward him glaring directly at her father. Nandini looked down as she approached the stern looking man. They walked through the garage and inside. There were five men in the room and two women. Anika scanned them quickly to see which one she was going to tell no.

"Please, please, everyone, this is my beautiful, young daughter, Anika." Her father held her shoulders mimicking affection, but she felt like she was being held so she would not run away.

"Hello. I apologize for my attire, but father has not told me what this is about." She turned and shot an angry look at her father which no one else could see.

"I wanted a surprise. I want you to meet the Mutti family." Her father pointed to each person and they nodded respectfully. "I work with this man, Mr. Mohammed Mutti, and this his wife, Yamani, and his brother, Doctor Ramesh Mutti, and his wife, Sanitri." He paused for dramatic affect. "And this is their son Ryan, who in medical school now. *Very* smart boy. And say hello to your Uncle Nitesh and cousin, Kazi."

Anika felt like an exhibit at the zoo as all eyes were on her. "My daughter the engineer! She is very smart too. She got big money job the day she graduated. All of us very proud. And she is beautiful like her mother," Mr. Laghari added boastfully.

Uncle Nitesh and cousin Kazi remained silent most of the night as neither usually spoke in front of strangers. Uncle was the kind of man who studied people carefully and listened to everything anyone said, but later might obsess over a single word, the way it was used or the subtle tone no one else noticed.

After a meal of traditional, northern Indian cuisine prepared by Nandini, the two families went outside to the covered patio to enjoy ice cream. Anika assisted her sister with the meal, serving to avoid any unwanted conversation. She tried to not look at Ryan who appeared to be younger than her and quite unattractive. His hair was combed straight back with long sideburns. He wore black rimmed plastic glasses and she thought he looked like a pedophile. His clothes were decent, but his shirt was too tight across his protruding belly. She saw his mouth with its crooked, yellowish teeth, and thought she could never kiss him. Though he was smart, he flaunted his knowledge of medical terms, knowing no one would question him. She looked over his parents and saw a typical, Indian mother and an overbearing father. She decided she would be pleasant tonight for her father's sake, but this marriage was not going to happen.

"Ryan will be doing his residency next year. We don't know where he will be. Maybe New York City? We don't know," Ryan's father said.

Anika smiled politely, and wondered what the family meant by that? Did they think she would be impressed by something that *might* happen? And who cares where?

"Yes, New York City." Ryan's mother joined in the fantasy.

"New York City would be something," Ryan's aunt said speaking for the first time all night.

"I went to New York City for a meeting one time," Ryan's uncle said.

Anika's mind was spinning in turmoil at how horribly bad the night was going. These were the most boring people she had ever met. They were literally talking about something that had little chance of happening.

"Can you assist me with a new drink, Anika?" Ryan broke the spell of the New York fantasy.

"Yes, of course." She stood and Ryan followed her to the kitchen.

"I wanted to be alone to tell you that I think you are beautiful, and I would do my best to make you a good husband," Ryan stumbled over what sounded like a memorized list of words.

"Thank you, but I am so sorry, Ryan. I don't know if I can marry you. Please realize that this is all very sudden to me. Let's just get through tonight and be nice to one another. Then we can let this experiment fail over time." Anika looked at him to try and read his face as she spoke. He was blank through it all.

"I understand. You are afraid to go to New York City." He incorrectly thought she was afraid to move.

Anika thought this was the most bizarre sentence she had ever heard.

"Yes, that's it. You nailed it, Ryan." She walked away back to the patio.

When Anika returned to her apartment that night, she had two messages on her machine from her father. "Please call me. We need to talk about how well it went tonight."

Anika knew she needed to tell her father the truth, and she also knew he would be upset. He seemed very excited about his possible future, doctor son-in-law. She also had a message from her friend Monica.

"Hey, I just needed to hear your sweet voice. Call me. I'm so tired with my new baby girl, and I want you to come see her. I am usually free from one to two in the morning, so give me a call." Monica ended the message laughing.

Anika dialed her back. "Hey, Monica . . . You will not believe what happened to me tonight. My father tried to sell me to a doctor named Ryan . . . No, I'm not kidding. You know how I have told you how strict he is and traditional? Well, that includes arranged marriages . . . Yes! . . . No, he was not cute. He is short and fat and has ugly teeth. You know I can't get past an ugly mouth . . . I know, you can't either. If men only knew how much they are judged by their teeth . . .

I do want to come visit little miss Janet Ann. . That is so cute! . . . I bet she is going to be as pretty as her mother . . . No, Dan is on and off. Oh, he's fine. It's just not clicking between us . . . Ha ha! . . . Love you, too."

Anika had first needed to vent to her friend, but now she needed to make the call she was dreading.

"Hi, father . . . No, I did not like him . . . Yes, it matters. Of course it matters! . . . I will not . . . I am not going to disgrace the family . . . just let me handle this . . . I don't care what Uncle says; I am not his daughter. I will see him once more, but that is it . . . Goodbye, father." She could not believe he was so upset with her for not immediately falling in love with that unappealing man.

Anika's Uncle Nitesh was the family patriarch. He was the first to leave their northern Indian village to come to the United States. He was twenty-three when he arrived in Houston in the early sixties having no money, few contacts, and poor English-speaking skills. He found work through a labor broker who took advantage of poor aliens trying to make it in America. These men found people like Nitesh through a vast system of informants stationed in bus terminals, docks, and even international air terminals.

Nitesh was not a good student like his younger brother. He succeeded in America the way many immigrants do—through crime. He learned from the labor broker how to take advantage of his own people. He learned the system quickly and started his own black market employment service, working with American companies and importing his countrymen. He exploited the desperate and made a comfortable income and enough money to educate his younger brother back home in India. When it was time, Nitesh brought his brother and the rest of his family to the States.

Nitesh married a local Indian woman after a couple of years, and they had one son, Kazi. His wife disappeared under suspicious circumstances when the boy was twelve, but there was no investigation or witnesses, because no one wanted to anger Nitesh. He used his newfound wealth to buy old motels around the state of Texas and imported unsuspecting countrymen who paid him for the never-ending loan to live in America. It was perfect; they had a place to live and a place to work every day and Nitesh had a constant cash flow.

Nitesh did not want any attention brought on himself. He lived in a modest home and drove a conservative sedan. Kazi was a tender-hearted boy who grew up missing his mother but was never able to leave his father's overbearing influence.

1989

The two men arrived at the house in the early morning hours and parked in front of the neighbor's house. Anika was asleep on the sofa in the little living room of the small rent house when Uncle Nitesh and her cousin Kazi burst through the flimsy door with a steel crowbar. They were on her in seconds. They had brought rope and duct tape and appeared to be organized. In a matter of minutes, the two men gagged and bound Anika, dressed her little girl and placed the child in the car seat in Anika's car. Uncle drove her car and Kazi threw Anika in the back seat of his Corolla.

They needed to get away from the area as quickly as possible, but they appeared to have no clear plan of what to do after the kidnapping. Kazi had driven for an hour when he saw his father pulling over at an abandoned trucking company. He walked back to the car where Anika was tied up, and she had worked the gag away from her mouth where she could speak. The door opened and she screamed, "Don't kill my baby! Please don't kill my baby! Take her to Travis City! You can kill me, but please don't kill my child!"

She had seen a sign that Travis City was only twenty more miles, and she knew if Monica could somehow find out, she would take care of the baby. If only they would leave the child at the ranch house where she had gone after her friend's wedding, her daughter would be saved.

Kazi pleaded with his father to take the child to Travis City. After arguing for a moment Nitesh said he would. Kazi told Anika he agreed to take her daughter to Travis City. The child was not at fault in Kazi's mind and should be saved. The exit came up on the right and the two cars pulled off the highway and tucked in behind a remote convenience store. Anika saw her uncle jerk her daughter out of the back seat and retrieve the crowbar from the floorboard. Kazi's headlights shown directly at the little girl and Uncle with the steel bar. He pointed with his makeshift weapon to the side of a dumpster and in stenciled letters it said, Travis City Waste. He suddenly struck the child on the side of her head sending her reeling to the gravel driveway. She lay motionless as Anika screamed in horror at the sight of her child being lifted by her uncle as he pushed over the dumpster lid and threw in her limp body. He walked back to the car, pure evil burning on his face and opened the door.

"I did what I said. I brought your daughter to Travis City. I always do what I say." He slammed the door shut against Anika's slumping body. The lead car pulled away and Anika's stunned cousin could only follow. An old, unmarked road appeared on the right with no evidence of any buildings or houses around. They drove up the road until the rough trail ended. Uncle got out and opened the trunk of Kazi's car and got out a can of gasoline and two shovels. Kazi opened his door and reluctantly walked over to his father.

"Start digging a spot, and we will do it here," the older man instructed his complicit son. Anika lay in the back seat, her hands and feet bound. She knew what was coming. She was to be killed for the sin of disobeying. She had brought great shame on her family name and disgraced her father before the whole world. She had seen her daughter killed in front of her and her tiny body tossed away like trash. She looked forward to death which was the only thing that would remove the state of her ultimate sorrow. The door opened and her head fell out and she felt rough hands grab her neck and drag her along the stony ground.

She lay on her back opening her eyes for the last time to see her uncle standing over her, emptying the gas can on her body and lastly her face. She could taste the gasoline on her lips, felt the dreadful pain in her nose, and lastly felt the cold liquid burning her eyes. She saw the flash of light, and then immediately felt the heat. She knew in her mind it would be over soon, but her last moments were agony. Death did not come as fast as she hoped as she fought the bindings while she twisted and thrashed on the rocky ground. She managed an involuntary scream before there was no more breath.

The two men stared at the pyre with a twisted fascination. Neither had seen this before and the smell was as horrible as the sight of burning flesh. Kazi threw up. Soon there were just a few bones left that were easily crushed to powder by the two shovels from the car. The last bits were swept with the sides of their shoes and covered with dirt as the sun rose in the eastern sky. It was over. Their job was done.

CHAPTER 52

LOURDES STARED AT the woman she now knew as her relative. Nandini had completely borne her soul to soothe her guilt, but there was nothing that could erase the horror of what had happened. Lourdes mind spun at the blunt description of her mother's murder. Her mother who never knew her child had survived.

"What was my name?" Lourdes finally managed to ask in a cracked voice.

"Your name was Amrita, but she called you Lotus like the flower. Oh, she loved you so much." Nandini was crushed and exhausted by recalling the past.

"Lotus? I think I remember that. I wish I could remember more," Lourdes cried softly.

"Lourdes and Lotus are close. Do you know why they named you Lourdes?" Nandini wondered.

"I never asked why. It was just my name. Do you know when my real birthday is?"

"February 24, 1986. It actually snowed that day," Nandini recalled. "I told Sudhir I was having female problems and had to go to the doctor, but I secretly met Anika at the hospital. She had called and left a message at the front desk in code. We used messages to communicate, and Sudhir never caught us. You were born early in the morning, and your mother thought you were the greatest blessing she had ever received."

"Did you know my father? He was white according to my DNA test." Lourdes continued to press for more answers.

"No, she would not tell me. I never understood why."

"She never married him or anyone?"

"No, she just had you. You completed her." Nandini still marveled at her sister's strength.

"Where was I born?"

"Here in Harlingen at Mercy Hospital."

"There must be a birth certificate," Lourdes said beginning to feel hopeful at the possibility of more information. "What was my full name?"

"Amrita Laghari, daughter of Anika Laghari born in Hidalgo County, Texas, USA," Nandini answered sounding official as she could.

Lourdes had tried to absorb the story of her mother's life and her own history as she visited with her aunt. Nandini talked of how wonderful she was as a child and she wished she could have known her better. Lourdes suddenly became aware that she may be in some danger.

"Where are your uncle and cousin now? Would they try to kill me if they knew I was alive?" she asked anxiously.

"All are dead. My father died last year. He smoked as many cigarettes as he could every day until they killed him. Uncle was killed in a dispute over a candy machine by one of his motel partners. At least that's what was reported. Our cousin Kazi was the saddest one. He killed himself. Kazi was a good boy, and he never got over the night your mother was killed. He thought you were dead too. There are no more demons out there," Nandini comforted her.

"Thank you for all you've done. I think I have everything written down. Here's my card and I have my cell phone here so you can call me anytime. There are so many things I want to know. One more thing. Do you have any photos of me or my mother?" Lourdes hoped for a connection to the mother she now knew had loved her.

"I do. Please wait here. I've had it hidden away for so many years." Nandini left the room and returned with a simple wooden box. She opened the box full of buttons and thread and pried the inside of the lid open at a crease and a wooden plate fell out revealing a photo behind it. She handed the color photograph to Lourdes.

Lourdes gingerly grasped the edges and looked at the snapshot of her former life. Anika was holding her baby on her lap. Lourdes was laying on her back with her head on her mother's knees as they both gazed at each other with pure joy and love. Lourdes tried desperately to remember that moment, but the long-ago memory wouldn't come.

"You were about three months old. A happy chubby thing you were. I took the picture when we met at her little apartment before she left to hide away from the family for good, or at least we hoped she would stay hidden." The older lady smiled as she looked at the photograph.

"Can I please have this? I'll make you a copy," Lourdes said through her tears.

"I don't need it anymore," Nandini said looking into her niece's face. "I have found where it belongs."

"Thank you for this. It means the world to me. I wondered for so long why a mother would throw away a child. It hurt me for years, but I had my parents who loved me through my pain. My mother didn't throw me away. She loved me." Lourdes felt her birth mother's love through the picture and a lifetime of questioning came to an end.

*   *   *

Lourdes sat a moment in the parking lot of the Hidalgo County courthouse. She had missed several calls and texts went unanswered as she tried to compose herself in the rental car. The only text she returned was Tommy's. The others would have to wait.

She had her notes in her purse, and she stole a look in the rearview mirror before working up the courage to walk in. Her makeup had been washed away by the tidal wave of tears over the past few hours. She did her best to make herself appear presentable before entering the courthouse. A security officer greeted her and accepted her purse as she walked through the metal detectors.

"I need a copy of a birth certificate. Can you tell me which way to go, please?" she asked the bored officer.

"Second floor halfway, down the hall on the right," he answered as he had hundreds of times before.

Lourdes nodded her thanks, seeing the main stairs ahead of her, she began the climb. Her heels seemed loud against the stone floor, and she could feel anxiety building as she reached the top of the steps. She glanced at her watch and the four hours before her flight was plenty of time. A line of about fifteen people had formed along a wall to her right, and she placed herself behind a woman with a baby in a stroller.

Lourdes suddenly perceived babies differently than before. She had a hidden terror before this day. The feeling she should never become a mother and a fear of her past. What if her mother had thrown her away and that an inherited evil against children was inside her soul? She could never be a mother if there was any chance she would do that to a child. She looked at the sleeping baby and for the first time in her life she desperately wanted a child. She knew she was not going to be evil; she was going to be good.

"What's your baby's name?" Lourdes asked as she leaned over to see the baby.

"Hannah," the woman answered with a smile.

"She's beautiful," Lourdes said never taking her eyes off the child.

"Thank you," the mother answered and pushed the stroller as the line moved.

"What's it like? To be a mother. What's it like?" Lourdes asked. She was suddenly curious about motherhood with a newfound possibility of becoming a parent.

"There's nothing better in the world, but it's very hard. You don't sleep, and you are scared all the time when they are sick," the woman answered honestly. "This one is my last. Four boys and one girl."

"Five children," Lourdes said in awe. "How do you divide your love among five children?"

The mother pushed her stroller to the next spot available and answered her, "You don't divide, miss. You multiply."

Maybe it wasn't really math, but Lourdes somehow understood the brilliance of her statement.

"Next." she heard the announcement. It was her turn and she walked to the next window.

"I need a copy of a birth certificate."

"I will need name, date of birth, and fifteen dollars," the plain woman with the plain voice droned for the one millionth time in her career.

"Amrita Laghari, February 24, 1986. Here's the spelling." Lourdes handed the clerk a note with the information. The woman typed on her keyboard with amazing speed and soon she heard the familiar sound of a printer under the counter. The clerk reached down and pulled the certificate from the printer placing it in a large brown envelope with Hidalgo County Texas printed on the front.

"Fifteen dollars."

Lourdes had a twenty-dollar bill and quickly handed it to her.

"Here ya go. Five dollars change. Next!" the plain faced clerk called for the next customer.

For the first time in her thirty years on earth Lourdes had her official birth certificate. She turned from the window and suddenly felt weak and overcome. She spotted a Coke machine next to a bench and slipped in the coins, pressed the iconic red and white logo, and heard the rumble of the can rolling to the bottom of the machine.

She sat with the cold soda can in her hand and sipped the sugary brown nectar. Her mouth was dry from nerves as she sat alone holding the envelope. The mother and baby came by as she tried to calm herself.

"You have a good day, and I promise you'll be a great mom one day. I just know it," the kind mother of five said to Lourdes as she walked past.

"You have a good day too and thank you," Lourdes responded and took another drink.

She lifted the brown envelope to her eyes and peeked in without removing the document to see if she could see anything. It was like some silly game. She laughed at herself and took another drink.

Her fingertips felt the paper inside the envelope, and she slowly exposed the official document to the fluorescent light of the courthouse corridor. Lourdes thought later of what the people walking past her were thinking when she gasped aloud. Her eyes went directly to the box for Father's Name: William Barret Downs IV.

1985

Anika heard a loud knock and wondered who was banging on her door this late at night. She glanced at her bedside digital clock and the red numbers showed 11:17. She got out of her bed and grabbed her robe hanging on the back of the bathroom door and went to see who it could be at such a late hour. She first thought it might be Dan Key, her on and off boyfriend, but this would have been out of character for him. She looked through the peep hole and saw her Uncle Nitesh. He appeared to be alone. Maybe something had happened to her father. She unchained and unlocked the door and opened it for her relative.

"Hi, Uncle. What's wrong?" She asked in her groggy voice.

"We need to speak of the matter at your father's last week. My brother has informed me you are going against the family and not marrying this man we have found for you," Uncle stated in a serious tone.

"I'm not going against the family. I am doing what is best for me. You don't get to decide my life. I am American, and I know my rights as a woman in this country," she responded firmly.

Uncle Nitesh stared at his niece with flashing eyes and slapped Anika with enough force to send her to the floor.

"*You* have *no* rights! You are the property of this family, and you will *obey me*," he screamed at her as he bent over to get in her face.

"You have two weeks to make this marriage work, or you will face the consequences of your stubborn American ways," he said gritting his teeth as he spoke in a growl and turned and left.

Anika knew how severe his punishment could be, and she knew she needed to do one of two things. Marry the medical student or run away. Where would she go? She had some money saved, but she had no time. She needed to pack and leave tomorrow. She could get Dan to help her move her furniture to his place or storage and she would cancel her lease. She had some vacation days at work and would see if they let her do contract work from home.

The next morning, she went to her job with a decent plan already formulated in her mind, but she had no idea where she could stay that was safe. Her sister and her husband owned the motel, but they would obviously check there. She was in her cubicle trying to focus on work when her cell phone buzzed. Monica was texting just to say hi, and Anika felt it was a sign and called her right away.

"Hi, Monica . . . I need help desperately . . . Thank you. I need a place to stay. My family is very upset and trying to force me to marry that stupid boy I told you about—the med student. If I don't it could be very bad . . . Yes, that's perfect. He's there now? . . . I don't want to impose . . . No, Port Aransas is close, but they would never think to look there. Thanks again. I'm unsure how long. Is that okay? . . . You are the best friend I could ever have. Bye." Anika hung up the phone with her rescuer.

Anika called Dan at lunch and explained the situation. They had not been together for a couple of months but remained friends. He was a genuinely nice man, but Anika had confused sex with love for a while, and when she realized she did not love him, the relationship had slowly withered. He did not seem to mind and in fact had moved on to another young lady.

"This is an awful lot to ask a man who no longer gets to see you naked," he joked which was one of his more endearing qualities.

"I get it, Dan. But think of our past activities as a down payment," she countered and laughed.

He chuckled and agreed. He had a couple of friends who would work for beer and would help move her. She submitted for her time off, spoke to her boss about contract work, and he agreed. That afternoon after work, Dan and two friends showed up and in a couple of hours, the one-bedroom apartment was empty. Things were going fast; she was relieved at how quickly her plan had come together. She had most of her things in storage in Dan's garage. She had a place to stay, and she had a job. Now she needed things to blow over.

Anika drove onto the ferry to the barrier island of Port Aransas, Texas, a tourist town of colorful beach houses and condos. Four's beach house was about four miles south of the small town on the Gulf side. She found the address easily with Monica's directions. There was no vehicle at the home, so she searched for the hidden key hanging on a nail behind the thermometer on one of the pilings. She ascended the stairs to the second-floor deck and unlocked the French door into the living area.

After a few trips up and down the stairs, she had the contents of her car emptied and stowed away in a guest bedroom. The interior was furnished in seaside décor with bright colors of aqua and coral. It looked like it had been recently cleaned with vacuum tracks in the carpet of the bedrooms and had coastal themed magazines carefully arranged on the coffee table. Time to call Monica and let her know she was here.

"Hi Mon, I'm here! . . . It is so beautiful inside. I can see your touches everywhere . . . No, I'm alone and the house is all cleaned up . . . I'm fine. I do feel safer now. I even parked my car where no one driving by could see it that well . . . Okay, love you too. Kiss Janet Ann for me. I cannot believe she is already one!"

Anika sat down and allowed herself to nap on the couch. She easily fell asleep on the late afternoon under the rhythmic ceiling fan. She was unsure how long she had slept when she heard a man's voice in her ear whisper.

"Found you."

Anika reacted to the voice with a swing of her arm before her eyes adjusted to a smiling Four, holding her arms to prevent her from hurting herself or him.

"Four, you scared me! You can't sneak up on people like that," she said rubbing her eyes and noticing it was dark out. "What time is it?"

"Close to ten. I got here three hours ago from fishing, but figured you needed some sleep," Four answered kindly. He was dressed in a short sleeved white fishing shirt and khaki shorts and was barefoot. He had a dark tan, and his hair was a little longer since she had last seen him at the wedding.

"You've been here for three hours? I must have been completely out of it. I never heard a thing." She pushed her hair behind her head with her spread fingers as a comb.

"I ate, took a shower, got dressed, drank a beer, and all the while, you were out cold, my darling. I have some food. Are you hungry? I have some leftover chicken."

"Yes, I am, but I can get it. Keep your seat."

Anika went to the kitchen and opened the refrigerator to find beer, orange juice, and sodas, along with some leftover fried chicken and Mexican food. She grabbed the chicken, a paper towel, a soda and returned to her spot on the sofa.

"I must look terrible. I wish you hadn't seen me looking this bad," she said as she began to eat.

"I don't think it's possible for you to look bad," Four was a natural charmer. "Monica told me you were coming and all the crazy crap with your family. You can stay here as long as you like and if I can do anything, let me know."

Anika thanked him and thought of how he and Monica met. Four had been Monica's knight in shining armor and now he was saving her. She needed one of those knights in her life, and she felt secure with him close. They visited for another hour and then Anika went for a shower and spent the night in a guest room.

Four and Anika went to a grocery store early the next morning where he paid for everything against her wishes. A two-week supply of everything imaginable was carried up the stairs in multiple trips and stowed away in the fridge and pantry.

"That should keep you for a few days until I return." Four stood in the kitchen with his hands on his hips.

Anika was overcome by his sincere kindness and hugged him and thanked him for the fourth time. She stood on the deck and watched him drive away and sat alone in a painted white Adirondack chair and listened to the sound of the surf in front of her a hundred feet away. She would call her sister at the motel and let her know she was okay using their special code and disguising her voice. They developed the code when Anika was leaving for college and were very proud of their system related to room numbers. If Anika said to the front desk, I have a message for room 110 that meant call me at home. Later they added room 114 which was call me at work. It was simple but very effective in maintaining communication initially to protect them from Sudhir's anger but now Uncle's wrath.

Anika woke early most mornings and enjoyed her retreat lifestyle the first few days. The sunrise was so beautiful from her view on the expansive deck. A new family had come to the house next door the day before. A young couple with two small children and an older couple. The light was piercing through low rain clouds on the eastern horizon when she saw the young mother walk out carrying the youngest child who appeared to be less than three months old.

The mother cupped her hand behind the baby's head and started to feed a bottle to her child. She was dressed in a simple white cotton robe and a long shirt type pajama. Her hair was pulled back in a ponytail, and she gently rocked back and forth softly singing to the baby who appeared to be aggressively eating.

The mother turned and saw Anika and was a bit startled to see someone out this time of day. She and Anika locked eyes and nodded to each other.

"How old is the baby?" Anika asked.

"Seven weeks," the woman answered trying not to shout the distance between them.

"Boy or girl?"

"Boy, named Jeffrey after my husband's father."

"Is he with you?"

"Yes, he and my mother- in-law own the house. Are you friends with Four and Monica?"

"Yes, I was actually in their wedding."

"I have met her a couple of times; she is so beautiful."

"She has a little girl now who just turned one," Anika informed her.

"She'll be a wonderful mom. I guess I better go back in, but we'll see you again, I'm sure. We'll be here a few days. I'm Ashley, by the way."

"Anika, nice visiting with you."

Ashley went back in the house with her baby boy leaving Anika wondering if she would ever be a mother. She came close with Dan, but he was not the fatherly type. He was the fun guy, but she couldn't picture him changing a diaper or even holding a baby.

The week went by quickly and the following Monday the neighbors were gone again. Anika had walked in the surf late in the day when most people were packed up or back in their rentals cooking hamburgers or frying fish and playing music. Joy surrounded her, yet she was alone. She was sitting on the living room sofa watching a bad movie while the sun was going down behind the west side houses when she heard the sound of a closing car door. She went to the window and saw Four getting out of his pickup. He was alone.

"How have things been while I was away?" he cheerfully asked her as she smiled to greet him.

"Good, I met the people in the house next door. They were nice. They have a cute new baby."

"Oh yea, last time I saw her she was big prego. I could use a drink. Can I get you something?" he asked his house guest.

"I suppose. I saw there was some wine in the pantry. That would be fine."

Four mixed a mostly vodka and some soda for himself and poured a stemmed glass full of red wine for her.

"Cheers!" he said as they sat in the living room.

Anika was not a big drinker—a glass of wine or two every once in a while, or a beer. One beer filled her up, so she was never a drunk. She drank some hard liquor in college and that had made her sick. Besides her family was very strict regarding alcohol.

"How are Janet Ann and Monica?" she asked.

"Both wonderful. That little girl has an attitude, let me tell you," Four spoke of his daughter with pride. "Monica loves being a mom. Let's sit outside and watch the sunset. It's my favorite thing to do down here." He stood and walked to the door, waiting for her to pass before following her out to the deck.

The two sat and felt the ocean breeze blow around their bodies and tasted the salty air as dusk fell over the island. The only sounds were a radio playing oldies music a few houses away and the constant waves clawing at the sand.

They talked of their time on Riverside Drive in Austin, the people they remembered, and the parties at the pool and Four's apartment. They talked about how he met Monica and saved her from a toxic relationship and how it was so sad to both of them that she had to endure that terrible time. Anika did not mention the secret, deep crush she'd had on Four in those younger days.

Anika felt the wine warming her from the inside. It felt comforting and soothing. She agreed when he came back out with the bottle for another pour. The wind died down which meant mosquitos would start biting, so they went inside. Anika excused herself to the restroom, and Four freshened his drink and topped her wine glass off with the last of the bottle. When she returned, she noticed but did not care.

She sipped the warm red wine which seemed to taste better with each swallow. She felt muscles releasing around her neck, and she stretched out her bare foot and legs, accidentally touching Four's thigh. His hand began to caress her lower leg, and she knew it was wrong. But in the moment, it didn't matter to her. It felt good.

His hand moved up her calf, and she kept her eyes closed to prevent herself from seeing the reality of what was happening. Soon he was laying on her outstretched body on the sofa, and she felt his lips on hers. She knew what was happening and made no attempt to stop it. The alcohol would be her excuse—their excuse.

The next morning, she awoke nude in the master bedroom with her best friend's husband. She was hungover and felt physically and mentally ill. The clarity of the morning was harsh to all her senses. She looked at him sleeping facing away from her, and she slowly and quietly exited the bed. Maybe he would not remember. Maybe he blacked out. She went directly to the guest bath and took a shower to wash off the shame. Maybe her uncle was right. She was an awful person.

She quickly combed the tangles out of her wet hair and dressed and opened the door hoping Four was still asleep. She knew they hadn't used protection, and she mentally calculated where she was in her cycle. Everything about what happened the night before could be bad. She smelled coffee from the kitchen and saw a string of discarded clothing on the floor leading to the master bedroom.

"Good morning, sunshine," Four greeted her cheerfully as if nothing happened.

"So, are we just going to pretend nothing happened?" Anika said with confusion and hope mixed together.

"Oh, it happened, and it was magnificent!" Four responded with enthusiasm, "But I'm all for pretending it never happened. I'm the married one you know," he tried to comfort her.

"Yes, you cheated on your wife!" she said without thinking.

"With whom?" he quickly asked.

"Her best friend . . ." Anika lowered her head in shame.

"So, we both have too much to lose in this deal. I figure it's like two countries with nuclear bombs. We both have one." She laughed at his flippant nature. It was done and over and nothing else would need to be said.

Monica and Janet Ann came with Four for a week at the end of summer. Anika and Four had not had any other moments together and both were back to normal around each other, with Monica none the wiser.

Anika loved playing with Janet Ann and could see herself being a mother someday. Monica told her she was pregnant again, and they were hoping for a boy. Anika left the beach house after a three month stay leaving her own pregnancy test results hidden in the outdoor trash can. She never told Monica or Four she was expecting a child around the same time as Monica. She would start showing soon, and she hoped things had died down with her family issues, because now she had a whole new problem.

She moved into a small apartment in Harlingen which Nandini found for her, and she was able to work from home. Her pay was reduced but she kept her health insurance. She wrote a thank you note to Four and Monica for their generosity, and she informed them she would be moving away to an unknown location until her family dangers subsided.

Anika's daughter, Amrita "Lotus" Laghari, was born on February 24th fifteen days before William Barrett Downs V. Both were healthy babies, and both had the same father.

CHAPTER 53

2016

L OURDES GATHERED HERSELF as best she could after reading the name that shocked her soul. The day had revealed her history, but she would never know *how* Four was her father unless she asked him directly. She walked in a daze to her rental car in the courthouse parking lot. She slowly shuffled her feet and her face looked like she had been hit in the gut with a two by four. She sat down and checked her watch. She had plenty of time to get to the airport to make her flight. She knew Tommy was at work, but she needed to be with him when she told him the truth.

She returned the rental car and waited at the terminal gate to begin boarding the first available flight home. She was in the A group and had a few minutes to review emails and messages before boarding. She texted Tommy that she was boarding the flight and would be home at seven thirty, and she couldn't wait to talk to him. The flight was routine. She sat on the front row next to a rotund, red-faced attorney who had been to a mediation. He was funny and kept her mind off the impact of the day as he talked about his children with his first grandchild on the way. He asked where she was from, remarking that he had an attorney friend named Oscar from Travis City. She normally did not enjoy plane conversation, but she welcomed the humorous stories that distracted her from her mental turmoil.

"What were you doing in The Valley?" he asked.

"Just seeing family," she answered.

"Family is important. At least what we define as family. I have three stepchildren. No children of my own, but I have had those three since they were very young. They had a daddy of sorts, but he wasn't much in their lives. I don't know why. Just sorry, I guess. You know what those three did for me? They all signed papers for me to adopt them." The man teared up as he spoke.

"They could not have made me any happier. They said I was the only dad they really ever had, you know? That meant something. So, family is who loves you, and that's all there is. I think the Good Lord puts people in your life at the right time and place. He sure did with me and my wife. You know what I mean?" he said with moist eyes as he turned to her.

"I know exactly what you mean." Lourdes felt a wave of sweet joy fall over her at the sound of those words of love, and she felt emotional for the hundredth time that day.

The plane began its slow descent, and she looked out the window at the Dallas skyline as they approached Love Field. She remembered how nervous she was when she first flew and how commonplace it was now. The aircraft noises that once raised her eyebrows were now almost comforting. The plane door was opened, and she stood up next to the round man with the sweet stories.

"Thank you for telling me about your children. I can see how very proud you are of them, and congratulations on the new grandchild. You will make a great grandpa."

"I can't wait, and neither can my bride. They live in the same neighborhood which is such a blessing. In two minutes, we can be there, or she can bring the baby to us. I'm setting up a nursery this weekend in our house. God bless you and very nice to visit with you," the man said brimming with happiness as they parted ways.

Lourdes walked to the parking garage to her car and cranked the engine, only to be startled by a loudly blaring radio. She quickly turned down the volume marveling at how she had just driven to the airport that morning. It seemed she had been gone days instead of hours. Before she drove to the airport exit, she texted Tommy, "In car heading home." He texted back, "On way home now too. I'll pick up food."

She smiled at the text knowing how thoughtful he was at little things.

She thought what the man on the plane had said about family, and she thought of Danny and Maria. They were her parents by choice. They put her on this path and molded her. Mr. Downs treated her like family and never knew she was his own granddaughter. Nothing good would come from this news being exposed. It would only hurt her parents and Monica. Would Four somehow be her new father? No, she had a father. It was not ever to be known by anyone in her hometown. She would only tell Tommy, knowing he would never speak of it.

She arrived at the condo and Tommy's car was there. She could hear the pinging noise a car makes when recently stopped confirming he had just arrived ahead of her. She took her purse and the brown envelope and walked inside.

"I'm home," she called out.

"Back here. Changing clothes," he responded.

She sat on the sofa putting her purse on the floor at the end of the sofa. She allowed herself a moment of silent prayer. "Thank you, God, for giving me the truth, and now I ask You for the wisdom to use it carefully."

She felt her husband's lips on her closed mouth, and she responded with a brief kiss.

"I'm so excited to hear what happened. Tell me everything." Tommy sat next to her.

"I'm going to change clothes first and then let's eat. I just realized all I've eaten today is a McDonald's biscuit. But I promise I'll tell you everything after that."

She changed and Tommy set the table with Chinese food from their favorite takeout.

"I need a glass of wine, too, if you don't mind. This is a big story." She sat at the table in her casual clothes.

She shoveled broccoli beef with steamed rice in her mouth as rapidly as she could. Tommy set the wine glass before her and she took a drink.

"Okay, I've been seriously thinking about what I learned today, and you will be the only one I will ever tell, understand? And you can't tell it either."

"I understand, baby." Tommy knew how important this was to his wife.

"I know who my real mother and father are. My mother is dead. My father is Four Downs."

"What?" Tommy fell back in his chair and stared at her in shock.

"I know!" Lourdes shook her head mimicking Tommy's disbelief. "I'm not used to all this yet myself. My birth mother was a friend of Monica and Four's from college. Her name was Anika Laghari. I met her sister today—Nandini. It's a long story."

Lourdes told her husband everything she learned that day. He sat entranced listening to the details of Anika's life and the horrible way it ended. Lourdes was exhausted when she finished telling him all she knew and lay back on the sofa.

"Are you going to tell the Downs family?"

"No. No one can ever know. What good would it serve, Tommy?" Lourdes was resolute in her decision. "It will only cause pain, and I don't want that. I have parents and it doesn't matter they are not blood relatives. They are the best two people in the world, and I love them so much."

"Then I'll never tell a soul. I love you, baby. I've never cared about where you came from. I've always known *who* you are. I have loved you since kindergarten and nothing will ever change that," he said holding her hands.

Lourdes rose and looked Tommy in the eyes. "I want to have children."

"How many?" he asked with a mischievous smile.

"Let's just start with one and go from there." She pulled her excited husband off the couch with an enticing smile.

CHAPTER 54

L OURDES SAT IN her office staring out the window at the rising sun. How often had she seen the sun pierce the horizon when she accompanied her mother to the bank in her younger days. She smiled at the memory of hearing Mr. Downs criticize anyone sleeping past daylight. "Wasting their lives sleeping!" She remembered the glimmer of gold and pink against the glass of the bank building facade, and how she never seemed to notice how beautiful it was back then.

She longed for that time—especially today. Mr. Downs had been her mentor and changed the direction of her life. Was it him or was it really her? He always said it was her. He would say he could pour water for anyone, but some just have better buckets to catch it in. She realized how much she loved the old man the day he took her home from the school after she hid in his truck. It had been her worst day, and he turned it into one of her best days.

He was her rock, her shelter in a storm. He saw all that was possible in her with no limits. Her parents loved her and cared for her but the prism they viewed life through was smaller. This limitation was not because they were bad people—it was simply all they knew. Mr. Downs saw no boundaries in her. He made her dream bigger than she ever thought was possible, because he could clearly see her life as being a huge success.

She smiled to herself with moist eyes. She knew this day would come as she turned to look at her University of Texas football helmet which was carefully placed on the credenza in the same lower right-hand corner as Mr. Downs had his old helmet. Her office was modeled after his. She looked at the Adam Smith quote on the wood plaque he gave her from his office. *It is not for the benevolence of the butcher, the baker, or the brewer we receive our meals.* It was one of her greatest treasures. The lessons learned at his desk were the ones she missed now more than ever. She called him when she doubted herself, and he would respond with firm advice tempered with some humor. He expected more from her than anyone she had ever met, and how wonderful it was to please him.

"Sports," he said, "are a great metaphor for life. No one knows the winner until the game is over." She recalled herself saying that games had definitive endings, but life does not. He smiled back at her and said, "Life does have endings, my dear, so play hard while you can."

She thought she had lost him for good now. It was so cruel how Alzheimer's had taken his brilliant mind. How he had wasted away as his body outlived the brain that ran it all. She had received a call from his nurse requesting her to come see him and was surprised to learn he had asked for her. Was his mind back? Would he know her, even briefly?

She opened her middle desk drawer and withdrew four envelopes with the familiar stationery. She had kept every letter Mr. Downs had ever written her and stored them in a safe place. But these four were special. One for her high school graduation, college years, time in New York, and her marriage to Tommy. Each one was carefully crafted with kindness and wisdom. She gathered the envelopes to her chest and caressed them lovingly. They were such riches, a connection to their lives together.

Lourdes drove down to her hometown after her last morning appointment. It is strange how time plays tricks on the mind. A drive you have made countless times can put you in some sort of trance, and her mind seemed blank when she exited to the highway to Travis City. Out of habit, her eyes cut to the left and she saw the dumpster behind the convenience store where her old life had ended, and her new life began. She had spent endless hours wondering why she was tossed away. Years of worry and doubt about her birth parents had consumed much of her life.

She was now in a good place. She spent every morning in grateful prayer, being thankful to God for all she had been given. Her father had taught her to focus on the good and extend forgiveness to others. Her blessed mother taught her self-respect and responsibility. She now knew the truth of how she arrived in the dumpster and in fact her birth mother had indeed loved her. She knew who her biological father was, and it did not matter if anyone else ever knew.

Lourdes was suddenly in Mr. Downs driveway, the last two hours lost to the universe. She parked her new black Mercedes sedan in the spot to the right of the garage. She glanced in the rearview mirror and checked her makeup. She exited the car, approaching the house with hope and knocked on the clean, white back door where most visitors entered.

The three-car garage was neatly kept. Mr. Downs' old pickup was there, dusty from lack of use, but with a little love it would come back to its full glory. Mr. Downs had said for thirty years he wasn't buying a new truck. This one was fine, and they are too damn expensive anyway. Lourdes knocked on the door suddenly feeling nervous about her visit. She was dressed from work in a gray plaid, fitted suit, white cotton blouse, and black leather heels. She wore the string of pearls Mr. Downs had given her at her wedding. Her stainless and gold Rolex watch fit loosely on her wrist, and she glanced at the time while she waited for the door to open.

Nora, the day nurse, welcomed her, "Hi, Lulu! I'm glad you came. He asked about you twice yesterday, but no words today. Sometimes I think he's doing good, but it comes and goes. He is in the den looking over the heifer pasture. He likes seeing the cows. They seem to make him happy." Nora strode briskly through the kitchen and dining room into the large den. Lourdes' heels clicked loudly on the hardwood floor as they found Mr. Downs in his wheelchair looking through the large glass windows toward the patio and fenced pasture.

"This is Lulu come to see you. Do you remember her?" Nora sounded kind and mockingly cruel at the same time.

Mr. Downs looked with little notice at the beautiful young woman he had known since she was ten years old. It broke her heart because she had so much to tell him. She leaned down and quietly said, "Hi, Mr. Downs." He did not appear to hear her. He was in a world of darkness and fog. Nora waved at Lourdes and left the room.

Lourdes pulled a small chair next to his wheelchair and end table facing the pasture. On the small dark wood table there was a note pad and pen, a box of tissues, a half empty glass of iced tea, and a Cattleman's magazine. A small wicker waste basket sat under the small table with a couple of scraps of paper on the floor in front of his chair. He was dressed in khaki pants and a short sleeved white collared shirt. He wore tan slippers without socks and his exposed ankles and lower legs were pale with blue veins rising against white skin. His hands with manicured fingernails rested on the arms of his chair—hands dotted with age spots and still wearing his wedding ring. His bare arms seemed too small to belong to the man Lourdes had known so long. His gray hair was mostly gone, but what was left was neatly combed. It was hard for her to look at him. He was so frail. Where was that man she knew? Was he still in there?

She thought about what she wanted to say and began, "My investment firm hit eight hundred million last week. I couldn't have done it without you." She paused and reflected on this seemingly tiny statement and the enormous impact it actually held. "Tommy is wonderful, and he loves me as much as I love him. My life is in a good place. I am very blessed. I just learned I'm pregnant. We are so thrilled." And then thought to herself, "I am having your great-grandchild."

Lourdes was facing toward the patio as she spoke, as if she was telling the story to the grazing heifers. Her hope of having him back was fading. She felt this was her last time to see him alive, but the definition of alive was now a technicality. She sat quietly and prayed, "Thank you, God, for this man who changed my life. Thank you for the lessons he taught me and the things he did for so many others. Lord, let him have peace."

Lourdes looked toward him with a melancholy smile. Then she noticed the trash on the floor. Standing she took a step toward him and bent over to pick up the wadded paper placing it in the basket.

While she was standing by him at the little table, she absentmindedly organized the few items.

Suddenly Mr. Downs asked her, "Where did Coca Cola stock close?" He was looking directly at her with a newfound clarity.

Lourdes was overcome. She knelt in front of him and smiled. "Up .22 cents at 58.47, Mr. Downs."

"Good, that was your pick. You did good, girl. At least I did one good thing in my life." His voice was weak, but clear. "I am very proud of you. If you're loved, you know the true definition of rich . . . I love you."

I love you. Tears flowed down Lourdes cheeks as she could not push out enough air to even make a sound. She was still kneeling in front of him, and she leaned over and gave him a hug and kiss on his cheek. He heaved a long sigh as she embraced him.

And then Mr. Downs was gone. His body slumped and his aged face lost color. The moment of connection had been brief, but somehow it was all Lourdes needed. She was loved by so many. Loved by those whose blood she shared and even more who loved her by choice. She defined rich.

"I love you too, Pop," she whispered into the old man's lifeless ear. It was the only time she called him anything but Mr. Downs. It was not important that he had never known she was his granddaughter. He had treated her better than family. He held her to a high standard, more than his own children and grandchildren. At the end, out of all that he had done for so many, he had thought of her as the one good thing he had accomplished.

Looking through the bay window, Monica was surprised to see Lourdes' car pulling into her driveway. She walked to the side porch door to meet her.

"Hey there, Lourdes. What are you doing in town?" Monica greeted her in her usual friendly manner.

Lourdes had been crying since she left Mr. Downs and her face showed it. Monica could see her red and swollen eyes and rushed down the steps to her.

"He's gone," Lourdes choked out. "Mr. Downs is gone."

Monica hugged her in a way she felt like Lourdes needed it more than she did. Monica had seen the decline and knew how bad things had been the last several weeks. He very rarely knew her or Four. Monica had grieved his loss in her mind, but this was the ultimate finality.

"It's for the best, Lulu. He has not been with us for a long time. He's at peace. And he loved you so much." Monica teared up doing her best to comfort Lourdes. "Come in. The world will know soon enough. Four should be here in a few minutes. I'll wait to tell him in person." Monica led Lourdes into the house.

The television in the den was on and the now four-year-old boy of Barrett's was sitting on the floor snacking on apple slices and watching a cartoon.

"What's wrong, Monny? Why you cryin'?" Willie turned and asked with sweet concern seeing the tears of the woman he knew as his mother.

"Oh, I'm fine. We just had some news. Pop went to heaven." Monica lifted him up and held the boy.

"In the sky? Way up to the top?" He pointed his little arm to the ceiling.

"To the very tip top." She smiled through her sadness. "Just like we talked about."

"It's okay, Monny. He will have lots of friends to play with," Willie responded with the confidence of a toddler.

"Yes, he will, my baby boy. Yes, he will."

"The funeral home was coming when I left. Nora took care of everything. She called me yesterday and said he was asking for me," Lourdes told Monica after Willie was back in front of the television.

"Did he know you?" Monica asked.

"Yes. It was brief, but very special for me."

"I am so happy for you, Lulu. I had a few little moments the past few weeks. I treasure them all."

"I don't want to do this today, but I don't want to forget when all the arrangements begin. Dawn and I were left instructions for you to meet with us in Pop's office after he died. There is a sealed envelope in his desk with your name on it. He informed me and Dawn on the same day. It was after he was starting to have some trouble, but while he was still very much aware."

"What is it?" Lourdes asked. "Did he say anything else?"

"No, just to tell you after he died."

* * *

Visitation hours were scheduled from four in the afternoon until as late as the family wanted to stay. Daisy flew in with her latest husband who seemed nice but very uncomfortable with the ceremony of death. Monica and Four's friends had sent so much food to their house, they were sending the excess to the ranch for Daisy and her husband who were staying there. Janet Ann and her husband and children arrived as quickly as possible to assist and to stay with Monica and Four.

Lourdes and Tommy were staying at her parents, and Lourdes had a very strange feeling of being with a man in her childhood bedroom. Lourdes' old room remained preserved from her senior year in high school, the walls decorated with band posters, snapshots of smiling friends making crazy faces, shooting trophies, and medals. And of course, she had the traditional staple of every Texas girl's childhood bedroom—a homecoming mum. Lourdes' mum was a giant art piece of a silk mum flower surrounded by ruffled layers of ribbon with long, three-foot streamers decorated with charms of little footballs, tiny megaphones and literally, all the bells and whistles. Tommy had dutifully given this to Lourdes to wear when they attended their first homecoming football game as a couple. It would probably remain enshrined in her bedroom until she was forty.

Tommy looked just as uncomfortable as Lourdes when they entered the pink bedroom. They unpacked and hung their clothes up in her old closet which was now apparently used as overflow for her mother's older, smaller clothing sizes.

"This feels really weird. Like your Dad is going to come racing in here and shoot me," Tommy joked.

"How do you think I feel?" Lourdes laughed.

They showered and dressed and were ready to leave by three p.m. They needed to get there early to help Dawn with some unknown project. The young couple walked into the living room to find Maria ready and waiting on Danny.

"You look very nice, Mama," Lourdes complimented her mother. By now, Maria was basically the same measurement around from her chest to her hips. Lourdes had bought her a new dress that her mother was sure was too big, but it wasn't.

"Thanks, Lourdes. I do like this dress. Come on, Danny!" Maria called back toward the master bedroom.

Danny came out wearing tan-colored jeans, a tightly wrapped blue button-down shirt and a navy blazer. Lourdes and Tommy dressed like this every day for their jobs, but her parents did not. Lourdes had on a short sleeved black linen dress with two large pockets on the front and red heels. Tommy wore gray plaid slacks, starched white button-down shirt, black wing tip shoes, and a black blazer.

"We can all ride in Mom's car," Danny said grabbing keys off the kitchen counter on the way out.

Maria sat in the front next to Danny placing Tommy and Lourdes in the back like chaperoned middle school kids going to a school dance. They were mostly quiet on the drive over. Danny knew a good parking spot they could slide into so they could go through a back door into the chapel. They entered the sanctuary and saw Dawn coming from the main entrance with her husband Paul following behind carrying a cardboard file box.

"Hi, Miss Dawn," Lourdes called across the room.

"Hey, Lulu! Glad y'all are here. I have a little project," Dawn responded.

"What's all this?" Tommy asked as they watched Paul open the heavy box which appeared to be full of letters.

"Letters—lots of letters. For the last forty years I have kept a copy of every letter Mr. Downs asked me to proof and mail for him. There are maybe four hundred in here. I thought we could decorate the walls of the sanctuary with them. What ya think?" Dawn smiled and handed each of them a roll of tape.

The six of them each took a stack of letters and spread out around the room with their tape. It took an hour, but soon enough all the walls were papered with the old man's correspondences. They stood admiring their work when Janet Ann walked in followed by her husband, Ben. She spotted Lourdes and ran toward her for a hug.

"This is great! What a good idea," Janet Ann exclaimed at the sight of the letters.

"Yes, it is. It was all Dawn's idea." Lourdes immediately gave Dawn all the credit.

"Thank you, I'm the only one who has read all of them, and I know how wonderful they were for the people who received them." Dawn smiled at Mr. Downs' granddaughters.

"He wrote me too! Does anyone know where mine are?" Janet Ann asked with excitement.

"I saw your name on that side under the Ten Commandments," Lourdes said.

Janet Ann rushed in the direction of her memories, as Daisy and Four came in together through the side door beside the grand pipe organ. Monica followed behind with Daisy's husband, trying to explain his role tonight. Monica was the first to notice the letters, and she covered her mouth with her hands in astonishment.

"Look, Four! Daisy, the walls are covered in letters your daddy wrote. We all got some, but I had no idea how many he wrote over the years. Who thought of this?"

"Dawn did it!" Janet Ann called out from the north, interior wall.

"Where's Willie?" Dawn asked deflecting attention from herself.

"Susan's keeping him with Robert and Molly. Dawn, you are the very best! He would have hated this so much!" Monica laughed.

"Oh, he would fire you from the grave if he could. But I could not be happier," Four said with a proud smile. "You have shown everyone what the people of this town meant to him. I love it. Thank you Dawn."

Soon the front doors of the church were opened to the public for visitation. The open casket had been placed in front of the raised pulpit and the line of those paying their respect came down the center aisle of the sanctuary. Four was first in line, then Monica and Daisy, and last was Janet Ann and her husband Ben. Daisy's husband sat on a pew alone nervously observing the Southern tradition of honoring the dead unfold before him.

Each visitor, greeted by the family, would offer their condolences. Dawn and a few others from the bank stood as secondary greeters along with Dub Daniels representing the ranch. The night was filled with humorous stories and tales of kindness. The constantly progressing line lasted for hours. People lingered and read the letters in amazement, most knowing the recipients in the small town. The crowd would wave others over to see a letter written to them, and they would remember the time and place in which Mr. Downs had written it.

Lourdes and Tommy sat with Danny and Maria watching the scene unfold around them while many would come and speak to them as well. Lourdes recognized classmates and the customers of her mother's cleaning service. When she turned toward the entrance to see how long the line was, she saw Claudia with her parents. She stood, waved her over, then went to greet her former enemy.

"Good to see you. You look fabulous, babe!" Claudia hugged her warmly.

"You look great as always. You come alone?" Lourdes said quietly so Claudia's parents would not hear.

"Yes. I'll explain later. Too much drama even for me!" Claudia whispered back.

"We definitely need to talk based on that statement," Lourdes chuckled.

The last of the line evaporated at nine-thirty. The greeters who had been on their feet for hours now sat down to rest. The crowd had dwindled down to about twenty people when Monica asked them all to come to her house for a late meal.

As the group was exiting, Danny noticed Maria was not with them. He turned to see her standing at the casket alone viewing the old man. He handed his keys to Tommy and told the others to go on while he went back down the aisle to comfort his wife.

"He changed our lives, Danny. He taught us to be bigger than we ever knew how to be. He told me once that I was his hero, and I never really thanked him. I never knew how. He appreciated hard work, and he made sure we knew he did. He was so proud of both of us, and he treated Lourdes like his own. What do we do now?" Maria's voice broke as she finished.

"We do what he would have wanted. We stay here and make this town better. We pass on the opportunity to the next generation. We become an example for others. He helped us, but we did the work.

We'll help those who do the work too. I think that's the best way to thank him." Danny kissed Maria on the cheek.

"Let's go, Maria." Danny gently pulled her arm. "They're waiting on us."

"My letter is on that wall and so is yours," she said weakly and walked with her husband out of the church.

* * *

It was standing room only in the First Baptist Church on the Tuesday afternoon of William Barrett Downs the Third's funeral. Daisy sat on the front row with her husband still looking uncertain of his role. Beside them were Four and Monica with Willie on her lap, Janet Ann and Ben, and their two small children, Robert and Molly. Monica, despite her age, was the most beautiful woman there. Sitting behind the family were employees from the ranch and the bank who were also considered to be part of Mr. Downs' family. Dawn, who had not stopped crying since entering the building, was sitting next to Randy and Vickie on the second row.

The service began with everyone present standing to sing the hymn How Great Thou Art. The pipe organ filled the sanctuary with the majestic notes soaring over the singing congregation and church choir. There were people from all strata of the community there to pay respect to the man who had shouldered the town for so many years. Men in jeans and worn boots, crusted with cow manure from the sale barn, sat next to the president of the Federal Reserve Bank in Dallas. Widows and orphans sat alongside pillars of business because they all had one man in common. The Skeet Club sat with the people from the Health Clinic, and each had their own cherished personal story of how he had impacted their lives.

Following the hymn, the pastor of the First Baptist Church walked to the pulpit centered in front of the choir loft with three chairs on the stage as the choir director passed him to take his seat. The row of stately engraved chairs were placed like thrones, one each for the pastor, choir director, and Lourdes "Lulu" Sanchez Adams. Lourdes was wearing her string of pearls with black heels in a beautiful black dress. When she dressed earlier that morning, she thought how much Mr. Downs would have loved seeing her wearing his pearls.

The pastor stood behind the ornate wooden pulpit. "Please bow with me. Our dear heavenly Father, we ask you to bless this time of celebration of the life of one of your faithful servants. We humbly pray for comfort for those who are hurting now as they face the loss of this beloved man but let us remember where he has gone. He has no more pain. His mind is clear and his body perfect. He joins his bride, Janet, his parents, and grandson, Barrett, in a joyous reunion. In Your Name we pray, Amen."

Dawn stood up in the second row as planned and walked to the pulpit. Lourdes rose and greeted her with a hug that was hard to break. Mr. Downs had been so important to them both. Dawn released the embrace and Lourdes returned to her seat, tissue in hand, blotting her eyes. Dawn was now in her late sixties and her hair was just as big and gaudy, only now it was a wig.

"We sat in adjacent offices for a great many years," Dawn began. "I spent more waking hours with Billy Downs than any of my husbands . . . And there were a few of those just for the record! He told me when I married my fourth husband, 'I have a good feeling about this one.' He was wrong." Laughter erupted in the sanctuary. "But he was always nice about those bad choices of mine. He never judged. He would just say he was lucky he found Janet . . . He loved her so. I suppose in a way, I kept searching for what he had. He had a way of making life look so easy even when it wasn't. He had a temper, but only when it came to certain things like a child being hurt. He loved children. Now, how many people here got a letter from Mr. Downs? Please stand."

There were about four hundred people filling the sanctuary and it appeared that three-fourths stood as recipients of Mr. Downs' notes.

"If you have lost that letter, don't worry. You will see the walls are covered with them. I tried to keep a copy of every single letter. He never knew I did that, and yesterday we had this little wallpaper project. The letters will be taken to the bank, and if you lost yours, come by and we will get your copy restored. now I want to read this letter from him I received one Christmas." Dawn unfolded the letter she had brought and began to read.

Dear Dawn,

I wanted to express my sincere gratitude for this past year. I am unsure how I made it through. It passed in a blur of unrelenting sorrow after Janet died. It has been almost a year, and I don't know what else to do but work. It is the only thing that gives me comfort because I have you as my guardian. You have kept me going. So much more than you will ever know. You protected me when I needed it, and you cried with me when I could do nothing else.

Dawn paused as her voice broke, and she took a deep breath to continue.

I wish you a very merry Christmas and hope next year will be better for us both. I guess you will want to retire at some juncture. For some strange reason people want to do that. And if you do want to retire, I will require a one-year notice. I'll need that much time to find anyone who could be half of what you are to me.

Love, Billy

Dawn looked down to gain her composure.

"I have never worked anywhere else but the bank my whole life, so I don't know what other places are like. But last night I showed my oldest daughter this letter and she said, 'How special of him to write you a letter and just say thank you. People don't do that anymore, especially bosses.' I said to her, 'I have forty more from him. He thanked me *every* Christmas.' If you want to run a business that has the same employees their entire career, thank them. The appreciated employee never leaves you. At least I never could, and I am really good at leaving men." The crowd laughed again.

"On the program you may see a young lady will also be giving a eulogy today, but some of you may not know her. She met Mr. Downs when she was just ten years old and worked for him cleaning the bank with her mother, Maria. Later she was our high school valedictorian and earned a scholarship to the University of Texas where she earned a double major in mathematics and finance. She worked in New York on Wall Street but returned a few years ago to Texas and opened her own investment firm based in Dallas. Her name is Lourdes Sanchez Adams, but Mr. Downs called her Lulu. Lulu, would you please come up and say a few words about our Mr. Downs?"

Lourdes and Dawn hugged again as Dawn returned to her seat, and Lourdes stood behind the pulpit.

"I remember the day he gave me the name Lulu. I tricked him into giving my mother and me a raise. Four dollars a day, mind you. Big money for us at the time." The audience chuckled. "Mr. Downs could be tight with his money, or so we all thought . . . He wasn't. In fact, he was quietly the most generous person I know. With the family's permission, we wanted to tell you a few of those acts of kindness and anonymous charity he and Janet did that we never knew about. He taught me charity is not really charity if you do it for attention for yourself. He preferred to be accused of being greedy than show off his offerings. I have a small list of donations that were made by Mr. and Mrs. Downs over the last fifty years. The church organ that fills this building with beautiful music—they paid for it, but there is no plaque that says they did it. The Health Clinic building—the government paid about a third, but Mr. Downs wanted it much nicer, and it is because of him, we have a beautiful clinic instead of a typical government-issue building. We unearthed fifty-three scholarships that were given to children from Travis City and one to a lady who was able to get her Physician's Assistant license, but she never knew where it came from." Martha Stall wiped away tear and the entire health clinic crew nodded in appreciation.

"There were loans paid off for widows and cars given to single mothers to assist them in transportation to jobs and schools. There were countless out of pocket loans to people whose credit was bad, but he knew they would pay him when they could, because they were good people. There were rents paid for when things got tough for young working families. He would gather boxes of clothes and shoes to take with him on White-winged Dove hunts in Mexico to donate to the villages. Mr. Downs created an opportunity for kindness even when he was on a trip for fun. Janet assisted missions of all denominations on the border and in San Antonio to help distressed women and children. They also paid off medical bills for people in need. Mr. Downs gave away a fortune, but he would say he never *gave* a dollar. He *invested* in people and his hometown."

"Mr. Downs was there on the worst day of my life. Or so I thought it was my worst day. I was hiding on the floorboard of his truck in tears as my world had crashed around me, and I thought my life was over and worthless. He said, 'You get to decide your own fate, not the others. You get to decide your path. Sometimes we are thrown down hard, but we must get back up and keep pushing.' I will never forget his words. He would not let me quit that day . . . Or any other day for that matter. Skeet shooting, school, business, he was always there for me. I called him when I was in college and needed guidance thinking life had cheated me. Mr. Downs said let it play out. Bad people are exposed faster than you think. He was always firm, but kind. He gave me the ability to think I could accomplish anything. He would say in his big booming voice, 'You can achieve anything. You just need a plan!' So, being a smart-alecky kid, I said, 'Can I be a football player?' And he said, 'Sure, just not a good one, and you may get killed the first day of practice.'" The congregation laughed.

"He taught me to question everything. Don't accept the first or even the second answer. Keep digging to find the real answer. He taught me respect for work because *all* work is noble. He taught me sacrifice and time. I asked him once what he wanted to be known for, and he said, 'I want people to know how many times I failed.' I couldn't understand what he meant by that, so he explained failing is important, because it is how we learn the best lessons. He said a child learns to walk by falling and learns faster if parents aren't holding their hands the whole damn time. Sound familiar? Warm and fuzzy, he was not." The audience erupted again relieving their grief through laughter.

"But maybe the greatest thing he ever did was write all those letters to encourage and thank people. I have some from him, and I would say they are my greatest treasure, because I will never get another one from him." Lourdes began to lose her voice. She took a few deep breaths and steadied both hands on the pulpit. "I will conclude in the way Mr. Downs would have liked—with a letter. It is from me and everyone else here today."

Dear Mr. Downs,

I am besieged with grief. Your town is in mourning. Our hearts are broken. You gave your best each day for so many of us. We will be eternally grateful for your sacrifices and time spent here to make our town an honorable place. Our town is known for a single letter by a man who was willing to give his life for what he believed. You will be known for giving a lifetime of many letters for what you believed.

In your remembrance, we will take up our own pens and write our own letters to encourage and console our fellow citizens and family. We will not let the gracious art of letter writing die with you. It was important to you. We know now, how important it was to us.

Your town will remember the name William Barrett Downs the Third as it will echo off our brick buildings and swirl through the branches of our oaks and blow across our green pastures and still waters. You have fought the good fight, and we submit you to the hands of God. I can hear our Heavenly Father saying to you now, *Welcome home, my good and faithful servant. Welcome home.*

Very truly yours,

Lulu and the people of Travis City, Texas

Lourdes returned to her seat and the choir stood. The song leader stood behind the podium and announced, "Please turn to hymn 312, Amazing Grace. Join us as we sing all five verses."

The choir and the congregation blended with the piano and pipe organ to raise the emotional melody across the town through the open doors onto Main Street for the crowd outside. When the song was finished the pastor returned to the microphone and simply said, "This concludes our service. The family asks for privacy at the internment to follow."

The ushers from the funeral home started at the rear of the church and each row was asked to stand and walk to the front and pass the casket as they exited through the side door. The old man lay in one of his dark suits, crisp white shirt, and red tie with his Stetson lying over his folded hands. Most reverently walked slowly past, nodding to the family seated to the right and the six pallbearers to the left. The pianist softly played Ode to Joy, one of Mr. Downs' favorite songs, as the crowd paid their respects.

When the guests were all gone, the family including Dawn and Lourdes all approached the casket one last time to say their final goodbyes. The pallbearers consisted of three employees from the bank, two of the guys from the ranch, and Danny Sanchez.

Mr. Downs earthly remains were placed in the back of the hearse and the procession followed it to the cemetery where he was buried next to Janet. The pastor finished the graveside service with kind words to his closest family and friends. Lourdes sat in the back seat of her mother's SUV as they pulled away from the cemetery, sharply feeling the wave of finality hitting her. She had been with him when he took his last breath, but now it was real. Mr. Downs was gone.

An eighty-year-old man sat alone under the graveside canopy holding his hat, summoning the strength to stand. He finally rose and stood in front of the casket as two funeral home workers waited at a respectful distance, their hands held behind them in a reverent pose. He looked down solemnly, sighed, and slowly uttered, "Bye, sum bitch."

CHAPTER 55

LOURDES CALLED MONICA and Dawn the next morning to arrange to meet for the opening of the envelope which was to be done after Mr. Downs' death. She left her parent's house and drove to the bank with her mind spinning, trying to discern what he could have wanted her to read. The rear parking lot held a few scattered customers' and employees' vehicles, but no one dared park in Mr. Downs' place. Lourdes walked through the rear entrance like she had done so many times, allowing her fingertips to feel the coarse walls of the familiar brick hallway as she turned right into Dawn's office.

"Good morning, Mrs. Adams. I'm Kay." A pretty young lady in her early twenties stood from behind Dawn's old desk and extended her hand.

"Nice to meet you, Kay. Have you replaced Dawn?" Lourdes asked.

"No one can replace me!" Dawn's voice was coming from Mr. Downs' office.

"But by golly, she may be as pretty as me," Dawn said standing in the doorway. "She's going to be great at this job. I ought to know. I hired her."

"Come on in, Lourdes, and close the door behind you," Monica called out from the sofa in Mr. Downs' office.

"Sorry. Kay. Private meeting. Let no one pass," Dawn instructed, finishing with an ominous tone for humor's sake.

"Please sit at the desk, Lourdes," Monica directed.

Dawn and Monica sat on the sofa beside one another as Lourdes reverently sat in the old, leather swivel chair.

Monica pulled out two letters from a folder lying on the cushions and handed one to Dawn.

"We each received these instructions over three years ago. As we talked at visitation, we learned they are identical. I suppose he wanted some redundancy in his plans. Our letter says this.

Dear Monica,

I have thought carefully regarding my departure from this earth. When Janet died, it seemed my path to the great beyond became more real. I have a will regarding all items that are to be given to my family, but I have a single request regarding my Lulu. I ask that as soon as possible following my internment, you instruct Lulu to come to my office. Have her sit in my chair and open the middle desk drawer. I want you and Dawn to be there when this is done in case Lulu has any questions. When she opens the drawer, ask her to feel directly under the desk for an envelope taped to the underside.   .

I respectfully ask you leave her alone after she has located the letter to read in private.

W.B.D. III

Lourdes stared at Monica, as she heard the cryptic words, her hands began to shake.

"Go ahead and find the letter," Dawn encouraged.

Lourdes could only nod, her mouth was suddenly parched as she pulled the drawer which held scattered pens, staples and notepads. She felt above the contents of the drawer and soon touched the unmistakable outline of an envelope. She pushed her fingernails under the taped paper and pried it from its secret home. She withdrew it carefully, and the two other women stared at her hands as she brought the document to light.

"We will leave you, but we will be back after you have some time."

Monica stood and walked out with Dawn who closed the door behind her.

Lourdes instantly recognized the stationery from Mr. Downs' past letters and used a letter opener on the great desk to slice open the envelope. Pulling out the trifold parchment, she opened the single page.

Dear Lulu,

As you read this, I have already left this world to meet my Maker. You entered my life as a smart, little girl who God Almighty placed in our small town. You were truly blessed with your parents, Danny and Maria, and a sharp mind. You have proven yourself at the highest level and can do anything you set your heart to accomplish. I have been proud of every high moment in your life and even more proud at your toughness in the low moments.

I am asking a favor that I do not have any right to ask. I want you to come home, to sit here at this desk. This town needs you to take up the mantle. You and Tommy have spoken of raising children here, and I have great hope you do. My family does not need any more money, so I want you to take our partnership and use it to make things better and to secure the future of the bank and the town. Giving to people in need will be the greatest reward you can imagine. Let me make this very clear. Assist those that are trying. Support those who want to create something and who will sacrifice to meet their goals. They will reap the greatest return.

All my bank stock, as well as the Lulu Partnership has been ceded to you. I know you thought you were paid your part many years ago when you started your company, but I hid one thing from you. For each dollar you presented out of your hard-earned income, I multiplied it by one thousand. This should be adequate to make you very comfortable and assist this town as you work to lift its families, institutions, churches, and businesses.

There is a separate letter to the Board of Directors in which I am naming you as my successor since all my shares are going to you. This is very selfish of me, and I know I have no right to assume you will lower yourself to return to this little town, but you are needed.

God Bless you, my darling Lulu.

WBD III

CHAPTER 56

THE BOARD MET with Lourdes for an emergency session. They were all thrilled when she accepted the position of chairman, and they pledged to work with any schedule she wanted. The bank had been on autopilot for a few years and was doing well under longtime loan officer Josh Simmons who had been named president when Mr. Downs health began to fail. All but ten percent of the bank stock belonged to Lourdes and hers was the final vote on all crucial matters.

Kay Johnson was named Lourdes' assistant, and she had been fittingly trained by Dawn. Kay had grown up in the same old neighborhood as Lourdes and was proven to be an excellent student. She had completed one year of her associate degree when the money ran out, but she showed the kind of promise Lourdes loved. A scholarship would be coming soon.

Lourdes and Tommy's first child was born six months after she began working at the bank. The little girl was named Anika Maria Adams. They called her Annie. When asked about the name, Lourdes simply said she heard it once and thought it was beautiful.

Danny Sanchez's business had grown to include four shop buildings and sixteen employees, but at age seventy, he still worked every day. Maria's business was doing well enough on its own, so she retired to keep Annie when Lourdes returned to work.

Maria arrived around six in the morning to Lourdes and Tommy's new home so Lourdes could walk out the door before the sun rose, her Open Road Stetson perched atop her head. Her covered parking spot at the bank was next to Mr. Downs' truck which was parked there like always. It had been Four's idea that it should be parked in the same spot as a memorial, and it felt comforting to the townspeople. Lourdes walked to the rear door with her keys in hand and felt the lock release. Her routine had been established by years of watching Mr. Downs. First, she would turn off the alarm pad, and then head to the kitchen where Kay had readied the coffee pot the night before.

When she crossed the hallway to her office, Lourdes would glance to the lobby where she envisioned her ten-year-old self on the floor picking up trash. She would smile. Sacrifice and time.

Lourdes carried the white mug through Kay's office and into what was now her domain. On her desk was the first draft of a letter thanking Beth for taking over the daily management of The Letter Financial Services. She preferred to write in the quiet, early morning just as Mr. Downs had done. Taking off her hat, she hung it in its rightful place, and placed her hand on her stomach. Her new son would arrive just in time for the reading of The Letter. Who would read it next year?

EPILOGUE

February 24, 1986

Harlingen, Texas

NANDINI SMILED AT her sister, Anika, laying in the hospital bed with her swaddled, newborn daughter gazing into the infant's foggy, dark eyes.

"She is just perfect," Nandini said with a single tear dropping from her eye.

"I don't think I can love anything more than this little bundle—my little Lotus flower." Anika could only stare at the miniature features of the scrunched, tiny face.

"What do you hope for your daughter?" Nandini mused.

"I hope she is smart, and beautiful, and loved her whole life. I hope she one day has a little girl too, so she can feel just like I do right now," Anika said with her eyes focused solely on the sweet infant.

"Did you know it snowed this morning? It hasn't snowed here in thirty years." Nandini gazed out the window at the unexpectedly white ground. "I think it's a good sign."

Travis City, Texas

A rare snow had blanketed Travis City the night before, the cold weather pushing south across the state all the way to the valley on the Mexican border. Mr. Downs had been unanimously selected by the committee for the centennial reading of The Letter since the ceremony began in 1886, the fiftieth anniversary of the letter itself. His wife, Janet, sat proudly on the front row in a red wool coat, her collar raised to guard against the frigid wind as she nodded and waved with red leather gloves to her friends and neighbors. Four was seated next to his beautiful and very pregnant wife, Monica, with their two-year-old daughter, Janet Ann, in a white rabbit coat sitting between her parents swinging her legs back and forth the way children do to expel energy. Daisy was seated next to her mother dressed in a knee length black mink coat she had never worn in California.

Mr. Downs wore a charcoal pinstripe suit with a solid blue tie and a black overcoat and a new silver belly Open Road Stetson and black alligator cowboy boots. His clean-shaven cheeks were rosy from the cold air as he stood to address the record crowd of townspeople at high noon.

"It is my great honor to read The Letter on this one hundredth anniversary in our beloved hometown. My family came here in 1830 when there was nothing here but hope. They showed more grit and determination than I will ever know, and I can never repay them. Many of the people here today have family who helped create this place, and we stand on holy ground formed by their sacrifice and time. My hope is the children born to our families will never forget who came before them. My prayer is that we preserve all the good things about this place so the bright stars of tomorrow will stay and continue to serve for our future." He paused and looked at the throng before him.

"I pray our traditions are kept alive and a hundred years from now, a crowd will still gather to listen once more to the words of William Barrett Travis. I hope The Letter will be read by one of us, revered by all here, and preserved for the generations to come."

He again looked over the familiar faces of the town and his own family who applauded his opening words. Mr. Downs withdrew Travis' letter from his coat pocket and perched his gold frame glasses on the end of his nose and began.

"Commandancy of the Alamo, February 24th, 1836
To the people of Texas and All Americans in the World,
Fellow Citizens and Compatriots,
I am besieged . . ."

ACKNOWLEDGEMENTS

THIS STORY WAS inside me in that mysterious place only revealed through inspiration. The hand of God was truly on me as I poured out this story. I started it but God finished it. This book is a testament to the men of my Texas youth who set a standard of honor in our state and to the daughters in whom we see no limits. It is also dedicated to the men and women who know *all work* is noble.

My wife, Sandy, believed I could write a book, and I suppose she was right. She would also say Covid-19 in 2020 assisted in preventing a baseball season to watch and I had no other way to spend my evenings. Sandy has read this story more than anyone else and pushed me through the creative process. Barry and Susan were there to keep me going, reading passages as I wrote, and being my cheerleaders which was so important. My daughter, Alban, gave me guidance on the thoughts of girls born in the eighties and patiently listened to me flesh out the story. I owe my love of reading to my dear mother and storytelling to my entertaining, late father.

Joel, Tom, Jack, Ginger, Karen, Charlie, David, and others said it was good—really good—and pushed me to get it published. Rob listened to me talk about ideas for months over Mexican food lunches. John Jasper handed me his careful edits at church each Sunday until the last page was done and was always encouraging. He made this a better book.

Anna Middlebrook of Pencil Edits did the hard work of copy editing to insure the best version possible. Jennifer at Gatekeeper Press, who has the patience of a saint, dealt with my constant barrage of questions and took it to the finish line.

I hope this book will inspire its readers to write letters. Anyone can write a letter and just because you have never done it, is not an excuse. A letter is something you keep. It is preserved as a moment in time between the writer and the reader. It means so much to receive something from the heart which an email or text cannot replace. The initial surprise in the mailbox and the smiles created by the writer sharing their thoughts, is a warm, precious moment in our now cool, digital world.

I was so thrilled when my lifelong, dear friend, Kaki, wrote these heartfelt words after reading my book:

> *There is a place in all of us that is sacred. It is a place shared with no one. A place where we imagine ourselves larger than we are and at the same time humble and small. We carry this place deep in our souls, and when we are feeling weak and vulnerable, we find solace in this honorable place.*

Thank you for buying and reading my book. There is something wonderful about reading a good book and getting a friend to read it as well so you can discuss every detail. I pray you received a moment of joy and maybe even solemn reflection in reading this book. Thank you again.

God Bless,
Henry Taylor Millard